-THE LEGEND OF HULLABEE ISLAND-

GENEVA SOMMERS

and the Quest for Truth

C.J. BENJAMIN

CROWN ATLANTIC
PUBLISHING

For information regarding permission, write to:
Attention: Crown Atlantic Publishing
2000 Mariposa Vista Lane #104
St. Augustine, FL 32084

Copyright © 2019 by C.J. Benjamin
All rights reserved.
Published in the United States by Crown Atlantic Publishing

ISBN 9781791830304

Version 1.1
Printed in the United States of America
First edition printed, January 2019

To Dalton,
for being the most unexpected gift.

And to Philip,
whose unwavering encouragement,
optimism, and belief in me
is unfathomable.

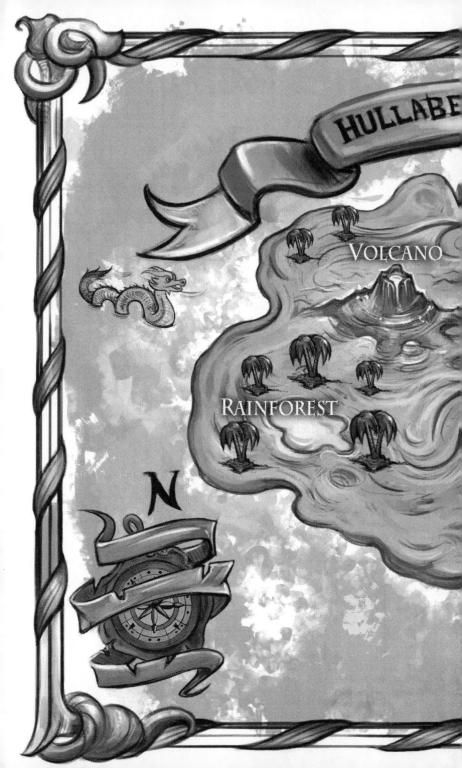

PROLOGUE

My name is Geneva Sommers. I didn't know that until today. Until today, I've lived the past thirteen years of my life as #65. Jane 65 to be exact. Janes, that's what they call us female orphans at the Troian Center. We live on Hullabee Island. Our way of life here is very simple, either you're one of the lucky ones, or you're not. I am not. Or at least that's what I thought, until I found out the truth.

1

Hullabee Island is massive; it would take you two weeks to walk end to end if you never stopped. It would take you just as long to hike to the top of its towering volcano as well. For the colossal size of the island, the population is rather small. It's made up of one beautiful sparkling city on the southern shore, called Lux. That's where the citizens live. They're the lucky ones. If you live on Hullabee, your biggest hope is to be a citizen. Then you could live the good life in Lux, in one of the beautiful white-stone houses that stare out at the glittering blue sea. The rest of us are called locals, we live on the outskirts of Lux in small villages. Our life consists of trying to clean up the mess from the Flood and keep things running smoothly for the citizens in Lux. The Flood, as we call it, happened over ten years ago, and that's how I became an orphan. There's a bunch of us orphans thanks to the Flood. We all live at the Troian Center right outside of Lux, in the town of Aveile. It's not such a bad life being an orphan, we spend a few hours each day learning lessons and then the rest of the day we work with the locals in the cleanup effort.

It may seem strange that after ten years we are still cleaning up from the Flood. Well, it wasn't just any flood that ravaged our island. We were flooded by a force that nature had never seen before. There was wind, water, fire and lava, and there was nowhere to run. I've heard so many stories about the Flood; it's almost turned into a legend around here. There's little else we have to talk about with the locals while we work, so they tell us all they can remember. They say it was like a monsoon, with a typhoon, mixed with an earthquake and a tsunami all rolled into one. Not to mention the molten lava spewing out of our volcano amid the chaos. As you can imagine, this event is responsible for wiping out most of the population on our island. There used to be big, lush settlements all over. Most of them were inland, sheltered from the harsh sun and weather by a canopy of thick, tropical trees and vegetation. These towns are all gone now. They were directly in the volcano's path and it's said that no one survived. Only the citizens of Lux were spared, along with a few lucky nearby villages of locals and us orphans.

Since the Flood I have lived here at the Troian Center. I have worked my way up through the years cleaning, sewing, and cooking with the other young orphans at the Center. When I turned eight years old, I graduated to Flood clean up. I have been helping sort through the rubble to find what is valuable enough to send to Lux. I've become a master at finding little diamonds in the rough, as we call them; pieces of gold, small jewels or precious stones, and metals. I find them and polish them until they look brand new. I don't mind the job much. I get to be outdoors in the salty sea air with the sun warming my back. It feels like a treasure hunt sorting through the piles of junk the locals bring in from the forest for us to comb through. It beats doing laundry! Working the rubble has made my legs strong from climbing the piles, and my feet sure and fast from scaling down the rolling, churning debris. My fingers are nimble from sorting and my arms toned from polishing. I cherish each beautiful sparkling thing I find. Each is more stunning than the next, and they're all more luxurious than anything I could ever hope to own. It makes me feel powerful to have something so beautiful in my hands. It almost feels like the gems speak to me sometimes, sharing with me their hidden secrets. Sometimes, when no one is watching me, I pretend they are mine and that I'm a citizen worthy of owning them.

Maybe if I were a citizen he would like me more ... Nova. I've had a crush on him since before I knew what a crush was. I've seen him in the Troian Center since I could remember. He was kind of hard to miss with that shock of blond hair and his tall frame. He was always a head above all the other kids. At first I thought it was because he must be much older, but I guess he was just blessed with being freakishly tall. Something I was in obvious envy of since I made a habit of walking around on my tippy toes to make up for my short stature, which eventually earned me the nickname "Tippy" from him.

W ell, if I'm going to tell this story, let me start from the beginning.

When I first had the pleasure of officially catching Nova's eye, I was twelve and he was fourteen. I was sorting rubble as usual and talking to a precious ruby I was polishing when he startled me.

"So, is that your best friend or what?"

I jumped at the voice behind me and dropped my stone back into the rubble pile. I whirled around ready to be scolded and beaten for slacking off on my job, but instead I was met with his blazing green eyes and the big grin on his sun-kissed face. His breathtaking beauty up close took me by surprise. I was at a loss for words, so at first I just started scrambling around searching frantically for the ruby I dropped. But then I heard his laughter, and my ears grew hot and I could feel my cheeks flush with anger. *Who did this John think he was anyway?*

"Why did you do that?" I screamed. "Now I have to find it and start all over."

"Jeez, sorry kid, I wasn't trying to scare you. I've just never heard anyone talk to a rock before."

"It's not a rock!" I huffed. "It's a ruby! And don't call me kid!"

"Okay, okay, I'll help you find it if you stop shouting about it. You're gonna get us sent to the locker!"

This shut me up momentarily because he was right, and that was the last place I wanted to go. The locker was where they sent us orphans if we misbehaved. If we slacked off on our job or lessons, or if we were being difficult, we were sent to the locker. Difficult is a funny word, it seems to mean a lot of different things around here. If you outgrew your clothes too quickly, you were being difficult. If your shoe came untied, you were being difficult. If you cried after a beating, you were being difficult. It seemed Nova was very difficult because he was in the locker a lot. I had only been there a handful of times and made it a goal of mine not to go back. It was cold and dark and damp in the locker, and there were no windows, no sounds—just you and the damp, cold, darkness for what seemed like an eternity.

"So what's your name kid?" he whispered as we searched for the ruby.

"65," I replied curtly.

"I'm Nova."

"What?" I squealed. "That can't be your name, it *has* to be John and your number," I said matter-of-factly.

"Well, Miss Know-It-All, my real name *is* Nova. But if that bothers you so much, you can call me 18."

"But, how do you know your real name?" I challenged.

"Well, that's a long story, maybe I'll tell you someday." Then he handed me the ruby and ran back toward the forest, leaving me flabbergasted.

He must have heard Greeley coming, because a second

later she was upon me. Our Headmistress Greeley is not known for her kindness, so it was a good thing Nova scurried away when he did or we'd both be headed to the locker. She is from Lux and seems to despise the fact that she has to spend her days here with us orphans. She couldn't even be bothered to learn our numbers even though they are sewn onto our tan, shapeless uniforms, as well as tattooed on our shoulder for good measure. To her, we were all just Jane or John. Not even worth a number.

"What have you got there little Jane?" Greeley croaked.

I slipped the ruby into her gloved hand and she gave a sly smile, exposing her vicious teeth and slipped the ruby into her pocket.

"I should give this one a closer look, don't you think?" she said with a wink.

At first I was confused, thinking she wanted me to reply, but she motioned to the pile I had in my basket and I quickly offered it to her. She did a quick survey, pawing through the valuable trinkets I had collected today, and then dumped them into her sack and sauntered away to the next orphan without another word to me. This is when I first realized she was stealing stones meant for Lux. I shook my head at her greediness, but also gave a little sigh of relief, knowing I had narrowly escaped Greeley's wrath and a sure sentence in the locker. Whatever she did with the stones wasn't my business and I was happy to keep my head down and survive another day. When she was far enough away from me, I gave up my sorting for a moment so I could turn toward the forest to try and catch another glimpse of Nova. I shaded my eyes with my hand against the hot afternoon sun and squinted, but he was gone, disappearing as quickly as he had appeared.

A fter that day, all I could do was think about Nova and wonder how it was that he knew his real name. I had always wondered what mine was. In school, each time I would read a new name in a lesson book, I would pause to wonder if it could be mine. I'd roll it around on my tongue and imagine my parents saying it to me. Maybe they would sing it each morning as they woke me up with kisses or each night as they gently rocked me to sleep?

I spent almost every waking hour thinking about my parents, imagining what they looked like, where we had lived, what they sounded like. I would usually get jolted back into reality pretty hard by the back of my teacher's hand. This always brought on a little snicker from the other kids. To everyone else it probably looked like I was just sitting there stuttering over the name. This added to my outcast status— since I did this often—as did the fact that I am the youngest orphan at the Center. My parents died in the Flood like most of the other orphans here, but I was barely a year old when they found me washed up neatly on the shore in Aveile. I was apparently happy as a shore bird, all swaddled in a basket, without a scratch on me. What a mystery, right? How does a helpless little baby survive the Flood when her parents and so many others weren't spared? I wonder about this question day and night.

I don't really have many friends at the Troian Center, not that that kind of thing is encouraged anyway. My closest friend, well my only friend, really, is John #26. He's in my year, and we are in all the same lessons and usually end up working the same jobs. You see, there's a strict system that we follow at the Center. All the kids are broken up by year. So all the thirteen-year-olds are together, all the fourteen-year-olds are together and so on. You spend all your life at the Center with the kids in your year, so if you're in a bad year, you're in for a rough ride. I should be in with the twelve-year-olds, but the problem is, there aren't any twelve-year-olds in the Center. I guess I was the youngest survivor of the Flood. So, they just threw me in with the next youngest group and I've been with them ever since. Right now we're all thirteen-year-olds, or I should say, they're thirteen-year-olds and I'm technically twelve. But I've been with them for so long—I consider myself one of them, even if they don't. In my head I'm thirteen-years-old. I think over time I've made up the gap of a year and am right there with them. I take all the same lessons, do all the same jobs; so, for all intents and purposes, I was a thirteen-year-old.

It has always been sink or swim for me, and I've really tried to swim! Being a year younger than all my peers may be a disadvantage, but I tried not to let it hold me back. I may have been a head shorter than them all, and my clothes didn't fit right—my scrawny shoulders always sticking out the neck hole of my work uniform and the rough, tan shirt being long enough to cover my shorts—but I made up for what I lacked in size with smarts and speed. I was one of the smartest in my year when I wasn't daydreaming, and I could outrun even the boys in my year. This showboating in speed often resulted in me getting bullied and tossed into the sand, but it was worth it for the brief second that I knew I was better than them!

I was trying so hard to be liked and to fit in that it seemed to have the opposite effect, so recently I've stopped trying. But not with #26, he's one of the good ones. He never gave me trouble for being fast or smart, or small and short for that matter. He never snickered when I stuttered in lessons. He never said much of anything really. He's very timid and doesn't talk much. He kind of reminds me of a marmouse. They're these cute, cuddly, large rodents that you can find all over the island and they often try to take shelter inside our Center when it rains.

Marmice are squeaky and brown and utterly defenseless, which makes them easy targets for the tarcats that patrol the halls. These vile, black-and-white spotted jungle cats patrol our school like guard dogs. They're cruel and ruthless and play with their prey in a tortuous way before they eat it. Headmistress Greeley just loves them. She even has a few favorites that she takes home with her each night, leading them by their big, sparkling collars. I think they're the only things that make her happy, besides sending us to the locker. She sent #26 to the locker once for a whole week when he was very young, and I think that's why he doesn't talk too much anymore. I think he must be scared he'll say something that will land him in the locker again. He's a great listener though, so I told him about my conversation with Nova while we ate in the dining hall today. This seemed to upset him. His big brown eyes got wider than usual and even welled up with tears at one point. I thought he was going to say something but he just sniffled and stared at me, so I kept going.

"Do you think he's lying? I mean, we're not allowed to have

names anyway, so why does he go around with this stupid story about his name being Nova? I think he thinks he's better than us because he has a real name! Everyone knows orphans don't have names. We're John or Jane with a number unless a citizen adopts us. But that will never happen, we're much too old for that, they only adopt the – "

"-emi," whispered #26.

My words stopped short as I caught the barely audible word slip from #26's lips. "What did you just say?"

"Remi," he said glancing around nervously, "My name was Remi."

"I don't understand," I stammered.

He grabbed me by the hand and pulled me behind him as we exited the dining hall at an alarming speed and scampered down the hall to the Jane's room. He slowed down every time we passed a Grift. Grifts are locals who work at the Troian Center because they're too weak to work with the other locals on Flood damage. Some were injured in the Flood and have missing limbs, some just seem like they're a little crazy in the head. Most of them are alright enough, but some would rat you out to Greeley in a heartbeat. Luckily, no one really paid any attention to us as we blended in with the other orphans in the halls while they changed lessons. I was out of breath by the time we were behind the stall door in the Jane's room. #26 crammed us both into one of the tiny, dank stalls on the far end. It was so small inside I had to climb onto the toilet bowl so we could both fit.

"What are we doing in here?" I whispered. "Are you crazy? We're both gonna get sent to the locker!"

For what felt like forever he just stared at me.

"You *are* aware that you're in the Jane's room right? And *you* dragged *me* here, after saying your name is Remi! You should be the one doing the talking now."

"Fine, will you please keep your voice down though?"

"Fine," I whispered.

"You should know that some of us know our real names. Like me, my name was Remi, that's what my parents called me before they were killed in the Flood. I used to have a little brother named Dhani, too."

"What? Why don't I know this? Why have you never told me?" I howled.

"Shhhh!" Remi clapped his hand over my mouth. "We can't talk about this!"

"Why not?"

"It's forbidden 65, that's why I haven't told you. I knew you would go on about it until it got you into trouble. I don't want to end up in the locker again."

"You're right," I sighed. Then something dawned on me.

"Is that why Greeley sent you to the locker for a whole week?"

"Yes, so you see why I don't want to talk about it? When we got here they basically brainwashed us into forgetting our names if we were old enough to know them. They told us that we were never to talk about our old names ever again, because it was disrespectful to the island gods because our family namesakes had been wiped out for a reason, and it would bring upon another horrible Flood if we went around speaking such names. You were too young to know your name when you arrived here, so they didn't bother with you. Plus, you know that if we get adopted the citizens will name us, so it's easier if we're not hanging onto our old names."

"No citizen is going to adopt us Remi, you know that. We're too old now. They only take the babies that the locals bring us."

"It could still happen, 65."

"Whatever you say," I fumed. "So why did you tell me your name just now when I was telling you about Nova?"

"I was jealous that he gets to go around boasting about his real name. It's the only thing I have left that reminds me of my family and my home. Sometimes I need to say it to myself just so I know it's real, that I really did have a life and a family before the Flood," he said.

"Do you know *my* name, Remi?" I whispered excitedly.

Silence.

"What?"

"I thought I heard someone. We need to go," he whispered.

"But, do you..."

"No! I'm sorry, no one does. You were too young. Now can we drop it and go?" he hissed. "And you have to stop calling me Remi."

I slunk down off the toilet I was perched on and sighed. "Okay, but let me go first so I can make sure the coast is clear."

I walked out to the hallway deflated. I looked around and there was no one in sight. The Grifts were elsewhere and all the students would be in the dining hall by now. It was almost time to start our Flood work for the day. I glanced to my left toward the buzz coming from the dining hall and then made up my mind that I had lost my appetite and I turned right, and headed to my room. By the time I reached the door to room 13, my eyes were watering. I knew our room would be empty so I barreled blindly through the doorway and tossed myself onto a bed. I buried my face into the mattress and tried to quietly sob for the next thirty minutes.

This is so unfair! I bet everyone else in the Center is walking around feeling satisfied knowing they had a name once and a family that loved them. I have nothing! No one! I will never have any answers and no one cares about me.

I was in the middle of a pretty good pity party when the

rest of my class started to stream into the room to change into their work clothes. I gathered myself back together as best I could and tried to wipe the tears away, but stupid Jane #31 saw me before I could. She was always picking on me. I hated the sight of her mean little black eyes and her silky raven-black hair.

She pointed at me and said, "Aw, is da wittle baby cwying? What's da matta wittle baby?"

"Shut up, 31," I mumbled.

I slung on my tattered tan linen shirt and faded brown shorts, jammed my feet into my shoes and stormed out into the courtyard where all the years were gathering to be escorted by Grifts to their jobs. I was busy scuffing the toe of my shoe into the sand when Nova appeared by my side.

"What's wrong now #65?" he said

I didn't even look up, but I knew it was him from his content voice and the way he smelled like plants and earth from working in the forest all the time.

"Come on," he said and he grabbed me by the hand.

"Wait, where are we going? It's time for Flood work," I protested.

"We've got time, and besides this will make you feel better. It always makes me feel better."

I felt the stiff breeze of the salty air, and as I looked past him I saw he was leading me around to the Southern wall of the Center that faced the ocean. It was the one way I could tell what direction I was facing even though I couldn't see over the tall coquina-shelled walls that surrounded the Center. I always wondered why it was so securely walled. No one was going to try to break in and steal a bunch of orphans. And it's not like we were going to break out with nowhere to go. We stopped at the far corner and Nova pointed to a big banana palm that had nestled its way into the corner of the yard.

"What? A stupid plant is supposed to make me feel better?"

"Not the plant, little Jane, look beyond it," he said pushing me toward it.

I felt a warm breeze rustle through the palms just then and could see a shimmer of light coming from behind the leaves.

"What is that?" I asked.

I leaned closer and danced on my tippy toes trying to get a better look. Nova smirked at me and slipped behind the tall broad leaves, disappearing from my sight. After a second my curiosity got the best of me and I followed him. Behind the palm there was a perfect eight-by-eight-inch hole missing from the wall, and you could see the white-sand beaches and crashing waves beyond.

"Ohhh...." I said, finally realizing what made Nova feel happy. *The sea always made me feel better too. How did he know that?* I wondered.

"Come take a look," he said moving aside so I could get a better look.

I grabbed the rim of the hole with my fingers and tried hoisting myself up while balancing on my tippy toes, but my eyes still barely cleared the opening.

"Ha-ha, don't you ever get tired of standing on your tip toes like that, little Tippy?" he laughed.

Before I could come back with a clever remark he scooped me up and slung me onto his back so we could both peer through the hole at the calm ocean. I could have stayed like that forever, with Nova's warmth radiating through my whole body as I clung to his shoulders and gazed at the sea while the salty air lapped at my long blonde hair.

He must have sensed my happiness too because he said, "See, I told you you'd feel better."

"Ok, so you were right," I smirked.

"So, what had you so upset there, Tippy?"

"My name I guess."

"Did you forget your name again? I heard you like to daydream, but that's bad," he joked.

"No, I didn't forget my name, it's Jane #65; only that's not the name I'm talking about. I mean my real name, like you and Remi."

"Oh. Who's Remi?" he asked.

So I told him all about my best friend, John #26, and about his real name being Remi. And how this whole thing had come about because I was telling Remi about how he had told me his name was Nova, and then about no one knowing my name, and then #31 picking on me.

"Tippy, I'm sorry. I shouldn't have said anything to you. I didn't know you were going to take the name thing so seriously," he said. "And your friend Remi is right, you can't go around talking about names. He sounds smart, so you listen to him, alright?"

"But..."

"And give 31 a break. I know she can be tough, but it's only because she's so sad over... well you know. We all lost a lot of people we loved in the Flood."

"I did too, that's no reason for her to be so mean. We all lost our parents!"

"Some of us lost more than that, Tippy."

"What do you mean?"

"Never mind," Nova said sullenly.

Sadness seemed to fill his eyes and he shrugged me off his shoulders and started to walk back toward the courtyard. I scurried after him.

"I'm sorry. I'm sorry. Nova, what did I do?"

"It's okay, Tippy, you didn't do anything. It's just ... you almost have it easier because you were so young when you came here that you don't remember your family, your parents, brothers, sisters. I still do and so does Jemma. We both lost our little sisters in the Flood."

"Jemma?"

"That's 31's name. Now don't go repeating that okay? You'll just give her another reason to go after you."

I couldn't believe what I was hearing. 31 had a name too? Was I the only one who didn't? I was lost in a thousand questions and had to jog to catch back up to Nova's long strides.

"I'm sorry you lost your sister, Nova," I added breathlessly when I caught him.

"Thanks," he said and gave a stressed smile for my benefit.

"What was she like?"

He stopped walking and just looked at me for a moment. I was about to apologize for being so nosy when he smiled and laughed.

"Huh, no one's ever asked me that before. She was a lot like you actually. Always under foot, too short and too curious for her own good!" he said, with a real smile this time as he poked at me.

And then he did something that no one had ever done to me before. He kissed me on the top of my head and trotted off to join the other fourteen-year-olds as they headed out to the forest for Flood work.

I stood there stunned for a moment. No one had ever kissed me before, and it made me feel funny. My ears burned again and my cheeks felt hot. I could hear my heart pounding in my eardrums. Suddenly Remi nudged me to follow him and the rest of my group out to the fields to sort through rubble. The rest of the day seemed to swim by. All I could think about was Nova. At first it was just in a curious way. Like, how did he know so much about the other kids and everyone's names, and the hole in the wall? But soon he was all I thought about, all day, every day. He slowly worked his way into my daydreams as well. I began to live for these dreams that brought me to this perfect fantasy world where we would go on hikes together into the rainforest and we'd hunt for gems and treasures among the ruins from the Flood. And we could keep anything we found. Or sometimes we would play on the beach and race into the waves. I would imagine that we'd swim out to sea and find our parents waiting for us on another island. They'd be so happy to see us and say that they never stopped searching for us.

4

mack! A crack with a rolled up stack of papers to the back of my head brought me swiftly back to reality. I was sitting at one of the large wooden tables in Miss Neilia's lesson. She was our reading and writing teacher, and I normally found myself in trouble with her because I always got so caught up in the stories we were reading that I'd end up daydreaming, just like I had today.

"#65, would you please pick up where #31 left off?" Miss Neilia said impatiently. Her round, brown eyes peered at me over the rims of her glasses.

Oh no, I had no idea where that was. Stupid Nova, getting me into trouble again. Why can't I stop thinking about him? I thought frantically.

"#65! Don't make me repeat myself again."

"Sorry ma'am, what page were we on again?"

"Miss Neilia, can I please continue reading?" #31 interrupted sweetly. "You know 65 will just stutter her way through the chapter anyway."

"Very well #31, you may continue," sighed Miss Neilia.

24

C.J. BENJAMIN

Then 31 grinned at me with an overly sweet smile and the rest of the class snickered in response as she began to stutter through the reading, imitating me.

"That's enough 31, let's all settle down and please continue," Miss Neilia warned.

I couldn't stop glaring at 31. I hated her in a way I never hated anyone or anything before. I had never done anything to her, but she hated me nonetheless. Anger was boiling up inside of me, blinding my thoughts. As I was feeling my eyes start to well up, the bell chimed and we were dismissed. I bolted into the hallway ahead of the others and was about to round the corner into the Jane's room when Remi caught up to me.

"65, wait up. Are you okay?" he asked.

"I don't want her to see me cry!" I choked out.

"Okay, c'mon. We'll go back to our room."

"No, I just want to be alone right now, okay?" I sobbed as I ran off.

I ran out to the courtyard, straight back to the hole in the wall where Nova had brought me. I curled up behind the shelter of the large palms and cried myself dry. Soon I heard everyone spilling out into the courtyard to get ready for work. I was in a foul mood, but I crawled out from behind the palm and met up with my year. I managed to hide through lunch, but skipping Flood work was not an option unless you wanted to get sent straight to the locker. I joined Remi and stood in line while the older kids got escorted out first. Nova gave my pony tail a tug as he walked by.

"Hey!" I yelled, but when I saw him wink and give that devilish smile, I couldn't help but laugh.

"So, that's him, huh?" said Remi bitterly.

"Yeah, why do you say it like that?" I asked.

"No reason, forget it."

"Okay, fine. What do you want to talk about then?"

"How about work so we don't get in trouble today, okay?" replied Remi.

"Fine. Are you excited that we get to go work out in the forest soon? It's almost time for the New Year Gala and we'll be fourteen! That's old enough to go into the forest!"

"Um, I guess."

"I'm excited," chirped the small girl in front of me.

I stopped for a moment to look at the tiny smiling girl. Her name was Jane #42 and she was in our year. She'd never really spoken to me before, but she seemed friendly enough with her shining amber eyes and her bright smile taking up most of her delicate face.

"See, 42's excited for the forest. This job is getting dull. We've been picking through rocks since we were eight. I'm ready for something new."

"I guess so," said Remi.

"Well don't forget we *will* get to go into the forest and see what all the fuss is about," I said in our favorite teacher's exaggerated voice. "C'mon you know you're excited to put all that boring reading from Plants and Poisons lessons into use."

This got Remi to giggle a bit because that was our favorite lesson. Our teacher Miss Banna was a little bit over animated. She would get so excited describing a poisonous plant to us and what it could do to a person, that she would get winded and have to sit down on her desk and fan herself while wiping little beads of sweat from her forehead with the old cloth she kept tucked in her shirt. We loved to mimic her frenzied voice when studying for her exams. We spent the better part of our walk to the fields having a great time impersonating her. Even 42 chuckled quietly as Remi and I joked.

"Well *I* have *never* seen such a *horrible... vile... suffering... infested... infection* as when someone mistakes a *cantamum* for a *crenia*!" I quipped.

"Having a good laugh, 65? You know I could tell the Grift on you right now and you'd go straight to the locker!" steamed #31. "You might not be so funny then, would you?"

She must have been walking behind us the whole way there. Remi froze, knowing that 31 was cruel enough to do it. I turned to face her.

"Oh give me a break, 31. I wasn't even talking to you, okay?"

"What's that supposed to mean?"

"It doesn't mean anything, 31. She's sorry, aren't you, 65?" said 42.

"What's this? Did you make a new friend, 65? That makes sense since you can't even talk for yourself. You have to make your little friends do it, don't you? Is it because you're afraid you'll st-st-stutter?" squawked 31.

"No, I don't have a stutter and I don't have a problem, unlike you, Jemma!"

Silence

Now I noticed that I was attracting a crowd, and for some reason this just infuriated me. Why was I always the freak show?

"What did you call me?" she hissed.

"You heard me. I know your name and that you act all mean and tough because you're really just sad inside like the rest of us—because you miss your little sister!"

Pain. Blackness.

After that, everything was a bit spotty.

At first there was a crunching sound.

Then more pain and more blackness.

Then I heard shouting.

Then I saw the sky. It was blinding.

Then Remi's head was in the sky.

Then blackness again.

Then it smelled like salty forest earth.

Then I saw Nova's head in the sky, eclipsing the sun. Did he have a halo?

"Nova?" I whispered.

Blackness.

It was black for so long that I started to panic and my mind raced away with me.

I must be in the locker. Of course I was in the locker. What was I thinking? How could I have said her name? I know better. It's just... Oh, she gets me so mad. What is her problem with me anyway? Ugh... I really shouldn't have said that. She's never going to leave me alone now. Oh no! What happened to Remi? And 42? I didn't mean to get them in trouble. Why did I have to say anything? Poor Remi, he's going to kill me, that is, if he ever speaks to me again after getting sent to the locker. Then I'll have zero friends. Nova! He's my friend, right? Why did he have to tell me his stupid name anyway? That's what started this whole thing. I'm gonna... Nova! Nova!

"There you are. We were starting to worry about you, little Jane."

Light!

I opened my eyes to see our nurse, Miss Breia's large face staring down at mine.

"You were out for a long time, little miss. And talking up a storm just a minute ago. What's Nova?"

Oh crud! What did I say? I wondered.

"What happened to me, Miss Breia?" I asked.

"Well, you fell off the rubble pile dear, and that's how you got that black eye. You don't remember? Must have been some fall."

"What?"

I popped up to try to look at my face, but it must have been too fast because the room started swimming and I felt all hot and clammy.

"You'd better stay lying down, dear. I think you have a concussion."

Suddenly it came back to me. I remembered perfectly that Jemma had punched me square in the face for saying her name and saying she missed her sister. I did NOT fall off the rubble pile. I've never fallen off. Who would make up such a story? I was gonna go with it though because maybe if no one knew the truth, I wouldn't end up in the locker.

"How'd I get here?" I asked.

"John 18," she whispered.

Why did women always whisper when they said his name? I thought to myself while I tried to absorb what she was saying.

"Oh, he brought me here?"

"Why yes, and he's been by to check on you quite often, always wondering if you're awake yet. Shall I go get him and tell him you're alright?"

"I... um... maybe..." I stammered.

"Yes, he'll want to see you. I'll be right back. Now stay put, okay?"

And she hustled out the door.

I was happy to stay where I was. I laid in bewilderment. I had so many questions. Like, how was I not in the locker by now? Where was Remi and 42? Where was Jemma? Surely she had to be ratting me out by now. There was no way she was going to let this go. She would bug me for days just for stuttering over a name or shedding a tear. But this, this was much worse. I suddenly realized I was shivering. I was shaking at the thought of what I was in store for as soon as I stepped out of the nurse's station. Maybe Jemma hadn't told on me yet because what she had planned for me was worse than a trip to the locker? Just as I was working through all the possible forms of harassment Jemma might be plotting, Nova walked in.

"Hey Tippy, you're awake! And about time, too," he jested. "So, how are you feeling?"

"I... well... you..." It was all I could get out, I was happy to see him, but then I remembered I was mad at him for the whole name situation in the first place. But then I felt hazy and couldn't quite connect the thoughts in my head with the words coming out of my mouth. Nova twirled the bedside chair around and straddled it backwards. His face was inches from mine. I instinctively felt myself stop breathing, as he placed his hand on my forehead.

"Miss Breia, I think 65 may have a fever. Would you be able to get her a frenlic palm that we can soak to draw the heat out?"

"Oh, of course 18, that's exactly what we need to do. You're so clever. I'll go get it this instant. You stay here with her, okay?" Miss Breia sprung into action as soon as Nova had addressed her. I'd never seen her move so fast. She bustled around the office seeming to not know how to find the door before she finally gave a nervous laugh and scurried through it.

Now we were alone. Despite this, he still leaned in closer and whispered to me.

"I have to do this fast so listen to every word I say, okay?"

All I could do was nod.

"Good. Now, I've made up this story and we're all sticking to it, so memorize it or we're all going to the locker. You were climbing the rubble pile and you lost your footing and fell. You fell into 31 on your way off the pile and that's why she has a black eye, too. I saw it happen and ran over to make sure everyone was alright. You were unconscious, so I brought you to the nurse's station directly."

I nodded again, not sure if there was more to his story or if I was supposed to speak.

"Do you understand that?"

Nod. Nod.

"Okay, what's wrong with you? Did you forget how to speak? I can never shut you up and I just told you a tremendous lie and you're just staring at me?"

"I... I don't really remember what happened. It's... foggy."

Nova stared at me for a moment and then started smoothing my flaxen-blonde hair back and out of my face. He tucked an unruly strand behind my ear and I really thought I might have a fever as my cheeks reddened.

"What do you remember?" he whispered.

"I got into a fight with Jemma. She was going to try to get us in trouble, so I yelled at her, I said her name, and I might have let it slip that I knew she lost her sister."

"Tippy!"

"It's your fault! You told me all that stuff and then she was just being so awful to me and it just slipped out. That's when she hit me."

"Okay, so how did you hit her back?"

"What are you talking about? I didn't hit her. What did she say to you? She hit me and that's all I remember. I think I hit my head and then I remember seeing Remi, and it was black and then I smelled you...."

Nova laughed at this and then said, "Okay... anyway. You really don't remember what you did to her?"

"Remember what? I just told you what happened. What am I missing?"

Just then I heard an out-of-breath nurse huffing toward us down the hallway.

"Tippy, listen to me, I don't have time to explain it all right this second," Nova spat out rapidly in a hurried, hushed voice that I'd never heard him use before. "You need to stick to the story I told you and keep saying you don't remember anything else if they question you. I'll explain it all later. They're going to let you go back to your room soon and I'll come find you. In the meantime, promise me you won't say anything to anyone! And stay away from Jemma."

I wanted to protest, but the stress in his normally carefree voice frightened me. I stared at him wide-eyed and nodded. He gave my hand a squeeze and met Miss Breia at the doorway of my room.

"Oh, 18... how is she? I got back as soon as I could, I've got the leaves!" She gasped, waving them triumphantly in the air for us both to see. She must have been running because she was still trying to catch her breath, and she looked more in need of the fever-reducing leaves than I did. Miss Breia is a sweet woman normally, but she was really turning on the charm for some unapparent reason. Nova put his arm over her shoulder and turned her back toward her office.

"I think she's doing much better, I have a few concerns though. Let's let these leaves soak and talk out here," he said leading her out of my room.

As I watched them stroll out of my room, I thought I saw Remi peeking in as the door closed behind them. I tried to sit up, but my head fought me and I felt woozy again. After the pounding in my ears subsided I could hear bits of what they were saying.

"Oh, hello dear, can I help you?" said Miss Breia's voice.

Then nothing.

Then, I heard Nova's voice but I couldn't make out the words.

Then Miss Breia again, "Yes, yes, you're right, she shouldn't have any visitors right now. I'll let her know you stopped by. Now run along so you're not late for lessons."

Then I heard Nova saying something else and Miss Breia gave a girlish laugh.

Then I must have drifted off to sleep.

5

I awoke with soggy frenlic leaves on my forehead. I was still in the nurse's station rather than the locker, so I took that as a good sign. I successfully propped myself up on my elbows without too much resistance from my head and surveyed the room. It was small and mostly the same grayish-tan color that made up the stone walls of the rest of the Center. You could tell Miss Breia tried to make it cheery though because there were bright-yellow curtains hung on the inside of the barred windows. I watched them billow in the breeze, mesmerized by the way the sunlight caught the checkered pattern. Next to my white linen cot bed was an old wooden chair, still facing backwards from Nova. There was a simple bedside table next to me, containing an oil lamp, a bowl of soaking frenlic leaves and a mug of water. I reached for the water and sipped as I looked around the rest of the tiny room. There wasn't much else. Just some generic medical posters on the wall and a washbowl. Just then Miss Breia popped her curly-haired head in.

"You're up! Very good, how about some breakfast?" she smiled as she carried a bowl of porridge and fruit toward me on a teetering tray. I smiled back and let her peel the leaves off my head and prop me up higher so I could sit facing her. She handed me my breakfast and put her hands on her big hips.

"Well, you do look much better. These frenlic leaves did the trick. That John 18 is something, isn't he?"

"What?"

"Never mind. How are you feeling this morning, little Jane?"

"Better, I think."

"Excellent, because if you can finish your breakfast I'm going to release you."

I swallowed as hard, dark thoughts of the locker rushed through my mind.

"Release me to where?"

"Well 18 and I think it's too soon to send you back to lessons and work just yet, but we think you'd be more comfortable in your room. I've already had a cot bed set up for you so you don't have to share a bed with the other children while you're recovering."

"Oh... um, thank you."

What was going on here? I was going back to my room and getting my own bed?

That never happened to any of the other orphans that I knew about. If what Nova said is true, I should surely be going straight to the locker. I thought maybe they were just making sure I was healthy enough to endure the pure torture of sensory deprivation that the locker offers. But never did I think I'd be rewarded with my own bed and getting out of lessons and work.

How hard did I hit my head?

None of this was making sense. Maybe I woke up in some alternate universe where orphans were treated kindly and there was no such thing as the locker. I had no idea why Nova was making decisions about my future. Miss Breia said that 'she and 18 think I'm not ready for lessons and work...they think I'll be more comfortable in my room.'

Since when did Nova help staff at the Center make decisions?

I choked down my porridge so I could get out of the nurse's care as soon as possible and hopefully get some answers to all my questions. Miss Breia was overly pleased to see I finished my breakfast. She helped me out of bed and even wiped me down with cool water before she helped me dress. I normally would have insisted I could do this all on my own, but I was still experiencing dizzy spells that would sneak up on me when I wasn't expecting them. I felt like I was just learning to use my legs for the first time. I almost knocked over the bathing bucket that Miss Breia was using to wipe the sweat from my boney shoulders. It was hard not to like her. She patiently steadied me each time I swayed and even hummed pleasantly as she bathed me. I didn't know how to receive such kindness. I just stared at her plump face, hoping she could tell I was grateful.

Now that I was clean, dry and dressed in my freshly laundered uniform, I was actually starting to feel better. More like myself, yet still wary of how well things were going for me. I was waiting for the floor to drop out from under me at any moment. I couldn't help feeling I must be dreaming when Miss Breia led me into the thirteen-year-olds' room. It was completely empty and looked just as I remembered it, minus the slim white cot bed under the foggy glassed windows.

"Is that for me?" I questioned.

"Of course, now why don't you just rest here until lunch, then I'll make sure someone from the dining hall brings you a meal," she said with a warm smile.

"Okay."

"Now if you need anything you come find me, alright?"

She turned to walk toward the door and I had an urge to call to her. Her name escaped my lips before I knew why I was calling her.

"Miss Breia?"

"Yes dear?"

"I...um...thanks."

"You're most welcome dear." Then she was gone.

I sat on my new cot bed cross-legged as I tried to make sense of what was happening to me. I gazed toward the sooty windows next to me and then untucked my shirt so I could use the bottom of it to try to clean a spot to see through. It was no use. The smudges and dirt seemed to be on the outside. I actually preferred the barred windows that were in our lesson rooms and dining hall better. You could see through them clear enough and you could always feel the ocean breeze. As I longed for the ocean breeze, I leaned up against the window pane and it budged! I sat bolt upright and looked around. I was still alone in the room. I turned back to the window and pushed on it again. This time the bottom pane tipped out and I could see the ground below. I instantly shut it and double checked that I was still alone. So far, the coast was clear. Just as I was turning back to face the windows, I heard his voice.

"You really don't know how to stay out of trouble, do you?"

I caught my breath for a second before I realized it was Nova.

"You scared me! I was just..."

"I know what you were doing. Very clever. You figured it out without me even having to tell you about it."

"You know about the window?"

"Of course," he smirked. "Who do you think unlocked it?"

"Nova, what's going on? You said you'd explain everything to me."

He walked toward me smiling. When he sat on my bed, I

could smell his sweet earthy scent. I felt my face heat up again as he put his arm across my shoulders.

"You're right, and I will. I have a plan for us. And it involves this window. I've gotten you out of lessons and work for the rest of the week, but we need more time."

"For what?" I said impatiently.

"This is the part where you listen and I talk, okay?"

"Okay!" I howled. "Just get to it already."

"For the rest of the week I need you to meet me behind our palm in the courtyard. I can tell you everything there. I don't want to say too much in here in case someone is listening to us."

I nodded for him to continue.

"At lunch today meet me out there. I'll knock twice at your door when I'm heading out to the courtyard, okay? Give me a few minutes head start and then meet me there. Don't tell anyone where you're going. This has to stay between us."

"Okay."

"Promise."

"I promise, jeez."

Nova shook his head at me and smiled that big, brilliant smile of his.

"What?" I prodded.

"Nothing... I'll see ya in a few," he said as he got up to stride toward the door.

I caught him by the hand. "Now it's your turn to listen," I said.

"I need to know what I did! And why I'm not in the locker! I know I provoked Jemma and she punched me, but you said there's more. I need to know what else happened."

Nova grabbed my face in his hands. His green eyes bore into mine and for a moment I felt like I was going to be swallowed up by them and drown in that deep-green sea swirling behind his pupils. "Trust me," was all he said and he left the room.

I sunk back down onto the bed and felt even more confused than before. Nova had helped me this far. He brought me to the nurse's station and he covered for me with his lie about falling off the pile. I guess I had no other choice but to trust him. I didn't have much chance to think about it though, because a moment later there was a knock on the door.

I rushed to it and whispered, "Nova?"

"No, sorry to disappoint you, it's just me," muttered Remi as he pushed past me.

"Remi! Oh I'm so glad to see you!"

"Yeah, well I brought your lunch."

"Remi, what's going on? Please tell me what happened. Are you okay? What about 42? I didn't get you into trouble, did I?"

He just stood there staring at me, holding my tray of food with a bewildered look on his face. At first he looked like he was angry, but then he took a few more steps toward me, holding my gaze the entire time.

"I don't remember what happened. I remember her hitting me and that's it."

Remi looked like he was deciding whether he believed me or not.

He must have sided with me since he put my tray down and sat down on my bed. I joined him.

"65, you hit her back. I think. I'm not really sure what happened either. One minute she was punching you in the face and the next second she was flying backwards."

"What do you mean?"

"Well, when she hit you, you put your hands up and she flew backwards. It was like you hit her too, but I was right next to you, 65. I never saw you touch her. You both just fell down and it was chaos. I was trying to see if you were okay, but I didn't have a chance. Nova swooped in and told everyone what to do."

"What did he say?"

"He told me and 42 to stay with you and told everyone else to get back to work so we didn't attract attention and get sent to the locker. Then he ran over to 31. To see if she was okay, I guess?"

"Was she?" I asked.

"Yes, she sat up and looked really confused. Nova talked to her for a while and then called two Grifts over to make sure she was okay. That's when he made up that story about you falling off the pile and knocking into 31 on the way down."

"Then what?"

"He told us the story we were going with and said to keep our mouths shut so we didn't all get into trouble. Then he picked you up and was gone."

I sat there taking it all in.

"I was so scared, 65. I didn't know where he was taking you. And you were knocked out. You hit your head so hard when you fell." He paused. "You're alright, right?"

"Yes, I think so. I just don't understand what happened. Nova says – "

"Why do you even talk to him, 65?"

"He's my friend! That's why!"

Remi rolled his eyes. "Well this *friend* has been getting us in an awful lot of trouble, hasn't he?"

"We're not in the locker right now because of him, so I think he's actually pretty good at getting us out of trouble."

"Well, I don't like him," Remi said angrily. He stood up and crossed his arms to face me. "Do you know he wouldn't let me see you in Miss Breia's office?" he huffed.

So, I wasn't imagining Remi being in the nurse's office?

I flashed back to the conversation I had tried to overhear after Nova and Miss Breia left my room. Why hadn't they let Remi see me? Maybe Nova didn't want Remi to get nervous and screw up the story he'd made up. I made a mental note to ask him about it.

"I'm sorry, Remi. I thought I saw you, but I was so out of it. I would have wanted to see you if they asked me. You know that. You're my best friend."

"I know," he smiled. "I'm sorry, I know you've had a rough few days. How's your head?"

"It's okay."

"Well, your eye doesn't look that bad," he lied.

"You're a terrible liar," I laughed.

This seemed to put us back at ease. We both laughed at the purple bruise covering half of my face. Then we hugged each other. What would I do without Remi? He always made me feel better. Just then there was another knock at the door and 42 and another John from our year peeked in.

"Hi, 65. Can we come in?" 42 asked timidly.

"Sure."

They looked around as they entered the room slowly and closed the door softly behind them. #42 looked as bird-like as ever as the sunlight streaming in from the windows danced across her delicate features. Her piercing-amber eyes looked worried as she swiftly crossed the room toward me. Remi and I were still sitting on my new cot bed, so she crouched down in front of me at the foot of the bed, folding her slender legs under her. She stared up at me expectantly. I looked over at the other John who had come with her and noticed he was staring at me too. It was starting to make me uncomfortable. I recognized him instantly from our year, John #22. He was one of the fittest boys in our year. He looked as solid as the stones they built the walls around Lux with. His short brown hair and deep amber eyes complimented each other and I realized I never really looked him in the eye before. I was in the habit of keeping my head down and minding my business. I deduced that he wasn't one of the Johns that roughed me up after I beat them racing through the fields, and he wasn't in the group that always tagged along with Jemma, sneering as she tormented me. Still I had no idea why he was all of a sudden taking an interest in me. This newfound attention made me uneasy and my cheeks flushed, giving me away. Luckily, 42 piped up.

"We just wanted to check on you and make sure you were alright. You took quite a fall."

She paused and looked from Remi to me and back. I couldn't take the silence so I finally motioned for 22 to join us.

"I know I didn't fall, okay?" I said.

"Oh! Good. I didn't want you to think we weren't going along with the story. But now that it's out, how did you do that?" 42 said.

"What do you mean?" I asked.

"With Jemma...that's what you call her, right? How did you throw her like that?"

"Yes, Jemma, but we really shouldn't say that to her face, you saw what happened, right?" I said pointing to my bruised face. I was trying to lighten the mood, but this just made 42 wince.

"I'm Journey," said 22, looking serious as he stood over our little group. This was the first time he'd spoken since entering our room. He didn't offer anymore, just his name.

"And I'm Sparrow," whispered 42. She had a huge grin on her face.

"Guys, seriously I think we need to lay off the names. It's just getting us into trouble," said Remi.

"She can protect us," said Journey with such a confidence I almost believed him, except wait—he was talking about me?

"What?" I asked, standing.

Sparrow scrambled to her feet as well. "65, that's why we're here, we wanted you to know we're on your side and we're with you, ya know? We'll help you," she said breathlessly.

"I don't know what you mean, there's no sides, I ... I..."

"It's okay 65. We're like you," she beamed.

Just then there was two quick knocks at the door. All of our heads spun toward the noise. Remi jumped and for an instant we froze. Then I remembered that it was Nova's signal. I ran to the door, turning back to look at their startled faces before I left the room.

"I gotta go, we'll talk later," I called over my shoulder.

I did a jerky walk-jog to the courtyard. I wanted to get there fast! I needed answers! But each time I started to run, my head would protest and I would get funny glances from the Grifts I passed. I skidded to a stop just in time to avoid slamming into a large tarcat as I entered the courtyard. It was Khan, I could tell from his jeweled collar. He was my least favorite because of his extra ornery disposition. He was the largest of all the tarcats at the Center and Greeley's personal favorite. He had paws the size of my head and teeth so sharp and long that he couldn't close his mouth all the way, creating a constant snarl on his face. He narrowed his bright-yellow eyes at me and twitched his long whiskers. I took a step back and bowed to him. This was how you must proceed if you don't want to offend a tarcat. They're very temperamental creatures. My heart was pounding as I continued to bow and my mind screamed.

Walk away, walk away, please, walk away, Khan.

He shook his snow white coat and sniffed the air. Something else seemed to have caught his attention because he turned away from me, and I ducked to avoid getting smacked by his black whip-like tail. I breathed a sigh of relief that he hadn't decided to drag me to Greeley's office. Finally, the coast seemed clear and I darted to our secret meeting place.

"Took you long enough," Nova joked.

He was leaning against the wall, chewing a blade of palm grass, looking like he didn't have a care in the world. This infuriated me. After my confusing morning, I was determined to get to the bottom of what was going on and I didn't want to play Nova's games anymore.

"Nova, I need to know exactly what's going on, right now!"

"Ah, she's getting tough, huh?" he teased.

"I'm serious. Remi just told me that I somehow magically threw Jemma without even touching her, and then 42 and 22 confirmed it, and said they're on my side, whatever the heck that means. Oh, and their names are Sparrow and Journey in case you're wondering. They came in just offering up names and help. What is going on? They said they're special like me...? Nova, I don't want to be special, I just want everything to go back to normal."

"Well, you can forget about that, my dear little Tippy. You're the one we've been waiting for and your whole life is about to change," he said with a proud smile.

6

Nova was right. Nothing was the same after that day. We sat behind our palm in the courtyard for hours while he filled me in on all the details that would change my life forever and set into motion a chain of events that would change Hullabee Island forever.

He recounted the confrontation with Jemma in the field when she hit me. That much I remembered, but the bizarre thing was how she suffered the same injury she inflicted upon me, without me or anyone else ever laying a hand on her. I was at a loss for how this could be possible, but Nova had some theories of his own. He proceeded to fill my head with the fairytales and legends of our island. I say fairytales because surely I thought none of it could be true. But as I later learned, Nova was just beginning to open my eyes to the strange and wondrous world of the island I called home.

Nova told me the legend of Lux, and how Hullabee Island had once been a flourishing land of peace, equality and harmony. Lux was so large and expansive that it dotted the entire coast of our island with its shimmering white-stone buildings. Everyone was welcome in Lux or anywhere on the island for that matter. There were no citizens or locals or orphans or Grifts, all people were cast of the same cloth and all were respected by each other. There were also tribal people on the island that lived a simple life, deep within the rainforest and were said to have magical powers that they used for good. These powers helped to keep the peaceful balance among all things on the island. The pleasant people, the bountiful crops, the ideal weather, the docile animals, all were thanks to the indigenous Beto tribe that dwelled in the lush depths of our forests, near the volcanic heart of Hullabee Island.

Of course, as every fairytale goes, things could not stay this good forever. A simple man named Ravin would ultimately destroy this utopic paradise. He was a man who always needed more. He always wanted to be the best at everything. He was never satisfied by what he already had, or where he'd already been. For Ravin, contentment didn't exist. He first focused on building his muscles and sculpting his body into the perfect specimen that even the gods would admire. After achieving the perfect body, he decided he needed the perfect home. He picked a site on the highest cliff above all of his neighbors. He spent years erecting his white-stone palace. It was the largest home Lux had ever seen and everyone came to admire it. Ravin loved the attention and bathed in the power it made him feel. But still he needed more.

He set out to find himself a wife to live in his enormous white palace. Of course not any woman would do, he was looking for the most beautiful woman on the island, and he was so arrogant in his quest that he abandoned the idea of loving his wife and held an audition to find her based solely on beauty. Women from everywhere flocked to Ravin, hoping to be selected as his wife. But Ravin wasn't impressed. All the women looked the same to him. They were all tan with dark hair and dark eyes, just as he was and as was everyone on the island. He wanted to have something special, that no one else had. On the third day of his auditions, he grew hopeless that he would ever find anyone that could be as beautiful and perfect as he was, and was about to settle on an athletic girl named Tonia when he saw *her*.

Her name was Mora and she was walking along the soft, sandy streets with her mother, carrying baskets of exotic fruit from the forest upon her golden-blonde head. Ravin had never seen something more beautiful than Mora and was instantly taken by her. He pushed through the crowd of women fawning over him and ran over to Mora and her mother. The hulking sight of this gigantic, muscular man running toward her frightened Mora and she hid behind her mother when he approached. Ravin tried to explain to Mora and her mother how lucky they were that he had spotted her from afar and instantly knew she was the perfect woman he was looking for to become his wife. This brought the Beto women to giggles and they tried to ignore this obviously raving madman and continue down the street. But their laughter angered Ravin and he told them that he was the most desirable man in Lux and that Mora had to be given to him. At this time Nevia, Mora's mother, spoke for the first time. She explained that she and her daughter lived in the forest with the Beto people, and while they were flattered by Ravin's admiration, they would both be returning home after they finished trading their fruit. Ravin was stunned by Nevia's boldness to defy him her daughter. He saw there was no use reasoning with the old Beto mother, so he picked up Mora and threw her over his shoulder and ran up the hills to his home. Mora was terrified of Ravin. She screamed for her mother the whole way to Ravin's home. He tried to quiet her and convince her that she would be happy with him, but she only begged harder to be returned to her family. So the frustrated Ravin locked her away for the night.

Each day he would try to win her over with lavish gifts and sweet words, but each day Mora grew more frightened. Nevia sat outside Ravin's home every day chanting and pleading with him to release Mora or she would have no choice but to summon the island gods for help. Ravin grew desperate that someone, perhaps even the gods themselves, would eventually come and take Mora away, so one night he took her from her room and led her out the back door of his palace. At first Mora was elated. This was the first time she'd been outside in weeks. She stared up at the bright moonlit sky and drank in the beauty of the stars. Her flaxen-blonde hair seemed to come to life in the moonlight, dancing across her slender shoulders and down her back. Ravin grabbed her wrists and pleaded with her once more for her to love him, but when she turned her clear-blue eyes away from him, he knew he would never win her, so he did the only thing he thought would guarantee that no other man could best him by winning Mora's heart. He threw her from the cliffs of his home into the dark, greedy sea. Mora's fateful scream awoke Nevia, and when she found out what Ravin had done, she was inconsolable with fury and rage. She returned to the Beto people and told her family of the grave misfortune that had befallen their beloved Mora. They were all shocked and devastated by the news, but none more so then her twin sister Nesia. Nesia and Mora were identical twins and she had always shared a special bond with her sister beyond their delicate, pale skin, blue eyes and blonde hair. Their connection was so deep that Nesia was said to have felt her sister's pain when Ravin held her captive and finally killed her. She went to their tribe's leader and demanded that her sister be avenged. Jaka, the Beto's leader, said the only way to appease the gods and restore balance after Mora's death would be to sacrifice Ravin into the volcano, and then everything would be forgiven and could start anew. But of course Ravin would not comply with such a thing, and secretly Nesia was happy because she believed Ravin deserved to suffer a death far worse than that.

So, the Beto people released a wrath upon Lux that had never been seen before. A war broke out between the people of Lux and the Beto tribe. Although no one in Lux condoned what Ravin had done to Mora, none of them would help the Betos stand against Ravin. The Betos saw this as a traitorous act against their people and went after everyone in their way to avenge her death. The people of Lux had no choice but to fight back and fiercely defend their homes and families from the ruthless Beto warriors that pillaged and burned their once-beautiful city. Without the Beto tribe using their powers for peace on the island, things quickly changed. There were divisions between the populations, the weather turned turbulent, and the citizens of Lux began to take notice of the treacherous wildlife that surrounded them. The regal tarcats they once revered became savage, blood-thirsty beasts. The indigenous plants of the island swiftly overtook the crops, and the hostile waters made it impossible to fish or trade by sea. For four years Hullabee Island was locked in this tumultuous battle that nearly destroyed all of Lux.

It is said that Nesia made it her goal to find Ravin and avenge her sister. She was fueled by such hatred that she became somewhat of a legend herself. She was feared by all because she no longer felt any allegiance to her people or those in Lux. She was ruthless and would kill anything that crossed her on her mission to destroy Ravin.

On her quest she found herself spending a great deal of time in solitude, hiking the cliffs and mountainous shorelines of the island in search of Ravin. One day she slipped and fell, injuring herself badly. She had lost all hope of rescue, when suddenly a young man appeared. He approached her without fear, although he surely knew who she was from her tribal attire and long blonde mane. He was wearing traditional white linen pants and shining gold cuffs, he was clearly from Lux and not a friend, but he helped her nonetheless. Nesia was confused by his kindness, and as she stared into his light-blue eyes, the light in them reminded her of her sister, Mora, and the kindness and love she had always shown others. Hadn't her own eyes looked this same way not too long ago? She began to weep at the thought of how much Mora would have hated this bloody war being fought over her.

Nesia began doubting her motives and spending more time with this man called Kai. She was stirred by the feelings she held for this kind stranger that cared for her and nursed her injuries. She soon found she was in love with him, and him with her. And what's a fairytale without forbidden love, after all?

Nesia and Kai tried to hide their love at first, but found it impossible as the fighting escalated between Lux and the Betos. Secretly they wed atop the cliffs where they met. They lived in blissful solitude far away from the fighting and started a family. It is said they had two daughters. One with hair as dark as the night sky, the other with hair as white as the sandy shores. They represented the light and the dark, the heavens and the earth, the balance that Hullabee needed to restore peace. Nesia went to the Beto leader Jaka and asked him if there was any way to stop the war, because she feared for her daughters and she believed they might be the key to bringing peace back to the island because they were created out of love between the Betos and Lux. Jaka was intrigued and asked to meet the daughters. He was shocked to find that they were as Nesia had said and more. He blessed them and said they were indeed proof that Lux and the Betos could live in peace once again.

After meeting Nesia's unique daughters, Jaka said he would sacrifice himself to the gods so the island could be reborn. The Beto tribe begged for another way, but Jaka explained that his people would have all they needed in Nesia's daughters. They were light and dark, sun and moon, heavens and earth; they had the power to sooth the unrest and heal the island. And with this he sacrificed himself to the volcano and the rest is history.

"What do you mean the rest is history, Nova? I've heard parts of this story before from the locals, but if it were true wouldn't we all be living in peace and harmony in beautiful seaside houses in Lux? It's nothing but an old folk tale."

"That's just it, Tippy. It's not that old, and I'm not done yet. Do you want to hear the rest or not?"

"Alright, but get on with it!"

"After Jaka sacrificed himself into the volcano he set in motion what we refer to as the Flood. He said the island would be reborn, but he neglected to say how. He said that those on the island who had become evil and poisoned by the war would be eliminated. That is what caused the rains, the winds, the lava, and the peril. Everything had to go so the land could be cleansed and start anew.

"Yeah, but we didn't all die, did we? You're still here and so am I."

"Exactly!"

I gave him an impatient look.

"You see we were the innocent, we survived the Flood because we were meant to."

He paused for a moment, looking into my eyes; searching for more understanding than I could give him. He leaned forward and took my face in his hands and continued.

"And some of us were meant to do even more," he said almost pleadingly.

I was mesmerized by the way he gazed at me. I found myself drowning in his languid green eyes. I felt my mind spinning and my cheeks flushing. My heart quickened again and I felt short of breath. Why did this keep happening to me? Damn Nova and his hold over me. I loved and hated it at the same time, and yet was powerless against it. Nova released his hold of my face and my soul simultaneously.

"Are you alright? You look flushed. Maybe this is enough for today. I've given you a lot to think about."

I shook my head. "Oh no, all you've done is tell me some old fairytale. None of this explains what happened between me and Jemma, and why everyone but me has a name, and why I all of a sudden have *friends* on my *side*? You need to do a little better than this."

"Ok, I will, I promise; but it's getting late."

I looked around and he was right. The shade from our palm had grown into a shadow that cloaked the courtyard in darkness. My time with Nova had slipped away too quickly as usual.

"Nova! You missed Flood work!"

"Let me worry about that, okay? Now, this is the deal. You remember how your window works?"

I nodded. Finally we were getting to the window!

"Okay, tonight and every night for that matter, at 11:00 sharp, you'll use the window and come meet me outside the Center."

"But how will I know when it's 11:00, Nova? And won't a Grift see me?"

"Tippy, a little trust," he smiled. "I'll call for you when it's 11:00 and I've taken care of the Grifts. Just do as I say and soon you'll have all the answers to your questions."

7

I didn't have any time to protest because Nova kissed me on top of my head and then slipped silently out behind the palms. I dusted myself off as I stood and stretched my aching limbs. We must have been sitting for longer then I imagined because my legs felt heavy with the static pain of pins and needles. I shook them out and pushed myself out from behind our palm's wide, protective leaves and into the deserted courtyard. Nova was gone, disappeared into the night. All I could do was walk slowly back to my room with my mind swimming in wonder.

I never imagined my world would be changing so rapidly. Just a few weeks ago I had only one friend in the world, I believed none of us knew our real names, and I had never heard of Nova. I was starting to wonder if the world was a safer place for me back then. I had a strange foreboding feeling in the pit of my stomach. Suddenly I was snapped away from my thoughts as I walked straight into Jest, one of the Grifts we all tried to avoid. His foul smell and yellow sagging skin was enough to keep you at bay, but his propensity to alert Greeley of our "difficult" behavior was what worried me the most about encountering him. I stumbled backward and landed with a thud on my rear.

"Oh... I'm sorry, I... uhh..."

I let a little gasping sound escape as I realized who I had bumped into, and that was a mistake because Jest always assumed that we were gawking at his missing limb. He lost his arm from just above his elbow in the Flood. I'd heard that it was so badly burned from the lava that it had to be amputated and that it accounted for his sour disposition. The stub that was left hung awkwardly at his side and was still a blackened, vein-covered mess, laden with sores that constantly attracted beat flies, menacing little biting creatures. He leaned toward me and my nostrils burned as his putrid smell encroached my space. His hollow grey eyes narrowed as he focused on me.

"So, who do we have here?" he growled.

I crawled on my backside a few paces before scurrying to my feet.

"It's just me, sir. 65. I'm on my way back to my room for the night, sir. I was just using the Jane's room," I quickly lied.

"Were you now, 65?" he questioned sarcastically.

I nodded quickly as I started to slowly take side steps in the direction of my room.

"Well, how is it that I find you past the dining hall when the Jane's room is in the other direction?"

Shoot! He was right, I was proud of my quick response, but hadn't thought it through. I was nowhere near the Jane's room, which was only a short walk to the left after leaving room 13. Jest had found me just outside the entrance to the dining hall, which was in the opposite direction of my room. There wasn't much past the dining hall other than lesson rooms, rooms for the other orphans, and the entrance to the courtyard. None of which I should have been visiting at this hour. From the way his colorless lips were curled into a grin Jest was surely relishing the idea that he caught me in a lie and was about to turn me into Greeley.

"I...I...um.."

"Come with me, 65," he hissed as he latched onto my shoulder squeezing it much harder than necessary. I couldn't help but let out a little whimper as I saw his jagged yellow nails dig into my flesh.

"Knock off your sniveling, Jane, you'll soon have something to cry about!" he snarled.

"What's going on out here?" I heard from behind me.

We both turned our heads to see Miss Breia pop her head out of her office.

"Miss Breia!" I cried. Why hadn't I thought of her? I was only a few feet from her office. I should have said I was on my way to see her because of my fall. Maybe she would buy that my head was hurting?

"I found this one sneaking around the halls," Jest said.

"Oh, 65, what's wrong? Are you feeling ill again?" Miss Breia asked when she saw it was me.

"I, I was just going to the Jane's room, but I got dizzy and...disoriented."

"Oh my dear, that's to be expected, you took quite a fall," she said as she bustled around me, feeling my forehead and checking my pulse. Jest released his grasp on my shoulder and backed away for a moment, but was growing impatient with Miss Breia's meddling.

"I'm taking her to see Greeley, she shouldn't be out here. She's nowhere near the Jane's room!" he grumbled.

"Oh no you will not!" Miss Breia said, pulling me toward her, almost smothering me in her oversized chest. Normally I would have squirmed away in protest, but anything that kept me shielded from Jest and Greeley was okay in my book.

"This poor little Jane has had a traumatic week. She's the

one that fell from the rubble pile and gave herself a good old fashion head knocking. She's had enough trouble for one week. I'll take it from here," she said as she sheltered me against her and headed toward her office.

I never felt so much love and respect for Miss Breia as I did in that moment. She had just stood up to Jest and delivered me safely to her office. Without her I would have ended up in front of a just-woken and extra-ill-tempered Greeley, and would have definitely been spending my night in the locker. Miss Breia released me and took a step back to look at me once we were inside her office.

"Now, what can I do for you, little Janey 65?" she asked cheerfully.

I couldn't help myself, I just stepped forward and hugged her, stretching my arms as far as I could around her broad waist. She laughed and hugged me back.

"Well aren't you a sweet one?" she chuckled. "Don't worry about old Jest. He's just cranky on account of that arm. I've told him I could treat it about a dozen times, but the old bog won't let me near it. No need for him to inflict his suffering on others. Anyway, are you still feeling dizzy? Because I can give you something to help."

"No, I actually feel much better now. I think I can find my way back to my room, I just want to get some rest," I said. "I can find my way from here. Thank you!"

"Dear, don't you need to use the Jane's room? Here let me take you."

Oh yeah, the Jane's room! I forgot that had been my excuse.

I thought about protesting but then, on second thought, it wouldn't hurt to have an escort in case I ran into Jest or anyone else in the halls. I followed Miss Breia to the Jane's room and she stood outside the door waiting for me. I figured I might as well use the facilities while I had the chance. I was going to have to sneak outside to meet Nova soon, and who knows what he had up his sleeve. I took the opportunity to wash up a bit while I was in there. It wouldn't hurt to look a little more presentable. I scrubbed a layer of grim from my skin and soaked my blonde hair with the cool water running through the sink basin. It felt refreshing and it seemed to relax me a bit. I pulled my hair back and quickly braided it to the side, tying it with a piece of twine I normally kept wrapped around my wrist for such occasions. I gazed at myself in the mirror for a moment, admiring how my normally bright-blonde locks looked almost brown when wet. It made me feel like I fit in a little more. I splashed some cool water on my face and stepped closer to the mirror to inspect my grooming job. The moon-light bounced across my freckled cheekbones and caught my eyes, lighting up my clear-blue irises like they were electric. There was nothing I could do to dull those eyes. I would always be different. I sighed at my reflection, feeling heaviness in my chest again.

"Are you alright in there?" Miss Breia called, pulling me away from my thoughts.

"Yes, coming," I replied.

I swiftly crossed the Jane's room to meet her at the door.

"Sorry to keep you waiting," I smiled. "I just wanted to wash up a bit before bed."

"No worries, love."

We walked down the hall the short distance to my room and as we were reaching the door I turned to Miss Breia.

"What time is it?"

"Why it's bedtime silly," she laughed.

"I mean, what hour is it?"

"65, are you sure you're alright? You know we don't keep hours that way around here."

"I know, it's just, I was curious to see if you maybe knew hours that way since you know medicine and all."

She looked at me quizzically.

"We learned about it in lessons and it made me curious, that's all," I lied.

"Sorry my dear, I've never had use for the hours here."

Great! So how exactly does Nova think I'm going to figure out when it's eleven o'clock?

"Never mind. Goodnight Miss Breia," I said as I slipped through the door to room 13.

Luckily everyone in my year seemed to be asleep, so I didn't have to answer any questions from them. I tiptoed to my cot bed under the window and lay there fully dressed, staring at the ceiling, hoping there would be some sign of when I was to meet Nova. I lay there wide awake for what seemed like hours, just replaying the events of the last few days. I had met Nova, found out my best friend #26 had a name – Remi. I also learned that the raven-haired bully of my year, #31, was actually named Jemma, and that she had a little sister that died in the Flood; which apparently she didn't like being brought up, because that resulted in my trip to Miss Breia's nurse station after my supposed fall from the rubble pile and my black eye. Not to mention the secret-invisible-magic punch that I apparently delivered to Jemma, and the new-found friends Sparrow and Journey, it attracted. Then Nova, who was supposed to help explain it all, just told me some crazy fairytale and that I was special or something. And now, I was supposed to climb out this window and meet him at 11:00 with no way to know when that actually was.

How did I get myself into this situation? Had I asked for it? I was always daydreaming about another life, where things were better and I wasn't an orphan. Had the gods grown impatient with my whining and chosen to show me I didn't actually have it so bad? Or, was this what I wanted? I was learning names, making friends. Maybe this was the path that would take me to what I craved – my name, my family, a life away from the Troian Center? And then there was Nova. I had a feeling I wouldn't trade any of the fear, pain or frustration of the past few weeks away if it meant I wouldn't know him. I had only scratched the surface of Nova. I felt that there was something special about him, something that made me trust him and drew me uncontrollably toward him. I knew in my heart that I would follow Nova into the mouth of the volcano if that was his intention. I had hopelessly fused my soul to his that day he scooped me onto his back and showed me his secret world behind the banana palm in the courtyard.

8

"*Tippy!*"

I bolted upright. I just heard someone calling me. Had I fallen asleep? I looked around the room. All was dark and still. The only sounds I heard were the steady breathing of the other orphans. I hung my legs off the side of the bed and they swung, still inches from the floor. I craned my neck toward the large straw bed to my right where all the Janes lay huddled together under their threadbare tan blankets. They all seemed much more comfortable without me taking up another space in the communal bed. The scene to my left was the same. All the Johns slumbered undisturbed in their bed. I could see my shadow cast eerily on the floor from the moonlight shining in from the window behind me. The angle made me appear tall and long. It made me smile for a moment, getting lost in the idea that I would one day grow out of the short, slight frame I inherited.

"*Tippy!*"

There it was again! This time I knew it was Nova. No one ever called me Tippy but him. This had to be the signal. But how was he calling me without waking the others? It was

almost as though his voice was inside my head! I scanned the
room for movement one more time, but no one stirred. I
pulled my legs back onto the cot bed and folded them underneath me until I was crouched in a sort of kneeling position,
facing the window. I slowly pushed on the bottom pane of
glass as I had done that morning. At first nothing happened
and I began to panic. I tried again with more pressure and this
time the pane swung out so suddenly that the top half of my
body went with it. I found myself dangling from my waist out
of the window, with the pane resting lazily on my lower back. I
began to wiggle my hips back and forth until I gained enough
momentum to slither the rest of my body out the window as
silently as possible. I landed unceremoniously on the sand
below. *Graceful 65!* All the sounds of the buzzing nightlife
around me stopped the instant I thudded to the ground. The
silence was unbearable. I sat for a while until the insects
picked up their songs again. Then I stood up brushing sand
off of me and smoothing my hair. I guess bathing was unnec-
essary after all.

It took a moment for my eyes to adjust to the darkness so I
could get my bearings. It appeared I was behind some foliage
right outside the Troian Center. I gingerly pushed through it
to the clearing ahead. The plants were thickly wound together
and they resisted my progress, roots tripping me along the
way. As I neared the edge I paused to look around. To my
right, I could see the sparkling lights of Lux in the distance; to
the left I could see the entrance to the courtyard. There
weren't any Grifts posted there as there should be. That
worried me, because maybe it meant they heard me and were
coming to look for me! This thought dropped me into a
crouch among the bushes.

"*Tippy! C'mon!*"

There was Nova's voice again. Where the heck was he? It

irritated me immensely because his voice kept startling me and interrupting the thoughts and conversations I was having with myself. *Well, now or never I guess? Nova said to trust him, so here goes nothing.*

I stood and broke free from the shelter of the plant life and darted straight ahead at a full sprint. I had gone a good distance when I realized I didn't know where I was going. I stopped and knelt down, suddenly feeling overexposed being out in the open. I looked over my shoulder at the dim light coming from the Troian Center. All was still. I stood again looking to the inky blackness of the thick forest ahead of me and slowly started making my way toward it. All of my senses seemed to be straining to overcompensate for my lack of vision. I heard the crunch of each footstep I placed and smelled the thick earthy scent of the forest approaching. I didn't know why I was walking toward the forest since Nova neglected to tell me where to meet him, but something was pulling me that way. It was as if a magnetic force grabbed a hold of me and was guiding my steps. As I reached the edge of the forest I felt all of my senses tingling. I was nervous and excited all at once. The damp soil and the heavy perfume of the tropical plants were intoxicating. The smell reminded me of Nova, and like that, he was by my side!

"Nova!" I squealed, half startled and half relieved.

"You made it! Great work. Come on we have a lot to do." he said as he grabbed my hand and started forward.

"Wait, what are we doing out here?" I whispered nervously as I pulled against him.

"I thought you wanted answers, Tippy?"

"I do."

"Ok, then let's go. Your answers await."

I could see his white teeth gleaming as he smiled at me and pulled me onward. As usual, he melted away my inhibitions with his charm. We walked a little way deeper into the forest and soon I felt that we had been swallowed by the night. It was so dark that I couldn't even see my hand in front of my face. Not even the moonlight could make its way into the thick forest. Just as I was about to protest that we go any further for fear we'd never make it back out, I saw a little burst of light. At first it was large, but then it shrunk to the size of an egg and danced in front of Nova. I clung to his side not sure what to do. As I looked closer I saw that the dancing yellow light was a flame floating directly above Nova's open palm.

"What the...?"

"Pretty cool, huh?" he said happily.

My eyes grew wide and my heart pounded louder as I stared in bewilderment at Nova. Was this some kind of magic trick?

"How did you do that?" I whispered nervously.

"This is what I was trying to tell you, Tippy. I'm special, just like you!"

"What?"

"I knew you'd never believe me if I just told you what I could do, so I figured I'd show you. That's what tonight is all about!"

I took a step closer to the ball of light bouncing steadily above his hand. It was amazing. It was the most amazing thing I had ever seen. Everything in me was telling me to be afraid, but I couldn't help myself, I was so drawn to Nova and his flame. I wanted to know all about it and I wanted to be able to do it myself. I circled around his hand with my eyes transfixed upon the flame. I wanted to reach out and touch it, but something held me back. I was trembling inside at the idea of it.

As if he was reading my mind, he said "You can touch it. It won't hurt you."

Startled, I froze and looked up at him.

"Nova, how do you do that? You always know what I'm thinking."

"Oh, that?" He laughed. "Well, yeah. I can do that, too."

I paused for a second to focus on Nova's face. It was illuminated in such a way that it took my breath away for a moment. The light bathed his tan face enough for me to see the bright sparkle of his green eyes and the joy that radiated over him as he looked at me. His smile was dazzling and white, and his dimples were in rare form. It had to hurt to smile that big, I thought as I stared at him. Then I shook myself from the Nova-induced spell that he always seemed to cast on me. I was so confused. I didn't know if I was happy or sad to learn these things. Wait, was he listening to my thoughts right now?

"You can hear what people are thinking?" I asked cautiously.

"Yes. I know it's weird, but I've always been this way. Ever since I was little. I thought it was normal, and everyone could do it. I've never shared this with anyone else, Tippy."

"Why me?" I asked.

"Because I trust you. You're different, you're like me!"

"Why do you keep saying that? I can't do this," I said pointing at his outstretched hand. "I can't make fire or hear what people are thinking!"

He smiled. "I have a feeling you can do a lot more than you think you can."

Nova set off again and I was forced to follow him or be swallowed up by the trail of darkness. He stopped shortly and sat on a fallen palm tree, patting the trunk for me to join him.

"You try it now."

"What?"

"Just do whatever you did when you were with Jemma," he encouraged.

"I keep telling you all, I didn't do anything when I was with her."

"Well, you definitely did something, maybe you just don't know how. That's why we came out here. We can practice until you figure it out."

For the first time since I joined Nova, I started to feel that heavy thing creep back into my chest. What if the only reason Nova wanted to be my friend was because he thought I had powers like him? Once he figured out I didn't, would he not want to spend time with me anymore? I began to feel panicky, like the air was being sucked from my lungs. Little beads of sweat broke out along my hair line. I wiped at them with the back of my hand.

"Tippy, it's okay. I know you can do this, even if you don't. Just believe in it."

There he went again, getting inside my head! I was going to have to remember to guard my thoughts more carefully when I was around him.

"Here, why don't you try this," he said grabbing my hand and dumping his bright little orb into my palm.

The instant it touched my hand it went out and we were once again bathed in darkness until Nova sparked another magical flame. My mind was reeling. I was learning so much, but was more confused than ever. Nova had magical powers, he's convinced that I do, too; and who knows, maybe I do? But my trial run wasn't going so well.

"You have to believe in yourself, Tippy. Let's try it again, but don't be scared this time."

I held out my right hand, palm up and open and steadied it with my left hand underneath. This time it stayed lit, but as soon as I felt the tingling sensation take hold of my hands I panicked and pulled them back to my sides, dumping the little flame, which extinguished when it hit the mossy ground.

I let out a deep sigh. "I'm no good at this. Let's just go back, okay? I've had enough."

"No, Tippy, come on! Concentrate! I know you can do this!"

"Nova, I can't!"

"Ok, calm down. We need to think about this. Maybe you need to be in the right frame of mind to be able to do it. I've had years to practice so it just comes naturally to me, but you need to take your time and figure out your triggers."

"Triggers?"

"Yes, that's how you tap into your power. It's usually tied to emotions or nature."

I stared at him wide-eyed. It was like he was speaking another language and he might as well have been because I hadn't the first clue what my trigger was or how to find out since I'd never done anything magic before. Well, except for when I hit Jemma apparently.

"Jemma, that's it!" he said.

"Oh, you've got to stop doing that! I don't like you reading my mind!"

"Sorry, bad habit," he smiled. "But I'll try harder to stay out of your head, promise."

"So you think Jemma is my trigger?" I asked.

"Maybe? That's the first time you did anything magical, right?"

"Yeah, I guess. But what are we gonna do? Jemma's not exactly my biggest fan, she's not going to help me figure out if I have powers!"

"Hmmm... let me think," Nova said, pacing back and forth silently on the damp forest floor.

I sat on the log tapping my foot impatiently. It figured that Jemma would be standing in my way of something great. She never could stand me.

What did I ever do that was so awful to make her hate me so much? Ugh, I'm not going to let her take this from me. Whatever these so-called powers were, I wanted them. I stood up and paced around with Nova, too. It felt more productive than sitting at least. I stopped by a tree and gave it a hard kick to release some of my frustration. Nova's light suddenly brightened. We both turned to look at each other.

"What was that?" I asked.

"I think it was you! What were you just doing?" Nova demanded.

"Walking around thinking about how much I hate Jemma. I took my anger out on this poor tree," I said, patting its trunk regretfully.

"That's it. It's your anger toward Jemma!" he said excitedly. "Come here, let's try it again. This time think about Jemma and how much you can't stand her."

"Okay, I'll try," I said, sounding a bit unconvinced.

I raised my hands again, palms open and cupped together this time. It was as if Nova was passing me a fragile insect considering the delicacy he used transferring the flame to me this time. It touched my palms and he continued to support me by placing his hands underneath mine. The light danced and flickered but it didn't go out. I concentrated hard on staying still although I could feel the powerful sensation of the flame tingling up my arms. Nova and I stood there with our arms outstretched toward each other cupping the licking flames.

"I'm going to let go now, Tippy. Keep concentrating."

He slowly pulled his hands away from mine and took a step back into the shadows. I felt the flame start to dull, but I was determined not to lose it, so I dug deep into my memories of all the horrible things Jemma had done to me over the years. That seemed to work because as my cheeks flushed with anger from those memories, the flame strengthened. It was like a fire had been ignited inside of me. I felt hot and powerful, like my whole body was glowing.

I smiled without taking my eyes off the flame. "I'm doing it!" I whispered to Nova, but as I spoke the flame began to dull and then I heard it – that voice in my head again.

"Jemma! Jemma! Jemma!"

It made me jump and I lost the flame completely. I was swallowed in the heavy cloak of blackness that dwelled in the forest. I froze in place. I wanted to call out to Nova but lost sight of him before the flame went out and I was scared of the voice I just heard in my head. What if it was coming for us?

Light!

"Oh, thank the gods!" I gasped and ran toward Nova, wrapping my arms around him. I was out of breath and shaking.

"Tippy, it's okay. You did great! What's wrong?" Nova asked as I clung to him.

"That voice! Did you hear it too? It was shouting in my head, and it's not the first time I've heard it. I think it's what led me out here tonight. I think we might be in danger, Nova."

"Tippy, don't be mad okay? You have nothing to be afraid of."

"What do you mean? Why would I be mad?"

"It was me that you were hearing in your head. Just now I was trying to help you concentrate on Jemma, and earlier it's how I told you it was time to meet me. It's another power I have."

"What? You not only can read minds, you can control thoughts? What are you? What do you really want with me?"

I was shouting now and backing away from him. I felt overwhelmed and angry. I knew I was different, I'd always been the outcast, the one with no friends or family, but for once I thought I found someone who didn't care. But I was wrong. Nova just wanted to take advantage of me, too!

"Tippy, stop it. You have me, you're not alone now." he said, coming closer to me. "And you're not an outcast, you're special, look what you can do."

His words shook me and instantly brought tears to my eyes. Nova softly draped his arm over my shoulder and I began to cry.

He knew so much about me! It wasn't fair. I barely knew anything about him. Everything about him was mysterious. The fact that he knew his name, the secret hiding spot he had in the courtyard, the way he unlocked the window in my room, the magic flame, the mindreading, the way I hear his voice in my head...

Suddenly I stiffened. Nova was so open about his other powers, but he didn't say anything about being able to speak to me in my mind, only that he could read minds. What if he can implant thoughts? Was any of this real or was he just manipulating me? Was this all a trick to get me out here? I was suddenly frightened of him. I was alone in the forest with a boy I barely knew and he had strange powers. How had I been so stupid? Well, if he did have other plans for me I wasn't going to make it easy on him. I ducked from under his arm and took off running aimlessly into the forest.

"Tippy!" he shouted after me. "Stop, it's not like that, I swear. You have to trust me."

I didn't make it very far before Nova caught up to me. I couldn't see where I was going and kept stumbling and I eventually slammed my shin into something solid and fell down completely. Nova had no problem finding me with his handy little fire light. I felt cornered and vulnerable as he approached. I was breathing heavy when he stopped at my feet. He stood looking down at me for a moment and then just decided to sit on the large stump next to me. It must have been the source of the throbbing pain in my shin. I scrambled to a standing position and stared at him. Why was he just sitting there?

"What are you?" I shouted at him. "Why did you bring me here?"

He just sat there staring at his feet. This infuriated me. My fear was suddenly gone, replaced by anger, fueled by my need for survival.

"I don't know what your problem is, but I'm not a freak like you and I don't want you in my head anymore! Got it? Just leave me alone!"

"Tippy, I'm sorry. I understand how you're feeling, but I'm only trying to help you. I promise," he pleaded.

"You may be able to hear my thoughts but you don't know how I feel! I feel betrayed. I trusted you! And this whole time you were just messing around in my head? I don't even know what to believe anymore."

"Tippy, I promise I never messed with your head. I only talk to you. I don't make you do things."

"Yeah right! Like I'm supposed to believe the mind bender?"

I turned away from him and started to stomp off again, but he reached for me. As soon as I felt him touch my skin, I whirled around like a wild animal and lunged for him.

"Don't touch me!" I screamed as I swung out with both fists.

I hit him square in the chest with my left hand, but as I swung again with my right, he blocked me with his flame-wielding hand. Before I knew it, I was on fire! There was a burst of flames as soon as our hands connected, then the fire raced down my right arm and across my back. I could feel the heat and I closed my eyes in panic and screamed. As the sound escaped my mouth, something incredible happened. The flames transformed into a glowing light beam that shot straight up from my body into the night sky. The whole forest awoke with the burst of light radiating from me! Suddenly, I wasn't afraid anymore. I felt strong and powerful and light and fearless! I stretched my arms out in front of me. The light spread to both hands and I separated them shoulder width apart. The light continued in a beaming arc that connected both my hands. I laughed at the strangeness of the whole experience and the light grew brighter still. It sprang to life, leaving my hands and encircling me. I threw my head back in hysterical laughter. How was this happening to me? Had Nova been right all along? Could I do magic? I looked around trying to find him. All I saw was my halo of white light, breathing a glowing life into the dark forest around me. Suddenly, I realized I was no longer on the ground. I was hovering!

"Oh my gods!" I gasped.

"You're okay, Tippy. Stay calm," came Nova's steady voice.

Following the sound of his voice, I looked down to see him about ten feet below me.

"What do I do?" I shouted.

"Just stay calm and concentrate on coming toward me."

I locked eyes with him and heard him whispering in my mind.

"It's okay, you're okay, I'm right here."

I focused on his face and his calm, steady voice in my head. I could see his face coming closer, it was getting clearer. I honed in on each of his exquisite features. His golden-blond hair seemed to glow in the light I was casting; his deep-green eyes sparkled as the light picked up the flecks of gold in them; his sharply chiseled jaw and angular cheek bones were highlighted as the light danced across the bronzed skin of his face; and his full lips turned down and pressed together in concentration with genuine worry for me. That's when I first realized that Nova truly cared about me and that I should trust him.

He drew closer and closer to me and before I knew it, his arms were encircling me, holding me safely against his chest as it heaved up and down heavily. That's when I realized Nova must have been scared, too. Even though his voice was strong and calm, he must have been just as frightened as I was. I looked up at him and the relief on his face was radiating in his smile. I hadn't realized my feet were on the ground until that moment. I still felt like I was floating while in Nova's embrace. We both just stared at each other for a moment and then we laughed until we collapsed.

"Well, this was quite a night!" said Nova between fits of laughter.

"I'll say!" I gasped.

"I told you, you could do it," he boasted.

"Okay, okay, you were right. But I think I'm done for tonight."

"I agree. You scared me for a little bit there."

"Me? *You* scared me! I thought you were turning my brain to mush or something!"

"I know, I'm sorry about all that. I've never shared these secrets with anyone and I guess I didn't think about how you might react. I'm sorry, Tippy," he said sounding downtrodden again.

I scooted closer to him and grabbed his left hand, gently scooping out the little flame he was controlling.

"All is forgiven," I said, resting my head on his shoulder. "And I'm sorry I called you a freak. I guess we're both freaks, huh?"

Nova smiled and shrugged, "I like the sound of that."

We sat like that for a while, trading the light back and forth with each other. In Nova's hand it was a flickering flame, in my hand it transformed into a blue-white, gaseous orb. The beauty of it mesmerized us. Each seemed a fitting representation of us. Nova's flame was bright, bold and fiery, and my orb was ever-changing and seemed a bit unstable. Strangly, I started to feel more like myself than ever before. I couldn't explain the feeling of ease and contentment I felt playing with this magical source of light on the damp forest floor with Nova. It was like coming home, even though I had no recollection of my actual home. This feeling gave me strength, courage and peace that I was doing the right thing. And it gave me trust in Nova, like I had never had for another person before. I felt as though our souls were meshed together like the flickering flames before us and that he would always be a part of me. Nova gave me a reassuring sigh of contentment. I guess he was feeling the same way, or perhaps reading my thoughts.

I turned to look at him.

"Can you tell me everything about you? I don't want any more surprises and I won't overreact, no matter what you tell me. I promise. I just want to know you."

He smiled at me and reached out his empty hand, pulling us to our feet.

"Nothing would make me happier, Tippy," he murmured. "There's a lot to tell, but we better be heading back, I think your light show woke up the whole forest. We're going to have to go deeper next time. You're a lot more powerful than I even imagined."

I beamed at his praise of my powers, and followed Nova, brushing the mossy forest floor off my legs as I walked. I let Nova light the way, and held his hand to keep on the trail. As we walked, Nova started to tell me about his life. How he had grown up in a small village on the edge of the rainforest called Leone. As farmers, his family worked alongside the Beto people to learn the best ways to farm the land. They had a great relationship with the tribe, and Nova remembered playing in the fields with his little sister, Ivy, and their friends from the forest while their fathers worked. When the Flood came, his father brought him, his sister, and their mother into the forest to find higher ground, but they never made it. When they entered the forest it had already begun burning from the lava. Nova's father told him to climb a nearby tree and not to stop until he reached the top. That was the last he saw of his family. He thought they were climbing the tree as well, but when the storm was finally over and he could cling to the tree no longer, he slid to the ground to find he was completely alone. At first he thought they may have climbed other trees nearby, so he searched and he searched and soon realized that the trees held nothing for him. He wandered aimlessly around the forest until he was eventually found by the Grifts and brought to the Troian Center.

"And you know the rest," he said.

I pondered this for a moment. I still had so many questions.

"When did you find out you had powers?" I asked.

"I think it first started right after the Flood. After I couldn't find my parents I was so alone and had no one to talk to in the forest, so I just did a lot of thinking in my head and I remember I kept thinking, '*Please find me, I'm right here, I'm right here.*' And that's when the Grifts found me. They said I was calling them, but I knew I had never uttered a word. Then, back at the Center, I figured out that I could hear what people were thinking. Like if one of the orphans were scared I'd be able to tell and comfort them. Or if one of the teachers were in a particularly foul mood, I'd know why, and how to cheer them up or if I should just steer clear of them all together. It's like a sixth sense I guess. We can all read people's feelings, I'm just really in tune with them and I think that helps me hear their thoughts."

"What about the whole mind bending thing, where you can get inside people's heads?"

"Well, that happened by accident at first. Like in the forest when I was begging someone to find me, I guess my thoughts were so strong they were able to enter into the minds of the Grifts. But I would find myself thinking things in my head and someone near me would start responding, like they thought we were having a conversation. I tested my theory out on a few innocent Grifts. It was harmless fun really, like sending them into Greeley's office when she hadn't called them, or telling them to walk in circles. You know, pranks and stuff. Soon I realized it was a pretty powerful tool though, and I decided I didn't want to use it unless I had to."

"Like to tell me when to meet you?"

"Yes, and other times. Like having Miss Breia set up that cot bed in your room and having it positioned right under the window. And telling one of the Grifts to clean the window and leave it unlocked. And also telling them, they had to use the John's room at the precise moment you were escaping from your room."

"You used it to make everyone think Jemma and I had just fallen off the rubble pile too, didn't you? That's why we didn't end up in the locker!"

Nova just smiled and shrugged, but I caught his wink.

"Wow! That really is handy! Do you think I have that power?"

"I don't know, Tippy. One step at a time, okay?"

"Okay," I sighed. "So, what about your little flame here?" I said pointing to the fire light dancing in his hand.

"Well, that has been the best part of this whole thing, and it's what led me to you!"

"What do you mean?" I asked.

"Well as you know, I've spent my fair share of time in the locker." I nodded for him to continue, because everyone knew Nova was a fixture of the locker, yet he always seemed to return unshaken, unlike the rest of us. I was dying to know his secret.

"Well, the first time Greeley sent me there I tried to get into her mind and tell her that she didn't want to send me there, but it didn't work! I was so confused and I sat in the darkness stewing about not being able to control her and I just kept thinking that I needed '*Light, Light, Light!*' Then bam! There was a light hovering over me! I reached out and touched it and it dropped into the palm of my hand and since then, all I have to do is get into my own mind and tell it that I need light, and viola!" he said, and with a snap of his fingers the light disappeared and then reappeared with his second snap.

"That's so cool! I can't wait until I can control it like you!" I squealed!

"Patience, Tippy. There's still more to the story."

"Oh yeah! Like how the light told you to find me?"

"Exactly. When you have light in the locker, it's quite an interesting place. It's not scary. In fact, it's rather exciting. All the walls are filled with the history of our island and the legend of Lux."

"Really," I asked skeptically. "How come I've never heard that?"

"That's the way they want it. They want to keep us in the dark, literally and figuratively. I don't think they even know that the legend is down there on the walls or they wouldn't chance sending us there. Especially not you."

"Why me?" I asked.

"Well," he stopped walking and turned to look at me. "Because I think the legend is about you."

I stood there stunned. Normally, I would think he was joking, but after tonight I was beginning to believe anything was possible. I had magic powers after all, so why couldn't I have a legend?

"Why do you think it's about me?" I asked cautiously.

"Tippy, I still have so much more to tell you, but not tonight. We stayed out much later than I anticipated and we've got to get back into the Center."

I looked around and realized we were at the edge of the field where we had entered the forest earlier in the night. The inky black sky was starting to show signs of brightening as it became washed with a glowing deep-sea color. It would be dawn soon. Everyone in the Center would be rising and I didn't even want to think about what would happen if they found us missing. That had never happened before that I knew of and I wasn't about to find out what the punishment for such actions would be.

"Okay, what's the plan?" I said so matter-of-factly that Nova chuckled.

"We go back the way we came. I'll help you sneak back into your room through the window and we'll meet the same time, same place tomorrow."

I hated the idea of having to wait a whole day to be with Nova again. I wanted to learn more. I wanted him to finish his story and tell me about my legend and teach me more powers. It was as if a sponge had replaced my brain; it was wrung dry and thirsty to soak up all the information about my new life. I felt like from today forward my life was truly starting. If only I'd known how right I was.

Once Nova was sure the coast was clear, we sprinted across the open fields to the Troian Center and scurried through the bushes in front of my window. Nova pulled open the window pane from the bottom and before I had a chance to say a word, he kissed me atop my head and pushed me through. I landed on my cot bed with a thud. I froze, fearing someone had seen me enter the room, but as I scoped out the scene everything seemed just as it was when I left. I let out a breath of relief and slowly removed my shoes and slipped under the covers, falling instantly asleep.

9
_____

The sunlight streaming in woke me before the morning bell. I sat up and stretched. I felt so stiff and sore and—oh wow—I had a lot more scrapes on my legs than I usually did. I reached down to examine the one on my shin and it all came rushing back to me. The whole crazy night! Nova, talking in my head, escaping through the window, meeting in the forest, his magic flame, my magic beam of light! Oh my gods, I can do magic! I clapped my hands over my mouth even though no sounds had escaped. I really needed to pull it together before someone saw me acting stranger than usual. Just then, the morning bell rung and everyone began to stir.

I sat on my cot bed, already dressed, watching all the other orphans in my year mill about. They continued to ignore me and got on with their day. Dressing, gathering up books for morning lessons, and chatting easily with each other. I always envied that; the ease they all seemed to have with each other, the way they were comfortable and had a sense of belonging. I always hoped that one day they'd let me in and I'd be one of them. But today was different. Today, I watched them without jealousy or longing. I was simply studying them, finally embracing my outsider status, and viewing them in a new light. With each Jane or John that passed me, I found myself wondering if they possessed any magical powers waiting to be discovered. I strained to get some sort of vibe from each of them, hoping I'd pick up on something special.

"Hey."

I jumped at the sound of Remi's voice and turned to see his big brown eyes staring at me more quizzically than usual.

"What?" I asked. "Why are you looking at me like that?"

"I was just wondering why you decided to wear your work uniform this morning rather than your Center uniform?" he said.

"What?" I said puzzled for a moment, until I looked down and realized he was right. I was still in my work clothes. I had worn them to the forest with Nova last night and fell asleep in them. I was so groggy when I woke up that I only took note that I was dressed, not paying particular attention as to what I was dressed in.

We have strict rules on our uniforms. As orphans we were already the lowest grade of people on the island, so Greeley always told us the least we could do was look presentable. We wore the Troian Center uniform during the day for our lessons, which consisted of a tan-linen tunic with a red sash. It left our right shoulders exposed so you could see the tattooed numbers that branded us orphans. And we had our work uniforms that we wore whenever we left the Center to do Flood work. The shirts were made of the same itchy tan linen, with brown long shorts to tuck the shirts into. This is what I was currently dressed in. None of the uniforms ever seemed to flatter my scrawny shape, but I looked worse than usual this morning in my rumpled work clothes, still covered with dirt and bits of moss. Remi was staring at me, probably scrutinizing my sanity.

"Oh yeah, I ... Well, I was talking while I was getting dressed and I guess I wasn't paying any attention," I stammered, quickly walking away from Remi and toward the Jane's wardrobe. I went right to the shelf labeled with my number and exchanged my shabby work clothes for my Troian tunic. I balled up my dirty shirt and deposited it into the laundry bin. Our orphan numbers were stitched into the hem of each item of clothing we had so that if we lost or ripped or soiled anything, we could be punished for it. I was fretting over the state of my shorts when Sparrow came up to me.

"Here, let me see those," she said, pulling the shorts from my hands before I had time to protest. She shook them a few times and rubbed her hands over the stains and they seemed to vanish before my eyes.

"There we go, good as new," she smiled and dropped them into the laundry bin.

"How did you do that?" I asked in astonishment.

"You can heal anything with a little love," she said with a wink and then skipped away.

I stood there stunned. Sparrow was special too. She was like me! I knew it! I knew there were more of us, more like Nova and me. Sparrow said she was like me, but witnessing her powers with my own eyes confirmed it! I was so excited that my heart was pounding and once again I didn't notice Remi come up next to me.

"What was that all about?"

"Jeez! You've gotta stop sneaking up on me!"

"I'm not sneaking, you're just extra jumpy this morning. What's going on with you?"

I turned to him, longing to tell him everything. I felt like a river ready to spill over its banks when Remi asked me what was going on with me. I wanted to tell him about my powers and my amazing adventure last night, but I distinctly remembered Nova asking me not to tell *anyone* about us. Remi wasn't just anyone though, he was my best friend, yet still I felt I would be breaking Nova's trust if I told Remi. My eyes searched the deep-chocolate oasis of Remi's, begging him to understand what was happening, but he blankly blinked back at me. I sighed deeply and said, "Nothing, I'm fine. Come on, we don't want to miss breakfast."

Remi didn't seem to buy it, but he didn't argue and he followed me, and the rest of our year into the dining hall. The large drafty room in the middle of the Troian Center served as our dining hall. We got three squares a day there. The food was simple and always the same, but I never complained. It kept my stomach from growling and it was served to us by weary Grifts who would probably not take too kindly to any criticism of the menu.

I got in line with Remi and a bowl of porridge and fruit was unceremoniously slopped onto my tray. We walked over to our usual table and saw that Sparrow and Journey were already sitting there. Remi stopped short when he saw them, but I nudged him in the back and whispered, "Don't be rude." I swung my legs over the bench and sat next to Sparrow. Remi approached the table like he thought it was going to bite him and eventually decided to settle himself across from me, but still as far away from Journey as possible. Sparrow beamed at us and offered a chipper greeting.

"Good morning, friends!"

"Morning," I said doing my best impression of her hundred-kilowatt smile.

Remi just stared at her, so I kicked him under the table and he jerked enough to break his gaze and mumble something that sounded like good morning as he scowled at me.

The whole time Journey silently ate his breakfast as if us sitting together was the most normal thing in the world. I couldn't say I blamed Remi for his bewildered reaction because no one had ever sat with us in the dining hall before. It had always just been the two of us at our little table in the corner for as long as I could remember. I can't say I minded. We got along great and always had something to talk about. Well, I did most of the talking, while Remi tried to get me to study; but still, we liked our little world. It was comfortable there with just the two of us in it. This morning it felt like someone had ripped a hole in our safety net, letting Sparrow and Journey waltz in and make themselves at home. A week ago, I would have probably been reacting like Remi and felt a bit put out by their intrusion, but now it just felt like a natural progression. Like we were supposed to be friends. Maybe they would teach me something about myself just like Nova had. And right on cue, Nova appeared, sliding in next to Remi and pushing him uncomfortably close to Journey.

"What's up, gang?" he asked cheerily.

"Morning, 18!" Sparrow beamed. I straightened up and offered a dopey grin. Journey gave a nod of acknowledgement and Remi just squirmed.

We ate our breakfast together while Sparrow made small talk with everyone.

"18, I don't think we've properly met before, but I'm 42," Sparrow chirped.

Nova smiled. "I know who you are, 42. But, nice to officially meet you."

"Oh wonderful!" she exclaimed. I didn't think it was possible for her to be any happier, but she seemed like she might explode with joy at any second, based on the fact that Nova knew her, so I took over the introductions for her.

"And you've met Re.., I mean 26 before, and this is 22," I

said gesturing to Journey who nodded again. I was beginning to see he was a man of few words. "Everyone this is 18."

Nova smiled at everyone, but sent a wink in my direction before focusing back on the tray of food in front of him. It felt too bizarre to be sitting at an almost full table with people who I guess I could call my friends, all of whom knew their names and some who had magical powers, yet we all sat pretending we were just enjoying a casual breakfast. It was killing me. I felt all the questions I had burning inside of me, yet I knew this wasn't the time or place to discuss anything. It seemed we were on the same page, because as I looked around the table, I saw we were all looking at each other, smiling cleverly. Even Journey had a smirk on his rugged face. And then there was Remi. He hadn't even touched his breakfast and he looked so uncomfortable that I feared he might become ill. Sparrow must have noticed it too, because she asked, "Are you okay, 26?"

"What?" he said, suddenly startled that we were all focused on him. "Yeah, I'm fine."

I looked at Nova, pleading with him in my mind to let me tell Remi. He was obviously the only one at this table that didn't seem to know what was going on. Somehow Sparrow knew I was special and trusted me enough to show me her little laundry trick this morning. And I still didn't know what was up with Journey but Sparrow trusted him and he seemed comfortable hanging out with me. But poor Remi was turning green wedged between Nova and Journey. He looked so small and frightened, like a mouse cornered between two predators who hadn't yet discovered his presence. Then I heard Nova's voice in my head again.

"No! Tippy, not yet. This is too important. I need to explain more to you first, okay?"

"Fine," I said.

Remi looked at me pleadingly. "Who are you talking to?"

Nova just laughed and said, "You know Tippy, always talking to herself."

The whole table gave a good-hearted chuckle and then we were saved by the bell.

At the sound of the metal chime we knew it was time to clear out and head to lessons. Nova gave me a scratch on the head and a wink as he jogged off. That left the four of us to make our way to Plants and Poisons. Sparrow rambled on the whole way to lessons. It made me appreciate Remi's silent qualities even more, as it was impossible to think with her chattering in my ear. I only caught portions of what she was saying. Something about Nova being cute, maybe something about what we were reading about in P&P today, blah, blah, blah. I was really just going through the list of questions I had for Nova. I couldn't wait for the day to be over so we could get another chance to go to the forest and get some answers.

The day dragged on. I made it through Plants and Poisons, and Reading and Writing without a hitch, but Mr. Greyvin called me out of my daydreams in our History and Trade lessons. "65, care to give your take on the value of precious stones trade?"

'*Oh no, here we go again,*' I thought. I was totally lost in thought and had no idea where we were in the lesson. I looked around for help but found nothing. I stared blankly at Mr. Greyvin, hoping he'd take mercy on me. He was famous for making examples out of students that didn't pay attention to him.

"Miss 65, why don't you go to the board for us and write down the top five trading gems that our island was founded on since you obviously know so much about our history and trade that you don't need to bother paying attention to our lessons."

My cheeks flushed as I slowly stood and walked to the chalk board. It felt like I was walking to my death sentence. By the time I reached the board my palms were sweating and beads of perspiration had formed on my forehead. I picked up the piece of stark-white chalk and wiped my forehead with the back of my hand. I stared at the empty abyss of blackboard in front of me, and it felt as though time stood still. I heard my heart thundering in my chest, the fly buzzing around the lesson room, the flipping of book pages, then suddenly I heard voices, streaming at me all at once. At first it was just a chaotic static noise, but I took deep breaths and strained to make out individual voices.

"She's so screwed."

"I bet she's going to get sent to the locker."

"Thank the gods I'm not up there!"

"You can do it, remember the code S.E.R.G.A"

S.E.R.G.A! That was it! It's what Remi had made up to help me remember the top five trading gems for our exam. It was his voice I was hearing! He was sending me help, trying to save me from humiliation and the locker!

I quickly scribbled the answers on the board and then trotted swiftly back to my seat. There on the board in my scrawling handwriting was Sapphire, Emerald, Ruby, Garnet and Amber, in perfect order. I felt electrified! I not only figured out the answer to Mr. Greyvin and my classmate's surprise, but I had discovered another power! I was like Nova! I could hear thoughts! I sat at my desk tingling, smiling at Remi who was sitting to my right.

"Very well, 65. It seems you have learned something from me after all," said Greyvin sarcastically. "Moving on... Your homework will be to read pages 114 to 142 for tomorrow's lesson. Please be prepared everyone." And he shut his book and sat down just as the bell chimed.

I grabbed my books and Remi's hand and darted out into the hallway ahead of everyone else.

"Come with me!" I hissed at him when he pulled against me.

I dragged him into our room and shut the door behind us. Room 13 was deserted, as the rest of our year was making their way to Math and Calendars, our last lesson of the day.

"Remi! You did it! You helped me remember the stones!" I squealed hugging him.

"I know, I was so impressed you remembered. See all the studying pays off," he said smiling. I released him from my embrace and grabbed him by the shoulders, looking as serious as I knew how.

"No, I didn't remember on my own. I was up there panicking, and then I heard you!"

"What?" he said taking a step back.

"I heard you! You were thinking it over and over in your head. S.E.R.G.A, S.E.R.G.A.! I never would have remembered it without your help. I was too scared standing up there to think straight, but I started to hear what people were thinking and I heard you, and you were helping me. You saved me!" I said, hugging him again.

Remi pushed me away from him. "What are you talking about? You can't read minds, you just finally remembered something that I drilled into your brain."

"No, Remi, it was you! I heard *you*!"

"Okay, I really think you're starting to lose your mind. Maybe you've been hanging out with these new friends of yours too much or maybe you hit your head really hard when you fell off the rubble pile, but we're going to be late for lessons. Let's go."

Remi walked out of the room, leaving me standing there alone.

I was stunned. Remi was my best friend. I thought he would believe me. I would have believed him if he told me something like this, wouldn't I? I stood there hoping that I would, but maybe not? Maybe I only believed it because of all the incredible new things Nova had opened my eyes to recently. Maybe Nova was right, I shouldn't tell Remi about my powers yet. Maybe I would have to show him. Yes, I would show him, and then he'd have to believe me. I needed Remi to believe me. I really needed my best friend with me in this crazy new life I was discovering.

I made up my mind that I would tell Nova that we had to let Remi in on all this when the second bell chimed. '*Shoot!*' I was late for Math and Calendars. I sprinted out of Room 13 and ran straight into Miss Breia.

"Dear Jane! Are you alright?"

I had bounced off her and landed square on my rear end. "Yeah, I'm fine," I said as I stood, dusting the sand from my uniform. "Sorry, I wasn't watching where I was going."

"Well, you'd better come with me. We'll need to get you a late pass so you don't get into trouble for wondering the halls, dear."

I followed Miss Breia into her office and sat in the chair while she bustled about her desk looking for a late pass.

"So, how has your head been treating you? Any more dizzy spells?"

"No. I think I'm cured, thanks."

"Good, good, very good to hear," she said distractedly. "Ah-ha, here they are. Alright then, where are you headed, little Jane?"

"Mr. Hookturn's lesson."

"Here you are," she said handing me the little square stone that she had just written my number on.

"Thanks," I said taking it from her, letting my hands run

over its worn smooth edges, avoiding the sticky black cretil ink. We learned about this ink in P&P lessons. It's made from the sap of a cretil plant and the black lava rock found on the island. It's washable with a particular solution, so it's perfect for the stone passes we use in the Troian Center. You need them to go to the nurse's station, the Jane's room, Greeley's office, or anywhere other than where you're supposed to be.

I walked into Mr. Hookturn's lesson and handed him my pass, then headed for my seat next to Remi at the long table in the back of the room. He glanced at me questioningly and I shrugged at him putting my books down. We sat silently next to each other through the whole lesson, quietly working on filling out our calendars and equations. I could feel the distance between us and the tension that was building. It made me uncomfortable to have secrets from Remi and I was hoping after today that I could come clean and we'd be on the same page again.

10

Finally the bell chimed. I gathered my books and rushed back to room 13 to change for Flood work. The rest of the Center was heading to the dining hall for lunch, but I needed to talk to Nova and was desperately trying to call him with my thoughts. I sat on my cot bed in my over-sized work uniform with my eyes squeezed shut.

"Nova, I need you! Nova! Nova! Nova!"

"Meet me in our spot."

I jumped at the sound of his voice in my head. It worked! I'd called him and he heard me! I was so excited and proud of getting the hang of these powers. I laced up my shoes and ran to the courtyard. Nova was already behind the banana palm when I arrived. He was staring out the hole when I breathlessly climbed through the leaves to meet him.

"I did it! I called you and you heard me! I had to talk to you! So much is happening. I think I'm like you! I mean I know I am, but I can do mind stuff like you, I heard voices today. I think I was reading minds! I read Remi's mind in History and Trade and he gave me the answers while I was at the board! It was so AMAZING! And then..."

"Whoa, Tippy. Slow down. You're talking a mile a minute. Take a breath."

"Okay, okay, sorry."

"Why did you need to meet with me? Are you alright?"

"Yes, I'm great. I just wanted to tell you that I read minds today!"

"Really? That's impressive. How did it happen?"

"Mr. Greyvin called me up to the board to write down the top five trading gems and I panicked. I was just standing at the blackboard shaking and sweating, and all of a sudden it was like everything slowed down and I could hear everything around me, the flies, the pages rustling, people breathing, and then their thoughts started rushing at me."

"So, you were afraid?" Nova asked.

"Yeah, but that's not the point," I said frustrated.

"It's important, Tippy. We're still trying to figure out your powers and what triggers them, remember? I need to know what you are feeling and doing when you discover new powers."

"Well then, yes, I was scared. Do you think that's what could've done it?"

"Definitely, fear is a very powerful emotion. What happened next?"

"I took a deep breath and focused on the voices and I could start to pick out different ones, and then I was able to focus on them one at a time and make out what they were thinking. That's when I heard Remi, I recognized his voice instantly because it was so positive. He was giving me the answer. He kept saying it over and over again in his mind."

"Hmm," Nova mused while rubbing his chin.

"What?" I asked impatiently, but got no response from Nova.

He seemed lost in thought and suddenly I was lost with

him. I had touched his arm to get his attention and at that same moment was in his mind with him. I could see, hear and feel his thoughts. It frightened me to be inside his head like that, so surrounded and consumed. I jumped out as quickly as I could, gasping for air.

"Tippy?" Nova said, grabbing my arm to steady me.

"You think we can't trust Remi!" I sputtered.

"How did you do that? You were reading my mind, weren't you?"

"Yes, I think so, but it was different. Not like in lessons. I, I felt like I was you! I could feel your emotion, and see what you were seeing and hear your thoughts... it was... I don't know what it was. Is that normal? Is that what you do?"

Nova looked at me, smiling and shaking his head. "No, Tippy. It's not what I do, but it's okay. You're perfectly normal for a freak," he laughed.

"This isn't funny, I don't know what's happening to me!"

"You just came in here bragging like super-girl a minute ago."

"I know, but it's all happening so fast!"

"It's fine, we'll practice more tonight. One step at a time, remember? You just need to stay calm."

"But what if something crazy happens?"

"If you need help just call me. We know we can talk to each other telepathically now, so you'll never be alone."

That did reassure me actually. I took a deep breath and started to feel a little better.

"Okay, so what now?" I asked.

"Just get through your Flood work and meet me at night like we planned."

"Okay," I said, starting to slide my way out from behind the palms.

"Tippy, stay away from Remi for now, okay?"

"He doesn't know anything, Nova."

"How can you be so sure?"

"Well, he's my best friend for one, he gave me the correct answers in History and Trade, and I told him that I read his mind and he just told me I was crazy and walked away."

"You what?" Nova exclaimed.

"I was so excited that I just read minds that I had to tell someone, and he helped me, so I thought maybe he knew I could do it or something and he was trying to help me."

"You can't go around talking about this, Tippy. There's so much you don't know. There's people who will want to hurt you because of who you are and what you can do. We'll talk about all this tonight. But for now, please stay away from him. He knows too much already and we need to be careful."

"Jeez, okay. I'll try, but it won't be easy."

Nova shook his head at me and pushed past me into the courtyard. I watched him stalk away. Wow, I was really having that effect on everybody today. I started the morning with four friends, that's three more than usual, and now with how I was finding ways to annoy Nova and Remi, it seemed I was down to two. Not a good track record. The orphans were starting to make their way into the courtyard to line up for Flood work. Great, I had missed lunch, too. Now I'll be starving while I dig through the rubble piles. I fell into line and listened to the sound of my stomach growling when suddenly I felt something round thrust into the palm of my hand. I looked behind me to see Sparrow grinning at me.

"I didn't see you at lunch, so I figured you could use this."

I looked down to see a bright green avocado in my hand.

"Thank you," I said in amazement.

At least Sparrow was still on my side. She was proving to be a great friend. We followed our Grifts out to the fields and I decided to join Sparrow on a rubble pile instead of going to my usual spot with Remi since he was still looking sour. This would give me a chance to talk to her more anyway. Nova hadn't said anything about staying away from Sparrow. We grabbed baskets and climbed up the pile, working in silence for a while before my curiosity got the best of me. Sparrow was polishing a rather large emerald she found when I scooted over closer to her so we could talk without attracting attention from the Grifts. They frowned upon fraternizing, saying it slowed down our work, but if you kept it to a whisper, you could usually get away with it.

"Sparrow, can I ask you something?" I whispered.

"Of course."

"This morning, when you, um," I paused trying to think how to phrase it.

"Helped you with your uniform?" she finished for me.

"Yes! What was that?"

She just smiled cleverly at me. From the gleam in her eye I knew she knew more than she was letting on, so I pressed on, taking more risks this time.

"You can do things can't you?" I asked. "Special things that not everyone else can do?"

"Yes," she said smiling at me.

"I can do special things, too," I whispered excitedly.

"I know."

"You do?" I asked cautiously. "But how?"

"I've been watching you, 65. There's always been something that made me extra aware of you. I couldn't put my finger on it until I saw you and Jemma get in that fight. That's when I knew you were like me."

"But why didn't you say anything to me before if you've been watching me?"

"I wasn't completely sure about you until that day with Jemma, and I had to be sure. I couldn't risk exposing myself if

I was wrong. Once we were sure, we came to you in your room, remember?"

"Yes, you and Journey came to see me, and told me your names. But I didn't really understand what was happening to me yet. And how do you know about what I did to Jemma? I thought Nova took care of that?"

"I knew he was trying something with us. He tried to bend our thoughts, didn't he?"

"Yes," I said sheepishly. "Nova did try to bend your minds. I didn't know he as doing it though. I'm sorry."

"It's okay," she said with a sly smile. "But you might want to let him know that his mind bending doesn't work on us."

"Us? Do you mean Journey, too?"

"Yes, he's like us, 65."

"What can he do?" I asked.

"I think we'd better let Journey tell you, or better yet, show you on his own terms."

"Oh, fair enough," I said.

I sat there silently for a moment, pondering this new information. I was right about Sparrow. I knew she had powers and I had been right to trust her. I was starting to trust my instincts more. But why hadn't they alerted me to Sparrow and Journey? She knew there was something about me, but I had been completely oblivious to her and Journey until they came to me. I needed to get to the bottom of this. But, something else was still bothering me. If it was true that Nova couldn't bend their minds with his ridiculous story about Jemma and me falling off the rubble pile, why Sparrow and Journey gone along with the story? I had to ask.

"Sparrow, how come you went along with Nova's story?"

"Well, it's complicated. I knew he was trying to do something to us, but I wasn't sure what. Nova hadn't been on my radar, but I suddenly felt that I should trust him after the way he was caring for you, so I just went along with what everyone else was saying had happened. That's when I figured out he was bending minds and he must have powers, too. I knew exactly what I saw, yet everyone was acting as if something else entirely had happened. That's when I put together that Nova was trying to protect you, and he must have suspected your powers as well."

"Great, so it's obvious to everyone but me that I have these crazy magic powers?" I asked sarcastically.

"No, not everyone silly, just us Truiets."

"Truiets?"

"Yes, that's the word the Betos use for people who were gifted with powers from the gods."

"So you, Journey, Nova and me, we're all Truiets?"

"Yes. I believe so."

"Okay, so if I'm a Truiet, I should be able to locate other Truiets? That's how you knew there was something about me?"

"Well, it's kind of tricky. Truiets all share a bond and we can feed off each other's powers. Once we locate each other we form bonds that link us together and are almost unbreakable. Like you and I, if we used our powers together then we'd be bonded for life."

I stared back at her with a confused expression.

"Okay, let me put it like this. If you and I decided we were going to focus all our power on this rubble pile and turn it into a tornado, we would be doing magic together. That's something very powerful and it requires us to share a bit of our souls, kind of twisting them together so that after that, no matter how far apart we go, we will always be connected to each other. We'd know where the other was, and if they were in danger. Stuff like that. Do you get it now?"

I nodded my head. This explained the feeling I had with

Nova. In the forest I felt like I bonded with him in the most powerful way. It was so strong I couldn't even explain it. That must be what I was experiencing. That was s relief. I thought I was just madly in love with him. I gave a little snort of laughter and looked back at Sparrow.

"What's so funny?" she asked.

"Nothing, I think I know what you're talking about. I've experienced it and I'm really glad you explained that to me because I was definitely mistaking those feelings for something else."

"Glad to help clear it up then."

"Could we really turn this rubble pile into a tornado?" I whispered.

"Wouldn't that be a show for Greeley!" she said, sending us both into fits of laughter.

We worked silently for a while with the Grifts nearby. Sparrow was merrily polishing her stones and humming a little tune. Her basket was nearly full and mine was looking like a pretty poor example next to hers. Maybe the Grifts were right, talking really did slow down our productivity. I scurried around sifting through rubble until I found something worth polishing. I clambered back up to sit by Sparrow again and to my surprise my basket seemed to have taken on powers of its own. There were now about a dozen stones, gems and metals all glistening in a neat little pile. Only minutes ago there were about six poor specimens.

"Sparrow! How'd you do that?" I exclaimed trying to hide my astonishment in a whisper.

"Just gave them a little love is all."

"That's what you said this morning too with my uniform! How do you do it?"

"I'm a healer, 65. That's my gift. I can restore things back to their original form."

I was amazed. What an incredible power! I wondered if I could do that as well?

"Can you heal anything? Even people?" I asked

"I've never tried to heal anything more serious than the occasional scrape or burn," she said suddenly sheepish now. "I'm not that great."

"Are you kidding? I think you're incredible!"

"Well, it does make this job a little easier."

We both laughed at that and continued to work on the rubble pile together while she explained more about herself to me. She came to the Troian Center after the Flood like the rest of us orphans. Before that, she had lived in Lux, in one of the glimmering white houses by the sea. Their home was swept away in the horrible Flood and she and her family were washed out to sea. She awoke to find herself drifting on a piece of debris in the ocean. She clung to it until it took her ashore. That's where she found Journey. He must have washed up on shore and was lying unconscious in a heap of sea kelp and weeds. She ran to him and stayed with him, comforting him and stroking his tangled brown hair until he woke. Even after he came to he still wouldn't speak to her, but they were inseparable despite his lack of communication.

They lived in a secluded area of the beach for about a week, surviving on fruit and berries until the Grifts found them and brought them to the Center. She told me that when she first arrived they tried to separate them, thinking that Journey was older than Sparrow because of his size. He threw a fit and clung to her, saying that she was his twin sister and they couldn't take her away. This astonished even Sparrow because up until that moment she had never heard him speak, but knowing no one else at the Center, she went along with it. This made me laugh out loud, because saying Journey and Sparrow were twins were like comparing a

tarcat with a dortrib. Sure they were of the same species and
had the same coloring, but dortribs were scrawny little
felines that the locals kept as pets. No one would ever
confuse one for a lethal tarcat. It was true that Journey and
Sparrow both had similar features, like tan skin, amber-
colored eyes, shiny bronze hair, but that's where it ended.
Sparrow was almost as thin as me, but a bit taller, giving her
a lanky bird-like fragility. Journey, on the other hand, was as
solid as a stone. His neck was as wide as his block head that
sat atop his muscular shoulders, giving him a menacing
appearance.

I worked quietly, soaking up everything Sparrow was
saying. She was a wealth of knowledge and seemed trustwor-
thy. I only spent a few hours with her working on the pile, yet I
already knew she would be my friend for life. I wanted to
spend more time with her and I thought the perfect opportunity would be for her to come with me to meet Nova tonight. I
had a feeling he wouldn't be happy about me bringing along
an unannounced guest, but she was one of us. Maybe she
could help me figure out my powers faster.

"Sparrow, I have something I want to tell you. But, it's a
secret."

"You can trust me, 65, we're sisters now."

I smiled, loving the sound of the word sisters. I always
dreamed of having a sister. I repeated the word, letting it roll
off my tongue. That sold me right there. I was definitely going
to tell her about Nova's secret plans to meet in the forest.

"I want you to go somewhere with me tonight."

"Where?"

"Well, that's the secret part. Do you trust me?"

She nodded.

"Okay, then tonight we're going to sneak out of the Center,
so wear your clothes to bed so you're ready to go."

Surprisingly, she just nodded at me and her only question was if Journey could come.

"I don't know if that's such a good idea. We don't want to attract too much attention."

"Yes, but I don't think I can actually sneak away without him noticing. It might be better to just clue him in on it so he doesn't give us away by mistake."

I weighed it over for a moment. She was probably right; those two really were joined at the hip. Even now I could see him just one pile over from us, always keeping her in his line of sight. I watched him sorting through rubble effortlessly, discarding rocks for the locals to haul away like they weighed nothing at all. I just didn't know him enough to completely trust him yet.

"You can trust him, 65. I promise," she said. "He's one of us."

"Okay fine. You tell him to be ready and not to tell anyone else."

Just then the Grifts blew their whistles, signaling the end of our work day. Wow, it really flew by. What's that saying? Time flies when you're having fun? It should be time flies when you're discovering you have magic powers! All the Johns and Janes filed into the dining hall. We filled our trays and went to our respective tables. Dinner was always my favorite meal of the day. In addition to the fruits we ate at breakfast and lunch, we also were served fresh seafood. It was usually boiled into a thick stew with roots and grains, but every once in a while we would luck out and the seafood would be served breaded and fried until it was golden and crispy. I always said if I ever found the Grift that made that meal I'd marry him! However, he mustn't have been in the kitchen today because I was slopped a healthy portion of fish stew.

I exited the line and headed to my usual spot. My quiet

little table in the corner was already bustling with excitement. Nova, Journey and Sparrow were deep in conversation when I joined them. I scanned the room for Remi after I sat down, and spotted him in line. He was just starting to make his way over to us, looking glum as ever at the prospect of another meal at his newly popular table.

I tried to focus on the conversation going on at our table while Remi approached. Sparrow seemed peppier than ever. For a moment I panicked that maybe she was excited about our secret trip tonight and was filling Nova and Journey in on it. That would ruin everything.

"What are you talking about?" I asked nervously.

"The New Year Gala!" she squealed. "They just posted the songs!" she said handing me a sheet.

"Oh, great," I replied faking a smile.

My relief that she wasn't spilling my secret was short lived. I dreaded singing at the New Year Gala. It was an annual festival in Lux to celebrate the New Year and since we didn't celebrate birthdays, it also marked the turning of our year. We would all be one year older when we returned to the Center. It was actually quite a lovely event. We got to dress up in lavish white robes and be on the inside of the shimmering walls of Lux for a change, but for me, all of that was overshadowed by the fact that we had to sing. I hated singing. I was horrible at it. Remi never poked fun at me except for on this occasion. He couldn't help it I suppose. Everyone laughed at me in rehearsals. Last year, our teacher Miss Sprigg actually asked me just to move my mouth around like I was singing, but not actually make any noise. She said it sounded better that way.

"26, over here!" waved Sparrow.

I looked up to see Remi staring at us, standing planted a few feet from our table. Probably trying to decide if there was anywhere else he could sit. But now that Sparrow had drawn attention to him, he seemed guilted into joining us. He sat at the end of the table, closest to Sparrow and me.

"Did you get your song sheets yet?" she asked him when he sat down.

"No, I didn't know they were up yet," he replied.

"Just went up! I got you a set."

"Thanks," he said glancing at me with a little hint of his usual smirk. I bet he was loving the fact that he knew I was squirming inside.

"What do you think, Tippy? There seems to be a good selection this year, huh?" Nova asked, flipping through the papers.

"Yeah, *Tippy*, I bet you're *very* excited," jeered Remi.

I glared at him.

"I bet we'll get to sing the same part," Sparrow said grabbing my hand. "Are you a Soprano? I am."

"Um, I don't know. I'm not really that great at singing," I said. This made Remi choke on his food. "Okay, I'm plain awful alright!" I shouted at him. "Happy now?"

After he had his little laughing, coughing spell, he said, "Yes, actually thinking about you singing really did cheer me up."

"Very funny."

"See, you can't be that bad if you cheer 26 up," said Sparrow.

"He was being sarcastic," I said.

"I remember you from last year! You're the one Miss Sprigg made stand in the back and just mouth the words, aren't you?" asked Journey.

Great, so the guy who never says much has a mind like a trap! Figures. "Yes, that was me. I told you I wasn't good."

That gave us all a laugh actually. It was kind of fun to be laughing with friends about my horrible singing skills rather than being laughed at. It helped take the pressure off. Unfortunately, our light heartedness didn't last very long. It was interrupted by Jemma and her band of followers. I could feel her unpleasant presence even before she opened her mouth. I think I had sensed her. Was that part of my powers? Maybe I could sense evil?

"Well, look at this cheery little group. Having fun are we?" she sneered in her usual acid tone.

I'd managed to steer clear of her since our fight. I guess my luck had to run out at some point.

"You must be looking forward to singing again at the New Year Gala, 65! Should I advise Miss Sprigg to put you front and center this year? No one will want to miss your spectacular voice," she laughed. "Maybe someone will do us all a favor and finally adopt you."

This ignited a round of laughter from her little henchmaids. That was my word for the Janes that fawned over her.

"Give it a rest Jemma," I warned.

"I thought you would have learned not to use my name again, but I guess you're even dumber than I thought!" she whispered over my shoulder. "Don't think I've forgotten about your little stunt in the fields. You won't always have your friends around to protect you."

She took a quick step closer to me, intended to frighten me I guess. All it did was bring, Journey, Remi and Nova to their feet. Sparrow sat there wide-eyed, staring at me.

"Don't get up on my account, Johns. I was just leaving," she sneered. And with that she flipped her long black mane and marched away.

"Well, that was pleasant," sighed Sparrow as the boys returned to their seats. "Are you alright?" she asked.

"Yes, I'm fine, and thanks for sticking up for me guys, but I can handle Jemma on my own."

"I agree with Tippy," said Sparrow. "I think she's just trying to get a rise out of her and you guys reacting that way is exactly the attention she wants."

"Hey, I just didn't want a repeat of what happened in the fields," said Nova.

"I don't think any of us want that," I muttered under my breath. All this Jemma talk was ruining my appetite. I stood abruptly, grabbing my tray. "I think I'm going to go get a jump start on studying. See you all later."

11

Nova caught my eye as I was walking past him. "*Don't forget about tonight!*" called his voice in my head. Like that was possible. I gave him a nod and kept walking. I got back to my room and sprawled out on my cot bed. I flipped over onto my back and stared at the ceiling. I had so many thoughts, most of which were questions, whirling around in my head. I wished it was 11:00 already so I could be on my way to getting answers to some of them. I felt like I had learned so many new things about myself in the past twenty-four hours that I couldn't keep them all straight. I lay there with my mind spinning until someone came into the room. I popped up on my elbows to see it was only Sparrow, so I slumped back down onto the bed.

"You forgot your sheet music," she said, cheerily waving the papers at me.

"Oh, thanks," I mumbled sitting up to take the papers from her. I stared at them sulkily as she sat down next to me, curling her delicate legs under her.

"You know I could help you practice. I'm sure you'll get better at it."

"That's not what's bothering me actually," I sighed.

"Is it Jemma?" she whispered.

"Not that either at the moment. I've just been trying to keep everything straight, you know? I feel like there's so much for me to learn still, about what I can do. But I've already learned so much and I have all these questions. I just feel really confused. How did you deal with it when you first found out you had powers?"

Sparrow smiled at me and grabbed my hand. "First, it's going to be okay. You have me and Nova and Journey to help you with all of this. Second, you need a journal. That always helps me make sense of my questions and keep track of things."

"A journal?"

"Yes! I have a spare that you can use to start with," she said as she bounded over to her shelf in our wardrobe. I started to argue that we weren't allowed to keep personal things, but she was ignoring me with her head shoved deep inside the closet. She probably couldn't even hear me.

"Here it is!" she said, dusting off a notebook and bringing it over to me.

"This is just one of our lesson notebooks," I said flipping it over in my hands as I inspected it.

"Well what did you expect? Something spectacular? It has to blend in with our things, since you know we're not allowed to keep personal things," she said mimicking my whinny voice.

So she *had* heard me after all. This got a smile out of me.

"Okay, so what do I do? Just empty my brain right here on the pages? What if someone finds it?"

She smiled wide and grabbed a pencil. "Watch."

She started scrawling her name on the first page, then she

wrote the date, and underneath she neatly wrote: *Today I give this journal to 65, so that she may begin her quest to greatness and learn the true gift that has been bestowed upon her. Sparrow.*

She handed the book back to me so I could inspect what she'd written. Then she closed the cover and held onto one end of the notebook, thrusting the other end in my direction.

"Okay, now hold on, close your eyes and repeat after me."

At first the room was completely silent. I sat quietly waiting for her to say something and then I heard it.

"Restore!"

My eyes flew open! She could speak to me telepathically too! I quickly shut my eyes again and concentrated on speaking to her with my mind.

"Restore, Restore, Restore."

"Okay, open your eyes," said Sparrow, with her amber eyes gleaming at me. "Now for the moment of truth. Open it."

I slowly pulled the notebook back toward me and opened it to the first page. It was completely blank! I must have missed a page? I flipped, faster and faster. Every page was blank! I flipped it over and started from the back. Blank, all blank!

"You did it!" she squealed.

"Did what?"

"Okay, okay, I'll show you the best part. Repeat after me," she said, once again grabbing half of the notebook.

"Reveal!"

This time I heard her right away and repeated back to her with my mind, *"Reveal!"*

We opened our eyes and stared at each other. Her face was bright with her twitchy smile as she jutted her chin at me, motioning for me to open the book.

I hesitated for a moment, feeling silly, but when I folded the smooth cover back, the first page revealed what hadn't been there a moment ago. There in front of me was Sparrow's note!

"How?" I exclaimed almost jumping away from the words on the page with surprise.

"It's part of my powers." She smiled. "And it's essential for keeping a journal. Like you said, we don't want anyone else reading it."

"But can I do it?"

"You just did."

"Yeah, but you were helping me."

"Try it again on your own this time."

I repeated the process, *"Restore, Reveal,"* and to my surprise it worked exactly the same way. I was so excited I could barely contain myself. I felt like I was doing real magic! This was even better than the flaming light Nova showed me. That felt so detached from reality. Almost like it was a dream, not something that actually happened. But this, this was right out in the open, in my everyday life. I was sitting in my room, making words disappear and reappear! I grabbed the pencil and scribbled in the notebook under where Sparrow had written. *Sparrow is amazing. She just showed me an incredible trick! I can't wait to explore everything I learn in the safety of this journal. Sparrow, you are truly incredible!*

"Restore, Reveal." It worked again! I was positively glowing, and when I looked over at Sparrow, so was she. I reached forward, drawing her into a fierce hug! I hadn't felt this happy in, well, forever!

"How did you know I could do this?"

"I had a feeling about you. When you told me about how Nova could read minds and telepathically communicate and that suddenly you could too, I thought you might be a Parallel, someone who can mimic other's powers. It's very rare, but then again, so are you."

"Parallel? So I can do all the things you and Nova can do?"

"Potentially. Once we reveal a power to you and show you how to use it, you can absorb it and replicate it. Some things are simpler than others. Some will require a lot of practice."

"What else can you show me?" I asked excitedly.

"Well there's lots, but I think we better talk about that later," she said gesturing to the door.

I could hear activity in the hall, meaning that the rest of our year would soon be returning from dinner.

"I'll leave you to your *homework*," she said with a wink and then she hopped off my bed and went over to the large table in the center of our room and piled her lesson books there to begin on her own homework. I sat curled up on my cot bed, resting my back against the cool window panes as I began to write my first true excerpt in my journal as the rest of the orphans filed into our room.

Dear Journal,

Today is my first official entry. I've decided to use you to help me keep record of the new and exciting things I'm discovering about myself. Until recently, I thought I was a less-than-average girl, living in an orphan center on Hullabee Island, wishing with all my heart that I would someday know my family and my real name. I have lived here all my life, with barely any friends or anything to look forward to. I always felt alone, like there was no one on my side and my hopes and dreams would never come true.

My life has changed very suddenly, after forming an unexpected friendship with a boy named Nova, who up until now, I thought I had a major crush on. But, as it turns out, he has special powers and can do magic! It seems I've been misconstruing his powers as this unavoidable attraction I had toward him. It's a relief to know I'm not hopelessly in love with this unattainable, seriously beautiful, older boy, because he seems to have become my new mentor, because get this, I have powers, too!!!!

Nova brought me to the forest for the first time last night, by summoning me with his mind. I think this is called telepathing, at least that's what Sparrow called it. I'll tell you about her in a minute. Okay, back to Nova, this telepathing thing is one of Nova's powers.

Next, he shows me how he can produce a flame out of thin air and he wants me to try it. After a few failed attempts and some misunderstanding, I actually could do it, and more! I produced light, it wasn't a flame, I don't know how else to explain it other than it was bright and powerful and tingly, and it made me so happy!

Then Nova also explained about another power he has, where he can manipulate people's thoughts. This power frightens me the most and I have so many questions about it. I don't even know what it's called, but I've been calling it mind bending because I thought he was doing it to me and I truly felt like my mind was all meddled around in and my thoughts were bent in so many directions that I couldn't think straight. But it turns out that's just how your brain reacts when you've been a nobody your whole life and all of a sudden you're special and you have powers, and can do things you never even dreamed of, and you are getting this unfamiliar attention and new friends!

I used to be able to count John 26 as my one and only friend, and if you asked me last week who my best friend was, I would have laughed at you and said, my only friend would be my best friend, what a silly question. But I've found out that he hasn't even been completely honest with me. He's been hiding the fact that he knew his real name from me; it's Remi. It just hurts because I want to know my name so badly and Remi knows his name but never even shared it with me. I suppose he was just trying to protect me, because apparently I might be the only orphan who doesn't remember their real name since I was so young when I came here. Even the other Janes and Johns that know their names don't dare speak them because it's taboo here in the Center and will land you in the locker, and perhaps bring on the wrath of the gods. I had pretty much forgiven Remi for not telling me about his name, but now we have something else coming between us. I get the feeling that he doesn't really like my new friends for some reason, and I also tried to tell him about my powers and he doesn't believe me. He just thinks I'm acting crazy because I've been hanging around with Journey, Sparrow, and Nova.

Journey and Sparrow are the newest of my friends and they are like Nova and I. They have powers too! Well, I know for sure Sparrow does. She's great. She said we were sisters and she's the one who gave me this journal to help me manage all my thoughts and questions. She has one herself and she even taught me how to enchant it so that no one else can read it. That's the coolest thing I've learned so far and definitely my favorite power. She also showed me how she heals things by restoring them back to their origin, which came in handy with my dirty uniform and with our Flood work. I haven't learned how to do these things yet, but I think I will because Sparrow also told me she thinks I'm a Parallel. I guess that's the name of someone who can mimic other people's powers. So far I've been able to mimic the journal thing and the telepath thing. I sort of read Remi's mind too in History and Trade lessons, even though he doesn't believe me, so maybe I'm a mind bender, too.

So, you see this is a lot to take in and there are so many things I want to know more about. I just have so many questions. I'm going to meet Nova in the forest again tonight and I'm bringing Sparrow and Journey with me. I hope Nova's not too mad that I'm bringing them along. But I figured if we're all out there together maybe I can get more answers to my questions.

. . .

QUESTION 1 – Will I ever learn my real name?

    Question 2 – Will I ever know anything about my family?

    Question 3 – Do I really have a crush on Nova?

    Question 4 – What is the deal with Nova's mind bending power? Can I do it? Is it dangerous?

    Question 5 – Will Remi ever believe I have powers? Will he still want to be my friend?

    Question 6 – Can I trust Journey?

    Question 7 – Can Sparrow actually teach me to sing?

    Question 8 – What really happened when I hit Jemma and why does she hate me so much?

    Question 9 – Am I really a Parallel?

    Question 10 – Who else has powers?

    Wish me luck journal. Hopefully the next time I write to you I'll have answers to these questions.

As I closed my journal and secured it with my restore enchantment I felt lighter and more confident than ever before. Sparrow was right; this journaling thing was a good idea. I could feel it helping me already. I felt like I had my thoughts collected all in a row and would surely be able to formulate some answers tonight. I looked around the room at all the other orphans in my year. They were scattered about, most of them working on their homework lessons. Some were leafing lazily through books on their bed, and others were gathered in little clusters chatting away to each other. Everything seemed utterly ordinary. I scanned the room for Remi. He was sitting alone at the far end of the table studying his lessons. I felt my cheeks flush instantly when he looked up at me. I hated that we were fighting and I knew I was going to have to be the one to make the first move to right this situation. I hoped off my cot bed and walked over to Remi, pulling up a chair next to him.

"Whatcha working on?" I asked nonchalantly.

"History and Trade, and you should be, too. Greyvin gave us a lot of reading if you don't recall."

"Oh yeah, I should get on that. Let me go find my book and I'll join you."

I scurried away to grab my book before he could protest and was back in a flash.

"So, what pages were we supposed to read again?" I asked.

"You really are hopeless," he said with a hint of a smile. "Here," he said, pushing his notebook toward me. "These are the notes from lessons today and our reading assignment."

Now he really was smiling. It seemed like he had already forgiven me, even without the apology I had been readying. He was such a good friend. I always admired his kind heart and it made me feel worse that I'd been fighting with him to begin with. I reached for his hand and leaned in close to him and whispered, "Remi... I'm really sorry I – " but he cut me off before I could get anything else out.

"I know. Don't mention it, okay?" He stared at me with his big brown eyes and squeezed my hand.

"So, we're good?"

"We're good," he smiled.

This made me grin too.

For a little while we worked side by side on our reading. I would interrupt him occasionally to have him clarify his notes.

"You really should practice your penmanship," I joked with him. "This is *atrocious!*" I said, mimicking Miss Neilia's high-pitched accent.

"Like yours is any better," he said reaching for my journal.

Before I could stop him he was fanning through the pages. His expression slowly changed from playful to confused.

"I don't get it. You were writing in this all night, but it's empty."

"Oh, that was a different notebook," I said snatching it back from him.

Gong!

Saved by the bell again! This chime meant it was the end of our day and we had about twenty minutes to get changed and into bed before the final bell, signaling lights out. I leapt up out of my chair startled by the sound and grateful for it all at once. I grabbed my things and smiled at him before turning to head to the Janes' wardrobe. He continued to stare at me suspiciously. I could feel his eyes on my back as I disappeared into the crowd of Janes milling about as they got ready for bed.

I pulled my oversized nightshirt on over my work clothes and quickly hopped into my cot bed and under the covers before anyone noticed how lumpy my long grey nightshirt looked. As I lay in bed I had to concentrate on slowing my heartbeat that was surely loud enough to give me away.

Gong!

The final bell rang and the room went dark. The struggling electricity ceased its laborious buzzing and began its nightly slumber, leaving us in an eerie silence without its powerful hum. I lay wide awake bathed in the moonlight from the window. I was even more nervous tonight because not only did I have to escape, but Sparrow and Journey did, too. I wished I could talk to her to make sure she was still coming. Wait a minute, I could! I could telepath her!

"Sparrow! Sparrow!"

"Yes?"

"Oh great, it's working. This is how I'll tell you it's time to go tonight. You're still coming with me, right?"

"*Of course!*"

"*What about Journey? Did you have a chance to talk to him about it?*"

"*Yes, he's with us.*"

"*Okay, be ready to go when I call you again.*"

12

I laid awake for what seemed like an eternity before I heard Nova's voice. It hit me like a lightning bolt, sending a current of excitement tingling through my whole body. This was it, time to get Sparrow and Journey and go.

"Sparrow, it's time."

"Okay, what do we do?"

"I'm going to climb out the window and once I'm clear you can follow, one at a time."

"Okay, good luck."

"You too."

I sat up slowly and scanned the room like last time. No one stirred. I slipped off my nightshirt and stuffed it under my pillow. Still no movement in the room. I turned toward the window and took a deep breath, giving it a good push at the bottom pane. This time I was able to push it open far enough to slip out in one attempt. I still landed with a bit of a thud, but was more graceful than last time. I scooted over to the right of the window, waiting for Sparrow and Journey to appear. It seemed like it was taking too long. I was holding my breath when suddenly Sparrow slipped out the window. She was so silent and graceful that she didn't even interrupt the insects' night song. I was instantly jealous. She crawled over to me just in time to avoid being crushed by Journey. Even he managed to be stealthier than me. I really needed to work on that.

"Okay, follow me," I said.

I pushed my way through the bushes to the clearing ahead, where I stood to check that the coast was clear. It looked as calm as it had last night, so I motioned for them to follow me and I took off at a run across the field. I ran all the way to the forest line without stopping. Once there I turned to look for Sparrow and Journey. They were a good ways behind me still when I felt Nova grab me and jerk me in beyond the tree line.

"Nova!"

"Shhh...we've got company."

"Um yeah, about that..."

"What did you do, Tippy?"

"Don't be mad, I asked them to come."

Before Nova could scold me, I slipped out of his hold and waved them over to me. Sparrow was out of breath and looked nervous. "What are we doing out here?" she asked.

"We're meeting Nova," and right on queue he waltzed out of the forest calmly.

"Well, now that the gangs all here," he said glaring at me. "Shall we?" he asked motioning toward the forest.

"Come on," I said to Sparrow and Journey. "We need to get under cover."

We followed Nova silently into the depths of the dark forest. I could feel the tension among our little group. Nova was definitely a little miffed I had just sprung Sparrow and Journey on him. And Sparrow and Journey seemed on edge about being in the forest. Finally, Nova stopped and produced his flame, eerily lighting our faces.

"Well, I'm sorry guys, if I'd known we were having a party I would have been more prepared," said Nova, directing his sarcasm at me.

"Okay, I'm sorry I didn't tell you they were coming, but it's not exactly like we have the time to discuss these things at the Center and I figured this would be the best opportunity for us to learn from each other. Sparrow has already taught me so many things today and if we all put our heads together, I bet you can get me up to speed even faster."

Everyone just looked around at each other in the little circle we formed.

"Come on, you guys. I really want to figure out my powers and learn how to use them. You all know we'll accomplish more together," I pleaded.

After a long pause, Nova took a deep breath and turned to Sparrow. "What did you teach her?" he said accusingly.

"What did *you* teach her?" she fired back.

"I asked you first," Nova said taking a step toward her.

Before I could try to intervene, Journey placed himself in front of Sparrow, blocking Nova's path to her. There was something about the way his amber eyes glowed almost red in Nova's firelight that stopped him in his tracks. I think he could have stopped a charging elephant with how intimidating he looked right then. His jaw was set and his huge shoulders were squared, poised to attack if necessary. I couldn't even catch a glimpse of Sparrow behind his hulking frame. I had to do something to diffuse the situation and fast. I started by trying to push my way between them, but they seemed oblivious to me.

"Nova, please, it's fine. They're on our side. Journey, we're all on the same side. Guys, please!"

No response.

They both stood there, squared off, waiting for one of them to make a false move. I was so angry. This was not at all what I wanted to happen. I needed some way to break this standoff before something horrible happened. I wedged my way between them and was preparing to try to produce my orb but something unexpected happened. I produced light, but it wasn't in the form of my little bouncing orb this time. This time my whole hand was glowing, and so was my arm for that matter. My whole body was glowing. It looked like my skin was bursting from the inside out with light. It was pulsing through every pore in my body, flowing out of me effortlessly. I turned my palm over and back, watching the light reflect off of the forest around me. It looked like gazing up at the sun from under the clear-blue waters of the sea. Light was bouncing and dancing around me. I caught sight of Nova and Journey, who had now backed more than a few feet away from each other. This hadn't been my plan, but it had the desired effect anyway. I sighed with relief and my light instantly retreated back within as I lowered my arms.

"What was that?" exclaimed Sparrow.

"I don't know! But it was pretty cool, huh?" I said smiling.

"How did you do that?" Nova asked.

"I'm not sure. I was trying to produce my orb but that happened instead."

"Okay, remember what I said about triggers? What were you thinking about right before you started, well, glowing I guess?"

"I was just angry at you all for being so pigheaded, and I felt frustrated and desperate to stop you two from getting into a useless fight."

"Good, so it was emotions again. Anger, mixed with frustration and desperation. You need to remember these triggers, Tippy."

"You should write them in your journal," piped in Sparrow.

"In her what?" Nova asked.

"Oh, that's a great idea, Sparrow," I said smiling at her. I turned to face Nova. "That's what I've been trying to tell you. Sparrow is helping me with this, too. She showed me how to keep a journal about all the new powers I discover. I can write down the triggers that cause them so I can keep better track of how this all works. It's been helping me figure out how everything works and I can write down all my questions."

"Do you really think it's such a good idea for her to write down all our secrets?" Nova asked Sparrow.

"I taught her how to enchant it so no one else can read it."

"It's so cool, Nova. I just tell it to restore when I'm done writing and everything disappears. And then I say reveal and it all comes back!"

Nova looked impressed. "You're a healer?" he asked Sparrow.

She nodded.

"That's impressive. I've never met one before."

"See, this is what I mean. We can learn so much from each other."

"And I think she's a Parallel," Sparrow said gesturing to me.

"Really? That would make a lot of sense actually," Nova said. "She's picked up everything I've shown her really quickly."

"Exactly. I showed her how to use my healing power on the gems in the rubble pile and on the journal, and she got it on the first try."

"I showed her how I produce my flame and she ended up

almost setting the whole forest on fire with her light source! And we all just saw her little glowing trick."

"Don't forget about the whole mind reading and telepathy, too," I chimed in.

They both turned and looked at me, like they had forgotten I was there. Then Nova smiled at Sparrow and asked, "Shall we?"

"Why not? I bet she can do it."

"You're on," he said shaking her hand.

"Hey, are you guys telepathing about me? Not fair!"

"We have a little test for you, Tippy. Sparrow's going to show you something and we want to see if you can do it. I want to test this Parallel theory. Can you give us a little more light?"

"Sure," I said with a smile.

I produced an orb this time and grew it to about the size of a watermelon. I watched it hover above my hands and decided to try something. I willed it to stay afloat while I backed away and it worked. It bobbed slightly suspended about four feet above the forest floor. I lifted my hands still concentrating on the orb and it lifted higher off the ground. Once it reached a good height to illuminate a large enough area of the forest I commanded it to stay. When it complied, I smiled and wiped my hands back and forth matter-of-factly. "How's that?" I asked.

"Let's not get cocky just yet, Tippy," Nova said, but he was smiling too.

"Okay, Sparrow, go for it."

We turned our attention to her as she broke into a run. She was heading straight toward a large tree and I started to worry she was about to smash into it, when she took a step off of its mossy trunk and propelled herself upward. She was bounding diagonally off of trees, soaring between them effortlessly. She looked like the monkeys that traveled through the forest canopies. She wasn't exactly flying, more like gliding and floating between wide expanses that would have been impossible for a normal human. I was intrigued and in awe of Sparrow's grace. I wanted to do that too, and that's when I remembered this was a test to see if I could. *Well, here goes nothing* I thought as I broke into a run toward the same tree that Sparrow had vaulted off of.

It worked! I was soaring, bounding higher and higher into the tree tops. I couldn't believe I was doing it. I didn't know how I was doing it, but my body seemed to take over like it was the most natural thing in the world for me to be bouncing from tree to tree, clearing impossible gaps. I landed on a precarious limb and steadied myself, pausing for a moment to find Sparrow. It was harder to see so high up here. My orb looked about the size of an apple so far below. I needed more light. I produced another orb and let it float in front of me. Then I smiled, having a brilliant idea. I shoved off and headed for another tree, producing orbs as I went, leaving a trail of bouncing balls of light behind me. This quickly lit up my play ground and I found Sparrow bounding to a tree below me. I quickly set off to catch her and I landed on the same limb as she did simultaneously. Out of breath and giggling, Sparrow gave me a big hug.

"You did it! You were amazing!" she gushed.

"I can't believe I did it! That was so much fun!"

"Come on, let's go down and see how impressed the boys are!"

We bounded down to them, still laughing and smiling.

"So?" I said.

"Okay, I'm impressed, Tippy."

"Me too," said Journey.

That was a huge compliment coming from him since I rarely heard him speak at all.

"Thanks," I said. "It was so much fun. Oh wow, look at my lights!"

We all leaned our heads back, admiring the light trails I strung among the tree tops. It reminded me of the stars in the night sky that were blocked out by the thick vegetation of the dark forest. They twinkled beautifully high above our heads. I sighed, reveling in the idea that I had created this magical scene.

"It reminds me of the New Year Gala," said Journey breaking the silence.

"Yes, you're right. It's just like the candles and paper lanterns at the New Year celebration," I said.

"Well, maybe we can have our own New Year Gala out here now that we know what Tippy can do," joked Nova.

"If it means I don't have to sing, I'm in!" I said.

This made us all laugh. I was so happy this night turned around. It had been a rocky start, but it was turning into everything I knew it could be. We were working together and getting along, and I was learning new things at a rapid pace. I mean, I had just about flown through the treetops and lit up the forest with my string of glowing orbs. What a night; and I had a feeling it was just getting started.

I looked at Journey. "Okay, your turn, what can you teach me?" I asked him.

He looked at Sparrow for confirmation that he should share his powers with me and she nodded to him. He looked doubtful, but he took a few steps toward me and picked up a stone from the forest floor and crushed it in the palm of his hand. When he opened it there was nothing but a pile of dust.

"Wow, I'm glad we didn't end up coming to blows," said Nova, with a nervous laugh.

"You expect me to crush a stone," I said looking at Journey like he was slightly crazy. I already knew he was massive and insanely strong just from looking at him. Was this really something he needed magic for?

"Okay," I said sounding unsure. I searched around for a medium size stone and picked it up. "How do I do it?" I asked.

He reached for my hand. "Pull strength from me."

I closed my eyes and held Journey's hand with my left and the stone in my right. I closed my fingers tightly around the stone and felt it resist as I tried to clamp down further. Then I felt a surge of power rush through me from Journey's direction and I knew I would have no trouble crushing the stone. I tightened my grip around the stone and felt it crumple as if it were made of nothing more than sand. I opened my eyes and smiled at him. I slowly opened my palm to show the others and watched the dust slowly fall through my fingers.

"That was awesome! I could feel your strength when I needed more power to crush the stone," I said to Journey.

It felt amazing and I almost wanted to hug him, but I was still a little unsure of him, so I just smiled and patted his shoulder.

"Try it again without his help," Nova said in a serious tone.

"Alright."

I picked up another stone. This one was larger and heavier than the last one. I had to use two hands just to hold it. I pushed my palms against the cool hard surface and felt the stone resist. I pushed harder and this time I could feel little fractures beginning to form. I channeled my energy and focused on pulling the inner strength I felt from Journey. I could feel it surging through me and I knew soon the stone would crumble under my pressure. Sure enough it did, bursting into pieces of rubble and dust.

"I did it! That's so cool, Journey! What else can you do?"

"I've got a fun one for you to try," he said. He was actually smiling, and I saw a flash of the young boy that must've been lost behind his massive façade.

"You'll need to turn off the lights for this though," said Journey. "And I'll need your help as well," he said looking at Sparrow and Nova.

He must have telepathed something to them because they both nodded.

"Lights!" he said, and I went to work.

I walked to the center of our little meeting spot and looked up at my orbs. There had to be hundreds of them. I didn't really know the best way to do this, but raising my arms seemed to be a good start. I could instantly feel the sensation that I commanded over the orbs. It was empowering to know they responded to me. I pulled my hands together into a loud clap and instantly it was dark. It was as if all the light in the world had been vacuumed out. I stood in the inky blackness listening to the gentle rustling of leaves and the soft footfall of my friends. Where were they going? This must be part of the test.

"Journey?" I whispered.

"Over here," he answered sounding nearby. "Can you see me?"

"I can't see anything," I replied.

"Look for my eyes. Focus."

I scanned the emptiness in front of me. Nothing. I turned searching, pleading myself to find him. Then out of nowhere his eyes appeared! I was so shocked I jumped backward and fell flat on my back. When I sat up they were still there, a pair of bright red eyes staring back at me, blinking calmly.

"Journey? Is that you?" I whispered in amazement. I really hoped it was him or I was about to get eaten by something with glowing red eyes because they started to advance toward me.

"You try."

"Try what? To turn my eyes red?"

"It's more than that. You'll see. Grab my hand and slow your breathing. Let yourself be absorbed into the shadows and truly see your surroundings."

I felt him grab my hand, which I was grateful for because I would have been groping aimlessly for his. I could feel his calm and steady composure wash over me. I felt instantly at peace with the darkness of the forest. Like it was a comforting cloak resting over me. I could hear my heart beating, slow and steady, humdrum, humdrum, humdrum. Then I heard Journey's join in the percussion. Humdrum, drum hum, humdrum, drum hum. It had a catching beat. I looked over at him and to my surprise I could make out his features. An ashen glow cast over his whole body, but he was there, every detail. His short brown hair, his chiseled face, broad straight nose, and his wide-set glowing-red eyes.

"I can see you now," I said.

"Good, you need to use sight and sound for this exercise and we need to communicate like this so we don't scare our prey."

Prey? I didn't like the sound of that.

"What are we hunting?"

"Sparrow and Nova."

That's what I was afraid of. I knew this was just a training exercise, but why did Journey have to make everything sound so menacing? I tried to think of it as hide-and-seek as we spread out into the forest. It had always been one of my favorite games to play at the Center when I was younger. I would still love to play it now, but such foolishness would never be tolerated by orphans our age. Eager to play, I decided to make the best of this test and reverted back to my childhood memories of crouching in the fields, and hiding behind trees as I moved silently through the forest in pursuit of Sparrow and Nova.

I tried to focus as Journey taught me. I slowed my breathing and listened to the sounds around me. I pushed the hum drumming of my heart into the background and that allowed me to truly hear what was around me. There seemed to be so much more life in the sleepy forest than I was aware of before. I could hear civer ants marching nearby collecting leaves for their colony. I could see the tree frogs waiting patiently for an insect to land within reach of their sticky tongues. There were even families of lemurs touring about the tree tops. How had I missed all this before? The forest had a nocturnal life that I never noticed before.

I pressed forward, listening painstakingly to every inch of forest around me. Soon I heard another heartbeat. It sounded just like mine, but it wasn't. It was louder and faster than mine. I walked in the direction of the sound and suddenly Nova's blond hair gave him away. It appeared shockingly white with my newly acquired night vision and almost seemed unfair that he didn't know it was sticking high above the palmetto palms he was crouching behind. I crept silently behind him, unable to help myself from launching a surprise attack on him.

I pounced. "Gotcha!"

"JEEZE! Tippy, you scared me to death!"

I landed on his chest and got a full glimpse of the panic on his face. I was rolling in a fit of laughter. "You should have seen your face! That was great! This is so much fun!"

"Yeah, yeah. Laugh it up, Tippy. I'm glad you're enjoying yourself."

"Oh come on, you have to admit this hide-and-seek part was pretty fun. It reminds me of being little. Imagine if I knew I could do this stuff back then! I would've been unstoppable!"

"From what I remember, you were pretty good back then, too. No powers necessary."

I sat up and looked at him. He was inches from my face and I could feel his warm breath on my neck. Could he really have remembered playing hide-and-seek with me all those years ago? I always went after the older kids, loving the challenge, but they never took me seriously. Even after I tagged them, they'd just keep on playing, waiting for someone worthy to find them. But not Nova, I remembered finding him hiding high atop a tree and he said I'd have to climb it to tag him...

"Or it wouldn't count," he finished for me.

"I can't believe you remember that."

"I remember a lot of things about you, Tippy."

Oh no, I was having those feelings again. The flushed cheeks, the pounding heart, the goose flesh. Was this really just because of the powers we'd shared, or was there more?

"Found her!" shouted Journey from a few yards away. This broke me free of my Nova trance.

"We're right here," said Nova, producing his flame to give us some light.

He gave me a swift kiss on the forehead and a wink as he pulled me to my feet. I hated when he did that. It made me feel all fluttery and dizzy. I needed to remember to ask Sparrow if that was what she meant happened to her with the whole sharing powers connection thing, and if there was a way to control it. I didn't like feeling so off balance.

"Well, that was a success!" said Sparrow with her usual enthusiasm. "What's next?"

"I think we did great for tonight and we should probably start heading back since we went a lot deeper into the forest this time," Nova said.

"I want to try one more thing before we go," Journey replied.

I was impressed he was the one who was so open to training me. This was the most I'd heard him talk. He really did have a kind-heartedness about him. I was beginning to see why Sparrow trusted him so much. Behind his stern exterior and brute strength was a generous soul. He walked over to a nearby tree and wrapped his hands around the scrawny young trunk. Slowly, from where Journey's hands were, the tree began to transform. The trunk splintered and fractured, making loud snapping sounds. I took a few steps closer, mesmerized by what I was seeing. Radiating out from where he gripped the tree, Journey was slowly turning it to stone!

"Are you kidding me?" I squealed. "I want to do that!"

Even Nova seemed to have lost his 'I'm-too-cool' attitude as he gawked open-mouthed at the stone tree.

"Okay, okay! That's enough," said Sparrow walking in between us and edging us away from the tree. "Can we please practice this on something that's not living?"

She put her hands on the stone trunk and closed her eyes, restoring the bark back to its original form. When she was done, she took a step back to admire her work, confidently putting her hands on her hips and lifting her chin.

"There, that's better." She turned to look at us. "What? Trees have feelings too you know."

"Sorry, Sparrow," said Journey lowering his head.

I didn't want today's lessons to end without getting to try turning something to stone, so I picked up a dead log that had been claimed by the mossy forest floor.

"Here, we can try this!" I said, waving the crumbling log under Journey's defeated face.

He looked at Sparrow for approval, and she nodded. "That'll do."

"Great, let's try it!" I exclaimed. "Will you help me?" I asked Journey, reaching for his hand.

I took it as a yes when he grabbed my hand and gave me a sly smile.

"*I have a better idea. Drop the log and we'll do something more fun.*"

"*Okay, any hints?*"

"*Just trust me. This won't hurt so don't be scared, it just looks a little crazy.*"

"*Okay, thanks for the warning, I guess,*" I said and then laughed nervously out loud, which caused Sparrow and Nova to eye me suspiciously.

Journey closed his eyes and squeezed my hand a little. I looked down at it and began to panic as I saw my hand was turning to stone! It was spreading slowly up my wrist. My skin was turning grey and cracking and popping like sides of an erupting volcano. I didn't know what to do. I struggled to pull my hand from Journey's grasp, but he was holding me tight. I felt myself sweating, panicking, my heart was pounding. Suddenly Journey pulled his hand away from me, as if he burnt it on a hot stove.

That's when all hell broke loose.

13

"Oh my gods, oh my gods, what'd you do?" I screamed.

I looked at my arm and it had turned to stone all the way up to my elbow. I grabbed at it furiously with my good hand, not knowing what to do. This brought Nova rushing to my defense.

"What's wrong? What happened?" Sparrow asked approaching us.

"My arm!" Journey yelped holding it up for Sparrow to see. "It's stone!" He whirled around to face Nova, while pointing at me. "She's an Echo, I knew it, she's an Echo! You knew it too, didn't you?"

"How dare you play with her like this!" Nova growled advancing toward him.

"*ME?*" exploded Journey, waving his stone hand right back at me.

Sparrow quickly put herself between the two boys to prevent any further advancements.

"What did you do to her? Look at her arm," Nova yelled. "I knew this was a bad idea!"

He turned on Sparrow. "You better be able to fix her!"

"Don't threaten her!" barked Journey, puffing up his chest and trying to get closer than Sparrow would allow to Nova.

"Stop it! All of you! We need to calm down!" Sparrow yelled. "Give me a minute to think!"

We were silent for a split second. It was long enough for me to look back at my arm and see that the stone was receding and my flesh was returning. It looked pink and new, but it was definitely skin.

"Uh guys, look," I said holding up my arm.

We watched as my pink skin waged war against the stone. It retreated all the way to my fingernails and then finally surrendered completely. Then we all swiveled our heads, turning our attention to Journey's stone hand. We were all expecting his hand to turn back to flesh as mine had, but after about five minutes of waiting, Sparrow spoke up.

"I just realized something."

We all looked at her.

"Well she's a Parallel right?" She paused, seeming to expect us to get to the same conclusion as she had, but when we gazed back at her with blank stares she looked aggravated and realized she was going to have to spell it out for us. "She has my healing powers, so she simply healed herself."

"So then Journey needs you to heal him," I said.

"I've never healed a person before, I told you that," she hissed at me.

"We'll I'm sure you can do it if I can," I encouraged.

She looked nervously at Journey and then back at me.

"Maybe you should try it. It worked so well on your own arm," she said to me.

"She's not touching me!" Journey barked taking a step backwards.

"Alright, alright," Nova chimed in. "I don't care who does it but we need to do it quickly. We need to get back to the Center! We've been out here way too long."

"Journey, please let her try. I'm scared that I won't do a good enough job and we only have one shot at this. Please let her try. I'll never forgive myself if I hurt you," Sparrow pleaded.

I'd never seen her look so scared. She was always so bright and confident. What did she mean we only had one shot? If I screwed it up would he be stuck with a stone hand forever? Why was she afraid to heal people? She healed the tree just fine. I stood there watching Journey's face twist as he fought back his emotions. He was obviously upset that Sparrow was so frightened, yet he really didn't want to let me try out my newly acquired healing skills on him. I couldn't say I blamed him, but I was pretty sure Sparrow was going to win this one.

I was right. Journey stormed over to me. "You better do this right," he growled.

Sparrow was by my side. "You can do this. Just concentrate, okay? I'll be right here," she said as she took my hand in hers.

I took a deep breath and swallowed hard as I slowly grasped Journey's awkward stone fist and closed my eyes. I had no idea how this happened, but I truly hadn't meant to harm Journey. I liked him. He was one of us. Whatever *us* was. He was helping me learn about my powers and I'd be damned if I was going to let a little thing like this ruin my chances of learning more about myself. Somehow I knew that I was going to need Journey in my quest, and I needed him whole, so that meant two working hands.

Sparrow's tightening grasp startled me and my eyes flew open. I looked down at Journey's hand. My hand was gripping his newly pink flesh.

"You did it!" she said sobbing, as she flung her arms around me. "I knew you could!"

"Thanks," said Journey, slipping his hand through mine so he could examine it better. I wasn't quite sure how I'd managed to heal Journey so perfectly, but I didn't have a chance to find out.

Nova gave us all a stern look and said, "Now let's go."

14

It was a silent walk back. We all moved single-file through the forest at a brisk pace. I had my eyes and ears alert to all the normally hidden sounds of the nocturnal forest. It seemed I couldn't turn off the hunting power that Journey gave me. Instead of it heightening my awareness, I just felt like it was congesting my head. What happened with Journey's hand tonight? How did I do that? Why did he try to turn my hand to stone? Did he think it was a joke? He had to have known that Sparrow might not be able to heal it. So why did he take such a reckless chance with me? And what was an Echo?

Tonight did not go as I planned at all. I had more questions than ever before. I was brooding mad when we reached the edge of the forest. The sun was threatening to overthrow the night sky. Nova was right, we had been in the forest much longer then we should have, but I refused to take another step until I got some answers.

"I'm not going back," I said.

"Quit playing around, Tippy. We need to go right now," Nova said.

"No! I need answers. I know there's so much more you're all not telling me and I'm sick of it!"

"We have to go, Tippy. Please! We can't be caught out here," Sparrow pleaded.

"Tippy, please don't make me force you to go back. I promise you that we'll keep doing this. We'll all come out here every night and you'll get your answers, but we don't have any more time tonight. We have to go back, now! Right now, Tippy, I mean it."

I could hear Nova's voice loud and clear in my mind, but instead of entrancing me as he usually did, he only made my blood boil. I glared at him as he spoke to me like I was a toddler. How dare he say he would *force* me to go back! He promised he'd never use his mind bending on me only last night and tonight he was already threatening to go back on that promise. How was I supposed to believe any of his promises? And Sparrow and Journey were so frightened by me tonight they'd probably never go back to forest with me. What if they were so scared that they told Greeley about me? No, no I couldn't go back. I wouldn't! Not without learning more. This could be my only opportunity to learn the truth. My eyes narrowed and my hands clenched. I could feel my heart thundering with anger in my chest. My fury boiled over and something took over me. I heard a scream escape my lips that sent a chill down my spine.

"NO!" I screamed.

The sound was coming from me, but the voice sounded so foreign it startled me. It was low, and guttural. It sounded more like the growl of a tarcat than a human. Suddenly there was a burst of bright blue light. It was like lightning, only it started from directly above my head and spanned out quickly in a ripple. I stared up at it, thinking it looked just like the little rings that follow after you drop a pebble into a puddle, spreading wider and wider until they disappear. Everything seemed so calm and quiet as the light spread slowly away from me. I lowered my gaze to find Nova and the others. They seemed frozen. They were all staring at me with expressions of surprise, or maybe it was fear. I wanted to ask them why they weren't looking at the sky. It was so pretty, I couldn't believe they were missing it, but every word I formed seemed to be swallowed up before it could roll off my tongue. Every movement seemed to be drenched in molasses. I could barely move. It seemed like I was in a dream world of slow motion. I focused on Nova and I could see his eyes were animated, tracking me, but he was still locked in his awkward stance. I forced a step toward him and then felt a searing pain in my head. Suddenly the light ripple retracted at lightning speed. It rewound rapidly, sucking its blue light back into itself and disappeared with a final blinding burst of blue light and a whip-like crack above my head.

Blackness.

15

I woke up in my cot bed rubbing my head. My eyes were out of focus when I opened them and everything seemed brighter than it ought to be. I sat up and rubbed the sleep out of them. When I pulled my hands from my face I was startled to find Sparrow staring back at me.

"Are you alright?" she whispered.

"Yeah, why?"

She just stared back at me. I caught movement in the corner of my eye and turned to see the yellow and white checked curtains of Miss Breia's nurse room billowing above me.

"What? How did I...? But..." I stammered.

"Shhhhh...." Sparrow hissed. "You'll wake her," she said motioning toward the door to Miss Breia's office.

"We brought you here last night, do you remember?"

I thought back, I remembered our trip to the forest, and all the things that Journey taught me; including the not-so-fun turning my hand to stone trick and everything turning to chaos. Then I remember being really mad that it was time to go because I wanted more time and more answers. Then there was that blue light in the sky!

"The light," I said quietly.

"Yes, the light. Good, you remember."

"I didn't think you saw it, you were all just staring at me and I wanted you to see it. Then I, I...." I let my voice trail off because the rest was fuzzy. "How did I get here?" I asked Sparrow.

"Nova redirected the Grifts so we could sneak you back in. Journey carried you to Miss Breia's, saying you woke up in the middle of the night complaining of a headache and asked for her before you passed out. She was nice enough to let me stay and wait for you to wake up."

"But, I don't remember any of that. I only remember that weird blue light and everything seemed like slow motion, and then there was a horrible pain in my head, then a cracking sound. What was all of that? I've never seen anything like it."

"Neither have I," she said solemnly, with a look of concern that was uncharacteristic of her usual chipperness.

"What's wrong?" I asked nervously.

"Tippy, you did that. You made the light. You froze us all." She paused waiting for me to understand what she was saying before she continued. "It's called a fissure and it's a way to stop time. It's very dangerous and I've always thought it was sort of a myth. No one has ever seen a fissure like that," she said with her eyes brimming with tears.

I could feel the fear she was emoting, but it wasn't for her self, but for me. She was afraid for me. She was afraid that my powers would hurt me. This frightened me more than anything. I never thought of it like that. I thought it was an amazing gift. Some sort of reward for putting up with the rough life of an orphan with no friends. An answer to my prayers, something good. But what if Sparrow was right? What if this was all too much for me? What if I couldn't control it? Maybe I would hurt someone or myself? I didn't even know what a fissure was or that I could do it. What else didn't I know about myself? Was this more than I could handle?

I felt her fear wash over me. I absorbed every ounce of it and it shook me. My eyes welled up and I reached for her hand. She took hold of it and squeezed.

"Did I... Did I hurt you?"

"No, no. It'll be okay. We'll help you. We'll figure it out."

"Please... Please help me."

Then we collapsed into a sobbing heap on the cot bed.

16

T he bell chimed, signaling... wait what was it signaling? I had lost track of time again. I didn't know if it was the morning bell or the breakfast bell or if it was time for lessons already. Before I could ask Sparrow, Miss Breia bustled in with a tray of fruit and porridge answering my question.

"Good morning, Janes! I was hoping you'd be up, 65. I brought you some breakfast. 42, you had better run along so you don't miss out on your own meal."

"I will, Miss Breia. Thank you for letting me stay with her." Sparrow smiled as she patted my hand affectionately before turning to leave. *"Meet me for lunch. We all need to talk,"* she telepathed.

I nodded at her and she left me to my breakfast. I was suddenly in a rush to get back to my room. All I wanted to do was get ready for lessons and grab my journal. I wanted to write down everything I could remember from last night while it was still fresh in my mind. I gobbled down my food and finished my juice in three giant gulps, wiping my mouth with the back of my salty hand. I thanked Miss Breia and ran out of her office before she could detain me.

When I got back to room 13 it was deserted. The rest of my year was enjoying meal in the dining hall by now. I quickly changed and grabbed my books. I instantly felt like I could breathe easier when I laid hands on my journal. I checked to make sure my enchantments still worked and then headed down the hall to Reading and Writing. I knew I would be early, but I wanted to avoid everyone and get some alone time to work on recounting last night.

The rest of the day flew by in a blur. I journaled all through lessons. Remi gave me some suspicious stares, but I ignored him, scribbling away.

DEAR JOURNAL,

Last night was interesting to say the least. It started out rocky, as I suspected. Nova wasn't happy that I brought Sparrow and Journey along. It was pretty tense for a while, but then we made some real progress.

Sparrow taught me how to fly, well sort of. I was able to bound from tree to tree. It felt like I was flying, soaring above the forest floor. It was so much fun.

Journey was amazing. He has so many interesting powers and he was really eager to share them with me. He is even stronger than he looks. He showed me how to harness my inner strength and channel it. I was able to crush a stone into dust with my bare hands! He taught me how to hunt, as he calls it. I learned how to tune out the apparent noises and distractions so that I could really hear what was going on around me. And he taught me how to see in the dark, it's some kind of nocturnal vision, I guess like animals have.

Things were going great up to this point. Even Nova seemed to be relaxing and enjoying playing with our powers. Then Journey tried to teach me another power and everything went wrong. He tried to turn my hand to stone, but I turned his hand to stone by accident and everyone went crazy. All the progress we made was gone, Nova was ready to kill Journey, and Sparrow was crying, and then all of a sudden I started healing myself! It was amazing. I guess I picked that power up from Sparrow. Then I had to heal Journey, but he seemed like he didn't want to trust me. He had to and I did heal him, so that sort of made things better, but Nova had enough and ordered us home.

On the way back I started to feel strange, like I couldn't shut off the hunting trick that Journey taught me. I could hear everything; every breath and heartbeat of every living thing in the forest. It was so distracting and it made me mad. I wanted to think clearly and I wanted to know more. I didn't want the night to be over. But Nova said it was time to go, and he was right. I realize that now. I should have listened to him. Why does he even put up with me? Why do any of them? All I do is cause trouble. I brought Sparrow and Journey with me, without telling Nova. I almost got us all into a rumble by accidentally turning Journey's arm to stone. Then, to top it all off, I threw a temper tantrum on the way back and caused some sort of time-stopping fissure! Oh, and as if that's not bad enough, I passed out and made my friends carry me back. And, they had to figure out a way to clean up my mess once again.

I'm just really glad we didn't get caught. And it seems like Sparrow is still my friend, which leads me to believe Journey will be too, or at least he'll come around to the idea of it if Sparrow says he has to. But what about Nova? He has to be ready to kill me. I need to see him. I really just need to talk to them and get it all out in the open. I need to know what I am and what I can do, before I hurt someone!

Sparrow really scared me when she was talking about the

fissure. I could see how scared she was. I could feel her fear. I don't want to make anyone feel that way ever again.

And what about the Echo? I almost forgot that Journey called me an Echo. I don't know what that means, but that made him react like Sparrow did about the fissure. He was frightened. Frightened of me.

Did I get any answers last night?

I still don't feel like I'm any closer to knowing my name or anything about my family, so Question 1 and 2 are still open.

Question 3, I guess I can say that even if I have a crush on Nova, I'm doing a great job at ruining any chances I'd ever have with him by acting like a crazy, stone-forming, fissure-slinging freak. So that takes care of him wanting to trust me and tell me about his mind bending.

I almost could answer Question 6 – Can I trust Journey? I would have totally said yes before he turned my hand to stone and all that. Now I should revise that question to: Can Journey trust me?

What about being a Parallel? That was Question 9. I think everyone was pretty convinced, because if I understand it right, it means I can absorb a power from someone else and then I'm able to have that power as well. I did a lot of that last night and everyone seemed pretty impressed. But what about Journey calling me an Echo? Was that the same thing as a Parallel or was it a bad thing? Everything else was going to have to take a backseat to that question.

Question 11 – What's an Echo? Am I one?

Question 12 – Am I strong enough to control all of this?

17

The lunch bell finally sounded and I scurried to the dining hall as fast as I could. I wanted to get my food and get to our table quickly so I'd have as much time as possible to talk with Sparrow and the others. I heard Remi calling after me as I ran down the hall, but I put my head down and kept going, pretending not to hear him. It made me feel bad to ignore him and my cheeks burned with shame.

I was the first one to arrive at our table. Sparrow and Journey joined me shortly, and then Nova. He looked worried, which totally threw me off because that wasn't what I was expecting. I thought he would be pretty peeved after last night, and I had a whole speech prepared that I was going to telepath to him, apologizing and explaining that I was ready to work with everyone so we could get my powers under control. But this, this whole worried, timid-looking Nova was the last thing I'd expected and it perplexed me. I just stared at him, unsure of what to do or say. We all sat there silently glancing from one to the other. I could feel the uneasiness and it was making me squirm because I knew I was the cause for it.

They were all unsure of me, maybe even scared. And who could blame them? I was the unpredictable one, turning hands to stone and stopping time on a whim. I was scared of me, too. I looked down at my small, rough hands on the thick, dark wood of the dining table. They looked so fragile compared to the oiled, aged wood. Its marred complexion looked like it could stand the test of time, while my hands, well, they looked so plain and ordinary. How could they be the hands of such power and possible destruction? I had to quickly clasp them together to stop them from shaking. I was quivering in my very soul, as I tried to fight back the tears that were beginning to form.

Nova reached out and grabbed my hands. He felt steady and warm and I felt his familiar comfort soothing me. I pulled one hand away so I could place it atop his to show my appreciation. Slowly Sparrow added her hand to the top of mine, and then Journey followed suit. I could actually feel them, feel their support washing over me, calming me, giving me courage—and more importantly—hope. Hope that I would be able to find out the truth behind all of this, and hope that I would be able to handle it all, with their help. Even though we could have had a perfect conversation through telepathy, we didn't need to. For the first time we communicated to each other perfectly through our unspoken bond. Somehow, I knew we each completely understood each other and had the same goal: to understand what my powers were and how to control the magic so we could figure out the truth.

I was oblivious to the fact that Remi walked over to our table until he cleared his throat.

"Well, I guess I'm not a part of this pact so I'll just find somewhere else to go be excluded," he said in a huff.

His words broke us all from our trance and we pulled our

hands back. I tried to protest as he turned to walk away, but Nova cut me off. *Let him go, Tippy.*

I didn't know how long he had been standing there watching us all holding hands, staring at each other. It must have looked pretty strange. I looked around the dining hall to see if anyone else had noticed us, but everyone seemed oblivious, caught up in their dull little cliques that I not so distantly longed to be a part of. I stared after Remi and watched him until he disappeared into a crowd milling about in the opposite end of the hall.

"It's better this way," Nova said softly.

"How?" I asked bitterly.

"Well, it's safer," offered Sparrow, back to her glass-half-full optimism. "You don't need to drag him into this mess until we have it all figured out. That way you can't hurt him."

"I'm pretty sure I just did," I sulked.

"Yes, but he'll recover from this. A stone arm? Not so much," ribbed Journey.

We all glared at him.

"What? Too soon? Aw, come on, it was my arm she maimed and I'm okay with it. Let's move on," he said putting his hands behind his head looking bored.

"Yes, lets," I said. "What's the plan?" I asked looking to Nova.

"I have one, but we need to test a few things out first. I want us to meet in the forest every night for the next week at least and we'll see if we're ready for the next step."

"Is there anywhere else we can work together besides the forest? It doesn't leave us much time with all the sneaking in and out we have to do," I said.

"Well, we have breakfast, lunch, and dinner to discuss things and plan. Anywhere else would look too suspicious," Nova said.

He must have been reading my mind again because I was already thinking of suggesting we go to our secret place behind the palm in the courtyard. He was probably right though. If we were always disappearing together it might draw attention. Plus it would be harder for all four of us to get there. With all of us trying to avoid the Grifts and tarcats someone would surely get caught. And I guess it would be kind of cramped back there anyway.

"Okay, breakfast, lunch, and dinner to plot, and the forest each night to practice. I'm in," I said grinning for the first time all day.

"Me too," said Sparrow.

Nova and Journey just nodded.

"One more thing though," I added. "I have to know the plan."

"I thought you might say that," said Nova. He was grinning now, too. He leaned in and lowered his voice, drawing us all closer, held by suspense. "You want answers, well we're going to get them. We're all going to the locker!"

"What?" we all exclaimed simultaneously, pushing back from Nova.

"Are you mad? We don't need much of a plan to get sent to the locker! And I thought we were trying to avoid getting caught!" I said in a rushed whisper.

"The locker is the only place you're going to get the answers we all need. Remember the legend of Lux I was telling you about? Well, how do you think I learned it? All that time I spent in the locker has paid off. It's not such a dull place to be when you shed a little light," he said slyly.

"That's right!" I said, suddenly remembering what Nova told me about the locker. I had almost forgotten about that with all the chaos of last night.

"What are you saying, Nova?" asked Sparrow.

He leaned in again, serious this time, speaking in a whisper. "The legend is down there. It's written on the walls. We need to go to the locker to read it. It'll help us understand Tippy's powers, because if she's who I think she is..." he paused. "Well, there's just a lot we need to learn."

I looked around at our little group. *"Are you all still in?"*

"Yes."

"Yep."

"Of course."

"Okay, well it's settled then. We will meet back here to come up with the best way to get in and out of the locker and we'll practice those skills when we go to the forest. We need to do it soon though because the New Year Gala is coming and we need to have this figured out by then," said Nova.

Gong!

18

Our little group of four worked tirelessly over the next few days. We plotted together over each meal in a hurried whisper. We practiced all our powers in the forest at night, but there never seemed to be enough time. Mostly because I slowed us down with all my questions. I didn't know enough about the Truiets and how everything worked.

"Isn't there like a Brief History of Truiet Magic she could take?" Nova joked one afternoon.

"I know, I know, I'm sorry," I said.

"Well..." Journey spoke up grabbing our attention. "I might know someone who could help her."

"Have you been holding out on us, Journey? Is there another one of us here?" Nova said, suddenly hostile.

"No, not exactly. I just have a hunch about this. When we've been going to the forest, I've been seeing signs."

"What kind of signs?" Sparrow asked.

"Well, the old Truiet markers. Carved into trees and rocks."

"Yeah, I'm sure there are old signs still out there."

"Well, that's what I thought at first, but it's been so long and I'm sure the Flood destroyed most of them. And then last night I saw a new one."

"How do you know it was new?" asked Nova skeptically.

"It was glowing. They only glow blue like that for about two days."

"How come none of us saw it?" I asked.

"You have to know what to look for. The Truiets hid their signs to protect their people. This way only those with Truiet powers could find them. I can show you the markers tonight so you know what to look for," Journey said.

"So you're saying there are Truiets living in the forest?" Sparrow asked.

"Yes," Journey said slowly.

"That's impossible. They were all killed in the Flood," she said.

"I actually agree with Journey," Nova replied, shocking us all.

"What?" I asked.

"Well, I've been working out there for a while now and I sometimes get this feeling that I'm not alone, like there are other power sources somewhere. I could never figure it out or see any signs of anyone other than us orphans and Grifts. I just had a feeling. But what you're saying confirms it."

"Okay, so even if this is true, we can't just go hand Tippy over to a Truiet and say, 'hey, can you teach her all your secrets?'" Sparrow said.

"Why not?" I asked.

They all just looked at me, shaking their heads.

"What? Come on, I'm sick of being in the dark about how all this magic power stuff works. It's slowing us down."

"She's right," said Nova, again surprising me that he was on board. "When we go out tonight, show me the markers and

I'll try to get a bearing on it tomorrow during Flood work. Maybe I can find someone and see if they might be open to helping us."

Journey nodded and we all got up from the table as the bell chimed.

19

I thought I caught a glimpse of Remi across the dining hall as I was leaving. I didn't know who he was sitting with, or if he was hiding all alone somewhere. I pushed that thought out of my mind because it made me feel guilty for neglecting my best friend. I just needed to get to the bottom of all of this. Maybe once I did, I would be able to tell him and he could help me! Remi would be the perfect person to tutor me on the Truiets if he knew about them. He's so smart and always did such a good job helping me concentrate on our studies. Speaking of studies, they've really been suffering this week without Remi. We had exams coming up before the New Year, but I could hardly ask him to help me cram after excluding him from everything else that was going on in my life.

I tried to put Remi out of my thoughts as I went back to our room to get ready for music rehearsal, but I just about smacked into him on my way to my wardrobe.

"Uh, sorry. I..."

"You just were looking right through me. Don't worry, I'm starting to get used to it," he scathed.

"Remi, no it's not like that! You're my best friend."

"Really? Because I thought friends talked to each other, included each other in their lives. It's like you've been living in another world since you started hanging out with them. I never see you anymore and you're always with them, whispering. What is going on with you, 65?"

"Remi..."

I longed for him to understand me. I begged forgiveness with my eyes and pleaded mercy with each beat of my heart, but it didn't work. The damage was done. He knew I wasn't going to tell him anything and he was hurt and angry and I couldn't blame him. I watched him shake his head and walk away from me as my heart was breaking under the pain I had caused him.

It was as if I could feel his pain. My chest was tight and heavy, and I had a lump in my throat that tasted of bitter despair, threatening to suffocate me. It choked back my words and thankfully my tears. I felt dizzy and confused, like I was lost at sea with no North Star for guidance. Remi was my North Star, but I had just cut him loose to wander aimlessly in space. It seemed the star and the sea didn't know what to do without each other.

20

*G**ong!***

It was time for music rehearsal. Luckily I was able to get by so far by faking that I was singing. I stood next to Sparrow, whose sweet voice rang so clear and bright that she would surely drown out my imperfections even if I was singing. The first time I heard her singing voice up close it took my breath away. It sounded like what I imagined angels to sound like. Each note was crisp and effortless. Her voice rang out like a shiny perfect bell; each note was attached to the next with a fluid quality that couldn't be taught. She was naturally gifted with this melody. I remember thinking if I sounded that good I would sing everything. I would sing instead of talk. I would never stop.

Today I took my usual spot next to Sparrow, who was beaming and flipping through the sheet music.

"She's going to assign the solo today."

"Oh, you know you're totally going to get it! You're amazing, Sparrow."

"Oh, thank you, Tippy. But will you be okay without me?"

"Sure, I can fake it pretty well," I smiled.

Just then Miss Sprigg came into our room and called us all to attention. She looked all business with her normally unruly mop of brown hair twisted into a neat little bun, high atop her head. It almost made her look taller. I bet that was her intention, because her tiny stature was easily lost among some of the taller Johns of our year. I'd always liked Miss Sprigg. She almost reminded me of myself; a quiet outcast even among the Grifts. She was so short and frail, and all the other Grifts paid no attention to her. I imagined that I would probably look just like her when I grew up, save for my flaxen hair. It was a shame that she was our music teacher though, because my lack of musical talent probably ensured my feelings toward her weren't mutual.

She'd been teaching us and all the other orphans to sing for as long as I could remember. She had a decent singing voice and must have had a true passion for music to volunteer to teach our lot. She had been putting up with the likes of me and some other less-than-talented orphans for a long time. Each class had one song to learn and perform at the New Year Gala. After I performed and released all my nervous jitters, I actually looked forward to hearing the other orphans sing. It was our only chance to listen to them sing since each class rehearsed and performed separately. Last year, Nova's class sang a beautiful song about the sea. Its melody was so sad and heart-melting that it brought me to tears. Of course, Nova was the one singing the solo that year. He had a voice as perfect as his flawless features.

I sighed thinking back to his performance. Was there anything he wasn't good at? Miss Sprigg brought me abruptly out of my daydream when she cleared her throat.

"Everyone, let's get started. Johns on the left, Janes on the right. Today we're going to be arranging you into sections and I'll be assigning the solo, so I hope you've all been practicing."

This caused quite a buzz among us. I heard moans and groans, amongst the other orphans. Perhaps some of them were dreading this as much as I was, or more likely they were just reluctant to be separated from the comfort of their cliques. There was actually some clapping and excited laughter and squealing going on, too, though. I could practically feel Sparrow's elation about the solo selection as she squeezed my hand and danced in place. I tried to give her a grim look, but her joy was infectious and all I could do was grin back when I looked at her big bright amber eyes that were lit up by her gleaming, white smile.

"You're insane, you know that?" I laughed.

"I'm so nervous!" she squealed

"Why? You're clearly amazing! You're going to get the solo."

"I hope so. Jemma got it last year."

"That's because everyone was always too scared to audition against her."

"True. Maybe I shouldn't. She's been leaving you alone lately, maybe I shouldn't stir up any trouble."

"No! You're incredible and you deserve the solo. I'm sick of Jemma always intimidating us. It's time for everyone to hear your voice."

"Thanks, Tippy. You're a great friend."

"I know," I smiled with a little wink. It felt great to be called a great friend, but only for a second, because it instantly made me think of how I was being far less than a great friend to Remi.

"What's wrong?" Sparrow asked. My face must have given me away, so I quickly put on a smile.

"Nothing. Go get 'em!" I said.

As usual, Jemma was the first to volunteer to sing the solo. Her gaggle of henchmaids fawned over her performance, oooing and ahh-ing and giving overly enthusiastic applause. I rolled my eyes as she bowed. I couldn't wait for her to see Sparrow sing. She probably thought she had this in the bag since no one had ever dared to try out for the solo, for fear of the wrath of Jemma.

"That was wonderful, 31. Just lovely," Miss Sprigg said. "Alright, shall we move on to the next part? Johns, lets..."

"Uhmmmm!" I cleared my throat and gave Sparrow a shove forward. I was afraid Miss Sprigg was going to move on without giving her a chance if I didn't act fast.

"Yes, 42. Can I help you?"

Sparrow glared at me.

"Um, I'd like to try out for the solo, too," she mumbled quietly.

"Excuse me dear? Speak up."

"I'd like to try out for the solo," she said more clearly this time.

This caught everyone's attention. Everyone stopped talking and stared at Sparrow. Everyone except me. I had my eyes trained on Jemma. She was standing there, mouth open, eyes wide with disbelief. She only lost her composure for a brief moment, but I caught it and it was so gratifying. The ice queen was shocked! She quickly narrowed her eyes as if looks could kill, but she covered that up with her sweet-as-poison smile and said, "Well, how sweet. I've inspired someone to sing. Come on, 42, let's hear it."

This seemed to be what Sparrow needed because she had previously been standing shakily in front of us all, nervously shuffling through her sheet music, shifting her weight anxiously from foot to foot. But after Jemma's taunt, she lifted her chin and thrust her music to Miss Sprigg, who seemed to be confused as to what was happening.

"Alright, 42, please take it from the top."

Sparrow burst into song. Her notes were clear and crisp

and perfect as I knew they'd be. She sounded better than ever. Our entire class was spellbound, speechlessly gawking at Sparrow as if they'd never met her before, and I guess they hadn't, not this Sparrow anyway. This Sparrow was more confident, more alive, and was absolutely glowing. I looked over at Journey and he seemed to be as happy as she was. He gave me a smile and then focused his attention back on Sparrow as she finished up her solo.

When she ended with her final high note, she took a deep breath and beamed back at us. The mood our room was emoting was complete adoration. No one knew what to do or say and I could see the look of panic setting into Sparrow's dainty face.

"You did great," I telepathed to her.

"But no one is saying anything."

"You just shocked them is all." I started clapping hysterically to break the silence, just as Jemma's groupies had, except Sparrow's applause was deserved. This seemed to break the trance and everyone else followed suit, clapping and hollering for her. Even some of Jemma's clique clapped until they caught sight of Jemma's seething look. I couldn't help but laugh. Finally someone stood up to her.

"That was inconceivable, 42! Where did you learn to sing like that?" Miss Sprigg asked, wrapping her arm around Sparrow's shoulders. Sparrow just shrugged and smiled.

"Well, I think we've just found our soloist!"

Everyone continued to clap as Sparrow rejoined me.

"Told you," I said.

"Oh, thank you so much for convincing me to do that!"

"Okay, okay, everyone we really need to get to the rest of our parts, so unless there's anyone else that has been hiding a voice as pristine as 42's, let's move on," Miss Sprigg said half joking, but then someone else was pushing their way to the front. I strained to see over my classmates, but it wasn't until he emerged in front of us that I could see who it was. I drew in a panicked breath. Remi! What was he doing? Was this some sort of stunt to get my attention? I had no idea what could have possessed him to stand up in front of our entire class to sing. He was by far the quietest John in our year, maybe in the whole Troian Center, and I wasn't even sure if he could sing. I mean I'm sure he was better than me, but it's not like he went around humming tunes day in and day out.

"Well, 26, let's hear it," Miss Sprigg said stepping back looking annoyed to give Remi the floor.

At first he was completely silent. I felt every cell of my skin crawling. It was as if I was up there instead of him. My palms were sweating and little beads of perspiration were forming on my forehead just as they were on his. I could hear his heart racing in unison with my own. I was terrified for him, or maybe with him. I wished so badly that I could offer him some sort of help, or come to his rescue like he did for me with Mr. Greyvin. All I could do was stand here helplessly and hope that he could pull this off.

It was silent for so long that some of the other kids started to talk and snicker. Miss Sprigg shushed them and gestured to Remi to get on with it. His big brown eyes looked like chocolate saucers as he tried to hide them behind his sheet music, but then something incredible happened. Sparrow left my side and joined Remi in front of us all. She grabbed his hand and started singing softly. Remi eased into the song along with her, lowering his music and looking straight into Sparrow's confident eyes. Their voices swelled and intertwined beautifully with each other, casting a hush over us as we were once again astonished by their unknown talent. I caught Journey's eye, but he only raised his eyebrows questioningly and shrugged. I guess he didn't know what was going on either.

When they were finished singing, we all broke into applause again. This time Jemma didn't even try to stop her cohorts' praise for Remi and Sparrow, who were excitedly hugging each other. After their embrace, they quickly returned to the group, being swallowed up by admirers. Remi was getting high fives and pats on the back. I even saw someone tussle his mop of dark brown hair. It was good to see Remi smiling like that, getting praise from our peers. Sparrow was getting more of the same among the Janes as she pushed through them toward me.

"What was that?" I whispered.

"What do you mean?"

"Why did you go up there to sing with him?"

"You asked me, too."

"What?"

"You kept saying 'help him, help him.' I thought you were talking to me."

"Oh, yeah," I said not very convincingly. Great now I was telepathing accidently? I had been thinking that I wished I could help Remi, but I thought I was just thinking it to myself. At least this hadn't backfired like most of my other accidental magic tricks. Sparrow was still looking at me questioningly. I'm sure I had a perplexed expression on my face so I quickly tried covering it up with a smile. Luckily, Miss Sprigg saved me by speaking up before Sparrow could question me any further.

"Well, it appears we'll be having a duet this year! I'm excited by all of this new talent! Now let's get to work on the rest of this song."

The rest of the lesson went smoothly. We practiced our parts without any more interruptions. The basses, tenors, altos and sopranos all were rehearsing their parts dutifully. I was put with the altos, which at first disappointed me because it meant I wasn't with Sparrow. But when Jemma and most of her band of merry henchmaids were sorted into the sopranos, I was actually relieved to not be in their group. My part was mind-numbingly easy, which was fine with me. I repeated my words on beat and generally in tune, and was happy when the bell finally chimed, signaling the end of our rehearsal.

"Great work, everyone. Please continue to practice. We only have a few more lessons before the New Year Gala," Miss Sprigg called after us as we disassembled.

I grabbed my journal and retreated to my cot bed to write as the rest of my year gossiped about rehearsals and studied for our exams. I looked up a few times to check on Remi, who seemed to be enjoying his new popularity. He had a group of Janes and even a few Johns surrounding him, chatting energetically. I shook my head in disbelief. It seemed the impossible was becoming increasingly possible recently.

Dear Journal,

Today was interesting. Well, I guess I should stop saying that because suddenly everything in my life is new and unexpected. I know I've been asking for my life to change and I guess that it's actually happening. I think I'm learning to watch what I wish for. I at least need to be more specific anyway.

I wanted to be popular and I guess I am now. After I hit Jemma everyone seems to know my name, well, my # anyway.

I wanted friends, and now I actually have some. Nova, Sparrow and Journey. But in the gaining of new friends, it seems I have lost an old friend. Remi and I have been fighting. I don't know what to do. He's been my best friend since, since I can remember. I don't know what to do without him in my life, but my life is so crazy right now, I can't possibly bring him into all this magic power stuff. I don't even know how to answer my questions about what's happening to me, let alone the questions he'd have. Plus, it's not safe. I'm not safe. I don't want to accidentally hurt him. I know keeping away from him is for his own good. It's the only way I know how to protect him. I just hope that I can figure all of this out soon before it's too late, before he moves on and doesn't want to be my friend anymore.

He sang today, with Sparrow, and they sounded amazing. Like they had been singing together their whole lives. It was unreal. I didn't even know he could sing. How could I not know that about my best friend? I'm beginning to think there's a lot I don't know about Remi. For starters he didn't tell me he knew his real name was Remi, or that he'd once had a brother named Dhani, or that he even remembered his life from before the Flood. I know he said he was protecting me and I believe him. I just hope he can see that now it's my turn to protect him.

He seems to be enjoying all the attention he's gained from his little duet with Sparrow. All the Janes in our year are fawning over him like he's this new sensation. It may be making him happy, but it's driving me nuts. Hello, he's been here all along. You've lived with him since the Flood you oblivious twits! You've shared a room, a desk, a life with him! Oh, I really hope this is short lived because I can't stand that he's talking to them. We used to despise them, but I guess he'd rather talk to them than to me. How backwards it that? I guess my whole world is pretty much upside down, so it shouldn't surprise me.

Tonight we're going to the forest again to practice. I'm getting better at controlling my powers and I haven't had any more accidents. We're all telepathing flawlessly and I can produce and control my light orbs with ease. I can even change their color, which Nova doesn't seem to appreciate. He's not the usual lighthearted Nova I know him to be lately. He's all business. He's starting to take the fun out of playing with my new powers. He just wants me to be able to do everything on command, there's no more fun hide-and-seek or *reminiscing. I know he's right to keep us focused. Going to the locker is a serious matter and we need to be prepared so we can be sure to find what we need while we're there.*

We're also going to look for some special markers that may or may not lead us to some surviving Beto people? Yeah, it sounds even crazier when I write it down. Journey says he's seen their markings with his hunter vision and that if we can find a Beto person, they can get me up to speed on the history of Truiets and my powers. Hopefully, we can find someone to enlighten me. I'm ready.

Well, wish me luck.

21

It was finally it's time for our nightly meeting in the forest. We'd gotten remarkably good at sneaking out. Journey's sly hunting skills rubbed off on me and it really helped being able to see in the dark. We moved silently and swiftly now, like tarcats stalking prey. When the four of us united at our usual meeting place, Nova got right down to business.

"Lights," he said.

I produced my orb on command and didn't bother trying to dazzle him with the cool colors I could turn it to now. I posted my blue orb of light above us and commanded it to follow us through the forest.

"Okay, Journey, where did you see the markers?" Nova asked.

"This way," he said taking the lead.

We continued on, deeper into the forest. We'd been this way before; I remember it from the clusters of moss-covered tree trunks and limbs that lay scattered about the forest floor. It was such a quiet place that seemed to emote sorrow from the mass grave where the old and tired trees had come to rest and be reclaimed by the soil that had nurtured them all their lives, until the Flood devastated the area. I didn't much care to hang out here. I didn't like the feeling I got from the eerie silence. Even under the thick steamy blanket of forest air, the haunting place made me feel cold. But of course, this was where Journey said he'd seen the Beto markers. He searched around for a moment while we stood clustered together watching him. He moved slowly, methodically from tree to tree until he found what he was looking for.

"Here," he said waving us over.

At first none of us seemed to know what caught his attention. He was pointing at the base of a thick, moss-claimed stump. It looked just like all the other unfortunate areas of the decaying forest, but apparently we were supposed to see something special. I was growing impatient though. I hated this part of the forest and I wanted to move on, so I tried to speed up the process a little since it seemed obvious that none of us had as keen an eye as Journey.

"So, what exactly are we supposed to be looking at here?" I asked.

He turned to look at me, and then to Nova and Sparrow. Realizing none of us got it, he sighed deeply. Then he turned his focus back to me. "65, you should be able to see this. I taught you how."

"Yeah, well all I see is a big mossy stump," I said impatiently.

"Focus. Really *see* it," he said.

I squinted my eyes and focused all my energy on the stupid stump. I somehow managed to shut down the uncomfortable vibe I was getting from the forest and just tried to see it, as Journey had taught me: See with all your senses, like a hunter. And then it suddenly jumped out at me, causing me to gasp. A small blue symbol was painted on a single leaf at the base of the mossy stump. A normal person would never see it. It was so small and inconspicuously placed, but with my training my eyes picked it up. Its blue tint and straight lines stuck out sorely in such a natural place. I knelt down to get a closer look so I could make out the shape. It looked like a diamond turned onto its side, with a circle at the center and a dot in the center of that. It was an eye! It was peering back at me, right through me actually. I was spellbound by it and reached out to touch it. Journey lunged to stop me but he was too late.

As soon as my fingers grazed the leaf, the marker burst forth with a blinding blue light. It made me jump back and my eyes seared with pain. I was using my night vision when the light exploded toward me and I was sure I was now blind. I rolled on the forest floor clutching my eyes. I could feel someone comforting me, cradling me. It was Sparrow, it had to be, and she was healing me. Perhaps I would have been able to heal myself, but I was too consumed by the pain to think straight. Slowly the pain subsided and the throbbing white light started to diminish from my line of sight. I rubbed my eyes hard to bring everything back into focus.

I saw the three faces of my friends staring back at me with concern. I only focused on them for a moment though, because beyond them, I could see glowing blue eyes dotting my field of vision. I shook my head, thinking my eyes must still be suffering, but when I took a second look they were still there, forming a path that led deep into the forest. I slowly rose, looking beyond my friends, who where murmuring questions, but I could scarcely hear them because I was so focused on what was before me. I pushed past them and came to a stop a few feet from the leaf I touched. Could they see this, too, or what it just me? Surely Journey could see it, right? I turned to ask him, but all three of their expressions confirmed that they were looking at the same thing I was. Sparrow's mouth was open and she was gripping one of Journey's strong arms for support. Nova just looked focused, dangerous, like he was ready to go into battle.

"Guys?" I paused waiting for response, but none came. "What is this?"

Journey stepped toward me.

"It's the Truiet path to the Beto people."

My heart skipped a beat. That meant it was a path to the truth! To all the questions I had about myself and my new powers. Maybe even the answers about my family, my name, who I truly was. I smiled and started off toward the next marker.

"Tippy! No!" came Nova's voice behind me. "What if it's a trap?"

I turned, poised to yell at him. Ready to tell him he didn't have to follow me, but I was going to get my answers, but I didn't have to. Journey spoke up before I could, giving me the excuse I needed to keep going.

"Nova, you know it's not. Only a Truiet can see the markers of the Betos for their own protection. They would never risk revealing themselves just to create a trap. They're trying to communicate with us. Why would they leave these markers here if they weren't? They know only one of their own can read them. They won't hurt us if they know we're one of them."

"This is why we came here, Nova. We wanted answers, right?" Sparrow asked.

"Alright," he said reluctantly, "but let Journey go first," he call to me.

22

Journey led us along the path of glowing markers. I was glad he was in front of me, because every time I got a glimpse of the creepy, blue, glowing eyes I couldn't help but feel the goose flesh crawling up the back of my neck. I was hoping Journey knew what he was talking about because this really did feel like a trap. If I looked behind us, all of the markers we passed disappeared; slipping into the blackness, widening the abyss with each step we took.

We walked for what seemed like forever, and I kept having to check myself mentally to keep thinking positive. It was far too easy for dark and twisted thoughts to consume you out here. Plus I could feel Nova in my head, keeping an ever watchful eye on me and I didn't want him to know I was scared and doubtful. I had just finished running though my positive mantra when suddenly the markers all vanished and blackness engulfed us. Even my orb had been snuffed out. I stopped in my tracks and felt the others crowd around me. I was shaking by the time Nova flicked on his flame, illuminating our little group.

"Everyone all right?" he asked.

He got a murmur of acknowledgement from us. I began to feel foolish for panicking. I needed to remember to rely on my powers. I should have used my night vision or just flashed on another orb. Why did I always let fear get the best of me? Nova was right to bring me out here; I needed more practice before we went to the locker. What if when I got down there I was too scared to remember what to do? What if they separated us and my friends weren't there to rescue me, like they had tonight?

Wait a minute, was this what he was doing? Was this Nova's plan all a along? This whole night was just a training exercise and I was failing miserably? I felt so betrayed; they had all been in on it, playing their part! This was my test to see if I was ready for the locker! They were throwing things at me left and right to see what I would do. Would I panic under pressure or would I succeed and use my powers? Well, I wasn't going to let him do that to me. I wasn't going to fail! Not now that I knew what was going on!

I drew from my anger and a new confidence settled over me. I produced a large orb and spread it above us, expanding the light all around us.

"Okay, Nova, what's next? Do you want me to fight off a tarcat? Maybe mind bend a monkey? What else have you got?" I yelled, hearing my voice reverberate around me.

My friends were looking at me like I was crazy, but I didn't care. I started kicking the plants that were threatening to tangle my feet. I stalked off of the path still kicking and yelling.

"Come on, what else is hiding out here for me? What's out here?"

Then, as I was about to take a swipe at a tall spade leaf, it moved on its own, revealing a dark round face. I leapt backward, barely able to stifle my scream. Suddenly Nova and the others were by my side again. Swooping to my defense.

Darn it! I was caught off guard again! I marched forward, back to the spot where I'd seen the face. I pushed the spade leaves apart and this time it revealed a whole body.

"Who the heck are you?" I asked annoyed that I had been duped again.

No response.

I took a step closer and grabbed hold of his dark brown skin and pulled him wriggling from the bushes.

"I asked you a question! Who are you?" I demanded.

"Eja. My name is Eja," he replied.

His eyes were large and he was obviously frightened. I instantly felt that I had been wrong about tonight. The mood of everyone was so tense and fearful that this couldn't have been part of a training exercise. Who was this boy that materialized in front of us? It dawned on me that I was still tightly gripping his arm. I let up a little and decided that I should release him. Instead I offered him my hand.

"I'm 65," I said.

He hesitantly took my hand with both of his and closed his eyes. When he opened them he was smiling at us.

"You came!" he exclaimed.

"Were you expecting us?" I asked looking back at my friends.

"Yes. Yes. I was hoping you would come. I heard you calling for me so I left you a trail to find me. I knew if you were who you said you were, you could find me," he said excitedly. "You're all Truiets aren't you?" he asked, talking faster now as he walked past me to Sparrow and the others.

He took each of their hands, as he had done with me, somehow verifying that we were who he thought we were. He was as thin as I was and probably around the same age, but much taller and his skin was so dark; it was the darkest I'd seen, gleaming almost black, under the blue light I had cast above us. He was wearing nothing but a thin cloth around his waist and his jet-black hair pulled back at the nape of his neck. It made me shudder for a moment because it bared such a resemblance to Jemma's hair. The thought of her out here in the forest made me cringe. I shook the image from my mind and tried to refocus on Eja's babbling.

"Eja, you said you heard us calling you? What do you mean by that?" I asked.

"I heard you. Just you," he replied, beaming. "I've seen your lot in the forest for a while. You make a lot of noise you know?" he said looking at each of us. "But I'm a Beto, and I'm not permitted to show myself to locals. Not unless you call me."

We all just looked at each other while he smiled at us.

"But Eja, I didn't call you. I didn't even know you existed."

"Ah, but you did. You talk to me all the time, you say you wish to know the truth, you wish to learn more about yourself, your power, your family; but finally you ask the right questions, you ask to be enlightened!"

"Truiet means enlightened ones," Nova telepathed to me.

"Yes, Yes! Very good," Eja said.

"You can hear our thoughts?" Nova asked.

"Yes, I just told you, I heard her calling me."

Nova and I looked at each other and I couldn't stop smiling. I finally found someone who could help us, someone who could help me find out the truth. I was brimming with excitement; I didn't know where to start! I turned back to Eja and he was smiling as big as I was.

"I will help you understand, 65. Take my hand and I will show you," Eja said.

As I reached for his hand I heard a twig snap suddenly and we all jumped. I whirled around again to find Eja had disappeared! Journey went into full hunter mode and telepathed for me to turn off my light. I did as he asked and stayed huddled together with Nova and Sparrow. I staved off my panic and used my powers to see my surroundings as Journey taught me. I tuned out everything around me, and then slowly let certain sounds back in as I was able to identify them. The humdrum of my heart, the slightly faster flutter of Sparrows, the steady beat of Nova's, the powerful pumping of Journey's, and then another nervous humdrum. It must be Eja's. That gave me hope that he was still nearby and hadn't vanished into thin air. But then I heard one more nervous pitter patter not too far off. Although it was going at hyper speed, it was definitely a human heartbeat and something seemed familiar about its nervous beating. I was drawn toward it and telepathed to the others that I was going to help Journey. Not knowing what I'd caught wind of, the others didn't fight me. I relied on my vision now to make out my surroundings. I spotted Journey a good ten yards ahead of me. He was going toward the sound of the desperately beating heart as well. He must have been getting closer too because the beating picked up, becoming more sporadic. Still, I had an unsettling feeling that I knew who it was, but I couldn't put my finger on it.

How could I possibly recognize the heartbeat of a stranger? That was it! I couldn't. This wasn't another of the Beto people or some local or Grift, it was someone I knew, someone I had connected with closely enough to know the sound of their heart, someone wise enough to follow me out here... In an instant I knew who it was.

I lunged forward as fast as I could to reach Journey before he cornered his unsuspecting prey, but I knew I would be no match for his strength once he locked on and he had such a lead on me. It was imperative that I got there first. I didn't know what Journey would do if he reached his target before I did. I knew what I needed to do. I closed my eyes and

launched an orb between Journey and the sound of the franticly beating heart. It did the trick. He was blinded and
stunned as I had been when I touched the leaf. I would heal
him as soon as I got the chance, but I had a more important
matter at hand.

"Remi!" I called. "I know you're out here. It's okay. I promise, it's okay. Where are you?"

I heard rustling and footsteps, but still saw nothing.
Where was he? How was he hiding like this? It seemed odd
that I was unable to see him, even with my night vision. The
only thing that gave him away was his heartbeat. I recognized
its uneven beating as his nerves kicked in. It was his tell every
time we had a pop quiz, or when Greeley came around, or
even Jemma, and most recently when he decided to audition
for the solo.

"65?"

I heard his quiet voice right next to me and turned just in
time to see him materialize. He shimmered into view, head
first, slowly, like the surf retreating back to the sea. I couldn't
believe my eyes. Remi was standing before me, where only a
moment ago there was nothing. We both stood staring at each
other, wide-eyed. I didn't know what else to do, but I had an
overwhelming urge to hug him, so I did and he actually
hugged me back! For a little while I forgot we were standing
deep in the dark forest. We could have been in room 13 or the
courtyard or the dining hall. All of our familiar surroundings
rushed back to me, filling the empty space with our happy
memories. I hadn't realized how much I needed Remi until I
had him back with me that instant. I felt whole again, stronger
somehow. And so relieved that I could tell him the truth!

"Remi!" I squealed releasing him from my embrace. "Oh
my gods, I'm so glad to see you!" Then I remembered where

we were, that I just blinded Journey, and that poor Sparrow and Nova still didn't know what was going on.

"Come with me," I said, taking him by the hand.

I lit up the canopy with a large yellow orb, spreading it all the way back to Nova and Sparrow as I walked toward Journey.

"It's okay. It was just Remi. I've got to help Journey really quick," I telepathed.

Journey was sitting on the forest floor, rubbing his eyes. I was relieved to see I hadn't blinded him that badly, but I could tell he was still going to be really mad at me. I knelt down and put my hands over his eyes.

"Sorry, Journey. I knew it was the only way to stop you from ripping his head off," I apologized as I gently placed my hands over his face to heal him.

"There," I said stepping back. "Better?"

"Yeah, thanks," Journey grumbled, rubbing his eyes and letting them readjust to his surroundings.

He reached out for me to help him up, but as soon as I offered my hand, he yanked me to the ground and then whispered closely into my ear, "That's twice now... if you ever mess with me again, I'll make you pay."

There was a serious calmness about the way he hissed these words into my ear that sunk them into my mind, where I was sure they'd lay embedded forever. I had no doubt that Journey was serious. Ally or not, I pushed him too far. I knew it was the right thing to do at the time because I wouldn't have taken a chance that might put Remi in danger, but it seemed I had used my last pardon with Journey and I shuddered a bit at the thought of what he might do if I crossed him again. I shook it off as best as I could, because the others were coming toward us now.

"What happened?" asked Sparrow breathlessly, reaching us first.

"What the heck is he doing here?" demanded Nova glaring at Remi.

Journey was already on his feet and he extended a hand to me, with a stern look, but I accepted it and let him pull me to my feet. Remi stood behind me, shifting his weight uncomfortably while he waited for me to somehow explain how and why he was here. I turned to him and repeated Nova's question.

"Yes, Remi, what *are* you doing here?"

"You mean to tell me you didn't invite him?" Nova said, with a slightly nervous twinge in his voice.

"No, she didn't. None of you did. No one would tell me what you were up to and I needed to make sure that she..." Remi trailed off.

"That she was what?" challenged Nova, stepping closer to Remi.

But I heard the end of his thought. Somehow I could read Remi's mind. I could feel his genuine concern as his mind finished what his lips could not. He wanted to make sure I was safe. He was worried about me; he still cared about me, maybe even more than ever now; even after how I treated him lately. It made my heart swell. I pushed past Nova and hugged Remi once more.

"Well," I said, "I'm not sure how you got here, but I'm actually really glad you're here and that I don't have to keep this from you anymore."

"Yeah, I think you're going to have to do some explaining, 65. What are you and how can you do those things?" asked Remi wide-eyed.

"What about you?" shot back Journey. "Why couldn't I see you?"

"Because it's pitch black out here in case you haven't noticed," Remi said gesturing to the now brightly lit forest around us. "Well, it was before... Before, that thing," he said pointing at my orb of light.

"That was me," I boasted, smiling proudly. "I lit our way out here, but I couldn't see him either," I said turning to Journey who looked agitated. "That's not supposed to happen, right?"

"Right," Journey said. "Unless he's hiding something from us."

"Like what?" asked a confused Remi. "Are you mental? It's pitch black out here without that light. It was all I could do to follow you. Then the light went out and I panicked. I thought I was going to be lost out here forever."

"Remi, you know how I can make this light? Well, Journey can see in the dark and he's taught me how too. It's like how nocturnal animals see so they can hunt. We can see everything. It's amazing. But what's puzzling is that we couldn't see you. That's why Journey is confused. I think it's abnormal that we couldn't detect you following us."

"Nothing about this is normal!" Remi shouted.

"He's a Truiet," came a small voice behind us.

It was Eja. He reappeared again and was approaching us.

"How do you know that, Eja?" Sparrow asked.

"Same way I know you're a Truiet," he said, bringing his hand to his heart. "I feel it."

"Who is he?" Remi asked me with wide eyes.

"I can show him!" said Eja excitedly. "I can show you all."

"That would be wonderful, Eja," Sparrow said. "How do you show us?"

"In here," he said pointing to his head.

"Okay, I think it's time for us to be heading back," interrupted Nova sarcastically, not buying anymore of Eja's quirkiness.

"No!" I said stopping him in his tracks. "This is why we came out here. We all need this. We're in this together."

"Fine," Nova sighed. "Let's just do this fast. We can't stay out here all night."

"Sit, sit," Eja said, making a sweeping circular motion with his long, tanned arms.

23

We all took a seat on the damp, mossy forest floor. Eja sat next to me and held my hand, nodding for us all to follow suit. Once we were holding hands, he told us to close our eyes and he took his free hand and placed it on my forehead. There was a sudden flash of light and then rapid images began flashing before me. Images of the Beto tribe, their history, their way of life, morals, powers, beliefs, the fable about Ravin and Mora, the war with Lux, then the story of Nesia and Kai, and Jaka sacrificing himself to the volcano. And then I finally got the rest of the story that Nova never finished telling me. That a chosen one would come, one who would restore Hullabee Island to all its glory. The person would bring free will and equality to all of the island's people, and be someone destined for greatness. This person was called Eva, meaning new beginning, restorer of light among the dark. Then I gasped at what I saw next and recoiled away from Eja. This broke our little circle of knowledge and everyone's eyes flew open.

"What's wrong?" Sparrow asked.

"Tippy?" Nova said looking concerned.

The others just stared at me. Even Eja seemed shocked. I sat there wondering if they saw what I did. I saw myself as the image of Eva! It couldn't be true. There was no way I was the one to unite everyone and restore Hullabee Island. Maybe they all saw themselves. Maybe Eja was playing a trick on us so we'd help him with some devious plot. We didn't even know him; maybe Nova was right, we should have left earlier? We had no way of knowing who Eja really was or what he wanted from us. I looked to Nova pleadingly, but the expression on his face said it all. He *did* see what I saw. He saw me as Eva and he believed it. My eyes began to water. This wasn't at all what I wanted. I wanted to find out the truth about my name and my family, not be thrust into some crazy destiny to unite a ruined island! I wasn't going to let this happen. I stood up.

"We're done here," I said wiping my eyes. "Thank you for sharing with us Eja, but we need to go back now."

"You still seek the truth?" he asked. "You have a mission and I can help you."

We all looked around, wondering how he could know what we were up to.

"I share with your mind as you share with mine," he said.

"You were rooting around inside our heads just now?" barked Journey taking a menacing step toward Eja.

"That's how it works. I can't help it. Your minds were completely open when I was sharing my mind with you. It was impossible not to see your thoughts and plans," replied Eja. "I mean you no harm. I'm here to help and I can see you need my help."

We looked at each other for a few moments feeling uneasy. It was true that none of us liked the idea of being forced to work with this boy we barely knew, but he knew about our plan to get sent to the locker to learn about the legend of Lux.

He obviously knew we had powers as well. It seemed we had to work with him or risk that he would use this information against us. I could tell we were all on the same page with this. Well, all of us except Remi. He just seemed frightened and utterly confused. I spoke up first breaking the silence.

"Eja, can we trust you?"

"Yes, yes. I told you, I can help you. I knew you were here and I heard you asking for my help. That's why I led you here, so I could teach you what you need to know."

This was a step in the right direction, but the group still didn't seem completely satisfied. Sparrow approached Eja slowly edging her way past Journey.

"Eja, are you alone out here?"

"Oh no, no. I live with the others in the forest," he said nonchalantly.

"The Betos?" she asked.

"Yes, of course," he smiled.

"That's impossible," said Remi unable to keep quiet any longer. "Everyone knows that there are no Beto people left. Those who weren't killed in the war were wiped out in the Flood."

"That does seem to be what everyone thinks," Eja said with a sly smile. "And we like it that way because no one bothers us now. No one from Lux comes to fight with us anymore. It's almost safe again."

"So you mean to tell me that you and the rest of the Betos have been hiding out here in the forest all these years? How has no one seen you? We work out here everyday with the locals and the Grifts," Nova argued.

"Ah, yes. We see you out here. We know when you will be coming so we take caution and stay out of sight. We've had the Truiets help us charm the forest so that we will be alerted if someone is getting too close. We have gotten very good at hiding over the years. None of you saw me all the times you came out here at night. Not even the one who can hunt," said Eja, as he nodded his chin toward Journey.

"We can both hunt," I said defensively.

We were all silent for a moment considering the information Eja just gave us. He had a point. We had no idea he was out here watching us. Even our powers hadn't alerted us to him or any other Beto people. Again it was Sparrow's kind words that opened the lines of communication once more.

"Eja, can you teach us to be like you? So we can go undetected? It's very important to our goal."

"Of course! That's why I'm here," Eja smiled proudly. "But, I am more curious to know how this one went undetected by even me. Maybe we should have him teach us," he said pointing at Remi, who was turning bright red and backing away.

"Yeah, Remi, you've been avoiding the question. How did you manage to get here without being seen?" questioned Journey. "Even I couldn't see you when I was using my powers," he continued. "But somehow Tippy knew it was you."

"I don't know!" Remi croaked, looking more flustered than ever. "I don't know what's going on!"

I blocked Journey's path to Remi and tried talking to him on my own.

"Guys, can I have a minute with Remi?" I asked.

The group mumbled and nodded and gave us some space. I walked Remi a little further away and then began whispering in his ear.

"Remi, seriously. How did you get out here without us seeing you? Journey and I have this special night vision and we can see everything as bright as day, but I never saw you. The only way I knew it was you was by your heartbeat."

"My heartbeat?"

"Yeah, we can hear really well, too. I can block out all the other noise and just focus on one thing. It makes it easier to find your prey."

"Can you not use that word? I'm already freaked out enough," Remi said swallowing hard.

"Fine, but when I heard your heart beating it seemed really familiar and I figured out it must be you out here because I didn't know anyone else well enough to know the sound of their heart beating."

Remi just stared at me wide-eyed. He seemed stuck between admiration and sadness. It contorted his face in a twitchy way that made me think he was going to cry. I didn't want that to happen at all and I put a comforting arm around his shoulders. He looked at me with such honesty in his big *chocolate-brown* eyes and asked, "What's happening?" But before I could say anything else, Nova interrupted us.

"She can try to explain that to you later, but right now we need to be leaving. We'll return here again tomorrow to meet with Eja," Nova said.

He had such a commanding tone to his voice that for once I didn't challenge him. He reminded me of the war leaders we read about. He had such poise and confidence that we all fell in line like obedient troops, marching single-file through the dank forest, following his firelight. No one spoke, but I did keep a watchful eye on Remi, who seemed to jump with every snap of a twig or nocturnal sound that found us. I was subconsciously using my powers to see in the darkness surrounding us and listening to the strange sounds of the forest at night. I heard them so often now that they were starting to sound as comforting to me as the crickets outside my window. I hummed along to the night song as our merry band of misfits made our way back to the Troian Center. Even though tonight was overwhelming and had once again not gone as planned, I couldn't help feeling elated now that Remi was a part of our group. I was so happy to not have to hide things from him anymore. I was sure that once I found some time to fill him in on everything that was happening to me that we could go back to being best friends.

24

We were just a few yards from the opening to the fields when something stopped me in my tracks. Journey heard it too because he stopped and motioned for us all to come toward him.

"*What's going on, Tippy?*" Nova telepathed.

"*Not sure yet. I think there's something out here. I think it's a tarcat!*"

"*What?*"

"*Just stay with Sparrow and Remi. Journey and I will track it.*"

Nova gathered the others and huddled with their backs to a large mossy tree, while Journey and I fanned out, keeping in constant eye contact with each other. I kept hearing the heavy panting of a large animal nearby, as well as the frantic sounds of other smaller animals trying to scurry away. We swung wide off of the trail and were instantly upon it. There, with its back to us was a large tarcat with its face buried deep in the earth, rooting around for something. It was slashing its massive paws, with its long claws gleaming in the filtered moonlight. I was frozen with fear watching it thrash a marmouse it just pulled from a hole in the forest floor. The marmouse screamed in pain as the tarcat clamped its massive jaws around its helpless, writhing body.

"65, let's go. It's not after us and I think it'll be distracted long enough for us to get back to the Troian Center."

"What? No! I'm not going to let it murder that helpless marmouse! We have to do something."

"Yeah, and that something is get the heck out of here before the tarcat catches our scent. These aren't like the tame tarcats we're used to at the Center."

Journey reached for me, but I balked and gave him a threatening look. I knew better than to cross him again, but he also knew better than to force me to defend myself.

"You can go, but I'm staying here!"

I turned my attention back to the tarcat and knew I had to act fast, because the amount of blood pooling on the ground was spreading, flowing from the marmouse in massive amounts. I was frozen in place at first. In an eerie way, the pooling blood reminded me of when I spilled my ink well. Knowing how quickly the ink ran out sprang me into action at once. Without a plan, I produced a large orb and hurled the flash of blue light at the tarcat, temporarily blinding it. My orb was enough of a shock to cause the tarcat to lose hold of the marmouse, but the poor thing was so injured it could do nothing but lay panting in a pool of its own blood. The tarcat whirled around and laid its hungry eyes on me. He licked his blood-stained muzzle, exposing his dagger-sharp teeth. He was seemingly contemplating whether he wanted to mess with me or go back to the easier prey because he kept looking back toward the marmouse. Either the prospect of taking down larger prey seemed too cumbersome to him, or the metallic smell of blood that was filling the air was too powerful to turn away from; but whatever the case, the tarcat began to turn back toward the maimed marmouse.

"No!" I screamed.

Strangely this stopped the tarcat in his tracks. He looked back at me, curiously cocking his head to the side. Then the most shocking thing happened. The tarcat spoke to me.

"So you'd prefer to be my dinner then?"

I was speechless. I frantically looked around to see who else this comment could have come from. There was nothing, no one. Journey already left me and I was standing alone. I was unable to deny that the deep throaty voice was none other than the tarcat's. He stood before me, twitching his tail impatiently and took a threatening step toward me with a questioning look in his eyes. I knew better than to give up any ground. Tarcats feed on power and giving up even an inch to him would only encourage him to attack me. I'd become accustom to their temperaments since we were forced to encounter them daily as they roamed the grounds of the Troian Center. And I knew my best bet would be to show him respect and convince him that I was more dangerous than he expected. I took a step toward him, begging my legs not to fail me and gave a deep bow. This seemed to work. It stopped him in his tracks. We held this standoff for what was probably less than a minute, but it seemed like an eternity to me as I racked my brain for what to do next. I tried to steady my breathing and slow my heartbeat so I could concentrate and figure out what powers I had that could rescue me from this situation. I formulated the best plan I could on such short notice and decided now was as good a time as any to give it a try.

"I don't want to hurt you. I respect you and all creatures of the forest and that is why you must leave. If you do not leave, I will be forced to defend myself and that marmouse, which may end badly for you."

The tarcat lowered his head and glared at me, but I got the feeling he could understand me. He took a step back without ever taking his vicious eyes off of mine. I slowly stepped to my right until I was close enough to touch the large tree near me. I placed my hand shoulder height on its massive trunk and fanned out my fingers as wide as they would go. My hand began to glow and for the first time the tarcat wasn't looking at me as a meal, he was focused on my hand and the slow, grey matter that was spreading in crackling waves from it. The hairs on his back bristled and stood as he crouched lower and growled. Now the hard grey stone began to spread rapidly. It climbed the tree, wrapping its way around the trunk higher and higher, choking the life out of it as it went. The ear-splitting sounds of the wood splintering as it gave way to the infection I was spreading, echoed eerily through the forest. Soon, what once were bountiful branches were now heavy stone limbs that began to fall. One hit right in between me and the glowering tarcat, who let out a startled hiss and with that he made up his mind to retreat. And I made up my mind to do the same. I dove behind a large boulder that must have been remnants from the volcano. I balled myself up as small as I could behind it and waited out the storm of falling rocks that I created. I was beginning to feel pretty awful with myself for killing this tree. It was a majestic relic of the forest and it was obvious I'd done too much damage to heal it. Maybe this is what worried Sparrow when Journey taught me this magic. I was starting to see how I could quickly lose control of it.

I kept peering around the boulder to where the marmouse lay. I was terrified that one of the far reaching branches would fall onto it, finishing the job that the tarcat started. I couldn't take the chance of waiting for the tree to stop dropping stone limbs, so I took a deep breath and propelled myself toward the marmouse. I used the powers that Sparrow taught me to quickly bound through the air, which brought me to my target almost immediately. When I came upon the poor thing I tried to pick it up as gently as I could, but it screamed in pain and thrashed wildly. I could see panic in the whites of its eyes.

"I'm here to help you. I promise I don't want to hurt you. I know someone who can help me heal you. Just let me take you to her."

Her eyes were still bulging and she was laboring immensely to breathe but she didn't resist when I laced my fingers under her as delicately as I could. I took off running, holding her as gently as possible. I headed to where I had last seen my friends, shouting Sparrow's name.

"Over here!" Sparrow yelled to me.

They were closer now than where I left them. They were coming to help me! Journey hadn't abandoned me; he'd gone for help. I was glad to hear Sparrow's voice and I ran toward it. When I reached my friends, I could see the shock on all of their faces. I was panting and struggled to give them a rapid recount of what happened so that Sparrow and I could get down to business and heal the poor marmouse.

"There was a tarcat, he's gone now because I scared him by turning a tree to stone, but he injured this marmouse!" I said, gasping to catch my breath as I uncradled my arms, thrusting the marmouse toward Sparrow. "You have to help me heal her!"

Sparrow looked at me with more sadness in her eyes than I'd ever seen.

"Tippy, I think she's gone."

"No! She's not. She's still breathing," I croaked as my voice cracked, betraying my emotions. "We can heal her. Please help me!" I said as the tears started welling up, blurring my vision.

"Okay, put her down and we'll see what we can do," Sparrow said kindly.

I lay the quivering marmouse on my lap because even the mossy ground seemed too harsh for her ravaged body. Her fur was matted with blood and her sides were heaving as she struggled for each rattling breath. Sparrow and I lay our hands on her and we watched as the warm yellow glow from our palms slowly spread over her. Some of her more superficial wounds began to close up, but the deep, gaping ones seemed unable to find the means necessary to heal completely, leaving small ragged holes all over her body. I felt Remi's hand on my shoulder and looked up to see the sorrow that had washed over the faces of each of my friends. That was when I knew we couldn't save her and I began to sob.

"I promised. I promised I'd help her," I cried.

Everyone was silent, and I watched Sparrow move her hands away from the marmouse in defeat. Then I heard a soft, squeaky voice that could only belong to the dying soul in my lap.

"I must beg another kindness from you. Promise me to take care of my baby. I was protecting him from the tarcat. Promise you will protect him."

I nodded and softly pet her head, smoothing her silky fur away from her glassy eyes.

"I promise," I whispered.

Then, the marmouse gave her final shuddering exhale. I began shaking with uncontrollable sobs. It was so unfair that this poor animal had to die. It was so unfair that I had all these powers, yet could do nothing to save her. It was so unfair that my life was so messed up and seemed like it was no longer my own. But what I found most unfair was that there was a baby marmouse out there who would have to grow up never knowing its mother. I knew what that felt like and it ripped me to the core to know that I had let that happen to another.

I was shuddering and taking in rapid, sputtering breaths between my sobs. Remi, who was kneeling behind me, wrapped his arms around my shoulders and hugged me tightly. We rocked back and forth while I let Nova gently remove the dead marmouse's limp body from my lap. Sparrow tried to clean me up, but I could have cared less what I looked like. I knew I had to find the baby marmouse and deliver the bad news about its mother. The trouble was I didn't know how I would be able to find the strength to do so. I felt like a pile of worthless mush and would have been happy to just melt into the forest floor and disappear forever.

"You can't, Tippy. We need you. The baby marmouse needs you. You made a promise and I'm going to help you keep it."

I couldn't believe what Nova was saying. I knew he could hear my thoughts, but I didn't think he could hear what the marmouse was saying. It made me feel so much better that he understood her too. I felt renewed energy in the fact that he was on my side and would help me do this. He instantly lifted my spirits by eliminating the burden of fighting with him about why I had to rescue the baby.

I looked past the others to find him, but only caught a glimpse of his silhouette hunched over. At first it startled me and I stood up thinking he was hurt, or ill, but as I approached him, I saw something that melted my heart and raised a lump in my throat. Nova had dug a shallow grave for the marmouse under a tree and was working hard to carve a cross at its base. A new batch of hot tears streamed down my cheeks when he turned to look at me and I saw the way his eyes were welling up. It reminded me of the way the rain water pooled on the palms, creating a heavy sparkling droplet that swelled and stretched as far as it could before finally becoming too much and releasing into a free fall.

I knelt beside Nova and began patting at the soft soil he had dug up. He joined me in smoothing the dirt on her grave and when our sullied hands touched I felt the familiar spellbinding sparks that Nova gave me. We seemed frozen for only a moment, yet that moment told me so much. It was more than telepathy, it was more like seeing into the depths of each other's souls. It was shocking and comforting at the same time to see Nova's sorrow over losing the marmouse and how it correlated too closely to his own feelings of loss over his family, just as it had with me. We were more alike than I knew and that calmed me to have his understanding. He looked at me longingly for a moment and I grew hot as he stared into my eyes. Then he retracted his hand and used the back of it to wipe at his forehead, leaving a big streak of dirt. I realized I was holding my breath until that moment and finally released it, reaching up to brush the dirt from his forehead but stopped half way when I became aware that the others were gathered around us and decided to just point it out to him so he could wipe it off himself.

We all knelt and bowed our heads in silence, filling the air with our heavy sorrow. Although we hadn't been able to save her, we'd done right to send her off with our humble burial. My eyes were squeezed tightly closed when I heard Nova start to speak the most beautiful words I'd ever heard.

"Light to dark, bone to dust.

Our souls to you we trust.

Take us you may, to another day, not so far away.

I do not fear for the ones I hold dear are just around the bend, where there is no end.

Only love, light and eternity."

When he was done, I shuddered at the eerie beauty of his words and squeezed his hand with my thanks.

He nodded at me and said, "Shall we?"

I knew exactly what he meant, but the others seemed confused as they followed us back into the forest.

"Nova, what are we doing? We need to get back! You said

so yourself and that was before we stopped to fight a tarcat and bury a marmouse," Journey complained.

"Yes, Journey's right. If we don't leave now we may all be caught!" Sparrow added.

"There's something we need to do first and I need all of your help for this," Nova said.

I continued to lead us silently back to the spot where I encountered the tarcat. Soon we came upon stone limbs that lay shattered as if they were made of glass. Limb after limb covered the forest floor in piles of gray rubble. It looked like a stone graveyard and made me shudder. I almost couldn't believe that I was the cause of such destruction. I didn't have time to really see how bad it was before because I was so busy trying to rescue the marmouse and not get clobbered by falling branches. But now, standing in the totality of my damage, I could only feel shame burning hot inside of me as I looked up to where the once majestic old tree stood. Nova put a comforting hand on my shoulder and drew the others around me. Sparrow was staring, mouth open in shock, while Remi's eyes seemed so large that they were threatening to pop right out of his head. But Journey stood sternly with his arms crossed, looking annoyed.

"So, what do you need us to do?" he asked patronizingly.

"We can't leave the forest like this. It's too suspicious and we can't afford to draw any more attention to us. We need to clean this up. Journey, you need to crush as much of this as you can. Sparrow, Remi, can you pile the smaller pieces up so they just look like ruins that we would bring back to the rubble pile?"

Everyone nodded silently and got to work. Nova and I wandered around for a bit until I located the spot where the tarcat had been. At first I was disoriented since the surroundings all looked the same with the giant stone limbs everywhere, but once we stumbled upon it, there was no mistaking it. The ground was saturated with crimson blood. The smell was so strong that I could taste it and it made my stomach pitch violently. I felt my knees buckle under the weight of my sorrow. Nova once again came to my rescue, steadying me and pulling me into a quiet embrace. I could feel my body rattling and tried hard to fight the tears that were threatening to break through by burying my face into Nova's warm chest.

"It's okay, Tippy," he said while he stroked my hair. "Come on, we need to focus on finding the baby."

This seemed to bring me back to my senses. I straightened up and rubbed my eyes to refocus them on our mission. I turned toward the hole that the tarcat had been thrashing at. It was big enough for me to crawl into at the mouth. I gave a look back at Nova before I knelt to wiggle my way into the hole. It was hot and smelled strange, like musky earth. I gave myself a moment to let my night vision kick in. I noticed that the tunnel started to narrow as I moved further in. The mouth must have been so large from the tarcat's attack and I was beginning to get nervous that I wouldn't be able to go much further when I heard a squeaking to my right. I carefully turned my head and saw a set of tiny black eyes blinking at me. Its little nose twitched anxiously and it inched toward me curiously. Soon his coarse whiskers were tickling my face as his wet nose nuzzled my face. This filled me with such an overwhelming happiness and hope that I wanted to cry again, but this time because my heart was brimming with joy. The baby marmouse was alive and well. He seemed so happy and oblivious to what happened. He allowed me to scoop his warm little body up in my hands as I carefully backed my way out of the earth.

When I finally reached Nova, he looked as happy as I felt when he saw me holding the baby marmouse, who kept rubbing his eyes to adjust them to the sudden brightness of the world outside his burrow. We couldn't help but smile when we looked at him. He was so small and delicate. He fit perfectly in the scooped palms of my hands. His black coat was so silky and shiny and he had the cutest markings of toffee brown fluffy fur on his face that looked like an animated mask as he sniffed and twitched quizzically at his surroundings. He had the same shaggy brown fur on his long, slender legs and round under belly. His long silky black tail wiggled excitedly, but I think my favorite feature had to be his oversized ears. They were so large that he couldn't keep the top half from flopping forward and they were covered with a silver wispy fur that seemed as fine as if it were spun by a silk spider. It floated in even the most undetectable breeze and gave the appearance that it was alive, like tentacles collecting valuable information.

At the sound of my voice those ears would perk straight up in full salute for a moment before gravity would take over and they would fold over again, leaving his little silver wispies floating behind. I couldn't get the grin off my face as I stared at him. He was so full of life and confidence. So trusting and wondrous. The cruelty of the world hadn't spoiled him yet and I made up my mind right then that I was going to do everything I could to keep him that way. By this time the others had come over to see what Nova and I were doing. Sparrow squealed with delight when she saw the tiny marmouse in my hands.

"Ohhhh, its so cute! Where did you find it?" Sparrow asked.

I didn't know what to say. They didn't know I could communicate with animals yet and I felt frightened to share that with the rest of them all of a sudden. Luckily, Nova sensed this and spoke up for me.

"She found him over here by his burrow," he said gesturing to the earthen lair.

"He's so tiny," Remi said coming in for a closer look.

"What are we going to do with him?" asked Journey craning his neck for a better view.

"I think Tippy has decided that he needs us to care for him," Nova said looking straight into my eyes.

"Is that the best idea?" Journey asked.

"Well, we can't very well leave him out here to fend for himself, can we?" chirped Sparrow who seemed completely charmed by the marmouse. "He can't be more than a few days old."

"We'll take him back to the Center with us and he'll need all of us to protect him," I said sternly. "I need to hear you all say you'll promise to protect him," I said looking directly at Journey.

They all nodded, even Journey, but I wanted more. I swore to his dying mother that I would protect him and I *had* to keep this promise.

"I need to hear you swear to it," I demanded, holding my hands out with the tiny marmouse in them. "Swear on him that you'll protect him."

They all reached a hand in, one by one and placed them upon mine, all touching the happy little marmouse as he inquisitively sniffed at them. And then in unison, they said, "I swear."

25

D*ear Journal,*

Last night was crazy! I know it seems I say that a lot, but last night was one of the worst and best nights of my life. We discovered that Beto people are alive and living in the forest. We met one of them. His name is Eja and he said he wants to help us, but I don't know if I trust him yet. He seems almost too eager to help. It was great that he was able to teach me so much so quickly about the Beto people through some sort of thought-sharing power. It was great up until the part when he showed me my destiny to become the savior of all the people on our island. Oh yeah, out of nowhere, Remi showed up! Journey almost took his head off, but luckily I found him first and was able to stop that from happening. I'm so happy that Remi knows what's going on now and that I don't have to keep any of this a secret from him anymore. I hadn't realized it, but not being able to share this with him was really keeping me from enjoying my new powers. I still have a lot of questions for him. Like, how did he find us and why couldn't I see him? And I'm sure he has a lot of questions for me, too. We haven't had any time to talk yet.

We were in a rush to get back to the Troian Center after staying in the forest so long, but we came upon a tarcat and, this is almost too painful to write down, but I guess I should if only to preserve her memory. Journey and I found a large tarcat attacking a marmouse. I did everything I could to save her, including destroying a huge tree by turning it to stone to scare away the tarcat, but it was too late for her. Sparrow and I tried to heal her, but she was too far gone. That was the worst I've ever felt in my life, but somehow I did find good in all of this. I rescued her orphaned baby and brought him back to the Center with me. We've all sworn to protect him and he's already charmed us all with his warm nuzzling and adorable qualities. I've named him Niv. It means survivor in Beto.

Last night also brought me strangely closer to Nova. I've never seen so much kindness and respect shown to another being as he showed to Niv's mother. He buried her and said the most beautiful prayer. I could see into the darkest shadows of his soul and how we were even more alike than I knew, both feeling the all too familiar sting of familial loss stirred up by the death of the brave marmouse. He also seemed to sense this connection and he stayed close to me all night, ushering us all safely back into the Center in the nick of time this morning and making sure we found a safe place for Niv.

Another crazy thing happened, too, and I'm reluctant to even talk about it, but this is my only escape, the only place I can get everything off my chest and sort out my feelings, so here it goes. Last night I figured out I have another power. I can talk to animals and they can talk back to me. Even writing this down it seems to be the most absurd of all my powers. Not that turning things to stone, or producing light out of thin air is normal, but this one happened while I was alone and Nova is the only one who knows about it. I was too shaken to tell the others after all we'd been through last night. Plus, I don't even think Nova knows this part, but what makes this all feel so strange is I think it's something I've always known about myself, and last night it became undeniably clear.

I've always felt a kinship to animals: been able to sing songs to the sea birds, show respect to the fickle tarcats, warmth to the hungry marmice. I even paid special attention to the crickets who sang me to sleep each night with their happy songs. Maybe these were all signs that were trying to prepare me for what's been happening to me lately, prepare me for my destiny.

At least last night answered one of my questions. Number 5: will Remi ever know I have powers? YES!

I may have a million more questions, but at least I answered an important one and it was the best answer I could have hoped for. As for the rest, I'm just going to keep working on them.

I WAS WRITING FURIOUSLY in my journal all through my first lesson. It seemed to make me appear studious because Miss Banna left me alone while she droned on about some useless plant or another. Before I knew it, the bell chimed and it was time to pack up and move on to Reading and Writing. I wanted to check on Niv before our next lesson, so I quickly slammed my books closed and ran to room 13 as fast as I could.

Niv was right where I'd left him. All cozied up inside a hollowed out book Remi helped me make last night so we could hide him in my cubby. I filled it with some straw from my cot bed and he settled right in. When I carefully opened the lid, he blinked sleepily up at me and stretched his little legs as far as they could go and let out a big yawn. He was so animated that I couldn't help but smile and scratch him under his chin.

"I'll be back in a little while, Niv. Keep quiet like a good boy and I'll bring you some lunch," I whispered and secured him back in his hiding place inside the wardrobe and then I ran off to lessons, sliding into my seat beside Remi as the bell gonged again. Remi gave me a sly smile and I couldn't help but grin, so happy to have him back at last.

26

W e met at our usual lunch table and reconfirmed our plan to meet Eja in the forest tonight for help with our plan to get sent to the locker and learn more about the legend of Lux. We also argued about whether Niv could come with us. I already intended to bring him to Flood work and the forest, thinking he needed the fresh air, but Nova thought it would be wise to leave him behind. We settled on bringing him to Flood work to see how he did. Then we ended up just gushing about how cute he was and what adorable things he did when we checked on him throughout the day.

We all saved our scraps from lunch for him and I carefully smuggled them back to our room. I packed the scraps and Niv in my burlap shoulder bag that I carried my Flood work gear in. Today I went back to my usual spot working alongside Remi on the rubble pile. When it was safe, I opened my bag to see how Niv was doing. I had to stifle a laugh because when I peered inside, he lay belly up on a pile of rags and my gloves, happy as a pig in slop. He obviously found the scraps of food I wrapped in a napkin and helped himself to them. He was covered in crumbs and was busy trying to collect them from his fluffy chin hair. He looked like a little, old man grooming his beard as he made soft grunting sounds. He paused for a moment blinking at me with his big brown eyes when he noticed me looking at him, but then he went back to work.

"Well, he seems happy," I said to Remi with a smile.

"What's he doing in there? I can hear him grunting," he asked.

"He snuffled his way into the scraps we saved him and ate them all. Now he's busy cleaning the crumbs out of his beard!"

This made us both laugh. It felt so good to laugh with Remi again that I couldn't help myself from blurting out my feelings to him.

"Remi, I'm so excited that you know about all of this now. I'm really sorry that I didn't tell you from the beginning. It was just so crazy and happening so fast, and I didn't know what to make of it myself. I wanted to tell you, I mean I even tried to tell you, but you were so mad at me and I didn't want you to think I was any crazier than you already did after Mr. Greyvin's lesson, and – "

"It's okay, 65. I get in now," he interrupted. "I'm really glad we're friends again, too, and I'm sorry for acting like a jerk," he said lowering his eyes.

"Let's just start over from here. Best friends again?"

"Best friends," he said smiling at me.

We worked side by side silently for a little while longer, occasionally checking on Niv and enjoying his antics. Finally, I got up the courage to ask Remi about last night.

"So about last night? How *did* you find us, Remi?"

"I followed you. I wanted to make sure you were okay. Like I said, you'd been acting strange, so I would lay awake trying to figure out what was going on. And then I caught a lucky break when I saw Journey get up. At first I just thought he was going to the John's room, but then I saw him go over to your window and climb out. I sat up and looked around and realized you were gone, too. So I got up as quickly as I could and went out the window the same way I saw Journey do it. I had a really hard time keeping up with him. I just saw you all walk into the forest together and was about to give up because when I tried following you it was too dark to see. But then there was suddenly light ahead and I just followed it, hoping it was you guys."

"Why didn't you call out to us to wait for you or something?" I asked.

"I don't know. I was afraid you'd be mad at me for following you and send me back. I wanted to find out what you were up to."

"But I still don't get how we couldn't see or hear you. Journey and I are really good at that kind of stuff. It's one of the powers we have."

Remi just shrugged and said, "I don't know, 65. I just kept as quiet as I could and was willing myself to be invisible, you know?"

I stopped polishing the stone I was working on for a moment. Something in his words gave me a strange feeling of déjà vu. It was as if I was trying to recall a dream. I had a foggy memory that was jogged by something Remi just said. 'Willing myself to be invisible.' *Could it be? Could Remi have a power, too?* A cold chill washed over me as I made the connection. It was Eja who shared the history of the Truiets and their powers with us last night. Invisibility was one of them. *That was it!* I was tingling with excitement. "Remi," I started, trying to sound as casual as I could. "What do you mean when you say 'willing yourself to be invisible'?"

"Just like wishing for it. Praying I'd stay hidden out of sight long enough to find out what you were up to," he replied.

"Could you do it now?" I asked.

"What?" he asked stopping to look up at me. "Why would I need to do that here?" he said sounding worried.

"Well, you wouldn't need to, but I was just wanting to try something," I said.

"Okay," he said hesitantly.

I crawled closer to him and glanced around to make sure no one was watching us. When I was sure we weren't on anyone's radar I grabbed his hand.

"Can you just try to recreate how you were feeling last night when you were trying to be invisible? I want to see if I can feel it," I said.

Remi looked at me suspiciously at first, but then he closed his eyes and I could feel him wash over me. I felt his fear, his insecurity, and his desperation to disappear. His emotions were so strong and real and he was able to tap into them so effortlessly that they must be kept at the surface and used often. This thought made my heart heavy. I could imagine that the hardships and teasing he'd endured at the Center had often made him wish he could just disappear, and then right before me, he vanished. It wasn't a slow withdraw, one second I was looking at him and then the next I was looking through the space where he had been. Although I couldn't see him I could still feel him. I could still feel the warmth of his hand beneath mine and feel his presence, and I could even hear his breathing. But even with being able to feel him I was so caught off guard that I let go of his hand to stifle my gasp. As soon as I did, it broke his concentration and he reappeared. He was just staring at me with those big brown eyes, swallowing me up with his questioning look.

"Remi!" I hissed in a rushed whisper. "Do you know what you just did?"

"I did what you asked me to do. You said to feel like I did last night when I was trying to disappear. What's wrong?"

"You really don't know?"

"No, but you're kind of freaking me out."

"You disappeared, Remi. For real, not just figuratively or in your mind. You disappeared right before my eyes!"

"What? Come on, 65, you're just messing with me now."

"Remi, I swear it. I swear it on Niv."

With that he sat up straighter, and I could tell he was starting to take me seriously.

"Watch me. I'm going to try to do it. I'm an Parallel."

He just stared at me blankly.

"It means once I connect to someone's power, I can do it, too. It sometimes takes some practice, but I'm going to try it, okay? Tell me if it works."

He only nodded at me with his look of concern growing. I closed my eyes just as he had and tapped back into his feelings. I felt them wash over me and could actually feel my body matter departing, becoming lighter. I opened my eyes expecting to see straight through where my hands were, but they were still there. All of me was still there. It made no sense. I could feel myself evaporating, but as I looked down at my body, I was clearly still there. I looked over at Remi and was about to apologize and say maybe I needed some more practice, but his look of pure terror stopped me dead.

"Remi, what's wrong?"

"Oh my gods!" he whispered.

"What? What is it?"

And with that I felt myself returning, the heaviness settled back in and Remi suddenly reached out to touch my hands.

"You did it," he whispered.

"Wait, you mean I disappeared?"

"Completely!"

"That's incredible! Remi, you're one of us! You just shared your power with me! It was so insane. I felt like it was working, but I could still see myself."

"Well, I couldn't see you. Is that really what I did?"

"I guess. Like I said, I didn't see you when you just did it, but when I was apparently doing it I could still see myself. Remi, that's magnificent. I bet that's why you never knew you had this power. Nothing changes for you. It's just others that can't see you."

We sat there staring at each other silently. I picked up a stone and handed it to him quietly so it looked like we were working because I noticed a Grift coming our direction. Remi idly rubbed at it with his ragged cloth, while I picked quietly through the pile, sorting the valuables into baskets. The Grift walked on by without a word and I was about to pick up our conversation when I jumped at the touch of something at my leg. I turned to see Niv nuzzling my calf.

"Niv! What are you doing out of your bag?"

Remi looked over at us.

"Well, do you suppose it's okay?" I asked. "He looks so happy scampering around out here," I said as he scurried past me, chasing a frightened acida bug. The bug wiggled its way through the crevices of the rubble pile and out of Niv's sight, which left him anxiously snuffing and snorting in every cranny he could stick his slender snout into.

"There's always birds and other rodents around out here. I don't think anyone will notice from time to time, but we need to be careful that no one notices him with us too much."

The rest of the afternoon was actually enjoyable as Remi and I continued to work, talking quietly about the possibilities of our powers, while we watched Niv play on the rubble pile.

It was almost too fun to even consider it work. The sun was setting, casting an orange glow and long, cool shadows. There was even a dry breeze that often wafted scents of sweet barley coming from the fields. Soon it was time to pack up Niv and head back to the Center with the rest of our year.

27

A t dinner, we all found each other at our usual table. We made small talk for a little while, discussing Niv's adventures on the rubble piles. This gave us all a laugh. From the outside, we looked just like all the other orphans, harmlessly enjoying a meal with our friends.

"Well, since you said he did so well at work today, I guess you can bring him with you to the forest tonight," said Nova lowering his voice.

I gave a nod, but there was something else on my mind. I wanted to tell them about Remi, but I felt a cold chill come over me when I noticed Jemma staring at us from her table of lackeys. I didn't know whether the chill was what alerted me to her stare or if it was her stare that gave me the chill, but either way I quickly averted my eyes and telepathed to the others that she was watching us. Remi jerked back as soon as I telepathed and I instantly realized what I'd done. From his look of shock, this was obviously the first telepathic message he'd heard and he was reacting about as crazy as could be expected. That was the last thing I needed. I didn't want him drawing Jemma's attention to us any further.

"Remi," I whispered, "Calm down please, we can talk about what just happened later, okay?"

He still looked startled but he nodded at me and slumped forward as he was before hearing my voice in his head. The rest of our meal passed pretty quietly, with only small talk here and there. The fact that I just discovered Remi's secret power, one that he himself didn't even know he possessed, made me suspicious of everyone. I was afraid that there were others like us. Maybe some of them were with Jemma and I was afraid they could be spying on us. I mean if Remi was able to follow us and see what we were up to, couldn't any of them do it? Perhaps we needed to come up with a better plan. When I looked across the table I saw Nova eyeing me. *Crap! Had he totally just heard my thoughts? Oh well, nothing I can do about it now.* I guess I'm an open book to him, and I'm fine with it right now since I could definitely use his help to safeguard us a bit more. He gave me a nod and a wink that signaled he was on it or perhaps already a step ahead of me.

Gong!

The bell chimed, signaling that dinner was over. I quickly collected everyone's scraps for Niv and headed back to room 13, dreading the grueling rehearsal that lay waiting for me.

Another night of rehearsing for the New Year Gala only meant another night of torture for me. We were broken into groups to sing our parts and as luck would have it, I was with Jemma and her henchmaids tonight. All rehearsal I listened to Jemma correct me and whine about how insufferable my pitch was, while her minions snickered at the seething comments she hurled in my direction.

"Honestly, 65, my ears are bleeding. Why don't you just give up and mouth the words for all our sakes?"

I'd be happy to, I thought to myself. As much as my voice pained her, it pained me more to spend time with her. I was busy looking down and trying to contain my anger and embarrassment when Miss. Sprigg cleared her throat to get our attention.

"Alright everyone. The New Year Gala is only three weeks away. I think it's about time we try putting all these pieces together and see how we sound. What do you say?" she asked cheerfully.

She was faced with grumbling and resistance, but she still managed to get us all together, standing in tiers so she could see all our apprehensive faces. Then she started flitting her long fingers back and forth, keeping time for us as the music swelled and we started our song. The basses set the beat, and the tenors added a rich sound and then it was our turn to sing. I started just mouthing the words until I could find my pitch and mix my voice as smoothly with the others as possible. Jemma would elbow me each time I would fall behind, all while keeping her sickeningly sweet little smile on her face. *How is it even possible to smile while you sing?* I was sneaking a glance at her out of the corner of my eye when I watched her expression change suddenly. It was as if I was looking at her for the first time. The smug little mask that she normally wore seemed to shatter, suddenly giving way to the ugly, darkness that I knew lay deep within her. It startled me and made me lose my place. I tried to follow her line of sight to see what had made her so angry and instantly saw what it was. Remi and Sparrow had just stepped forward to start their solo. I looked back at her and she had already composed herself, replacing her perfectly masked emotions.

28

After our singing lesson was over I felt exhausted. I flopped myself down on my cot bed while everyone else gathered their books to get started on studying. I wanted to wait a bit so I could go to the wardrobe after everyone cleared to feed Niv. While I was waiting, mindlessly flipping through my sheet music, Sparrow came over to join me.

"So, how'd we sound?"

"Oh, you guys were great. But..."

"What? Did I mess up the words?" Sparrow asked, suddenly anxious.

"No, I just wanted to tell you to be careful."

"Be careful singing? What do you mean?"

"I was standing next to Jemma today and I get the feeling she's really not happy you're doing the solo this year," I said.

"Oh well, Tippy what can she do? Miss Sprigg already assigned it to me and Remi."

"I know that, but just the look on her face... She just makes me nervous is all."

"Thanks for looking out for men Tippy," Sparrow said with a smile, patting my hand.

We sat quietly for a while, not an awkward quiet though. It was more like a comfortable, confident quiet. Like for once I wasn't the one on the outside looking in. I felt like everyone else was on the outside now. Even though my status around the Center didn't really seem to change too much with the other orphans, I knew that for the first time I was with the "in" crowd. Sparrow, Remi, Journey, Nova and I were the ones who truly knew what was going on, or at least we were getting there. The others didn't have a clue yet, but I had a feeling this was the calm before the storm, and soon everyone would be clinging to us for refuge. I'm not really sure what caused this foreboding feeling to wash over me, but it felt empowering and I liked it.

Sparrow nudged me, shattering my feelings of superiority, like a rock through a pane of glass. My thoughts fell away easily, revealing a dim reality. For now I would just have to be satisfied with sitting on a cot bed, with my friend, in a room full of orphans who were ignoring me as usual.

"Now's a good time to feed Niv," she whispered.

I looked around and she was right. Everyone was engaged in studying or lively conversations.

"Okay, but can you stay here and keep watch? If anyone is coming my way, telepath me," I said.

"Sure."

I made a beeline for the wardrobe and shuffled some of the books on my shelf around so I could get to Niv's, which I had hidden in the back. I hesitated a moment before opening it and then quickly flicked it open and dumped in the scraps of food we scrounged up from dinner. He yawned and stretched and made some sweet little grunting sounds. I wanted to scoop him up and hug him right then and there, but I knew it was too risky.

I scratched him under his chin and whispered to him. "Good boy. Eat your dinner and stay here just a little longer, then I promise to take you out to stretch your legs tonight."

I patted him on the head and closed the book, resituating it safely in the back of my cubby before heading back over to Sparrow. It amazed me how much the little guy could sleep, but I was thankful for it because I really didn't know where else we could safely hide him. We couldn't let him roam around the Troian Centery with the tarcats around. Plus the Grifts would be sure to see him and try to get rid of him or worse, tell Greeley. I wish I could trust the orphans in my year because then we could at least let him run around our room, but with Janes as cruel as Jemma and her friends, I was sure they'd sell him out just to hurt me. I was also worried that Niv would be getting bigger soon and then we'd really have to come up with a new plan. My worry must have shown on my face because Sparrow asked me what was wrong when I sat back down.

"Oh, nothing right now. I'm just trying to think ahead to what we're going to do with him when he gets bigger. He can't live in a hollowed-out book forever."

Sparrow smiled at me and said, "Don't worry, we'll think of something when the time comes. Right now we need to concentrate on our homework or we'll really have something to worry about."

This made us both laugh and helped take my mind off all my other worries. We got up and joined Remi and Journey at the table to begin tackling our assignments.

29

Finally, it was time to go. I managed to transfer the book with Niv inside to my shoulder bag before bed and now I was lowering it to Sparrow through the window. I quickly followed, and then Remi. Journey was the last one inside, standing guard with his night vision to make sure no one else was watching us. The three of us started making our way to the forest, knowing that Journey would catch up to us, but after a while, Sparrow stopped.

"Guys, I think something's wrong. Journey should have been here by now."

"Maybe he just got held up, Sparrow. Let's just get to the forest for cover and wait for him," I said. "Besides, he'd telepath if something went wrong."

She kept trudging forward with us but still seemed worried. We swiftly reached Nova at the forest's edge and explained to him what was going on. I was starting to feel uneasy about Journey's delay, too. I took Niv out of my bag and cradled him in my arms while he sniffed the air curiously. He climbed up to my shoulder and tickled my ear with his twitching whiskers while we all settled into the shadows to wait for Journey.

"This doesn't feel right," Nova said.

"I agree. Sparrow, will you try to telepath him?" I asked.

"Journey, what's going on? Are you okay? Do we need to come back?"

We waited patiently for a response and that gave Remi a chance to ask us some questions.

"So, how does that work? I can hear you in my head. It's creepy," he said.

"So, you *can* hear us?" Nova questioned with his perfect eyebrow dramatically arched.

"Remi, we can speak to each other telepathically because we're all Truiets and we're linked to each other through our powers. Once a Truiet shares a power with another Truiet they create an unbreakable bond that connects us to each other and allows us to speak to each other secretly. It was created to keep us safe," I explained to Remi.

"Well, look at you, Tippy! You learned a lot from Eja, didn't you? What a good student," Nova said playfully. "But as she said, Remi, you have to share a power with us in order to be privileged to our thoughts. I don't recall seeing you share anything with us," Nova challenged.

Remi looked between us nervously, settling his dewy brown eyes on mine pleadingly.

"He shared it with us without even knowing what he could do, Nova. I figured it out today while we were at Flood work and we tested it out to be sure."

"You tested it out at work?" he questioned, his joking tone absent.

"Yes, but we were careful. Anyway, it works, he can become invisible when he wants to and now so can I," I said, quickly calling on Remi's power to vanish me from sight.

"Show off!" Nova said, back to his jovial tone. He turned to Remi, "I have to admit, that's quite impressive. You really didn't know you could do it?"

"That's it!" Sparrow exclaimed before Remi could answer.

Up until that point she seemed to be lost in thought, and not really paying any attention to the rest of us, but now she was staring at the spot where I had been smiling brightly.

"What?" I asked, letting myself come back into view.

Sparrow walked over to me and lifted Niv off my shoulder, nuzzling him and stroking his shiny hair.

"That's how you can hide Niv!" Sparrow squealed. "I told you that you'd think of something."

"Oh! No way?" I exclaimed, suddenly catching on. "He disappeared, too, didn't he?"

"Is anyone else confused?" asked Remi.

Nova laughed. "I may be able to read minds, but sometimes even I don't know what these two are talking about."

Sparrow sighed, feigning impatience. "Earlier Tippy was worried about hiding Niv, because he's going to get bigger and we can't keep him in that little box forever. But she just made him vanish into thin air, so if she can share her power with him for long enough, then he can hide in plain sight at the Center!"

"Huh!" Nova said. "Ya know, that gives me an idea. We need to get to Eja though. What's taking Journey so long?"

"I don't know but something doesn't feel right," Sparrow replied staring back toward the Troian Center. "I think I should go back."

"Then we'd all have to go back," Nova said shaking his head. "Journey's a big boy, I'm sure he can take care of himself."

"Nova! He's one of us, we need to look out for him," I snapped. "Sparrow, if you want to go back, I'll go with you."

"No, if you're going back, we're all going back," Nova said rolling his eyes.

As we stood there arguing over who was going back, we finally heard from Journey.

"Everything's fine. Sorry, but I can't join you guys tonight. I'll explain later."

"See, I told you he was fine," Nova said triumphantly.

"What are you talking about? He doesn't sound fine. He didn't even tell us what's holding him up," Sparrow whined.

Remi piped up. "Okay, guys, this is going nowhere and neither are we. Do we go back or go find Eja?"

We all stopped bickering to look at him. He was right, so with slumped shoulders, Sparrow agreed to find Eja and worry about Journey when we got back. To make her feel better I let her carry Niv. It seemed to work because she had a smile on her face in no time as she cooed unrecognizable words to him, grinning from ear to ear when he would nuzzle her neck. We made it to the clearing to meet Eja much faster tonight and it was a good thing since we wasted so much time waiting on Journey. Eja was nowhere to be seen, but I could sense him. I quietly called his name and he dropped down from a tree behind me, making us jump.

"Hello!" he called cheerfully.

"Jeez! Do you have to do that?" croaked Remi.

"Sorry, habit. I can never be too careful out here. You should be better prepared though. I could have had the jump on you dropping down like that. Where's the big guy? I bet he would have seen me."

"Journey? He's not coming tonight," I said. "But we're all here, so how about you tell us how you can help."

"Who is this?" Eja said his eyes widening as he approached Sparrow. Niv was perched on her shoulder, looking back at him with his features twitching with excitement.

"Oh, this is Niv," she said. "We rescued him last night and we've sort of adopted him."

"Niv, what a curious name. Do you know what it means?"

"Yes," I replied. "Journey said it means survivor."

"Indeed. I guess it's fitting, isn't it? All of us are survivors, aren't we?" said Eja.

This made us all smile as Niv leaped from Sparrow's shoulder into Eja's arm and started licking his face, setting us all at ease. We settled into discussion with Eja as we let Niv forage around nearby. He was having quite a good time chasing insects and coming up with a snout full of dirt. He was so cute, ever mindful of where we were and if he strayed too far, he'd come darting back with his tail between his legs until one of us pet him and reassured him that he was okay.

Nova filled Eja in on his plan to get us into the locker so we could explore the legend of Lux. We all wore looks of concern as he spoke because of the apparent risks involved. One of us would hesitantly shoot down each of his menacing ideas.

"I don't think antagonizing the tarcats is a good idea. Not after what we saw them do last night," I said shivering slightly at the fresh memory.

"Yeah, and don't you think it might be a little obvious if all of us pulled something together? I don't want Greely to figure out that we're working together," Remi said.

"Well, from what you've just told me about your powers, I think you already have a solution to getting into the locker," Eja replied.

"What do you mean?" Sparrow asked.

"Will that work?" Nova asked, always a step ahead with his mind-reading abilities.

"Will what work?" asked Remi, frustrated again.

"You and Tippy can walk right into the locker anytime you want with your nifty little disappearing act," Nova replied.

"That's brilliant!" I exclaimed.

"Yes, that way only one of us will need to get sent to the locker and you two can follow," Nova said.

"What about the rest of us?" Sparrow asked.

"Well, originally I thought we would all go in, but it doesn't seem necessary. We can relay the information back to you."

"And besides we need someone to stay behind to take care of Niv," I said. The worried look in Remi's eye made me add, "Just in case," to that sentence. He forced a smile but still looked uneasy and I couldn't blame him after his last turn in the locker.

"Well, it's settled then," Nova said. "I'll use my usual charm to get sent to the locker and you two can follow me in. Then we'll get all the information we need about the legend."

"That all sounds great, Nova, but how will we get out?" I asked sounding worried now.

"Simple, Greeley will let us out," he said with a confident grin.

"And how do you think you're going to manage that?" I challenged.

"We're going to have to wait until the day before the New Year Gala. We'll have the day to get all the info we need and then Greeley will let me out because I have to perform at the Gala."

"Why will she care if you get to go to the Gala?" challenged Remi this time.

"I don't think they would risk leaving anyone behind all alone at the Center, but mostly because they would never leave their star soloist behind," he said, teeth gleaming as he winked at me.

"What? You're a soloist too?" squealed Sparrow. "Why

didn't you tell us? Remi and I have a solo also. This is wonderful! I'm so excited."

I had to force myself not to roll my eyes and look defeated. *Great, so all of my friends are brilliant singers?* I quickly shoved that thought from my head, hoping Nova wasn't paying attention to what I was thinking with all the racket Sparrow was making, chattering on about her and Remi's solo. After a few more moments I couldn't take any more Gala babble and had to interrupt.

"So, it sounds like we have a plan, but what are we supposed to do between now and then? We still have three weeks before the Gala."

"Well, we can keep coming out here to practice," Remi shyly suggested.

"I think we may have to cut back on that unfortunately, or we at least need to be more careful. We still don't know what held Journey up and if you were able to follow us, let's face it..." Nova trailed off with a shrug.

Remi narrowed his eyes at Nova, but said nothing in response.

"You're right," I said. "I've been thinking we need to find a new way to sneak out when we have to."

"Well, why don't we use your invisibility powers?" suggested Sparrow, looking at Remi and me.

"That will work for us, but what about you guys?" I asked.

"Yeah, you're not coming out here without me," Nova said.

"Maybe they won't have to," Sparrow replied. "Eja, earlier tonight, Tippy was playing around with the disappearing power to show us how it worked. She was holding Niv and he disappeared as well. Would this hold true, say if we were all touching her?"

"Ah, yes it should. She's a Parallel, right?" he asked Nova as though I couldn't answer for myself, which always made my blood boil.

"I'm an Echo, too, don't forget," I piped up.

"True. That's very rare. I'm afraid I've never met someone who possessed all your gifts, so it is possible all of your rules are yet to be written. What I do know is that as a Parallel you can absorb powers, and as an Echo, you can share them as well."

"Wait, so I can give my powers to everyone else, too?" I asked with excitement. "That's great!"

"Not so fast. You can share your powers with others, in a few different ways, but the simplest way would be through direct contact with you," Eja said, bursting my bubble. "And that only holds true for other Beto's, because it is meant as a means of protection."

"What about Niv?" I challenged.

"That is curious. Let me see you do it."

I called Niv over to me and stood up, cradling him in my arms. A moment later, we vanished. I could tell it worked by the impressed looks on everyone's faces. Niv looked happy as could be, giving me little kisses all over my face, making it hard to concentrate. I started to giggle when he wiggled his way into my shirt and suddenly I heard everyone else laughing. I must've been visible again.

"What's so funny?" I asked.

"Well, besides the fact that you have a marmouse wrestling around in your shirt, your face is covered in dirt," Remi said, barely able to contain his laughter.

"Oh," I said, instantly self-conscious and raising my hands to my face. "Niv!" The little bugger's face was covered in soil, so he left smudges of dirt all over when he was kissing me. *Great, now I a mess!*

"Don't worry, I'll clean you up," said Sparrow grinning.

All I could do was laugh as Niv popped his head out between my shirt buttons. We stayed in the forest a bit longer discussing the best possible options for sneaking out using the invisibility power. Nova cut our conversation short though when Eja started filling us in on other ways to share powers that included tethers and fissures.

"I think you've given us enough to think about for tonight," Nova said, rising to his feet from our comfy little circle on the warm forest floor.

"Nova, I need to learn about these things!" I said scrambling to my feet more closely to him than I intended, pushing me off balance.

Nova grabbed my arms to steady me and gave me a stern look that I knew would do me no good to argue against. By now the others were standing as well and Niv scurried over to see what was going on.

"I know we haven't been out here as long as usual, but we should really get back to see what kept Journey away. I'm kind of anxious about it still to tell the truth," Sparrow said sheepishly.

30

We thanked Eja and told him that we would be back to the forest as soon as we figured out the best way to cloak everyone with my new invisible power. He wished us luck and watched us as we trudged through the dark forest, until we disappeared from his view, the old fashion way. I slumped along behind the others deep in thought. I was wondering why it always seemed that although I would gain some great or valuable insight with each visit to the forest, I would always come away with more questions than I answered. I sighed deeply and scratched the silky long hairs between Niv's ears.

"At least we may have figured out a way to protect you," I whispered while kissing him on his snout as he gazed at me with sleepy eyes.

We reached the clearing to the fields that separated the forest from the Troian Center and stopped on Nova's signal.

"What's up?" I asked.

"I think we should try out your vanishing act," Nova said. "I feel like it might not be wise to send you back in through the window without knowing what stopped Journey from joining us."

We all looked back and forth at each other. I watched as Remi gulped in fear.

"It's as good a time as any to practice, I guess," I said with as much certainty as I could muster for Remi's benefit.

I tucked a sleepy Niv away into my shoulder bag and joined hands with the others. I concentrated on vanishing and I knew it worked because when I opened my eyes they were gone!

"Guys? This is so weird! I can't see any of you," I said nervously.

"I know, I can still see myself, but you're all gone," came Sparrow's excited voice.

"Well, I guess we know it's working," said Nova. "Shall we?"

"Remi, are you good?" I asked.

"I think so," he replied uncertainly.

"Okay I think we need to communicate like this until we get back to our rooms. Just because no one can see us doesn't mean they can't hear us," Nova warned.

"So, what's the plan?" I telepathed.

"Tippy, follow my lead. I'm going to bring us in right through the front gates. I'll be sure to redirect the Grifts and how about you take care of any tarcats that come our way," Nova added.

I could just picture him winking at me, which made me roll my eyes and smile. I hadn't told the others yet about my power of communicating with animals, so they probably all assumed Nova was talking about the tarcat I scared off the other night. Only I knew he was really playing lightheartedly with me to lessen my fears.

It felt strange to feel Nova's warm hand squeeze mine, but not be able to see it. I could feel Sparrow's cool, dainty palm in my left hand as well, and I could hear Remi's nervous breathing from further behind. We were walking single file from what I could tell, through the fields at quite a fast pace, and as the distance to the Troian Center decreased, the pounding of my heart increased. I could see two Grifts up ahead, casually leaning against the courtyard wall. We were still blanketed by the moonless night, but soon we would be close enough for them to see and we'd know whether we were really invisible or not. It was a frightening feeling, testing it out in the open like this. I felt very vulnerable, but even more determined because I needed to be able to protect my friends or we'd all end up in the locker, much sooner then we'd planned.

"I'm going to send one of them around the corner to check on something," Nova telepathed.

We paused a short while waiting for the Grift to stride to the corner of the wall and vanish as he rounded it. Then there was only one lazy Grift in front of us. As we got closer we could see he was mindlessly cleaning under his nails with a knife. The scene would have been nerve racking enough without there being a knife flicking about.

"Here we go, deep breath and then hold it until we're past. 1, 2, 3..."

I took a deep breath and then felt myself being pulled rapidly forward by Nova. At first I felt like a tiny tug boat pulling against the swell of the sea, but finally Sparrow and Remi caught speed and the four of us ran on our tip toes until we were well past the Grift and harbored in the long shadows of the courtyard walls.

31

"It worked! We'd made it past the Grift with no problem. He didn't even look up from his knife. It was so incredible, I wish you had been there!" exclaimed Sparrow in her high-speed whisper to Journey at breakfast.

"Humm...ts...ggud..." Journey mumbled as he stuffed his mouth with porridge and beans.

Ugh, he was so disgusting when he ate. I had to turn away for fear I would lose my appetite all together if I watched him sop up any more of his meal with the crusty hunks of bread he was stuffing into his mouth. I swear he didn't even chew. It didn't seem to faze Sparrow though as she leaned in closer to fill Journey in on all the things we'd done without him last night.

"So what held you up last night, Journey?" Nova asked. "You haven't said much this morning."

He took a few large gulps of juice and wiped his mouth with the back of his hand. He looked around the cafeteria for a moment, and then leaned in. "Jemma," he said quietly and my heart sank.

I quickly glanced past his shoulder in the direction of her

table and was cut by her icy stare. I wasn't expecting her to be watching us and before I could look away, she caught the startled look in my eye and a wicked smile slowly slithered across her face, baring her teeth the way a tarcat does right before it pounces. I swallowed hard and looked back to Journey.

"She's watching us," I said.

"Yeah, and I expect she will be for quite a while," he replied.

"Why? What happened?" asked Sparrow breathlessly.

Journey looked at me and told me to keep an eye on Jemma, and then he recounted what happened last night. Jemma had apparently gotten out of bed to go to the Jane's room. That's what held Journey up. He wanted to wait for her to come back to bed so she didn't return while he was trying to slip out the window. "I thought if she caught me leaving she'd alert the Grifts and then you'd all end up locked out or worse, because surely they'd come to our room and find you all missing."

"So what happened next? Did she take too long to go back to sleep or something?" Remi asked.

"Not exactly," Journey replied and then continued to fill us in on the rest of his night. "She came back shortly, and was about to climb back into bed when she stopped short. She turned slowly toward the windows and her eyes locked on the empty cot bed and froze. Then she looked around and saw that the rest of you were gone too and I was in a panic. I didn't know what to do. I was about to get up and grab her, but instead of going for the door like I thought she would, she crept over to the wardrobe. At first, I didn't know what she was doing, so I propped myself up to see better and I saw it."

While he was talking, goose flesh exploded up and down my spine, leaving the hair on the back of my neck standing even in the sticky morning heat that filled the dining hall. I already knew what he was going to say before he opened his mouth, no magic powers needed. I saw it in her wicked smile. She had found my journal.

"She had Tippy's journal in her hands."

With each word that rolled off his tongue, it felt like I was falling deeper and deeper into quicksand. Like the words themselves were burying me alive. The room tunneled around me and everyone's voices dimmed, like I was listening to them from inside a glass box. It was just noise and vibration. I missed the rest of what he was saying, but it didn't really matter. Jemma had found my journal. My completely empty journal, which I'm sure of because I was always careful to use the enchantment Sparrow taught me each time to erase my writing. But Jemma saw me writing in this exact book, over and over, she even made snotty comments about what a little bookworm I was becoming, always writing, writing, writing. I particularly remember one day in lessons when she was itching to sharpen her teeth on someone and she said, "Oh look, little Miss Nobody is writing to her imaginary friends, how sweet," right before she knocked it out of my hands while her minions laughed.

"She what?" exclaimed Sparrow, bringing me back to reality. Nova kicked her under the table, signaling for her to keep her voice down. "Sorry. She just has some nerve riffling around in your stuff like that," she said looking at me. Then she turned to Journey and hissed, "Why didn't you get up to stop her?"

"What did you want me to do? Tell her to please stop playing with 65's magic journal and go back to bed?" he retorted sarcastically.

"Journey was right to stay where he was. At least for now she only noticed the three of you were missing and she didn't see anything in the journal, right?" Nova asked looking at me. Sparrow nodded for me since I was too numb to move.

"So maybe she just thinks you tore the pages out or she found the wrong journal or something. You could have been out of bed writing in the courtyard for all she knows. The good news is she doesn't know we were out in the forest and she doesn't know that Journey saw her. We have a leg up on her. We just know we have to be extra careful now. I really think we need to suspend sneaking out to the forest because Jemma's going to be keeping a close eye on you. She may not know exactly what we're up too, but I have a hunch she's going to keep at it until she finds out," Nova said.

"But..." I started, only to be cut off by Nova.

"We already have our plan to get into the locker. Now all we have to do is wait for the time to be right. There's no use risking getting caught going to the forest. That would spoil the whole thing."

"I need to practice," I said, already sounding defeated.

"No you don't, Tippy. You're better than you even know you are. You got us back here safely last night."

"What about Eja? Won't he be expecting us?" Journey asked.

"I'll try to get a message to him while I'm at Flood work today. He'll understand," Nova said.

I stared at the table gloomily while the others finished their breakfast. I couldn't stomach any food even if I'd wanted to. I was too upset, stewing over what Jemma had done. I was stabbing my helpless fruit and pushing it around my plate while I sulked over how once again Jemma had managed to ruin my life. Why couldn't she just leave me alone?

"Tippy, it's okay. She doesn't have anything on us. We got off pretty easy. I mean, what if we hadn't taken Niv with us? She

would have found him and that would have been much worse,"
Nova telepathed to me.

I snapped my head around to face him, with my eyes as big
as saucers, already brimming with tears.

"Niv!" I squeaked.

This was too much to handle. Jemma could do what she
wanted to me and even my friends, but I couldn't let her get to
Niv. I promised to protect him and I already loved him so
fiercely that the thought of her finding him and taking him
away from me was unbearable. She had already taken so
much from me. I shoved back from the table and ran to our
room sobbing, leaving the others staring open-mouthed
after me.

I found Niv right where I left him, happily curled up inside
the hollowed-out book. He blinked up at me and gave a lazy
yawn, which actually made me smile and cry all at once. I
scooped him up and let him lick my salty, tear-stained face for
a second before I put him into my shoulder bag. I quickly
changed into my work clothes and slung the bag over my back
to head out the door right as Remi was coming in. I already
made up my mind that I had to protect Niv and I couldn't let
anyone get in my way. Not even Remi.

"65, where are you going?"

"I have to do something. Just cover for me, okay?"

"What? How? Where are you going?"

"I don't know, Remi. Just say I wasn't feeling well and went
to see Miss Breia or something."

He started to say something back to me but I didn't wait to
hear it. I pushed past him and at the door, I vanished. I could
feel it this time. It's hard to describe, but a feeling of transparency or lightness washed over me. I felt like a shadow,
moving effortlessly along, safe and unnoticed. I was really
starting to get the hang of this power and realizing how valu-

able it was. I crept carefully down the hall toward the court-yard. I saw the other orphans finishing up their breakfast, laughing and chatting in the carefree way I had always envied. I caught a quick glimpse of the others at my table. They sat quietly, looking drawn and worried. It seemed to age them, subtly setting them apart from the others. It was one of those things you'd notice, yet not be able to put your finger on. But I knew it, and I felt it. Every ounce of their stress, worry, fear; it all weighed heavily upon my invisible shoulders as I moved past them into the warm sun of the courtyard.

I pushed on, past the Grifts and into the wide openness of the fields. I could see the locals in the distance who had already started their long day, laboring in the fields. They tilled, pruned, plucked and cultivated the ravaged soil all day long to get enough food to sustain all of us on the island. Most of what they grew went to Lux. What was left they shared with the Troian Center or traded for supplies. Luckily the forest bounced back the fastest from the Flood and was back to producing abundant fruits and vegetation to keep us all going. I plucked a vine of wild grapes to eat as I made my way through the forest. I realized I was actually pretty hungry still since I didn't eat much breakfast this morning. Neither did Niv, who by now popped his little furry head out of my shoulder bag and was taking in the sights and sounds of the beautiful morning. I handed him a grape, which he kindly took and stuffed into his mouth, puffing out his cheek. He reached up for another and promptly stuffed it into his other cheek. His little face was so fat that I couldn't help but giggle as he greedily reach up for another grape.

"Niv, where are you possibly going to put another grape? Eat the ones I just gave you first."

He grunted and went to work on the grapes he was hord-ing. It kept him pretty busy for a while and we were deep in the forest in no time. Niv climbed out of my bag and up to his favorite perch on my shoulder when he was done with his grapes. We were far enough now that I probably didn't need to be invisible anymore. But I liked the confident feeling I had being able to go undetected, so I kept it up until we were at the spot where we met Eja. I revealed myself and called out to him.

"Eja?"

I waited for a response but only heard the calls of the forest wildlife in return. I sat down on the mossy ground and leaned my back against the cool trunk of a waxy palm. Niv scampered off my shoulder and started his favorite pastime of hunting bugs.

"Don't go too far," I called after him. "We have work to do."

He raised his head and looked back at me with his whiskers happily twitching. He had a look of understanding in his gleaming chocolate-brown eyes that melted my heart. I smiled at him as he telescoped his ears and scurried off.

I sat under the shade of the forest canopy for a while, amusing myself by watching Niv. I was beginning to think that Eja wasn't going to come. I had been calling him for a while now. The sun had risen fully over head and I would have to head back soon as not to miss Flood work. I was starting to contemplate whether life for everyone might be best if I just didn't return to the Troian Center, when suddenly Eja swung down from a tree above me.

"Tippy! What a surprise! What are you doing here? Is everything okay?" he asked.

"Eja! You've got to stop jumping out of trees like that! What took you so long?"

"I wasn't expecting you until tonight. I was on higher ground and had to sneak away to come see you. What's wrong?"

"Well, we can't come see you tonight. We may not be able to come out here for a long time. Someone noticed we were gone last night and it's going to make it hard for us to sneak out now."

"So you came all the way out here to tell me this?" he asked.

"Well, that and…" I paused. "There's something else too."

Eja just blinked back at me, waiting expectantly for me to go on. He almost gave me the impression that he knew what I wanted to ask him.

"Well, I wanted to ask you about something you said last night."

He nodded for me to continue.

"It's about tethering. Can you teach me how to do it?"

Now he was looking at me cautiously, not sure how to answer.

"Tippy, the things I tell you and your friends, they're just bits of history and knowledge about the Beto people that I can share with you because you're one of us and I want you to know as much as possible. But I don't know how to do all of these things, I don't even know if they are all intended to be used."

"Eja, I know you know how to do this. I could feel it when you were speaking about it and so could Nova. I have a feeling that's why he cut that conversation short."

"He's only trying to protect you."

"I know, but I can take care of myself, and besides there's someone more important that needs our protection right now," I said and then I called Niv over.

He came bounding over with his wispy hair damp and matted to his face from the dew. He jumped into my lap and rolled onto his back so I could scratch his round belly, snorting and cooing in delight. I looked back at Eja, who seemed be following me now.

"Tippy, this is dangerous stuff. It's not a game. You can only do this once and I've never heard of a human tethering themselves to an animal. They're too unpredictable and they don't understand the complications of what you're doing."

"Niv understands me. I can talk to him. It's another one of my powers," I said sheepishly.

Eja only stared at me.

"Please, you have to help me, Eja. I promised his dying mother that I would take care of him and protect him, and last night if I hadn't taken him with me... I don't even want to think what would happen if the wrong person found him."

"That's precisely why this isn't a good idea, Tippy. If the wrong person finds him and he dies, you die, too."

Niv stopped squirming in my lap and looked up at me with his big brown eyes as he seemed to have caught onto the serious tone of our conversation.

"Eja, please. I will find a way to do this with or without your help."

He sighed deeply and I tried hopelessly to contain my grin because I could see he was going to help me from the way he slumped his shoulders in helpless defeat.

"Alright, if you're going to do this, I better help you do it right."

32

I left the forest under my cloak of transparency, with a new feeling of triumph. For once I felt secure about something in my future, Niv was safe as long as I was safe and there was nothing Jemma could do about it. It was so happy that I was holding up my end of the bargain in protecting Niv. I felt that tethering myself to him would actually give both of us happier lives. He would be free to roam about under the protection of my invisible power, which meant he wouldn't have to stay hidden in a hollowed-out book or my shoulder bag. He could come with me to lessons, to work, to the dining hall, and to the forest, if we ever managed to find a safe way to get back there, that is. I sighed at the complications Jemma caused with our lessons in the forest, but decided to push those thoughts to the back of my mind for now and enjoy the beautiful day with Niv for a little bit longer.

We frolicked in the field, taking turns chasing and hiding in the tall wheat grass before pouncing on each other. I let Niv climb all over me and give me sloppy kisses and tickle me with his long whiskers. I knew Niv loved me for saving him, but I doubted he knew how much he was saving me. Having him in my life as a constant companion, who would never judge me or be disappointed in me was the most amazing feeling I'd ever had. I was beginning to understand what true, unconditional, selfless love was. I loved this little, furry orphan so much that I tethered myself to him forever. We would always be joined, connected to each others thoughts, emotions, and whereabouts. I could share my powers with him and protect him from harm. He could even protect me. As long as one of our souls lived on, the other would continue to live. We could heal each other effortlessly, we could telepath to each other, we could even terra bound, which is kind of like teleporting to another location, as Eja explained. I'm sure there's even more that we could do together that I still haven't discovered yet. Eja said each tether is unique to those who create it. tethering connected us in every way and I could see why it was such serious business, usually saved for your soul mate, but I was sure I'd made the right decision. I knew the others would be upset with me for doing it, but I made a promise to protect Niv and I meant to keep it by any means necessary.

After our fun romp in the fields I knew it was time to be heading back to the Center. If I hurried I might be able to get a quick bite to eat before Flood work. I scooped up Niv and headed that way, scratching his chin.

"Are you hungry, little guy?"

He replied with a lazy yawn and rolled onto his back in my arms so I could scratch his tawny belly.

"Well, I haven't been eating bugs all morning, so if you don't mind I'd like to get some lunch," I said as I smiled down at him.

He was getting so much bigger. I think that this invisible tethering business came just at the right time. He no longer fit in the palms of my hands. Now I carried him in the crook of my arm, with his long legs and scraggly tail hanging below. I had to shift arms every once in a while when he would start to get heavy.

I took a deep breath as we approached the Grifts guarding the entrance to the Troian Center and counted to three in my head before making a dash between them undetected. I knew I was still invisible, but it was still an eerie feeling to stare at them and sneak by right beneath their noses.

33

I made it back just in time to grab a few scraps from the dining hall as the rest of the orphans were emptying their trays and heading to change for Flood work. Sparrow spotted me and trotted over as I was quickly stuffing some bread into my pocket before the invisible Niv could grab at it.

"Tippy," she whispered. "Are you okay? You looked so upset at breakfast and then you weren't at lessons today. I was worried about you."

"Yes, I'm fine. Come on, we don't want to be late for Flood work," I said walking toward our room as she trotted along side of me wearing her worry. That was Sparrow, an open book, her emotions on her sleeve. I could tell she wasn't buying my story.

"We'll talk later, I promise," I whispered to her.

"Okay," she said, smiling now and seeming to perk up to her peppy self.

I waited for her to change and we went to the courtyard to head out to Flood work. Remi and Journey were there waiting for us when Sparrow and I joined them in line. Journey looked like his usual massive, aloof self, but Remi looked worried, or maybe preoccupied. As I got closer to him I could feel a mass of emotions radiating from him, one of which was guilt. I stared at him, confused as we followed our Grifts silently to the rubble piles. I was about the telepath to him and ask him what was wrong when I felt a warm rough hand firmly take hold of my wrist, and the strong smell of soil filled my nostrils. I knew it was Nova before he even had to speak and I knew he wasn't happy.

"Tippy, make us vanish and come with me right now."

I complied and side stepped out of our group heading toward the rubble piles. Sparrow, paused for a moment, looking anxiously at the now empty spot in front of her and stumbled when the John behind her walked into her back, but she shook it off and kept moving forward.

"It's okay, I'll be right back," I telepathed, not wanting her to worry.

I watched the others walk further away from me because I was almost too scared to look at Nova. I could feel his anger pulsing toward me through the firm grip he had on my arm. Finally, he spoke and I had to look at him.

"It's not okay, Tippy, and it's never going to be okay now. Tell me it's not true! Tell me you didn't do it!"

"Nova, keep your voice down," I hissed while looking around.

"I don't care who hears me! What have you done, Tippy?"

I was so confused. How did he know? Were he and I so connected he knew what I'd done? Or had he read my thoughts? I was so careful not to form a single thought about tethering until I found Eja. I didn't even let the words into my head. And then it hit me and I shook my head in anguish. Remi! That's why he was feeling so guilty, he figured it out and told Nova! He must have known what I was going to do. I guess it wasn't too hard to figure out after he saw me leaving our room with Niv after how upset I was by our discussion at breakfast. I actually wasn't even mad at him, I was relieved that Nova knew. I was going to have to tell them all anyway, because they would wonder where Niv had disappeared to.

"Tippy, do you realize what you've done?" Nova asked. His voice had lost its anger and now was rimmed with genuine concern.

"I had to, Nova. You know I had to. I promised. I can't let anything happen to him and Jemma would find him eventually and use him against us. You know she would."

"Don't you see now you've given her and anyone else all the leverage they'll ever need? Tippy, if anything happens to Niv, it happens to you," he said with his vivid green eyes boring into mine.

His intensity made me swallow hard and fight to keep the blood from rushing to my face.

"Nothing's going to happen to me. Niv is safer than ever. He can stay invisible and I'll know where he is at all times. He can have a good life now, not hiding in that stupid wardrobe."

"Tippy, you don't get it. Before I was only worried about you, but now I have to worry about him, too," he said pointing at the rambunctious marmouse that was digging near my feet. "If something happens to him, it happens to you. You get that, don't you?" he asked, angry again. "If he gets bit, you feel it. If he chokes on something, so do you. If he eats something poisonous, you get poisoned. He's just a stupid rodent. He doesn't understand the consequences and apparently neither do you," he said shouting again.

"He's not stupid! He understands me and besides, now I can protect him with my soul. If he gets hurt I can heal him."

"How are you going to heal him if you're both poisoned or worse?"

"That's the beauty of this whole thing, Nova. With our souls tethered, we keep each other alive."

Nova sighed and shook his head sympathetically at me. For a moment he looked like he might cry, but instead he pulled me toward him and hugged me tight. I closed my eyes as I felt myself melting into the warmth of his body as he engulfed me. But the comfort was short lived because I could feel the sadness and fear Nova was harboring for me. I felt an electric current take hold as I got a quick flash of Nova's thoughts containing horrible images of Niv and me dying and it made me pull away with worry. I struggled to catch my breath and then whispered to Nova,

"I screwed up, didn't I?" I asked, second guessing my decision for the first time.

"I don't think you fully understand how it works. Your souls are tethered together. They will live on forever because they can't be separated, but your bodies are still mortal and are susceptible to the same injuries as the rest of us."

"But... No... Eja said... I thought..." I was getting flustered now. This was supposed to be a good thing for both of us. Was Nova right? Did I put us both in more danger?

"This is dangerous magic, Tippy, Eja had no right to tell you about it."

This got my blood pumping. I jerked my arm away from his grasp and had my hands balled into fists to try to contain my rage. I hated when he treated me like a child. I was supposedly the Eva, the chosen one, or whatever it was, so didn't that earn me anything?

Now I was the one shouting. "If anyone has the right to know about this it's precisely me! This is why I can't let Jemma or anyone else stop me from coming out here. There's so much more I need to learn, Nova! I only got a crash course, but I need to know more and you know it's true. You know more than I do and I'm supposed to be the leader, the key to fixing our island? How am I going to do anything if you keep deciding what I can and can't know about?"

"Tippy, I'm only trying to protect you."

"You can't protect me from myself, Nova. You have to let me in, to all of it. No holding anything back. Not knowing the whole truth is what gets me into messes like this. You're not protecting me by keeping the truth from me. That's what makes me weaker. I've just made myself vulnerable because I didn't have all the information."

He sighed deeply and lowered his eyes in shame. "You're right, Tippy. I'm sorry, knowledge is powerful and you're smart enough to make your own decisions about these things or you wouldn't be our Eva."

I hadn't expected him to agree with me so easily and was taken aback by his concession. I found myself going to comfort him, when moments ago I'd wanted to fight him.

"Nova, it's okay, I know you're only looking out for me. I still need you to do that because I have a lot to learn. I just need you to open up to me and help me know the truth about things so I don't go into them blindly."

"Like today?" he said with his natural sarcasm.

"Yes, like today. I know it's not ideal, but I had to do something. You can understand that, can't you?"

"Yes, but you also need to understand why I'm so upset. If he gets hurt, you get hurt. If he dies, you die."

He said it with such finality that we both stood there silently for a moment, neither of us looking at each other. Our eyes found Niv and I could feel it in my heart that Nova was right, but I knew I would make the same decision again if it meant protecting Niv. When I felt Nova step closer to me and put his hand on my shoulder, I knew he understood why I did it and that he was going to help me keep him safe, for both our sakes.

34

I sat eating my breakfast and preparing to settle in for another awkward morning with Niv and the gang. Since Nova found out about the tethering, he ordered that Niv and I be under continuous surveillance. Nova made sure either Sparrow, Remi, Journey or himself were with me at all times. That even meant in the Jane's room. At first I fought it, not wanting to be babysat, but eventually I gave in to all their concerns. And it actually wasn't too bad at first, but lately I felt the task of guarding me was starting to become daunting to my friends. It was wearing worse on some of them than others.

I was trying to look on the bright side. At least I was stuck spending time with friends, so it wasn't all-bad. I really enjoyed all their company. Even Journey was growing on me. He knew a lot about the Beto people and always shared interesting little tidbits of their history with me. Sparrow and I spent our time together practicing our singing for the Gala and I was actually starting to improve and not dread our choir practice so much. But times with Remi and Nova were tense. Remi was getting moodier by the day and I didn't know why.

He seemed preoccupied and didn't laugh at my jokes anymore. I could tell that following me around was kind of getting old for him. It always seemed like there was some-where else he'd rather be. And Nova, well normally I would have loved the chance to spend more time with him, but he wasn't his fun carefree self anymore. He had transformed into an all-business bodyguard. One afternoon while escorting me to lessons, I sneezed and before I knew what happened he had me pinned to the floor. He was crushing me under his weight and I was crushing Niv, who, as ordered, was in my shoulder bag. In turn, with all of us being crushed I couldn't catch my breath. I was barely able to mutter for him to get off of me, as my face burned red from lack of oxygen and embarrassment. Everyone in our stuffy hallway stopped to gawk or laugh at us. Jemma was among them, scoffing snide comments to the rest of her groupies, who snickered wickedly in delight at my folly.

"Really, 65, you make it too easy," she said as she turned on her heel, deliberately spraying sand in my face.

Nova pulled me to my feet and dusted me off, and I had to assure him about a hundred times that I was fine so that he wouldn't drag me to Miss Breia's station again. I had already been there three times in the past week.

I was seriously considering asking Nova to change my assignment to just Journey or Sparrow when he joined me at breakfast. At least neither of them treated me like an invalid or pariah. But when Nova and Sparrow approached the table I could see a flicker of the old Nova in the glimmer of his eyes as Sparrow fluttered him with conversation. Journey was already sitting stoically beside me since he was on watch. Although I liked spending time with Journey, I was glad for some company to distract me from his repulsive eating habits. He was sloppily filling his mouth with more food than I thought humanly possible when they sat down at our table. I was grateful when Sparrow's chatter drowned out the sound of Journey's thunderous chewing.

"Where's Remi?" Sparrow asked.

"I don't know, I'm the one we're supposed to be watching remember?" I mumbled sarcastically.

This got a laugh out of everyone.

"Okay, what's up with you today?" I asked Nova, who was beaming.

"This is the week!" he said unable to contain his excitement.

Could it really have been three weeks already?

"Oh," was all I could say.

"I've decided what I'm going to do to get sent to the locker," he said grinning like a fool.

"I almost don't want to know," I said picking at my fruit.

"Well, I do," Journey encouraged.

"I'm going to hug Greeley on Lux day," he whispered with excitement.

I dropped my fork.

35

I gasped as soon as he said it because I knew it would without a doubt get him thrown into the locker, if he survived of course. It might not seem like a big deal to hug our headmistress. To most, a show of affection was certainly not something that should get you punished, but to Greeley this would be seen as a gesture so heinous that she wouldn't even blink before sending Nova straight to the locker, if she didn't feed him to her tarcats first!

You have to understand a few things about Greeley to see why this was such a big deal. Although she was our headmistress and entrusted with our well being, she despised us. She always said that she thought children were dirty, foul, grubby beings and she would never get very close to us. If by chance you encountered her in the halls, she would stop short and crinkle her sharp features as if she has come across a putrid smell. We always took care to give her a wide berth and keep our eyes averted to avoid being sent to the locker.

Another thing that was strange for our headmistress was that Greeley was sort of a recluse. She hid in her office all day long doing who knows what. She only ventured out sporadically, but the one time you could count on seeing her was for her weekly visit to the rubble piles. These weren't social visits though. She came out only to inspect the precious goods we were procuring for her. She would also take it upon herself to take a particularly lovely gem or stone, "for a closer look" as she would say. But we knew she was stealing them for her own collection because we would spot them either on Khan and Ria's collars or on the necklace she always wore.

That was another peculiar thing about Greeley, she was meticulous about her appearance. Even in the sweltering heat of summer, when you could see the horizon wavering like a mirage in the distance, Greeley would wear her long dresses, extravagant jackets and jeweled necklace. She always had her dark hair slicked back into a neatly braided bun at the base of her neck and she never went anywhere without wearing her gloves. She had them in every shade imaginable and they exaggerated her long boney fingers, making them appear pointed and sharp. Perhaps there were claws underneath; she was certainly vicious enough to have them.

All of the mystique surrounding the way Greeley behaved and dressed was enough to keep everyone at arm's length. Us orphans were all terrified of her. We knew even the slightest glance in her direction could warrant her reason enough to throw us in the locker. And the Grifts and teachers seemed to be frightened of her as well. None of them were chummy with her, that's for sure. Jest was the only one that I might call her friend, but even that was a stretch of the word. It was more like they shared a passion for punishing us. The only things that I could tell Greeley loved were the tarcats. Khan and Ria in particular. She adorned their massive leather collars with more gems than any of the other tarcats, and she would take them to Lux with her whenever she went. They would pad along lazily on either side of her like two black and white furry bodyguards. They pretty much followed her everywhere or would lay lethargically outside her office door.

Oh, wait, I take that back, there is one other thing Greeley loved: her sparkling necklace. It was made of gold that I'm sure orphans mined and collected, then melted down and hammered into a pocked bib necklace that she embellished with gems she confiscated from orphans over the years. By now, it lay heavy on her collar bone, gleaming in the sun, casting a dazzling display of colored lights that danced off her pointy features. It almost made her look beautiful on Lux days, as we called them, when she would wear her full-length white gown, the traditional uniform of the citizens of Lux. She would visit Lux once a week in her white attire and bring the treasures that we found during Flood work. She traded them at the port city for food and supplies that were needed to keep the Troian Center running. I had a sneaking suspicion she traded them for some of the extravagant dresses she wore as well. She must love Lux day because her white dresses were always starched and creaseless, making her carry her pointy chin a little higher.

It made me shiver picturing Greeley dressed that way because I knew it would mean it was time for Nova to attack her. Well, not attack really, just hug. But Greeley would see it as an attack. I don't think in the history of the Troian Center anyone had ever gotten close enough to Greeley to touch her. Especially not close enough to hug her. And Nova would surely be all sweaty and dirty from Flood work. I could almost picture the stains he would leave on her immaculate white dress.

"Nova, are you sure this is the best plan?" I began, begging him to reconsider with my mind.

"Tippy, don't even try to talk me out of it. I've thought of a million different things in my head, but this one is the best. It guarantees that I'll be sent to the locker and that you and Remi will be there to see it happen so you can both follow me in."

"But..." I paused shuddering again at the thought of it. "She's going to be furious," I concluded in a whisper.

"I'll be fine. Just stick to the plan. And fill Remi in on it whenever he decides to show up," Nova said rising from the table and walking out of the dining hall.

I sat there speechless for a moment, still tormented by the thoughts of Nova's plan. Sparrow broke my concentration and brought me back to reality. "Yeah, where is Remi? He's been really distant lately."

I shrugged, but she was right. He seemed to be pulling back from our little group and he was around less and less. I had way too much to worry about to keep track of Remi at the moment.

"I'm going to go check on Niv and see if he wants breakfast," I said.

"Oh, he's not here with us?" Sparrow asked sounding surprised.

"No, he hasn't been himself the past few days. He's sleeping a lot. He's curled up on my cot bed still. Hopefully, this fruit will brighten his mood," I said pushing back from the table.

I left Sparrow and Journey talking excitedly about Nova's crazy plan, but it was short lived because they both seemed to realize that no one was on Tippy duty and they rushed to dump their trays and catch up to me. I didn't get how they couldn't see how dangerous Nova's plan was. Maybe they were just happy that the time had finally come. Greeley hadn't gone to Lux yet this week. She would be showing up any day now at the rubble pile, all decked out in white. I slipped into room 13 with them on my heels and found Niv still curled up on my cot bed. The little indentation at the foot of the stuffed mattress gave him away. To anyone else it would just look like a lumpy mattress, but I knew better. I started clucking softly to him as I entered the room so I didn't startle him. It worried me that all of a sudden he had become so lethargic. He was usually bouncing with energy. Maybe he was just going through a growth spurt. I read that animals sleep a lot when they're growing. Or maybe he was hibernating. It was winter and I didn't know a whole lot about marmice. Whatever it was, it worried me. I gave him bits of fruit and watched as it slowly disappeared. It made me laugh every time. It was my favorite little magic trick. I felt like I was feeding my imaginary pet! In a way I guess I was since no one else could see him.

While Sparrow and Journey practiced for the Gala, I spent the rest of my free time journaling my concerns about our plan and looking out for Remi, who never showed up. Finally, I was forced to walk to lessons without him. He squeaked into the lesson room just as the bell was chiming.

Gong!

"Where have you been?" I telepathed to him.

He just looked at me with those big brown eyes and shrugged. He was out of breath and sweaty, so I knew he was up to something; but I knew he wasn't going to tell me, so I just dropped it. Sometimes he was so frustrating!

"Never mind, I have to tell you about Nova's plan," I said.

He rolled his eyes a few times while I was filling him in on the plan, but all in all he seemed to take it in stride as well. Why was no one else as concerned as I was? I sighed in frustration and tried to turn my attention to what Miss Banna was rambling on about, but it was no use. My mind was consumed by scary visions of Greeley, tarcats and the locker.

At lunch I put Sparrow and Journey in charge of Niv, in case today was the day we ended up in the locker. I didn't want

Niv to follow us so I told Sparrow to take him in my shoulder bag to Flood work and to not let him out of her sight.

"How am I supposed to do that when I can't even see him?" she asked.

"Journey will help you. He can hear him."

Journey nodded in agreement and that was settled. While we finished eating I gave them tips on the foods Niv liked and his favorite hiding and napping places. I caught Remi shaking his head a few times, but decided to ignore it. I was trying to think of what else I needed to tell them when Journey interrupted me.

"You're only going to be gone for a day," he said sounding annoyed by my fussing.

"Not if we get sent down there today! The Gala is still a few days away."

"Yeah, but you can leave any time you want. Isn't that the beauty of this plan?"

"And leave Nova down there all alone?" I asked appalled.

"You'll be invisible so you can go back and check on him any time you want," Journey added in an apologetic tone.

"But it's not like he'll need you to. He's a big boy, he can take care of himself," Remi shot at me with such hostility that we all stopped and stared at him.

I was so shocked I didn't know what to say. I'd never heard Remi so mad before. What was going on with him?

"I know that, Remi! That's not what – "

"Well you don't act that way sometimes," he interrupted and pushed back from our table and stormed out of the dining hall.

"What was that all about?" Sparrow asked.

"Beats me," I shrugged, trying to act as if it wasn't a big deal. But I was starting to worry about Remi's recent behavior.

I didn't have much time to think about it though because

Nova came strolling toward us a moment later, with a secretive grin lighting up his beautiful face. I could read his thoughts immediately and knew he was still basking in the excitement of his awaiting prank. I wish I could say I felt the same way, but all the stress of worrying about everyone was starting to get to me. Remi, Nova, Niv, not to mention myself and the added fact that Jemma always seemed close by, watching our every move. How were we going to get away with this?

It was a balmy afternoon at the rubble piles. On a normal day, I might have actually been able to enjoy the fresh air. But, I was so worried that today would be Lux day for Greeley that I could hardly concentrate. Every little sound made me jump and look around wildly. I felt like my whole body was on red alert, tensed and ready to react if need be. I was sweating despite the mild temperature. I glanced at Remi, who was working on my rubble pile today. Although he exuded a calm exterior, I could feel the worry pulsing through his body as well. I reached for his hand with my own trembling one, longing for some comfort in this miserable situation and to my relief he reached back, squeezing small pulses of hope back into me. I smiled at him and we communicated without words or telepathy, the way we always had, the way only best friends can. I could see he was feeling the same way I was and that although our future was uncertain, we were certain that we had each other and that washed away all my earlier doubt and worry about Remi's recent behavior. Whatever was making him act this way, I'm sure he had a reason for it and he'd let me in when he was ready.

I let go of his hand and turned back to focus on my work. We picked and sorted silently for the next few minutes before Remi said, "I have to tell you something."

"Okay," I said still working.

"I was only trying to protect you, so don't be mad, okay?"

"Okay," I said again, this time pausing to look up at him, but when I did, what I saw sent goose flesh racing down my spine, raising all the alarms!

I quickly put my hand over my mouth to stifle the gasp that I let escape. Remi turned to see what got a rise out of me and he froze, too. Just beyond the furthest rubble pile, I could see three figures emerging from the tall grass of the fields. Two of them were low and wide, moving with a slinking gait, and the third figure rose in between the other two. A tall thin pillar gliding toward us, all dressed in white.

36

You know how people say that time seems to stand still during a crisis, or you see your life pass before your eyes before you die? Well, I believe it now. I think they both happened at once for me. I was in a panic and my mind was racing as I watched the events before me unfold in slow motion, helpless to stop them.

Once I saw Greeley approaching with Khan and Ria, I got a lump in my throat, and I knew this was a bad idea. I wanted to abort our plan immediately. I turned to where Nova was hiding behind a nearby tree to tell him the deal was off, but he was gone. I looked around frantically and spotted him a few yards away, walking straight toward Greeley. The next thing I knew, my legs were carrying me forward rapidly. I was down the rubble pile and sprinting after Nova, waving my arms wildly trying to call him off. I always thought of him as old for his age, tall and masculine, but as he neared Greeley and the tarcats, he'd never looked smaller to me. I knew I was screaming, at least that was what my mind was doing as I closed the little ground between us. I was closing the gap, but it still felt like I was moving in slow motion. I remember seeing the long white linen of Greeley's dress fluttering toward me with each step she took and I was drawn to it. It was such a bright white that it seemed glow, almost blinding me. The billowing fabric flashed before me, displaying bits of my tragic existence upon it.

I was so close to Nova I could almost reach him, only a few more steps and... *Thunk,* I hit the ground hard. The last thing I remember was feeling my feet go out from under me. Now I could do nothing but watch from my horizontal vantage point as Nova carried out his plan. I heard Greeley shriek but couldn't look up high enough to see what was happening. It felt like there was something heavy on my back holding me down and in my mind I kept hearing *"Stay down, stay down!"* But I was so confounded that I didn't know who I was hearing or what was going on above me.

I looked on as feet and paws shuffled frantically a short distance from my head. There was more yelling from Greeley and angry snarls and hissing from the tarcats. I heard Greeley call for the Grifts and then there was an eerie moment of calm and silence that gave me a sick feeling in the pit of my stomach. A moment later that feeling was validated when Nova's head hit the same packed soil as mine had moments earlier. His eyes were closed and there were three large gashes bleeding before me on his beautiful face. The horrible sight was too much to take, so I squeeze my eyes closed and then my mind must have shut down because that's the last image I was left with before opening my eyes again.

37

The next time I opened my eyes I felt so unsure they were open at all that I had to feel for myself that my long lashes were indeed brushing past my fingers as I held my hands against my face. Was I dreaming? Was I dead? Nova! Where was he? Was he here with me? Or worse, was he...? I couldn't even bring myself to think it. I wanted to whisper his name but I feared what was out there, lurking in the darkness. I was somewhere cool and damp and it was pitch black. It wasn't the kind of darkness that your eyes could adjust to. It was an all-consuming blackness that could swallow you up whole, fears and all. I felt my instinctual panic starting to kick in, but all of my training in the forest paid off because I caught myself and was able to slow my breathing and racing heart enough to think clearly. I remembered that I had everything I needed at my disposal. I focused my mind on pulling forward Journey's hunting skills. I was able to call on my night vision and my surroundings came into focus. I was sitting on the packed earthen floor in the center of a large room. In front of me, it seemed to expand even further than I could see, but to my left I could see a stone wall glowing before me. I had no doubt about it, I was in the locker. I concentrated still harder and could hear the faint drumming of a familiar heartbeat in the distance. Nova!

I was on my feet in an instant, moving toward the rhythmic pulse when something stopped me in my tracks. It was a second heartbeat, this one was weaker, and irregular. Who else or what else was down here? I listened closer to try to get a bearing on where the beating was coming from. One was to my right and the other was straight ahead. I focused all my energy on listening to each heartbeat trying to identify who or what they belonged to. The steady familiar beat was louder, stronger, closer. All at once it hit me and relief washed over me, it was Remi, I was sure of it. It was the same humdrum beating that gave him away in the forest. He must have kept with the plan after all and followed us down here. I wanted to run to him, to tell him we were going to be okay, to tell him so many things, but my feet were cemented, resisting my urge to go to Remi, telling me to keep moving toward the other heart-beat. The one that was harder for me to place.

I was hesitant as I took a few steps closer so I could hear better. The heart was racing and in distress. I felt lured toward it, with a longing to help quiet its fear. It was the same way my heart often sounded when I reacted with panic in our training sessions in the forest. I made my decision to move toward the weak sound. Remi's heart sounded strong and steady. He didn't need me right now, but this other heart was aching and pulling me toward it. I half-heartedly hoped it was Nova I was moving toward, but I shuddered at my last memory of his beautiful face, marred by one of Greeley's tarcats. The frantic heartbeat ahead of me was so distressed that I almost didn't want it to be him, I didn't want to see Nova hurt or frightened. I swallowed the lump in my throat and pushed forward.

Nova was the one we looked to. I didn't like thinking of

him as helpless or frightened. That was a role I was used to serving myself. If Nova was really attached to the feeble heartbeat I was following, I knew I would find myself with a heavy weight upon my shoulders. After a few more cautious steps I stopped abruptly, covering my mouth with both hands to stifle a gasp that caught me off guard. Before me lay a heap of dirty, shivering fabric. I held my breath as I took another anxious step closer. I could see that the quivering mass was actually a human, and it was more than dirty, it was laying in a pool of dark, tacky fluid, that smelled of putrid rust so strongly that my eyes began to water. I followed the puddle back to its source and didn't like what I saw at all. I hadn't realized I was still holding my breath until I released it in a gush of horror as I saw the unmistakable shock of blond hair that parted to give way to a fresh supply of blood that was pooling below it.

"Nova!" I whispered, more to myself than to him.

I rushed to him, skidding to a stop on my knees. I knelt, hands trembling near him, not knowing what to do first. He looked so damaged I was afraid to touch him. I carelessly lobbed an orb above us so that I could better assess the seriousness of his wounds. I struggled for breath when I saw the slashes across his blood-stained face. Still worse was the gaping flesh on his chest that flapped vulnerably with each rattling breath he took. It took everything in me not to vomit as my stomach flip-flopped at the sight of his ghastly injuries. I buried my face into the crook of my arm and looked away until I could regain my composure. I took a few quick deep breaths and wiped away the tears that were streaming down my face. It was up to me now. I needed to pull it together to help Nova. I could heal him. Sparrow taught me how. I just needed to focus. Nova needed me and nothing else mattered.

I leaned close to his ear as whispered to him. "Nova, it's me, Tippy. You're going to be okay."

I didn't expect it when his eyes fluttered open, but the usual sparkle that greeted me was missing. They were dull and listless, but he did show signs of recognition as I spoke to him.

"It's me, Tippy. You're in the locker and you're hurt but don't worry, I'm going to help you. Just be still," I murmured as I stroked a safe looking spot on his forehead.

"Ti..pp..."

"Shhh, don't try to speak, okay? I can do this. You trust me and believe in me. I can do this."

I think I was saying it to comfort myself more than Nova, but it seemed to work. I rubbed my hands together over him and closed my eyes as I lowered them toward his chest.

"Please, let me do this," I whispered to myself right before I felt his bare flesh on my palms.

There was a sudden buzzing of energy vibrating through me. The room grew brighter as my orb glowed boldly above us as if cheering me on. I drew every bit of power and energy I had through my soul and channeled it to Nova. I opened my eyes, slowly, one at a time, almost scared to see if I was doing anything to better his injuries. I watched in horror as nothing happened. The bleeding had stopped and the slashes on his face seemed fainter, but the gaping hole in his heaving chest still looked threatening. I could feel my powers dim as I fought off flashbacks of Niv's mother dying in my arms. I didn't know what to do. I couldn't breathe as the strangling thoughts of losing Nova took hold of me. But then I felt something squeeze my hand and I looked down to see Nova staring back at me, with a look that could inspire anyone to move mountains. In the slight twinkle that had returned to his eyes I could see his confidence in me. His hope and faith stirred me deeper than I knew possible. He gave me a slight nod and I refocused all my energy on healing him and this time I pulled forth a new emotion, so powerful it scared me. It seemed to take over and squash all my fears. I felt a love for Nova pulsing through every vein in my body, breathing new life into him, healing his flesh, quieting his pain, making him whole again. This new energy was contagious, as it swelled inside me.

Nova's voice finally broke my concentration, and I slumped back onto my heels in relief when I saw him smiling back at me. He was breathtaking. Even in the dimness of the locker, he seemed to have a slight glow to him. I couldn't help myself, I leaped forward and hugged him, finally breaking down and sobbing into his perfectly formed chest.

"I... I thought... Nova... I was so scared!"

"Shhh...I know, I'm so sorry," he said while squeezing me tight.

Then he pulled away a bit and I tilted my head back, hypnotized by his eyes. He smoothed my hair back from my face and whispered to me, "Tippy... Thank you."

And then he kissed me.

38

I felt like I was floating, like I had momentarily left the planet. I had never experienced a proper kiss before. And as kisses go, I really didn't think there could be one better than this. But my bliss was short lived. Nova dragged me back to reality as he pulled me to my feet.

"There's someone coming. Listen."

"Oh, it's Remi. I heard him before I found you."

"Are you sure?"

"Positive, here I'll light the way," I said producing more orbs.

"Remi, we're over here! Are you okay?"

"65? Nova?" came Remi's shaky voice from the darkness.

"Right here," I called to him.

Remi emerged from the darkness looking paler than ever. Once he saw us, he ran toward us and gave me a powerful hug. Then he seemed to become self-conscious and released me, stepping back a few paces to take in Nova's appearance.

"You're okay?" he said referring to Nova skeptically. "You were a mess. I was worried you weren't going to make it."

"I probably wouldn't have if Tippy didn't save me."

"What do you mean?" Remi asked.

"She healed me," Nova boasted, beaming like a fool.

It made me blush, but I confirmed Remi's questioning glance with a nod. Remi stepped closer to Nova, circling him cautiously.

"That's incredible. You look impeccable," Remi mused.

Nova bristled up proudly as Remi inspected him, looking as though he was staring at a ghost.

"Remi, did you see what happened? I mean it's kind of foggy. I remember running toward Nova to stop him, and then I fell or tripped and..." I trailed off, shaking, as the last clear memory of Nova's attack flashed before me.

"Yeah, that wasn't part of the plan. You weren't supposed to chase me," Nova scolded.

"Well, I told you it was a stupid plan and you should have known better and called it off yourself when you saw Greeley had Khan and Ria with her!" I shouted. "What were you thinking?"

"Tippy, it could have been our only chance to get the information we need. I had to do it."

"What were both of you thinking?" cut in Remi.

Startled we both stopped our bickering and looked at him.

"You didn't trip. I tackled you," he hurled his voice at me. "I had to stop you from ending up like Nova. You're too valuable to be doing stupid things like that."

"He's right," added Nova gently.

"And I did see what happened to you, to both of you," Remi continued angrily, turning on Nova. "You barely reached Greeley before Khan took you out. Lucky for you Greeley was screaming and shouting so many orders that in the confusion I don't think she saw how badly you were injured. She called off the tarcats and had the Grifts escort her to Lux, but not before she ordered you both be sent to the locker."

"Both of us?" I asked.

"Yes, *both* of you. She thought you were the main culprit, and I'm sure that's how it looked to everyone. You were chasing Nova, raving like a lunatic. It looked like he was trying to get away from you. I was invisible during the whole incident so no one saw me trip you or follow you both to the locker, so I can go when I want, but you two are stuck down here."

I swallowed hard at the news that I had also been sentenced to the locker. As mad as I was when I first heard that Remi was the one who tripped me and held me down, I knew he was right to do it. If he hadn't I may have ended up as injured as Nova, or worse. Remi was so brave and smart, thinking fast in all that chaos.

"Well, at least Greeley doesn't know how badly you were injured," I said trying to find the silver lining.

"No, but Jest does, and so does half of our year. Everyone in the fields saw the tarcats nearly tear you to pieces and then Jest took you both to the locker and left you down here to die. He had to have known you wouldn't survive with those injuries," Remi said wide-eyed.

I shivered at the thought of it. But Remi was right, and I began to fear we would have a whole new set of problems once we got out of the locker. Tapping into my thoughts, Nova chimed in.

"He's right, Tippy. He'll probably think I'm dead. There's no way we can explain how I miraculously healed. Maybe we can use this to our advantage. But let's not worry about that right now. We have to get to work. We came down here for a reason and I'm going to make sure we get what we came for after all that we've been through."

"Okay," I sighed. "Where do we start?"

"Follow me." Nova snapped and his flame jumped to life in the palm of his hand lighting our way. Remi and I followed closely behind him to the far wall. "Here's where it starts," he said gesturing to the stone wall in front of us.

"It's just a wall," Remi said sounding confused.

"Look closer," Nova replied.

"I see it," I whispered.

My face was inches from the wall but I could see the distinct pattern of dark letters etched into the stone. I produced an orb of light to get a better look and leaned forward to rest my hand against the cool surface of the wall. Suddenly the wall lit up, glowing the same soft blue color of my orb. The light traced the letters, racing around the locker, lighting it up all around us. We instinctively backed closely together.

"Well, that's new," Nova said.

"Doesn't that always happen when you're down here?" I asked hoping his answer would be yes.

He shook his head and smiled at me. "Nope, but I'm not surprised by you anymore."

"I did that?" I asked.

Nova shrugged. "It makes reading a heck of a lot easier," he said as he moved closer to the wall again. "Some of this I haven't even seen before. Let's move down this way more," he said taking swift strides.

"But what about this part?" called Remi, still standing at the beginning of the glowing writing.

"It's mostly just the legend of Lux, the stuff we already know, but if you want to read it knock yourself out."

I looked after Nova, who was striding away from me, and then back at Remi.

"Why don't you start at the beginning in case we missed

something. I'm going to catch up to Nova and see what he finds."

The tortured look on Remi's face made it hard for me to leave him, so I made another orb and bounced it in his direction.

"Here, to light your way," I said as I turned, jogging off to catch up with Nova.

39

It felt like we had been reading for days. I was bleary eyed as I tried to focus on the glowing blue letters before me.

"Anything?" asked Remi, joining us.

"Not yet. You?" I asked.

"Just more about the legend," he sighed. "I need to go back. Sparrow and Journey are probably worried sick and I want to check on Niv."

"I'm sure they're taking care of Niv," I said. "But, yes, you should let them know Nova's okay."

"I won't be gone long and I'll bring you back some food. Is there anything else you need?"

I was about to shake my head, but Nova rattled off a well researched list of supplies that would help us down here, and once again I was grateful for his expertise. After Remi left, Nova told me to take a break and rest a while. For once I didn't fight him. I let myself slide down against the cool stone wall and I shut my eyes, blocking out the eerie blue glow of the illuminated letters and drifted off to sleep.

40

I remember being angry that something was shaking me awake, pulling me from the happiness and comfort of my dreams. I wasn't ready to leave yet, but when I opened my eyes only to be greeted with the beaming face of Nova staring straight back at me I decided that real life actually wasn't half bad. After all, wasn't it Nova I was dreaming about? It was fuzzy, but I was sure of one thing, I was relishing the moment that Nova had kissed me over again in my dreams. Just the thought of it filled me with the tingling lightness I felt in the moment his lips touched mine. I think I murmured a little sigh, but then quickly pulled myself together not wanting to be a total sap.

"Hey, Tippy, sorry to wake you, but I think I found something," Nova said softly.

I let him help me to my feet and I stretched my aching muscles and rubbed my eyes until the dreariness of the locker came back into full focus again. I yawned a little and then obediently followed behind Nova and his dancing firelight as he led me to a portion of the wall I hadn't been to before.

"Here," he said, pointing eagerly to the glowing paragraph before me. "I think this is what we've been looking for."

I stepped forward and read it aloud.

"Only the Book of Secrets can unlock the truth of the chosen ones.

It will never betray the truth to the seeker under the reign of the suns.

Locked away, high and safe, behind the one sworn to protect its secrets, who wishes to enslave the truths of the island, valuing self and greed over the greater good.

To gain what you seek, you must display bravery and strength where one hundred and forty warriors once stood."

"There's that 140 number again. Doesn't that number seem to be coming up a little too often to you?" Nova asked.

"Yeah, now that you mention it. Do you know what it means?" I asked.

"No, not yet, but I'm working on it. Anyway, that's not why I woke you up. Does anything else jump out at you?"

"Yeah, the *Book of Secrets.* This is the first time I've seen it mentioned. It's what Eja told us we need to find, right?"

"Exactly, and I think this tells us precisely where to find it!" Nova announced excitedly.

"Well, I'm glad you know where it is because I have no idea how to decipher this clue."

"Yes, you do. Read it again,and think of someone it might be describing to us."

I started from the beginning again, and this time read it more slowly, concentrating on each line, one at a time. Not during the sun's reign, so during the night then? And locked away, locked away. Where did things get locked away? In the locker? In a drawer? Behind a door? A door! Greeley's tall wooden door. That was high, and always locked and always guarded during the day.

"Oh my gods!" I gasped. "It's Greeley!"

"Yes!" breathed Nova, "It has to be! All these clues point to her! Her office is the only room in the Center that is always locked and always guarded by the tarcats during the day. The only time it's empty is at night. And she's tall, so it will be hidden high and she thinks of us as slaves, that's how we're all treated here at the Center. It has to be her."

"But what about that 140 warriors part?"

"I don't know how that fits in. Maybe it's from another part of the legend, during the war or something?"

"Well, I hope it's not too important because there aren't going to be 140 of us to stand against Greeley. More like five," I added under my breath.

We spent the next few hours going back over the script on the wall, making note of where the number 140 kept cropping up. There were passages about the strength of 140, the speed of 140, the fury of 140, and so on.

"It seems like it's part of the future rather than the past," I said.

"I agree. I only see it at the end of the legend in the prophecy."

"But that makes no sense. Who are these 140 people we're supposed to get to help us?"

"I don't know, Tippy, but I know we're right about Greeley."

"What about Greeley?" came Remi's voice, temporarily startling us.

"Remi!" I said, rushing over to help him.

He returned with a stack of supplies. He had blankets and food and notebooks. It was so good to see him again. We spread out the blankets and sat down to enjoy the fruit and bread he smuggled down to us. I didn't realize how famished I was. I tore the bread into hunks and stuffed them into my mouth and then washed them down with big gulps of water. Then I bit into a mango and let the juice run down my chin in delight. I was enjoying the meal so much I closed my eyes to savor it and laughed at myself, realizing how much I was behaving like Journey, gorging myself on the food before me.

"Sorry," I said sheepishly wiping my face with the back of my hand. "I must have been hungry."

"I'll say," Remi said with a laugh. "Just make sure you save a little for Niv."

"Niv!" I squealed with delight. "You brought him?"

"Yeah, Sparrow insisted. She said he'd been acting sad and she thought he might perk up if I brought him to see you."

Remi opened his shoulder bag and undid the invisibility charm as a sleepy Niv waddled out. He stretched and blinked, twitching his nose all the while. Once he got his bearings and caught sight of me he perked up and trotted over. He climbed into my lap and stood on his hind legs to shower me with kisses.

"Niv! Oh Niv, I missed you, too!"

I whispered a thank you to Remi. He always seemed to know exactly what I needed. Between Niv, the food and my two friends, I was actually able to forget I was stuck in the locker and spent an enjoyable evening chatting with Remi and Nova about what we'd learned from the walls. Remi agreed about Greeley after examining the wall for himself. He seemed to be deep in thought about what the number 140 could mean because he didn't say too much, until he excused himself for the night.

"Well, I hate to leave you down here, but I'm going to go back up our room. I want to fill Sparrow and Journey in on what you've learned. Maybe they'll have some helpful input." He stood to leave, but then turned back. "Will you be okay down here?" he asked us both, but I knew from his eyes he was really talking to me.

"We'll be fine," Nova answered, and graciously thanked him for the food and blankets.

I gave Remi a final reassuring nod and watched him vanish into the darkness.

"You know, you don't have to stay down here," Nova said after a while.

"I know, but I want to," I said with a shrug and I meant it.

I always cherished the time I got to spend with Nova and the locker offered us nothing but unending time. We settled in for the night, wrapping ourselves in the blankets Remi brought us. Niv burrowed his way down to my belly and snuggled up against me, making his little cooing noises that always soothed me. Nova nestled up against me and let me rest my head on his arm. Even though we were in the most dreadful place in the Troian Center, I have to say I had never been happier. I felt so calm and safe in Nova's arms. I let him play with my hair, smoothing it away from my face, lulling me to sleep.

When I awoke I didn't have any idea how much time had passed. Was it morning already? Afternoon? Or perhaps I only just shut my eyes moments ago? Not being able to see the sunlight was really starting to get to me. The peaceful complacency of the previous night had worn off. I anxiously untangled my stiff limbs from my blanket and stood, rubbing my arms to try to get some warmth back in them. Even Niv looked grumpy, with his rumpled beard and heavy eyes barely open, letting me know he was not ready to wake up yet.

"Fine, you stay there then," I grumbled as I started to pace around the room.

Not much had changed. We retracted my orbs and the glowing letters from the wall so we could sleep last night, so I was only using my night vision to get around, not wanting to wake Nova with my other sources of light. I had just reached the far wall, when I heard footsteps above. I turned to see Nova still contently asleep in his blanket. I strained my ears and then heard a heavy latch being lifted and suddenly a bright light beamed down into the room, temporarily blinding me.

"Nova!" I telepathed to him as I stumbled backward, but he was already up and by my side by the time I fully regained my vision. Someone was thumping loudly down the stairs. *"Niv!"* I silently shrieked to Nova. *"He's still in my blanket!"*

"Go, I'll buy you some time if you need it. Get rid of it all, Tippy."

He didn't have to tell me twice. I ran to where I left Niv and sighed with relief when he lifted his fuzzy little head to snuff at me when I reached the blankets. I picked him up and made him invisible right before stuffing him into my shirt. Then I piled up the blankets and things that Remi brought us and made them disappear, too. I wasn't sure who or why someone was coming down to check on us, but we couldn't let them know that we possessed all these supplies or they'd know something was up.

I was panting as I skidded to a stop near Nova on the far wall. We watched a shadowy figure reach the bottom step and bang something metal against the bars that held us captive.

"Come on then, rise and shine, it's you're lucky day, dearies," came Jest's raspy, wicked voice. "It's time to go back to work, for those of you who can," he said, laughing until he sputtered into a coughing fit.

"Why is he coming down here for us already?" I asked.

"Not sure, but I'm about ready to get out, so let's get out of here while we can."

"Okay, but you have to act injured remember?"

Nova winked at me and then slumped over, draping his arm heavily across my shoulders. I instinctively put my arms around his waist to steady him. I knew this was all part of the act to keep up the charade that Nova was still severely injured, but I wished he wasn't laying it on so thick. I was struggling to keep myself upright with his weight anchoring me down. Not to mention he must have accidentally squished the invisible marmouse in my shirt because now Niv was awake and angrily circling my torso, looking for a way out. I tried not to squirm at Niv's tickling as I worked tirelessly to guide an "*injured*" Nova out of the open section of bars, past Jest.

Once we stepped out into the hallway, we were bathed in the warm sunlight beaming down from above. It's comforting glow on my cold skin was short lived though, because as I turned to look at Nova, so did Jest and it was more than apparent that he was no longer injured. I had healed him too well. His shirt was still tattered and blood stained and even his hair was still matted with soil and blood, but his face was flawless. Where there had been gashes of flapping skin across his cheek only two days earlier, there was now perfectly formed skin without even a trace of blood left over. Jest seemed to notice at the same time I did. Thankfully, his brain moved at a much slower pace, as he tried to work out what he was seeing.

"Hey... wait a minute..." was all he got out before I swiped the heavy key ring from his hand and shoved him backward into the locker. I rapidly turned the skeleton key with my trembling fingers and grabbed Nova's hand before he could protest and dragged him up the stairs.

"Tippy!" he shouted at me the whole way. "What did you just do? That wasn't part of the plan!"

I stopped and turned to him when we reached the little room above the locker.

"He figured it out, Nova! He saw right through it. We were so stupid. I did too good of a job healing you to ever convince anyone that you were still injured. You can't see it but your face is perfect and you were a mess! A bloody, near-dead mess when they sent you down here. I'm pretty sure they sent you down here to die and now look at you! I had to think fast or

Jest wasn't going to let us out of there, and he'd surely tell Greeley something was up. Then they'd know. We can't let them on to us, not now when we're so close!" I said trying to drag him toward the door.

"Well, what do you think is going to happen now? Don't you think Greeley's going to notice Jest is missing? Listen to that ruckus he's making down there."

Sure enough Jest was making quite a racket. He was banging something against the metal bars and shouting at the top of his lungs. Even when I shut the trap door to the stairway it only slightly muffled the sound. I could still hear him. I was trembling as my rush of adrenaline started to waver.

"We'll just have to act fast," I said as panic started to set in. I turned to the door and rushed out.

I ran blindly down the hallway back toward room 13. I could hear Nova's footsteps following not far behind. From the warm, golden light that was brightening the gray hallways I could tell it was afternoon. Everyone would be at Flood work, which was perfect. With less people around it would be easier to break into Greeley's office and grab the *Book of Secrets*. I smiled, letting myself be hopeful for the first time, that I was actually going to get to the bottom of this and find out the truth about my parents and myself. I wanted to take advantage of our unplanned escape and go for the book now while the coast was clear. All I needed was my shoulder bag from my room so I'd have something to conceal it in. It was finally in sight. Only a few more strides... I reached for the door and collided with Miss Sprigg.

"There you are!" she shrieked. "You're a mess! Go get changed immediately, we're leaving for the Gala right now!"

I watched in shock and confusion as Miss Sprigg scurried away, giving me full view to the crowdedness of our room. Everyone milled about excitedly as Miss Sprigg continued fussing about how we are already behind schedule. I turned to see if Nova was still behind me, but he had disappeared. He must have heard Miss Sprigg when we got close enough and hid. *Some warning would have been nice,* I huffed to myself. At least I could still count on him to go after the *Book of Secrets.* He had to know this was our best opportunity. I sighed, but I still had hope that it would end tonight.

Sparrow rushed to my side and was busy whispering in my ear, but I wasn't paying any attention. My mind was preoccupied with questions. *How could it be time for the Gala already? How long had we been down there? I thought it was only two nights, had it been longer? It must have been.*

I was still busy trying to do the math when Sparrow's tugging interrupted me. "Come on!" she whispered louder towing me behind her. "We have to get you dressed."

Before I knew it she had me in the Jane's room. I looked at her for the first time and it took my breath away. She looked like an angel, dressed in her white tunic with a beautiful gold sash tied around her slender waist. Her mousy brown hair didn't look mousy at all. It was in a shiny braid and seemed to almost match the liquid amber color of her eyes. All I could do was smile at her.

"What's wrong with you?" she hissed as she unfolded my white tunic. "Wash yourself off quickly so we can get you into this dress."

"Here," I said, handing her Niv who I let become visible as I pulled him from my shirt.

"Hi, sweet boy," she crooned as she took him from me and I slipped away to make myself presentable.

"How is it time for the Gala already?" I called from over the stall door.

"Tippy, you've been down there for four days. We were all worried sick. It was the longest four days of my life!"

"Yeah, but Remi..." I trailed off as I stuffed my head through the tunic.

"Thank goodness Remi was able to check on you each night," she finished for me.

Something wasn't right. Remi had only checked on us once. But he told Sparrow he had been there every night? Where was he really when he said he was checking on us? I didn't have much time to think on it because I heard someone else walk into the Jane's room and the atmosphere suddenly changed. I could feel the panic and tension coming from Sparrow who moments earlier had seemed excited and happy. I felt the joy return to the air, but it was a sickeningly sharp happiness, laced heavily with bitter satisfaction and I knew even before I creaked the door of my stall slightly open who had walked in.

"Well, hello ladies," Jemma said with her eyes locked on Niv, making my heart drop. "Miss Sprigg sent me in here to hurry you along. We're lining up in the courtyard right now and I wouldn't want you to get left behind," she added with extra insincerity.

I stood silently trying to calm my nerves and control the urge to stuff Jemma into a stall and lock her there forever. I was waiting in painful anticipation for her to say something about Niv, but she didn't. She was ignoring his presence completely. Instead she went to the mirror to check her perfect appearance, smoothing her raven-black mane and smiling back at herself vainly. As if she sensed me leering at her, she turned on her heel and gave me a once over, letting a wicked smile slowly spread across her perfect red lips.

Well, you look... nice," she said softly, stifling a nasally laugh. I felt embarrassed that I let her comment automatically force me to look down, but my gown fit well and didn't have any stains or tears; but then I felt my face burn red as I followed her stare to my head where I'm sure my unruly hair was still a matted mess from the locker. Finally she turned to walk out of the room calling over her shoulder, "Don't be too long, Janes."

Sparrow seemed to take a breath for the first time since Jemma entered the room and I took two long strides before I was to her and Niv when I heard the click, click, clicking of Jemma's footsteps pause and my heart began to ice over as they came clicking back toward us, and she called, "Oh and girls, I would leave your little pet some place safe. It would be a shame if Greeley found it." Then she disappeared down the hallway, apparently satisfied that she had rattled us enough for now.

"Tippy!" Sparrow hissed in a frightened whisper that somehow echoed the exact amount of panic I was feeling at the moment. I took hold of Niv and hugged the oblivious little fool tight and then it was as if I had been struck by lightning. A blinding vision just sliced into my brain, paralyzing me momentarily and leaving me gasping for breath. It left as swiftly as it came.

"Tippy! What happened? Are you okay?" Sparrow whimpered looking desperately helpless.

"I don't know. I... I think I just had a vision."

"Of what?"

"I'm not really sure, but it was about Greely and Niv, she's going to find out about him."

"Oh no! Do you think Jemma will tell her about him?"

"She has to. We've got to go stop her."

"Wait, what do we do with him now?"

"We've got to keep him with us. Keep him safe," I said as I started for the door.

"Wait! Maybe that's what Jemma wants us to do. She did say *leave* your pet in a safe place. She wants Greeley to catch us with him. We should leave him here. I think he'll be safer. Just make him invisible again. She'll never find him that way."

I stopped, thinking about it for a moment and Sparrow was right. Jemma did say *leave* and my immediate reaction was to take Niv with me. She was always so good at pushing my buttons and manipulating me that maybe this was part of her plan. I didn't know what to do but we needed to make a decision fast. I could hear all the other orphans filing down the hallway toward the courtyard. The excitement in the air was growing and clouding my thoughts.

"Okay," was all I said as I hugged Niv once more and let him kiss my chin and neck before I turned him into empty space. I pushed out into the crowded hall and then into our now deserted room where I plunked Niv delicately on my bed and pleaded with him to stay out of trouble. I could see the indentations of each of his feet turn into one large dent on my cot bed and I sighed, slightly relieved that he seemed happy to sleep the rest of day away. I turned back to Sparrow and nodded to her that I was ready.

"One more thing," she said coming toward me and laying her hands on the crown of my head. "There, that's much better," she beamed.

"Thanks," I smiled back at her knowing she'd used her favorite magic trick to tame my hair.

We headed for the hallway. I paused to take one more look back at the empty space that was my sweet sleeping little marmouse and I gave an involuntary shiver. I couldn't shake the feeling of impending dread.

42

W e breathlessly reached the courtyard and joined the rest of our year. Journey raised his eyebrows when he caught sight of us and Remi gave me a goofy smile, but I chose to ignore them. I actually even allowed a tiny bit of the Gala excitement to catch hold of me. This was always our favorite day of the year at the Troian Center. We got to skip lessons and work to dress up and go to Lux. Minus the singing, it was actually something I looked forward to. Although I gave up the hopefulness of being adopted, I still enjoyed the beautiful sights and sounds of Lux. It was decorated so elegantly, with thousands upon thousands of candles illuminating the pristine city, lighting our path to the heart of the celebration. The sun-kissed citizens pulled out all their best jewels and most elaborate linens for the New Year Gala, celebrating the rebirth of their flourishing city into another year. My favorite part was the fireworks that lit up the inky night sky after we finished singing, signaling the start of the New Year. It seemed to be the beginning of the night for the citizens, but it's when we headed home, back to the Troian Center, back to being orphans for another year; another year of Flood work, another year of wondering where we truly belonged. I guess it's kind of a bittersweet day, but for that short little bit of time, I got to feel like we were more than just orphans, like we were part of something and I cherished each and every moment. I relished the sights, sounds, and smells of Lux, because even though I have no recollection of my family or my past, I felt most at home during our short yearly visits inside the exquisite gates of Lux.

My excitement was short-lived because Jemma lined herself up next to me, giving me a sly little smile and wink that made my stomach churn. I've shared winks with Nova and Sparrow before, but they signaled trust, friendship, or a secret. I didn't want to share anything with Jemma, especially a secret, because she was bound to save it for the precise time that it could hurt me the most. There was nothing I could do but stand alongside her and watch as the other years filed out of the courtyard ahead of us. I stood anxiously watching them pass. We would go last. We always went last. The oldest orphans would perform first, going in order of oldest to youngest until it came to us. We would close the show, ending with one of Jemma's solos. With her last perfectly timed note the fireworks would begin and applause would erupt. It did give me a small bit of satisfaction to know that Jemma didn't have the solo this year. I couldn't wait to see her have to applaud Sparrow and Remi with the rest of us. As I enjoyed this little victory I turned to look at Jemma, wanting to return a smile and wink of my own, but out of the corner of my eye I caught sight of Nova, marching tall and beautifully dressed, right past us with the rest of his year.

"*No!*" was all I managed to telepath to him as he passed.

"*Later, Tippy. We'll do it later,*" was all he telepathed back to me, obviously picking up on my disappointment that he was joining us at the Gala rather than staying behind to try to retrieve the *Book of Secrets*. I hated all of these delays. They just added to my agitation and that uncomfortable feeling that something was building, just out of reach, but dangerous nonetheless. I started to chew my nails as I watched Nova walk further away, but then he called back to me, *"And you look beautiful by the way,"* making me blush.

I found myself wondering what the heck Sparrow did to my hair. I guess I should have glanced in the mirror on our way out because I was getting some strange looks and now Nova was calling me beautiful. Maybe he was still recovering, or maybe I melted his brain when I was healing him.

"Mmm, John 18 looks great doesn't he?" Jemma said next to me, snapping me back to reality.

"What?" was all I could manage with my blood boiling as I stared at her questioning dark eyes.

Why was it that she couldn't let me have anything that made me happy? And why was she even talking to me. This was the most we'd ever conversed. I tried to gauge where she was coming from and for a moment I thought I saw her stern wall of unapproachability soften.

"I heard he got pretty messed up by Khan trying to pull some prank on Greeley, but he looks fine, don't you think?"

"I guess," I mumbled still staring straight ahead.

"Perhaps things aren't always what they seem," she replied looking straight ahead again with her emotionless wall back in place, battle ready once more as we marched on.

43

Our progress halted outside the giant white gates of Lux where we were inspected before we were permitted to enter. We waited while Greeley, who was seated comfortably in a plush covered carriage pulled by two jittery horses, passed us. While we were made to walk the vast distance of sun-cracked earth that separated us from Lux, Greeley always rode contently in her elaborate horse-drawn carriage. Of course Khan and Ria were afforded such luxury as well, which is probably what attributed to the nervous snorts from the horses. As I watched Khan pass by me I shuddered at the flashback of him mauling Nova. It was hard to believe the big tarcat, who was now lounging lazily behind Greeley with one massive paw flopping carelessly outside the cart, was the same one who almost killed my friend. And even Ria, who often seemed playful and sweet, with her slender body now curled up at Greely's feet, was in on the action. I realized we were foolish to underestimate them.

As we waited for the guards of Lux to give us the customary once-over, I found myself gazing at the massive gates that separated us from the citizens of Lux. It was almost bizarre the way these two solid doors were what separated us from the other; locals from citizens, luxury from lower class. I never noticed this before, but all of a sudden it seemed silly to me. These were just doors, highly structured ones at that, but still doors just the same. I guess it was what lay behind the doors that we coveted; the freedom and thrilling beauty of the sparkling city. It may have been just another seaside city before the Flood, but to us it was a land of secrets and mystery. Every time I had a chance to be inside the gates I would feel the excitement and allure catch hold of my heart. It had such a pull on me that it seemed like a place I was destined to be. As we finally started marching forward again, I kept hold of this thought; *Lux is my destiny*. Tonight I would find out the truth, no matter what.

44

The trusted guards of Lux deemed we were worthy enough to enter their protected city and gave us a long and ceremonious bow, which signaled the trumpeters to announce our arrival and the official beginning of the New Year Gala. As we passed under the shining arch that adorned the gated city I could feel my heartbeat quicken. With the sun setting, the gleaming white city emitted a beautiful golden glow. All the lavishly dressed citizens stopped what they were doing to line the streets and cheer for us, celebrating our arrival. Perhaps they were really only excited that the festivities had officially begun, rather than the fact that the local orphans were arriving, but I chose to believe the latter because it was my favorite part of the whole night. For that moment I felt special, important, loved. Each year it got better, too, because I got closer and closer to the front since the older years had moved on.

This year was just as wonderful as always. Upon entering the city I was hit with a sensory overload. I didn't know whether to look at the beautiful people layered in expensive jewels and fabrics, or to stare at the breathtaking beauty of the setting red sun, casting vibrant hues frolicking across the sea. I could see the pollen and dust caught in beams of pinks and oranges dancing slowly in the air, as if drunk off the beauty of the sunlight. The air was heavy with the intoxicating scents of sweets and spices. I could smell the mulled cider and brown sugar coated nuts roasting, and I swear if I closed my eyes I could almost taste the cinnamon date cakes. My ears were ringing from the applause and joyful shouts in our direction, until they were drowned out by the fast tempo of horns and percussion that swept us up as we got closer to the center of the chaos.

Yes, the sights, smells and sounds of Lux were dizzying, and even more wonderful than I remembered. They were like a dear friend I didn't realize I'd been missing until they came back home.

As I followed the others down the steep and winding streets, I kept reminding myself to watch my step because it was hard to keep my eyes from wandering to the thousands of pale paper lanterns glowing overhead. They lined the streets, stretching up to the cliff-side homes and all the way out to sea. Above my head they bobbed light and airy, in the soft warm breeze. In the distance they looked smaller, almost like they were floating unassisted, just like my shiny little orbs in the forest; and I couldn't help but smile. Then there were the starch-white homes, which were not to be outdone by the lanterns. They each boasted magnificent displays of candles burning brightly on their windowsills, vestibules and walls. Every little crevice of a ledge was filled with piles of white candles in varying sizes, set ablaze in melted, waxy arrangements. Tonight, Lux was a fireball of light.

As we reached the stage, I came back to reality a bit more. I always started to get nervous once we all crammed behind the stage curtains, cloaked from the excitement of the crowd beyond. They smelled musty to me, probably from being packed away all year long. Sparrow was instantly next to me the minute Jemma left my side. We gave each other a worried look and then went to find Journey and Remi. I found myself letting that old foreboding feeling creep back up to settle in its familiar place in my chest.

"What was that all about?" Remi asked, looking as engaged as I'd seen him in a while.

"Yeah, why were you walking with Jemma?" Journey asked with his eyebrows raised.

"I wasn't walking with her you dummy, she was walking with me!"

"Oh, there's a difference?" Journey half-heartedly challenged.

I rolled my eyes at him but dropped it. Instead, I turned to Sparrow and asked, "Are you ready for your solo?"

"Yes," she nodded nervously.

"And you?" I asked Remi.

"Yeah," he shrugged.

"Okay, well then we need to get a plan together for after the performance. I know where the *Book of Secrets* is and we have to get it tonight!"

"What? How? Where? Why tonight?" Sparrow sputtered while the boys just exchanged questioning glances with each other.

"Yes, it has to be tonight. Don't you guys see? Tonight is our best chance. There's so much going on that no one will suspect us. It's not a regular night where we'd look like we were obviously up to no good if we're out of bed late. Maybe we can try to sneak back to the Center early? Maybe we can – "

"That seems like an awful lot of maybes, 65," interrupted Remi.

I was about to protest, when I felt Nova behind me. He broke away from his year to join our little powwow in the back corner of the stage, where he comfortably slung his arm over my shoulders and I relaxed under the warmth of it. "She's right. If the book is where we think it is, tonight's the night. It's our best chance."

I smiled triumphantly back at Remi, but my gloating was short-lived.

"But, Tippy, we have to be smart about this," he said looking down at me before looking back to the group. "We can't try to sneak out of here early. *That* would be too obvious. We'll just leave the feast early," Nova added. "Agreed?"

We looked around at each other, knowing this was it. We were deciding to put forth a motion that couldn't be stopped once started. I could tell the seriousness of it was weighing heavily on each of us, and that was the way it should be. After seeing what happened to Nova I think we all realized this wasn't child's play any longer. His idea of leaving the dining hall tonight was definitely our best option. After the Gala we always returned to a wonderful feast at the Troian Center. This was often the highlight of the night for us orphans, but I was so preoccupied with everything else that it was far from my mind this year. I looked at the others and they were all looking at me for some reason, so I decided to step forward.

"Agreed," I seconded, reaching for Nova's hand.

The others nodded in agreement and joined hands with Nova and me, filling me with nervousness and calmness all at once.

45

Well, we had a plan. At least it was something. It seemed we were spiraling out of control since our last plan to get sent to the locker was hatched. I swallowed hard, hoping this one would work out better.

Remi and Sparrow headed off to practice their solos and Journey and Nova were deep in conversation about something. I walked over to them and almost wished I hadn't when I heard the subject matter.

"It really looks great. You can't even tell your face used to be shredded," Journey marveled.

"Yeah, Tippy did an incredible job," Nova said, sending a wink my way.

"How'd you do it?" Journey asked, focusing on me now.

"I don't know, I just did," I said roughly, immediately regretting my harsh tone.

"Sorry," I said, "It actually wasn't easy and it's not a great memory for me."

"Okay, I get it. I'm just really glad you were able to save

him," Journey said with more sincerity than I knew he possessed.

"I think you may have done *too* good of a job though. I swear I look even better than before," Nova joked, ribbing me a bit to try to lighten my mood.

"Yeah, we are getting some strange looks in our direction," I added with concern.

"Oh, well I think those are on account of how beautiful you look," Nova replied, giving my shoulders an affectionate squeeze, which instantly weakened my knees and made my cheeks burn scarlet red.

"Yeah, you do look really, uh... pretty...tonight," Journey said almost sheepishly.

"Alright, I'm convinced you've both gone mental tonight. I'm going to go see if Sparrow and Remi need any help rehearsing."

I left the boys to themselves and set off to find Sparrow and Remi. I had some things I needed to discuss with Remi, too. Like, where the heck he was going when he was supposedly checking on Nova and I every night? Maybe tonight wasn't the best time to confront him, but I was figuring out that I wasn't very good at leaving things unsaid and we promised each other no more secrets. I was rehearsing how to best approach the subject with Remi when I was startled by a passing reflection. I paused and took a few steps backward toward the mirror I just past. It was very old, covered in dust and utterly unremarkable in every way. It was dull and almost hidden by bolts of old fabric that were slung over it, but it was the strange face in its reflection that peaked my interest. My heart pounded as I walked toward the eerie image. I knew from the angle I should be looking at myself, but there was no way that the face looking back at me was mine. I didn't know her, yet she was somehow familiar. Her snow-blonde hair, intricately plaited, lit up the mirror, giving it an ethereal glow. I crept even closer, drawn helplessly to the light and beauty. The closer I got the more the feeling of familiarity grew inside of me. It tugged at my heart, begging my brain to make the connection. The reflection looked like me, yet not. The hair color was right, but it was so smooth, and shiny, and beautifully done. The eyes were similar but they seemed bluer, deeper, wiser, and more dynamic. The skin was the same tone, but flawless, and the lips were fuller and painted a beautiful shade of red. If I didn't know any better I would think I was meeting a relative, someone with the potential and opportunities that I never had. Someone confident and beautiful. I pressed my palm to the smooth glass and felt a jolt of iciness stab me in the heart, while in the same moment my veins seemed to burn hot. It took my breath away. Gasping for air, I pulled back from the mirror and sat down still facing it.

"Oh my gods," I whispered to myself. "I know who you are. You're Nesia."

I sat there reeling in my discovery. How was it possible that this mirror was turning my reflection into that of Nesia, the famous goddess of our island? I knew it had to be her. I had read so much about her and studied drawings and paintings. But the reflection of flesh and blood was new and harder to place at first, yet now that I had, it was impossible to shake. But why was she here, in my reflection? I was leaning forward for a closer look when Remi called my name, startling me.

"65! 65! I need you to talk some sense into Sparrow! Come on," he said pulling me to my feet and dragging me away from the mirror. I tried to interrupt him but he was babbling on and I was only catching bits and pieces as he tugged me through the crowed backstage.

"Remi! Stop! Tell me what's going on."

"That's the problem! I don't know what's going on. One

minute we're rehearsing and then Sparrow tells me she's not going to do the solo!"

"What?"

"That's what I'm trying to tell you! I went to go get some warm honey water for us and when I came back she was in tears. She said she wasn't doing the solo anymore and then she ran off. You need to go talk to her."

"Where is she?"

"She stormed off in that direction," he said, pointing to a dark corner of the stage.

I sighed and headed off in that direction myself. Sure enough I found her, kneeling in the corner with her back to me, fidgeting with something on the floor.

"Sparrow?" I asked softly. "What's wrong?"

She turned her tear-stained face to look up at me and then handed me a shoulder bag. At first I was confused but then it hit me that it was my shoulder bag and the moving bundle inside was Niv.

"He's okay!" Sparrow added quickly when she saw the panic in my eyes.

"How did he get here?" I gasped while stepping further into the shadows so I could see for myself that Niv was safe. His tiny black eyes peered back at me as he curiously sniffed the new smells of Lux. I nuzzled him and scratched briefly under his chin before securing him back inside the bag before anyone else had the chance to spot him.

"Jemma had him," Sparrow whispered.

"What? How?"

"I don't know, Tippy. She just came over to me a few minutes ago and said that I had something that belonged to her. I had no idea what she was talking about. I was about to say so, but then she said it was okay, because now she had something that belonged to me, so we were even. That's when she handed me the bag. She said, 'Even trade, don't you think?' And then she walked away."

I was speechless and seething mad, but unable to process how this happened. When I didn't respond Sparrow fell into her quiet sobs again.

"I'm so sorry, Tippy, I didn't know what else to do. I was afraid she'd tell Greeley on me if I didn't give in. She practically said so, with that smug look on her face."

"It's okay, Sparrow, none of this is your fault. I'm just sorry you won't get to do the solo now."

"I don't care about the stupid solo anymore," she sniffed, wiping her eyes with the back of her hands. "I'm just glad Niv is safe."

"And I think he'll stay that way now that Jemma got what she wanted, but we're going to need somewhere safe to hide him during the performance. Let's get back to the others," I said, taking the opportunity to return Sparrow's earlier favor by placing my hands on her head to restore her hair and make up to its pre-Jemma encounter.

I led Sparrow back over to the others and we filled them in on what happened. They were just as upset as we were. We were hastily discussing what options we may have to get Sparrow her solo back when Miss Sprigg rushed backstage, clearing her throat to try to get our attention.

"Gather 'round please! I said, gather 'round!" she squawked, stomping her foot to gain our focus. "Everyone please line up with your year, we're getting ready to begin any moment now."

Nova rolled his eyes at Miss Sprigg's dramatics, trying to lighten our tense mood, but the way he squeezed my hand as he departed our little circle told me he was just as concerned as I was. I sighed and relented to follow the others to line up with our year. I saw Jemma trot over, smiling from ear to vicious ear as she took Sparrow's spot along side Remi. My face burned and I gritted my teeth so hard with hatred for her that I was sure they would break. I was so angry with myself that despite all these special powers I had, there was nothing I could do. There was no way to get Sparrow her part back and give Jemma what she deserved. Not if I wanted to protect Niv. The only thing I had going for me was that it seemed that Jemma thought Niv belonged to Sparrow. At least she didn't know he was mine. I couldn't even fathom how she would plot to use him against me. Yet she still had me cornered, even if she didn't know it. At that very moment, I was beginning to understand the dangers of tethering my soul to Niv. Still, I knew I didn't really have a choice. Now I just had to do what was necessary to keep him protected. Well, both of us protected.

"Curtains!" came Miss Sprigg's high, nasally voice. A foreboding hush fell over us, leaving me shivering with a rush of goose flesh. She gave a little nod and then quietly said the same thing she said every year, but this time it held a different meaning for me.

"Let it begin!"

46

I stood quietly next to the other Johns and Janes in my year, feeling isolated and alone since I was separated from my friends. It almost felt like just another Gala, standing alone in the dark, terrified of what was ahead. But this time it wasn't the singing or stage fright that had me in a cold sweat. I was so busy concentrating on keeping Niv and my shoulder bag invisible that I didn't have any time to be nervous about those trivial things. It was Journey's idea to use the vanishing trick to keep Niv hidden. It seemed like the safest route because we all felt a bit uncomfortable leaving Niv unattended in my bag backstage. There were so many people around and we still didn't know how Jemma found him in the first place. Keeping him with us was the only way to know for sure that he was safe. The only problem was that I had to do it. Remi was the best at it, but he had a solo to do, so I was the only other option. Normally, I shouldn't have so much trouble with it, but for some reason it was taking much more concentration than usual. Maybe it was because I was distracted by Jemma's giggling. Each time she laughed it sounded like she was ringing little bells of victory in my ears. I took deep breaths to calm myself and was thankful that it was almost our turn.

Before I knew it, Miss Sprigg was scurrying around us, straightening our sashes, reminding us to stand up straight and smile. Then she ushered us forward. Typically, I dreaded this moment, but it signaled that this awful event was almost over, so I welcomed the bright lights and loud applause as we marched onto the stage. The air was much cooler and the sweat I had worked up felt like tiny beads of ice sliding cruelly down my spine. I shivered in the slight breeze that still carried the faint aromas that enchanted me upon our arrival. Below me was a sea of white and gold. From the height of the stage I couldn't make out the faces of the citizens, only their glowing linens and jewels, brightly illuminated by the warm glow of thousands of candles and paper lanterns bobbing and flickering lazily in the soft wind.

Moments after we took the stage the drumbeats started, then the strings and horns joined in and the sound swelled, drowning out any other thoughts I had. As soon as the music reached its peak, it was our cue to begin. I somehow managed to find my notes and muddle through the song. I can't say I even knew what I was singing, but I assumed I was doing alright since the Janes to my left and right weren't giving me any telling glares. I was thankful for all the practice sessions Sparrow put me through because my voice was able to operate on autopilot, while my mind concentrated on Niv. I was glad to be bunched up in the middle of the pack. It made me hard to see and eased my anxiety about anyone seeing Niv even if my focus slipped up. I felt his warm little body resting contently on my hip. It was comforting to have him so close. He always had a way of soothing me. I meditated on the steady thumping of his heartbeat and although it sounded more distant than it should, I found a way to relax a little more by melting into its beating rhythm.

I was pulled back to where we were when I saw movement ahead of me. Jemma and Remi were emerging to the front of the stage to begin their solos. Jemma's perfect black mane swayed effortlessly as she sauntered forward with the regal quality of royalty. I tried to avert my eyes and anger from her to only watch Remi. I focused on how proud I was that my best friend was getting his moment to shine. The smooth tone of his voice was beautiful. I never truly appreciated it until this very moment. His rich, warm tenor of melody hit my heart and seemed to make everything brighter. I felt lighter, like I could float along with his notes to anywhere they would take me. I leaned forward on the tips of my toes, straining for a glimpse of his face, but I could only see his profile. I wanted to share in this joyous moment with him, run to his side and hug him and tell him how wonderful he sounded. But my blissful moment was quickly shattered by the clear, sharp soprano that Jemma expertly delivered. I watched her take a step forward, trying to edge Remi out of view, but he surprisingly held his ground by taking a step of his own. Not to be outdone, Jemma took another step, but I watched in horror as Remi anticipated it and swiftly tucked his now invisible foot in her path, which sent her pitching forward. Her note flew high and off key as she fought to gain her balance—arms flapping— before her voice was finally silenced with a thud as she hit the hard floor of the stage, leaving only Remi's voice to ring in the New Year as the Gala fireworks erupted and paper lanterns took flight, waking the sleepy night sky.

47

Everything was exploding—the sky, my mind, Jemma's fury. Luckily, not too many people seemed to notice Jemma's fall since it perfectly coincided with the beginning of the fireworks. Even now, everyone's faces were drawn skyward, watching the spellbinding eruptions of color and light. I could feel the aftershock of each explosion boom through my chest and I was struggling to tell whether the alarm I felt was from the fireworks or that of Jemma's wrath.

Remi hadn't even taken time to bow. He was back in the pack and we were struggling to get to each other as our year was corralled off stage. I tried to stay put while the other orphans funneled around me, but I kept getting swept up in the crowd. It didn't help that I had to try to keep an invisible marmouse sheltered as well. I caught sight of Sparrow linking arms with Remi and I breathed a sigh of relief that he wasn't alone as I let myself get ushered backstage. It took a minute for my eyes to adjust to the dimly lit staging area again, and when I finally got my bearings in the swirling crowd of orphans I spotted Nova and ran straight into his arms. I couldn't help myself. I was fighting so hard to keep everything together that when I felt him wrap his warm arms around me I melted, completely dissolving into the true mess I felt like inside.

"Nova? What are we going to do?" I breathed into his chest. "Did you see what..."

"I saw," was all he said and then he pushed me back away from him and looked me in the eyes. "Are you sure you still want to do this?"

All the fury and determination I felt when we fled the lockers returned, surging through my veins, fueled even stronger by Jemma's wickedness tonight. It had to end tonight. No more excuses.

"Yes."

Nova nodded at me as the others arrived. We all gave each other tense glances, but then Sparrow fell into a fit of giggles.

"What's wrong with you?" I hissed, staring at her wide-eyed. But then Remi dissolved into laughter as well and we all couldn't help ourselves.

"You're mental, you know that?" I said, rolling my eyes at Remi as I tried to stifle my own laughter while giving him a playful shove.

"I don't even know what came over me. It just happened. But I wish you could have seen her face! I don't know what part was better, the shock as she fell, or the pure embarrassment when she got up," Remi snorted.

"Her voice was pretty great, too!" Journey added, grinning widely.

"Alright, I agree it was funny, but we need to stay out of her way for now because she's going to want revenge for getting embarrassed like that and we have more important things to worry about," Nova added, bringing us all sharply back to reality.

We recomposed ourselves and lined up for our final act of the night, the Troian Center Promenade. All the orphans had to line up by year and parade slowly across the stage showing the number boldly tattooed upon their shoulder, hoping some compassionate citizen would take pity on them and offer to adopt them. After an adequate time on stage we'd all bow and head back to the Troian Center, fading into the night, merely an afterthought to the citizens until the next year's Gala deemed us necessary again.

I always hated this part of the evening. It felt so degrading to walk across the stage one by one, showing every angle, with the hope that someone would find you worthy. It made me feel so vulnerable and exposed. Like I said, I didn't hold out any hope that I'd be fortunate enough to be adopted. In my experience the citizens only want babies or very, very young children that they could raise as their own. But by now, I'm sure their opinion of us was that we were all a bunch of lost causes. Nothing more than lowly, dirty locals, living in squalor and doing the manual labor that they would never dream of participating in. It was interesting to see how some of the other orphans were still hopelessly optimistic. They each had different strategies to get noticed. Most of the Johns would walk straight and tall and flaunt their muscular build, while others, mostly the Janes, would try to play on the sympathy of the citizens by looking meek and fragile, almost frightened. It was hard for me to hold back my aggravation when I saw this behavior from the same not-so-fragile Janes who helped Jemma torment me daily. Jemma, for as much as I despised her, at least handled herself with dignity on stage. She walked tall and proud and smiled brightly to the crowd, giving a little curtsy before she walked off.

When it was finally my turn, I tried to get it over as quickly as possible. Scurrying across the stage, spinning in my circle in the middle with a pause for a half-bow, before retreating to the darkness and safety of the curtains on the far side of the stage. I sighed, finally feeling relaxed knowing I'd made it through the evening, with Niv safely hidden and all of my friends still intact. So far, anyway. I'm sure Jemma would have more to say to us at the feast when we returned to the Center, but for now I was trying not to think about it. I breathed in the contentment I felt for surviving the night thus far, and took my final look at the sparkling city before we would depart on our journey back to the Troian Center.

48

The way we exited Lux was never as grand as how we entered. We left through a back door in the stage and filed silently uphill along a white walled passageway until we reached the gate, where we unceremoniously filtered out into the dark, cold night. The finality of the slamming gates rang freshly in our ears, and reminded us that we were not part of this beautiful city. We were just visiting and would will fade away from the citizens as unnoticed as the dissipating smoke from the fireworks.

The walk home seemed to go by quickly. Everyone was at ease with the performances behind them and eagerly chatting about the awaiting feast at the Troian Center. The other orphans were taking wild guesses at what kind of treats would be served this year, making wagers and comparing favorites. The Johns teased about what types of creepy-crawlies might be covered in chocolate, making the Jane's squeal and squirm. A debate about chocolate-covered civer ants versus chocolate-covered beetles broke out and seemed to be getting heated. Someone else was shouting that candied jellyfish beat both.

Despite the happy mood of the group and the fact that I

was walking with Sparrow, Journey and Remi, I didn't feel much like celebrating. I wasn't even looking forward to the deep-fried custard cakes that I dreamt of all year long. All I could think about was Niv and Jemma. My mind was still buzzing, unable to figure out how she found him in the first place, and I couldn't shake the feeling that she had more in store for us tonight after the stunt that Remi pulled on the stage. I was keeping a keen eye on her bobbing raven head in the distance. As long as I could keep her in my sights I felt a little less panicked.

Journey and Remi were still reliving Jemma's fall even as we entered the courtyard. They were hooting and ribbing each other. Remi's actions seemingly moved him up a notch in Journey's opinion, and the two of them were in cahoots more than I'd ever seen. Sparrow was rolling her eyes, but every so often she'd let her composure slip and a giggle would escape her pursed lips. I was grateful when I felt Nova nearby. I headed in the direction from which I felt his presence, wanting to talk to him as soon as possible.

"Quite a night, huh?" he said, eyebrows raised.

"I don't even know where to begin," I said smiling back at him.

Even with all the craziness we'd just encountered and knowing there was surely much more in store for us tonight, Nova's smile had a way of soothing me. For half a moment, I felt like everything was going to be all right.

"You okay, Tippy?" he asked giving my shoulder a squeeze.

"Yeah, I'm just a little shook up from everything that happened at the Gala I guess. I just want to get tonight over with. And I don't want any more hiccups."

Nova studied my face, narrowing his piercing-green eyes a bit. It always made my skin burn hot, feeling his eyes studying me so intensely.

"Tippy, what aren't you telling me?" he asked. "What else happened?"

"What do you mean?" I asked, genuinely sure I wasn't intentionally hiding anything from him at the moment.

"I don't know. I just feel like something's off. Something's got you spooked. What'd you see a ghost or something?" he joked, giving me a little nudge with his shoulder.

Just then my eyes lit up. The ghost! After all the commotion backstage, finding Niv, and Jemma tripping, I had totally forgotten about the figure I saw in the mirror.

"Yes," I gasped, feeling the icy goose flesh race up my spine and spread out over my cheeks.

"Jeez, I was joking with you, Tippy. What's the matter?"

"I think I really did see a ghost. I meant to tell you earlier so you could check it out, too, but I got so distracted. I found this mirror and when I looked at the reflection in it, it wasn't mine. I... I think it was Nesia," I whispered.

"Okay, I think you might need to sit down or something."

"No, I'm not crazy. Nova, I know what I saw and it wasn't me. The girl looking back at me wasn't even a girl, she was a woman, and she was beautiful. She had perfect red lips and ice blue eyes that almost glowed, and her blonde hair was even brighter than mine, and perfectly braided, and..."

I stopped talking when Nova took my chin lightly in his hand, softly brushing his thumb over my parted lips. I held my breath, not knowing what was coming next. But he released me and showed me the red smudge on his thumb. I stared at it perplexed, as he lightly touched the crown of my head, releasing my wild blonde hair, cascading down my back.

"Tippy," he said quietly. "You were finally seeing yourself tonight. You saw what I see, what we all see. You are so beautiful," he said reaching for my face again, inching his closer to mine, until I could feel his breath, warm against my skin.

"No," I whispered. "It wasn't me..." but then I couldn't finish, I was lost in Nova, totally absorbed in his closeness, wishing his words were true, as they clouded the sharpness of the memory of what I thought I saw in the mirror. I wanted to give in, I wanted him to be right, because I longed to be that beautiful girl in the reflection, but I still had a feeling that my eyes hadn't deceived me. I felt my breath catch as his lips drew closer to mine, and I closed my eyes. But before we could connect, the sharp *gong* rang out through the courtyard, startling us and signaling the beginning of our feast.

Shrieks of excitement erupted, filling the courtyard and infusing the air with so much jubilation that it was hard to recognize the Center as the same orphanage we resided in daily. Nova smiled down at me and shrugged, suggesting we should head in as well. We followed the crowd into the brightly lit dining hall. This was the one time that we weren't restricted to our normal order. It was such a chaotic scene that I had to laugh. Everywhere I looked there were orphans piling their plates with as much as they could carry, stuffing food in their mouths with sighs of delight, letting oozy syrups drip down their arms as they licked their fingers for every last drop of decadence. The scene was dizzying. The normally dim dining hall flickered to life with hundreds of candelabras atop our tables, which were covered in bright papers and tropical leaves. The whole scene was topped off by the strings of boldly colored lanterns draped with streamers hanging above our heads. This was by far the best day of the year at the Troian Center. It almost made the rest of the year seem bearable.

I sighed when I spotted the rest of my friends, already enjoying the splendor of treats before them at our table. They were cheering each other sloppily with mugs of mulled cider. It made me feel hesitant to ruin the moment by asking them to come with me to find the *Book of Secrets*. Maybe it would be better to do it on my own and let them enjoy their meal.

"Don't even think about it, Tippy," came Nova's voice in my head.

I sighed again, but this time I sat at the table and tried to enjoy a chocolate teacake, slipping pieces into my invisible shoulder bag when I could. After a few more minutes of celebrating I decided we needed to get down to business.

"Alright, if we've had enough to eat I think we should discuss our plan," I said, interrupting Journey and Remi mid-toast.

"Yea...awl't...ls'do-ts..." Journey mumbled with a full mouth. I stared at him no longer trying to disguise my disgust for his eating habits.

"He means, 'All right, let's do this'," Sparrow interpreted, with a shy grin.

"Okay, good. I'm glad somebody speaks 'Journey'," Nova joked. "Here's what I'm thinking. The simpler our plan, the better. Tippy and I will leave first and head to Greeley's office. Journey and Remi, you give us a good head start and then follow. Sparrow, we're going to need you to stay here as our lookout. If you hear or see anything suspicious telepath to Journey, okay?"

Everyone nodded, but started to look uneasy, realizing that this wasn't just talk anymore; it was actually going to happen.

"You're sure the book is in Greeley's office?" Sparrow asked.

"According to the part of the legend we read in the locker, that's where we think it will be," I said.

"What are you going to do when you get it?" Remi asked.

This made me pause for a second, realizing that I hadn't really thought beyond finding the book. "Bring it back to our room I guess. We can do the invisible charm on it until we can take it out to the forest with us."

"Works for me," Journey shrugged.

"Okay. Well, here goes nothing," Nova said, winking at the others as he got up from the table and sauntered out of the dining hall.

I took a last look around the table at my friends, thanking each of them with my eyes. I looked to Remi last, locking eyes with him, feeling his concern and fear for me in each frantic thump of his heart. I quickly looked down, not wanting to absorb his worry. I pushed back from the table and walked out of the happy dining hall, and into the dark hallway of my destiny.

49

I caught up to Nova in the hall. He was waiting for me outside the John's room. He was right, now was the perfect time for us to do this. There were groups of orphans wandering the halls; on their way back to their rooms, visiting with other years, heading back to the dining hall for seconds. We were able to blend in easily. The fact that we didn't look suspicious among the other orphans did little to calm my nerves. I think I actually would have preferred the halls to be empty as they usually were. All the commotion was unsettling. I felt like every set of eyes was on us, despite the reality that no one paid us a second look. They probably just thought we were a couple of lovebirds looking to celebrate the New Year together. This thought made my cheeks burn, so I put my head down and pushed forward through the crowd that was now thinning as we got closer to Greeley's office. Even though the other orphans all knew she was never here after hours, it still felt wrong to celebrate too close to her office. It was as if the shadowy atmosphere around it could choke the joy right out of the very air we breathed.

I slowed to a stop a good twenty paces from her door,

letting the heaviness of the situation settle in my chest. I read-
justed the invisible shoulder strap of my bag and froze. Niv! I
still had him with me. I had been in such a rush to get my plan
into action that I had forgotten about him! Perhaps it was
because he had been with me all night and having him close
was almost like a security blanket for me, soothing and
calming my anxiety. Yet in this moment I felt paralyzed that I
brought him so close to the mouth of danger. Nova stood
behind me, sensing my fear and reading my thoughts.

"It's okay, Tippy. I think he's actually safer with us right
now than anywhere else considering what Jemma did earlier."

"You're right. I just... I just worry about him so much. If
anything ever happened – "

"Nothing's going to happen," he cut me off. "The others
should be on their way here. Let's get started on the lock so
we'll be able to slip in as soon as they arrive."

I nodded and took a deep breath as I stepped out of the
protection of the shadowy corner I plastered myself into and
followed Nova to Greeley's office door. It only took a moment
for Nova to check the door. It was locked as usual. I was busy
staring at the worn spots on the floor where the tarcats
normally sat. Their constant pacing had worn a smooth, dark
trail from one end of the door to the other. Where were they
all tonight? I hadn't seen any on our way to the office. Thankfully, Nova drew my attention to him before I could let myself
slip into the dark thoughts of my last tarcat encounter.

"You'll have to unlock it."

"What do you want me to do?" I asked.

"Can you echo Journey's strength?"

"Yes, but that won't help with the lock. I'll just end up
breaking the door down."

Nova grinned at me with that old twinkle in his eye,
"What's wrong with that?"

"Um, won't that be a little obvious?"

"Hey, we've got to get into that room one way or another. Unless you know a better way…"

"Alright," I whispered. "Just stand guard okay, and make sure no one is coming."

Nova's face lit up again and he gave me a nod as he walked a few paces off to keep watch. I turned back to the door and took a deep breath as I reached for the doorknob. The iron was cold and rough in my hand. I closed my eyes and concentrated, feeling the same power and strength Journey taught me to harness returning on command. The warmth and light of the power rushed through my body and I channeled it all to the doorknob securely in my palm. With a slow whine, the knob cranked against the locking mechanism within, turning further and further, until there was a crisp *click*! I opened my eyes on baited breath as I watched the door slowly creak open as I released the knob.

"*Nova! We're in!*"

"Great job, Tippy! Such finesse. Although, I was kind of looking forward to some Journey-like destruction."

"Very funny. Let's go."

"Wait, I hear Remi and Journey. You go in and I'll meet them and show them in."

Before I could protest Nova was shoving me inside and the door was closing between us. I felt a moment of panic being in Greeley's office alone, but I concentrated on slowing my breath and calming my nerves. All the late-night forest training had really paid off. I pulled forth my night vision and got my bearings. Greeley's office was cold and dark. It seemed damp; bone chilling even. It was nothing like the other rooms in the Troian Center. The parts of the walls that weren't lined in bookshelves were smooth and curved. They were a silvery color that shimmered in a way that almost appeared wet. The floor was stone, rather than dirt and it was covered in layers of expensive-looking rugs. There were no windows in this room. For light, there were hanging candelabras and lanterns of different shapes and sizes. There were large torch fixtures bolted into the walls that seemed easy enough to light. I tossed an orb to each and soon the room was glowing as I transformed my light source to fire as Nova had taught me while we were in the locker. I walked forward to Greeley's massively ornate desk. It was as black as Jemma's hair and its scrolling details were encrusted with glittering stones and gems. Behind it was her plush, green-velvet chair, although throne may have been a more accurate word. The enormous chair looked like a castle, with its two spiked pillars rising high above me. In front of the desk were the all too familiar kneeling blocks, where we were forced to repent as Greeley doled out punishments to difficult orphans. I'd been on these blocks before and gave them a wide berth because of the bitter memories they were conjuring up. I could feel the sadness of this room. The atmosphere was heavy and old; perhaps remnants of all the emotions left behind by the terrified orphans who had come before our headmistress.

The door behind me creaked and I instantly vanished myself from view. A moment later, three familiar heads poked in and I breathed a sigh of relief to see Remi, Journey and Nova all file into the room.

"What took you so long?"

"Sorry, there were a bunch of Johns in the hallway outside. We had to wait until they left. What'd you find?" Nova asked.

"Nothing yet."

"What were you doing? Taking a tour?" Journey asked, trying to mask his nerves.

"Shut up," I hissed. "I was turning on the lights," I said gesturing to the glowing torch lights.

"Okay, let's get to work. We're looking for the *Book of Secrets,* so fan out. There's a lot of book shelves to cover," Nova said.

"Any hints here?" Journey called from a bookshelf to the right of the desk.

"Only the *Book of Secrets* can unlock the truth to the chosen ones," I called back. "It will never betray the truth to the seeker under the reign of the suns. Locked away, high and safe, behind the one sworn to protect its secrets, who wishes to enslave the truths of the island, valuing self and greed over the greater good. To gain what you seek, you must display bravery and strength where one hundred and forty warriors once stood."

"Um, okay, I said hints, 65, not riddles," Journey said, smiling for the first time since we'd entered Greeley's office.

I kept repeating the mantra softly to myself, willing it to guide me to what I was looking for. I was fairly certain that Greeley was the one enslaving the truth and protecting the secrets, which is why we were in her office to begin with. The legend said the book would be 'locked away high and behind...' I grabbed her ancient-looking chair and pushed it back from her desk toward the towering bookcase behind it. I climbed atop its soft, springy seat to get a better look at the higher shelves. The moment my hands closed around the clawed arms I felt a shock hit me in the spine, and I was blinded by a white light. The vision hit me hard, leaving me paralyzed and breathless by what I saw, and there wasn't even any time to warn them. I lay crumpled on Greeley's massive chair, sweating and gasping for air as the others crowded around me, calling my name.

"What happened to her?" Remi asked wide-eyed as he stared down at me.

"I think she had a vision," Journey said.

"What?" Nova barked, turning toward Journey.

"Sparrow said she's been having them," he shrugged.

I begged my brain to stop convulsing so I could warn my friends to run, but all I could do was look up at them and choke out a whisper. "I'm sorry."

50

"Well, well, well. What have we here?" came her smooth calm voice.

The Johns froze, and I watched as fear washed across their faces as they turned in horror toward the sound of her voice. My fall made such a commotion that it masked their entrance; three women, each wearing different expressions. Sparrow's slight frame emerged from the shadows looking terrified as her eyes wildly searched the room. When they landed on us, however, she dropped her gaze, unable to meet our eyes. Jemma stood boldly beside Sparrow, with her black mane swinging as she shook her head in satisfaction, giving us a sinister grin. But worse of all, behind them both stood the statuesque silhouette of Headmistress Greeley.

"This is turning into quite a party, isn't it? What can I do for you four?" Greeley asked as she snaked toward us.

Nova had pulled me from the chair and was slowly guiding us, taking cautious steps away from Greeley as if trying to counter her advances.

"John 18? We meet again so soon? I must say I would have

thought you might have kept your lesson learned a bit longer. Although..." she paused peering closer now, "You don't seem to look worse for wear," she finished with a twitchy smirk.

No one moved or said a thing. I was concentrating on an exit strategy, but something about the way Greeley was looking at us was giving me a sick feeling in the pit of my stomach. It was almost as if she knew something; knew what we were up to, knew what we could do. And then she gave me a wink and I widened my eyes with a sudden realization, my bag was no longer invisible! I could feel Niv restlessly pushing against me now that we were all crammed up against the bookshelves. Jemma opened her mouth and let out a little gasp.

"There!" she said. "She has it! 65 has the rodent."

"Ah yes, 31. I thought you said that it belonged to 42? No matter."

Greeley snapped her fingers and Khan and Ria came padding into the room. Ria stopped next to Greeley, allowing her to scratch her head while Khan stood, sniffing the air, looking curiously at me and my bag.

"Jane 65, you know the rules. We do not allow such vile vermin in the Troian Center. Hand it over."

"No," I whispered.

"Excuse me?"

"No!" I said forcefully this time and I vanished right before pushing myself forward into a run and barreling straight toward Greeley and the door.

Greeley, let out a high-pitched cackle and then snapped once more and the door slammed shut in front of me. Her laughter filled the room when I hit it full force and slid to the ground groaning and visible again. Jemma was staring at me, arms dumbly hanging at her side, mouth wide open in disbelief.

"What? How?" she stammered.

Greeley ignored her. She was occupied by the little marmouse that had escaped my bag and was running in circles on the floor.

"Niv!" I shrieked, only adding to his panic.

"Stop!" Greeley commanded and Niv froze in place.

I stared at her in wonder. Next she commanded him to "Come" and with a snap of her fingers he floated up into the air, tail first squirming all the way, whiskers twitching, eyes wide with fear. He let out frightened squeaks the closer he got to her. I longed to run to him and each call from him threatened to tear my heart open, but I seemed to be pinned to the door. I was unable to pull myself from its sudden magnetism. I looked around the room at the others, wondering if they too were stuck under Greeley's spell, because none of them made a sound or moved. All eyes were on Niv, including that of Ria and Khan.

"So, it has a name?" Greeley asked looking from Niv to me.

"Please... please, don't hurt him."

"Why would I do something like that?" she asked coyly.

"He hasn't done anything wrong. I'll let him go, put him back in the forest."

"The forest?" she said suddenly looking dangerous. "You found him in the forest?"

I didn't respond. Instead I swallowed hard and tried to telepath to Nova.

"We have to do something! Make her let him go!"

Greeley's laughter broke through my thoughts like icicles slicing through my brain. "He can't help you, little Jane. Not in here," she laughed and with a shrug she flicked her wrist and Niv went soaring. I felt a lapse in the magnetic pull and shoved off the door toward my flailing marmouse and as I leapt to catch him, I saw a black and white blur out of the corner of my eye pouncing toward me and before I knew what happened I was hitting the floor hard and empty handed while the air filled with a screech so loud and horrid that it felt like my head was about to split open. I rolled onto my back, still gasping for air, but I managed to scramble to my feet searching for Niv. I whirled around toward the tarcats and felt Nova's hands quickly fold across my chest as I finally spotted Niv, amongst the blood-red mass in Khan's powerful jaws. It happened so fast that my brain couldn't register what my eyes were seeing. Ria stood timidly by in a crouch licking her lips as she anxiously swatted at the scraps that Khan let fall from Niv's desecrated body. There was almost nothing identifiable left of him and I started to feel faint. I had to turn my head from the violence to fight the bile rising in my throat. This couldn't be real!

"NOOOO!" I screamed as I sank to my knees with Nova restraining me all the way. "NIV!"

I gasped as I felt the air rush out of me and hot tears streak down my cheeks. This couldn't be happening! But somehow it was, because I could feel each blow as if it were happening to me. The weight of Khan's paw was crushing my chest as his sharp teeth tore my soul from my very being. Everything went bright white as the pain became too much to bear. My heart was bursting with pain and fear. This must be it; this was the end of me as well as Niv because I had foolishly tethered my soul to my precious little marmouse that I had sworn to protect. A white-hot rage surged through me as the realization that I failed hit me. I failed Niv. I failed myself and my friends. I may have even failed all the people of Hullabee Island. The implications were too great and I felt myself bursting forth outside of the confinements of flesh and bone. My breathing slowed and my heartbeat steadied. Bright white light surged from me, taking over, cracking the walls and ceiling, silencing everything else in the room until nothing moved; everything was still and silent and I was finally able to see again.

I had unknowingly fissured our reality again. It seemed to happen every time I let my extreme emotions take hold of me. I surveyed the room that was now under my fissure, strewn with papers and books. My friends were all huddled near Greeley's desk with tortured looks on their faces; even Jemma was with them looking frightened. Greeley stood blinking before me, but she was frozen by the fissure too. I slowly made my way toward what remained of Niv's tattered body and knelt in front of him weeping my apologies, trying to take comfort in the fact that his death had been quick. *But what of my death? Wasn't I supposed to parish as well? Was there some part of Niv that was holding on still?*

I wanted to reach out to him, but his body was so ravaged that my stomach flopped. Instead I tore a piece of my white tunic off at the knees and delicately draped it over him, wrapping him in a proper burial cloth. The least I could do was take him to the forest and reunite him with his mother while I still had the chance. I didn't know why I was still breathing, but I wasn't about to challenge it.

As I stood to leave I noticed something. The bookcase I had been examining before Greeley caught us was in ruins. It was almost completely empty except for one book. I pushed through the heavy fissure air to where my friends were standing, clasping each other for support. I stared past them, up at the bookcase and it all fell into place! The Troian Center was the old prison on the island before the Flood. This must have been where our ancestors came to demand the release of their wrongly imprisoned people. If the legend is accurate, there must have been 140 of them. I looked around now, wondering how 140 people ever fit it this room, hoping it was a metaphor, because right now there were only five of us to unite and fight for our island. On a hunch, I reached out and took Nova's frozen outstretched hand and the lone book on the top shelf of the case began to glow.

"Oh my gods! I was right! We did it!" I gasped.

I waded over to the case and climbed high enough to grab it. As I pulled it off the shelf I could feel the fissure slipping. The room rippled, cracks of light began to form again and everything in it began to slowly move. Papers rustled, Khan's tail began to twitch, and it would only be a short time before it all receded. Perhaps this was what was slowing my inevitable death. This thought powered me into a frenzy. I ran with the book and grabbed hold of Nova and Remi, pushing and pulling them with me toward the door a few inches at a time before I went back for Journey and Sparrow. It was as if they were wading in tar with how little progress we were making. The closer to the door we got the easier things were. Soon they were fully animated and were able to drag themselves out. We were almost out when Remi paused, starting to turn back.

"What are you doing?" I shouted as pieces of rock cascaded down around us.

"Jemma's still in there," he said.

"Leave her!" I shouted with such ferocity that he didn't argue as he let me pull him back toward the exit.

Once we were all panting safely in the hallway, I turned and pressed my hands to the door, watching with satisfaction as it turned to stone and molded with the thick stone walls that surrounded it.

"I got it!" I said, breathlessly. "Let's go."

"Where are we going?" Sparrow whispered looking so fragile she might break.

"To the forest," I said looking down at crimson stain that was spreading on my linen shoulder bag.

51

No one argued, they just followed. We rushed down the hallways and out of the courtyard, not caring who took notice of us. It was liberating to take off on our own, away from the Center, not cloaked by darkness or magical powers. I'd made my decision as soon as I'd sealed the door to Greeley's office. I wasn't going back to the Troian Center. Unabashed by this new freedom, I found the strength to keep pushing forward, through the fields and brush, not stopping until being welcomed by the comforts of the forest. Here, with my lungs filling with the sweet nectar of forest air, I began to fully grasp our reality. I had nothing left to lose. I was supposed to be dead, but I wasn't. I still wasn't sure how these tethers worked. Maybe my death is coming, waiting slightly off in the distance, ready to strike. Either way, I had just revealed my powers to Greeley, who mind-blowingly enough had powers of her own! Even if I did survive the rest of this day, I could never go back to the Troian Center. It was never a home and now without Niv, I felt like I would never feel home again. I understood my own reckless abandon toward the future, but what about my friends? I'd dragged them into this, endangering their futures. They all seemed to be cautiously looking at me, waiting for me to have some sort of plan to make it all better. But the truth was, I didn't.

I slowly meandered through the forest on our usual path, feeling the heavy weight of our future upon my shoulders. Everyone was silent, leaving only the birds and insects to interrupt my dark thoughts. I couldn't get the image of Niv's final moments out of my head and I had to keep stopping to heave the empty contents of my stomach. Deep into the forest, I eventually came to the spot I was looking for and knelt down. Everyone gave me some space, realizing we were at the burial site of Niv's mother. I began pulling my stained bag delicately over my head when Remi put his hand on mine to stop me.

"Stop," he spoke softly.

"Remi, I have to..."

"No, you need to listen to me. I did something. Something I've wanted to tell you about for a while now. I even tried to tell you a few times and... It doesn't matter now, all that matters is that it's working."

"What's working?" Nova asked, stepping up behind us.

"What are you talking about, Remi?" I asked.

"Aren't you wondering why you're still alive right now?" he asked.

"I think we all are," Journey added.

"What did you do?" Nova asked Remi apprehensively.

"Just come with me. It'll be easier to show you," he replied.

Remi pulled me to my feet and we set off again, heading deeper into the forest, this time with Remi in the lead. I had to admit, it felt nice to just be following obediently. It took less energy, which was a good thing because I could feel my adrenaline fading and the hysteria settling in. I glanced at Sparrow, who seemed to be in a constant state of shock. She hadn't said anything since we left the Center. Her eyes were wide and glossy and she clung to Journey like he was an injured appendage. We had been walking for a while and I was losing steam. I stumbled on a root and thankfully Nova was there to steady me.

"Remi, how much further?" Nova called, sounding aggravated.

"We're almost there," he repeated for about the hundredth time.

"That's enough," Nova said stopping the group. "I think you had better tell us what's going on. Now!" he demanded.

"Fine, see for yourself then," Remi said pointing off the path just ahead.

Nova propelled his fire light ahead to illuminate the area Remi pointed at and we all heard a little shriek, followed by angry squeaking. My ears pricked up and my spine straightened. I would know that sound anywhere.

"Niv?" I questioned, tears already welling in my eyes, knowing I couldn't possibly be hearing my sweet little marmouse because my hand went instinctively to his maimed body inside my shoulder bag when I heard the noise.

"Remi, what's going on?" Nova shouted after seeing the obvious pain on my face was about to push me over the edge.

"It's called a shadow. Eja taught me how to do it. I started it right after she tethered herself to him. I knew there had to be a way to protect her. Eja told me that I could cast a shadow of Niv as a decoy, keeping the real one here, locked away and safe.

"So he's not dead?" I gasped.

"Not exactly. Since the shadow was killed, we just have to reunite his shadow body with the real Niv," Remi replied. When no one responded he started rambling at me. "I'm sorry. I wanted to tell you but I wasn't sure it was going to work and then I thought you would be angry with me for locking Niv out here all alone while you had an imposter, but I just couldn't take the chance that something would happen to you."

I ran to Remi and threw my arms around his neck, making incoherent noise, bouncing from laughter to cries and back. I released him and started toward Niv, only to return and hug Remi even harder. My best friend came through for me in the most insurmountable way. "This is where you've been going isn't it?" I whispered as I clung to him.

"Yes," he nodded sheepishly. "I had to feed him and check on him."

"Thank you," I said looking him deep in his chocolate-brown eyes. Before I released him from my embrace, I gave him a sincere kiss on the cheek and then ran to the spot where Niv was waiting for me.

"Niv! Niv! Oh my gods, Niv, you're okay! It's okay. We're going to get you out. Everything is fine now, little guy," I crooned as he stared eagerly up at me.

He was scratching at an invisible force field before him. I cautiously reached toward him and felt the empty space before me resist my advance. It was strong and it pushed back against me. I turned to Remi, who was already at my side along with the others. He asked us to back away and had me hand over my shoulder bag with the remains of Niv's shadow in it. I watched as he settled on his knees near Niv and repeated a line of foreign words. There was a tiny burst of red light, leaving a wake of smoke. I crept forward until I was even with Remi and as the smoke cleared, Niv came running toward me, leaping into my arms and showering me with sloppy kisses and coos! I felt a warmth and happiness radi-ating through me like never before. It felt amazing to be reunited with Niv after thinking I'd lost him forever. I felt like I could do anything! It was as if my soul had returned to my body, and perhaps it had. All I knew was that I would be forever grateful to Remi. Everyone crowded around me, laughing and taking turns loving on Niv. Sparrow spoke for the first time since we left Greeley's office.

"Oh thank the gods he's all right! I would have never forgiven myself. This was all my fault."

"Sparrow, what are you talking about? This isn't your fault at all."

"But it is. If I'd been able to stop Jemma none of this would have happened."

"What do you mean?" I asked.

"While I was keeping watch for you, she came over to me and asked me where Niv was."

Sparrow recounted her encounter with Jemma for us.

"Where's your little pet?" Jemma asked.

"Gone. I let him go."

"Really?" she laughed. "I highly doubt you would have parted with him so easily after giving up a solo for him. Anyway, he's none of my concern. Your friends however are. Especially that little boyfriend of yours. I have a score to settle with him. Where are they?"

"Who? #26? He's not my boyfriend. Anyway, I don't know where he is."

"Hmmm, I was hoping you'd choose the easy way, but I can find them without your help."

"What are you going to do?" Sparrow questioned.

"I'm going to find Greeley and let her know what you've been hiding."

"You don't have any proof."

"We'll see about that. I found him once before, don't doubt I can't do it again," Jemma threatened, turning on her heels, storming out of the dining hall.

"I followed her and she went the same way you had gone. It was uncanny the way she was trailing you. It was like you left her a trail of breadcrumbs or something. Then when it was obvious she was going to Greeley's I started to panic that she was going to find you there so I called out to her,"

'Wait! I'll tell you where he is. Just please don't tell Greeley on us.'

'Very well. As I said, I only need to get even with John #26.'

"I tried to lead Jemma away from Greeley's and bring her back to our room. I didn't really have a plan but I was just trying to get her far away from you and Greeley's, but she figured out I was misleading her because she got really angry and ran ahead of me. The next thing I knew she was back with a Grift, who took me to Greeley. Jemma told her all about Niv and how we were keeping him as a pet and that she thought we were pulling a prank with him and slipping him into your office. I don't know how she figured out you were in her office with him, but she did."

"It sounds like she's a tracer," came a voice, startling us.

"Eja!" I called to him, happy to see my Beto friend again.

We all exchanged pleasantries with him and brought him up to speed with the unbelievable events of our day. I also delved into my theory about Greeley's powers. She always prided herself on her citizen status, which is why her impressive display of powers shocked us all.

"Eja, is it possible that our headmistress is a Truiet?" I asked.

"Why do you ask?"

"Well, when she found us in her office, she wasn't surprised to see us. She acted like she was expecting us. But the craziest part was she has powers, too. I think she was able to see through the invisibility charm I was using to hide Niv. And that's not all, she knew where I was going when I was trying to escape her office and she somehow closed the door in front of me from across the room."

"That is curious..." Eja said while scratching his chin.

"But the worst part was when she made Niv levitate and she unleashed her tarcats on him," I said, swallowing hard as the all too fresh memory of Niv's murder surfaced again. "She could read my thoughts, too," I said as Eja pondered what I'd just told him. "But I don't think she's actually a Truiet because she doesn't use any of these powers for good. You said that the Beto people didn't use their powers for evil and Greeley is pure evil."

"Well, if she's not a Truiet, what is she?" questioned Journey.

"I don't know, but I have a hunch on how she gets her powers," I said cautiously.

Everyone looked at me, so I reluctantly continued. "This is just an idea, but I think she gets her power from the gems that we mine from the rubble piles." I was met with blank stares so I kept going. "They're supposed to be very valuable to Lux, right? Maybe they use them to power the city or something, who knows, but maybe Greeley is always stealing them because she knows what powers they hold or at least how to control them. I think that's why she has them on that necklace that she always wears. Think about it, she's never without it and she has them on the collars of all of the tarcats at the Center. I bet that's why I couldn't stop Khan and Ria. They obey her every order and I can't break through to them. I should have been able to stop Khan from attacking Niv in her office but he acted like he couldn't even hear me. There has to be a connection to the gems and all of this."

"I think you're very smart," Eja said with a smirk.

"So you think it's possible?" Remi questioned.

"Yes, I do. There are many legends about the powers of the

precious gems on this island," Eja said with his usual vagueness.

"Well, how do you suppose we find out if it's true?" Nova asked looking from me to Eja.

"I might have an idea how to test that theory," I murmured to myself with an eerie calm.

As I was pondering what Eja said, Journey questioned him about what a tracer was.

"It's a power that some Truiets have. Sort of like the hunting skill you and 65 share, but more powerful because it isn't reliant on your senses. It's a kind of sense all on its own. If you can set your mind on what you're seeking and connect to it, you can follow it anywhere."

"I think we know someone with this ability," Sparrow alleged.

"Jemma can't be a Truiet!" I yelled in bewilderment. "She's pure evil."

"Regardless, Jemma's the least of our worries right now," Nova interjected. "Greeley must be free by now and she's not going to let this go. They're going to come looking for us."

"He's right," seconded Eja. "We need to get you somewhere safe."

"Oh no! I mentioned the forest when I was talking about Niv. She'll come here first!"

Just as the words were leaving my mouth there was an explosion of fire high above us. The trees burst into flames, moaning as an eruption of ash showered down on us. Unsuspecting forest creatures were thrown into motion, fleeing the trees that had been transformed into a fireball.

"Too late, they're already here," Journey yelled above the commotion.

"What do we do?" cried Sparrow.

"Run!" Nova barked.

We all took off running, following Eja down seemingly endless trails, deeper and deeper into the forest, but no matter how far we went, the fire and fury seemed to follow closely behind. The terrain started to get steep and treacherous as we reached the heart of the island. We were at the base of the volcano now and we had nowhere else to go.

"Eja, stop!" I called. "We can't go up there. It's too dangerous. And if we actually do make it, they'll have us cornered. They've already destroyed half the forest."

"What do you suggest we do then," Journey growled, wiping the soot and sweat from his forehead.

I looked around at my friends. They looked battered and tired, and most of all frightened. They had done so much for me that I couldn't put them in harm's way anymore. This was my fight and I knew it. I was the one that revealed my powers to Greeley, not them. She was coming after me. I knew what I had to do. I gave Niv one last hug and handed him to Sparrow. I gave them my best smile and then pulled all the strength I could manage and vaulted into the cool night air. As fast as a lightning strike, it was done! I formed a bubble over them. A thick protective membrane encased them. Just like the one that had held Niv. Eja was probably the only one capable of getting out, but he seemed to understand what I had to do and he nodded to me. Nova went crazy, pounding on the invisible wall, throwing bursts of fire against its impenetrable force. I could hear him yelling but I couldn't make out the words. I turned my back on them and headed out to face my fears.

52

I bounded from tree to tree, staying high so I could get a better view, while avoiding the fires below. I could see the frontline at last. It was a small group of Grifts from the Center, with Jest leading the charge. There was no magic necessary for their kind of destruction. They held rifles and flame throwers and were blazing a wide path through the burning forest. Trees groaned and splintered as they fell into each other, overcome by viciously licking flames. I knew traveling the forest canopy would soon become impossible. I just needed to stay up here long enough to find Greeley. She had to be with them. Of course she would be sending the expendable before her, but I knew she wouldn't trust this job to anyone else. She would want to see the end of me, see the life drain out of my defiant eyes. Her insidious glare made that perfectly clear to me when I created the fissure in her office. Yes, I was sure she was out here, and soon enough I was able to confirm it when I caught sight of two large black and white figures slinking along below me.

Ah, where there's Ria and Khan, there's Greeley, I thought.

I knew now was my chance to catch them off guard. I

needed to act fast. I swung expertly from limb to limb until I was close enough to pounce. I wanted to land between Greeley, the tarcats and her first line of defense. *Now!* I swooped down landing steadily on my feet with a thump. The Grifts hadn't seen or heard me, but Greeley did. She stopped abruptly and narrowed her eyes at me. Ria and Khan were startled and crouched in positions of attack, hairs raised and bristled.

"Looking for me?" I called to her.

"As a matter of fact I am looking for you," she sneered. Then her voice turned sweet and patronizing. "And what of your friends? I was hoping to find them as well. What kind of headmistress would I be if I left you children out here all alone in the forest?"

"They're not out here. They... they didn't want to come."

"Oh, so you managed to frighten them away, did you?" she laughed. "Perhaps they're smarter than I gave them credit for. No matter, as I said, you're the one I've been looking for. You took something of mine and I intend to get it back."

"You took something of mine!" I shouted, holding my ground. "The truth about my life is in that book and I have the right to know it."

She rocked her head back and let out a shrill, terrifying laugh.

"Don't worry about your past, little Jane. It's your future that should concern you," she said.

And that was the moment I was waiting for. She gave the signal to her tarcats who were slowly pacing a wide circle around me. They were poised on either side of me, tails twitching, waiting for their master to give them the sign to attack. When it came, they were ready. They sprang forward, roaring toward me, teeth bared. I stood still, crouching low, waiting, with every muscle in my body tense and coiled. I counted each of their steps in my mind as they closed the ground between me. Then at last, just as they were about to reach me with their massive clawed feet outstretched in their final lunge, I leapt upward. I hovered above them as they crashed into each other, temporarily bewildered. Khan angrily snapped at Ria who shook her head in confusion. Then, before they knew what was happening, I strategically let myself fall, landing atop of them, balancing precariously on their haunches. I grabbed hold of their thick bejeweled leather collars and spoke to them as I turned the collars to stone.

"I don't want to hurt you. I'm going to set you free, but you must promise not to come after my friends or me. And there is one more thing that you owe to me before I let you go." I looked into their luminescent yellow eyes and could see that they understood what I needed them to do. Without another second, I crushed their now stone collars from their necks, releasing them from my hold and Greeley's simultaneously. I leapt up into a smoldering tree as they shook the stone from their pelts. I watched as Greeley shouted at them angrily, commanding them to attack me. But instead they started to close in on her and the last thing I saw was Ria pounce and rake a massive paw across Greeley's throat. She disappeared into a swirl of black and white fur that quickly became stained with splashes of crimson. The blood-curdling screams followed me as I retreated back into the forest.

Without Greeley driving them, the Grifts all scattered back toward the Troian Center. I held my position safely above them until I was sure they had all dispersed and wouldn't be any more trouble for us. I went to work retaining the fires they'd set and managed to put them out by turning the flames into bursts of light, that dissipated into harmless orbs, which I left hovering to light my way. Then I quickly returned to where I'd left my friends, in the safety of the translucent bubble. I was stunned to see another figure hunched over outside the barrier. She was covered in dirt and ash, her dark hair looked utterly disheveled. I cautiously approached her where she lay heaving for breath, worried that this must be one of Eja's tribe members injured in the fires. The others were all huddled near her on the other side of the translucent wall. They were nervously mouthing things to me that I couldn't make out, so with a wave of my hand I released them from their protective bubble and went to lay a gentle hand on the girl's shoulder. As I touched her she flinched and turned to me in shock. Both of us recoiled from each other in alarm. The frightened face that greeted me was none other than Jemma's!

I was blinded by rage and wanted nothing more than to call the tarcats on her, but Sparrow was shouting at me, tugging on my arm. Although I released them from the barrier that kept them safe while I dealt with Greeley, I still couldn't hear them, because my mind was reeling with fury, deafening me from the words of my friends. *How did she get here? Why was she here? Did Greeley send her to finish them off while she dealt with me?* I was seething mad and the only thing that brought me out of my rage was when Sparrow put Niv back into my arms. He wiggled around with his tail curing around my arm while he showered me with kisses, licking my hot, salty skin. I blinked a few times to bring myself back to reality. The others gathered around me, while Eja and Nova tended to Jemma. It angered me beyond reason to see Nova paying attention to her, attentively holding her hands while Eja treated her wounds. It seemed she had injured her ankle. She had a deep gash that was oozing an almost black-tinged blood. I wasn't disappointed one bit to see her suffering.

"What's she doing here?" I asked to no one in particular.

"She came to warn us that Greeley was coming," Remi said.

"Yeah right! Like she cares what happens to us! She's the one who practically delivered us to Greeley!" I shouted.

"It's true," came a foreign sheepish voice that I never associated with Jemma. "I was a fool to do that and I know you'll never forgive me, but I never thought anything like this would happen. I didn't know that she... or you... It doesn't matter. I know you hate me, but I thought I could at least warn you that she was coming."

"And how exactly did you know right where to find us? It's a little too convenient, Jemma," I scathed.

"I... I don't exactly know how I do it, but I just do. If I concentrate on someone hard enough, I just know where to find them."

"You're a tracer," Eja said smiling at her stupidly. Even in this state, her beauty still managed to charm without effort.

I rolled my eyes and said, "I'm not buying it. I think she was spying on us for Greeley. But you don't have to worry about that anymore because Greeley's gone," I said.

The group all stopped what they were doing to stare at me. It was painfully quiet. All I could hear was the smoldering crackle of the trees nearby. Nova walked over to me and looked deep into my eyes. It was as if he was reading my soul and I looked away, breaking the connection when it became too painful.

"You did what you had to do, Tippy," was all he said and he squeezed my hand, pulling me into an embrace.

I didn't want to dissolve into a puddle of tears in front of Jemma, so I stiffened and pulled away from Nova, shaking off my feelings of distress. I gave my friends the brief version of what happened to Greeley. Telling them that the only thing that mattered was that she wouldn't be coming after us anymore.

"Where's the book? Have you read it yet?" I asked wanting to change the subject.

"No, we can't get it open," Journey said.

"That doesn't make any sense," I retorted, taking the book from him.

I slid my hand across its aged leather cover. It felt cool and smooth against my hand. It was heavy and I sat down with it upon my lap and slowly ran my fingers along the binding, feeling for any sign of how to open it, but there was nothing. So I closed my eyes and hoped with all the strength I had left that it would open. As I reached for the edge of the cover and pulled it gently toward me there was a stiff groan and I felt the delicate pages brushing past my fingers. It was open! My eyes popped open, blazing into the ancient book lying unlocked in my lap.

"You did it!" Remi yelped.

53

Everyone crowded around. We all looked at the pages anxiously, only to be met by a foreign text. I could feel the wandering eyes around me looking to each other, not knowing what to do next. My eyes welled in frustration. We came all this way and now we couldn't read the language of the text! To be stopped now was too much. I pushed the *book off* my lap and stood up abruptly and stomped away from the group. I needed to clear my head. Niv hopped along behind me, squeaking until I scooped him up and let him ride on my shoulder. When I was far enough away, I stopped walking and slumped down on a lava-hardened rock. I looked at the smoldering fire around me. Daylight was breaking above the smoking tree line and the weight of the day finally became too great to bear. I broke down and let the tears fall. My tired body shook with tremors of fear and waves of disappointment. I let all the heaviness drain out and squeezed Niv tightly to my chest. After a while my well of misery ran dry and I caught my breath again. I looked down at my happy little marmouse, and he seemed more alive and healthier than ever. I owed all of that to Remi. I looked back to

my group of tattered friends and couldn't help but feel a small wave of comfort spread over me.

The day could have gone much worse. Niv was alive, as were my friends and Greeley would never hurt us again. So what if we couldn't read the stupid *Book of Secrets*. Maybe it was just as well. I was starting to feel like my friends and Niv were all the family I needed. I picked him up and headed back to the group. They were all still pouring over the *Book of Secrets* that was now resting in Eja's lap. They were so deep in discussion that they didn't even notice my return. Jemma was sitting next to Eja, injured leg outstretched. I knelt down in front of them and cleared my throat. This got everyone's attention. They stared at me. Sparrow's mouth dropped wide open, and Jemma's eyes widened. Remi stood and moved toward me. They all looked like they had seen a ghost.

"What's wrong?" I asked, letting that familiar sinking feeling rush in.

"65, we found you," Eja said. "The book is written in an old dialect of Truietian. I've been deciphering it and we found you."

"Where?" I asked anxiously walking around him to peer over his shoulder. "Where am I?"

"Everywhere," he said pointing to the heading of the page.

It was my tattoo LVX. #65. It was on top of the page he was staring at, as well as the next and the next. As he flipped all I saw was LVX. My heart pounded and I knelt down suddenly feeling weak. My mind was buzzing with white noise. This was more than I could have dreamed of. I had just about given up hope of ever reading the *Book of Secrets*. Thinking even if I did, I had to be prepared that it still might not be the answer to all my questions. But it seemed that almost the entire book was about me!

"What does it say?" I asked breathlessly.

"Well, there's a lot to read. Basically we were right in thinking you are the chosen one. It says only the Eva would be able to open the book."

"What else?"

"Well, you were right about the 140 needed to find the book."

"That doesn't make any sense, there were only seven of us in the room including Jemma and Greeley," I said, glancing skeptically in Jemma's direction.

"Ah yes, but you're thinking too logically. There were other numbers in that room, specifically the right combination of numbers," Eja said grinning.

I looked impatiently at the others' tense stares. They obviously already knew what he was getting at and I grew impatient with Eja's riddles.

"What are you talking about, Eja? Just tell me already!"

"Think about it, you each have numbers tattooed on your arms. The correct combination of your namesakes adds up to 140 and you were all a key part in locating and retrieving the book. You're all bound together. The gods meant for you to unite. It's necessary in order to save our people."

I was lost in thought, grouping together mathematical equations made up of all of our assigned numerical names. I was 65, Nova's 18, Sparrow's 42, Journey's 22, and Remi's 26, but none of them added up right.

"You're forgetting one," Nova said softly, obviously listening in to my thoughts again. I looked up at him and then to the person to his immediate left and all the breath left my body with a violent shudder, as the pieces finally fit together. *Me + Nova +Remi + JEMMA = 140!*

"No," I squeaked in almost a whisper. "NO!" I said again, louder this time, rising to my feet and backing away from them. "*She's* not a part of this!" I yelled, turning to look at each of my friends from the Troian Center. None of them would meet my eyes, none except for her, which only infuriated me further.

"Sit down, there's more to tell," Eja said calmly as he flipped through the book.

Sparrow was at my side suddenly and she was taking my hand, leading me back toward Eja. *"Please,"* she softly telepathed to me. *"It's important."* I conceded and followed her obediently, taking my spot again, kneeling next to Eja. Sparrow sat cross-legged next to me, still holding my hand supportively. "Okay," I nodded, signaling Eja to continue.

"Jemma is a major part of this and I see that you may not be happy to hear it right now, but just promise to keep your mind open," Eja urged me while he settled on the correct page. "Here," he said, pointing to two foreign symbols. "These are Jemma's parents," he said. "Nesia and Kai."

My eyes immediately misted up. After all the research we'd done on the legend of Lux –although I had resisted it – I had apparently let the thought seep in that the legend could be about me. And that these mythical parents could be mine. I angrily shook the thought from my head. I had been foolish to think I would have a fairytale ending, but it made me sick to think that Jemma was getting more than she deserved as usual. In bitter frustration, I leveled myself on the thought that my parents may still be in this book, too. And then I immediately felt resentful that we were wasting time on Jemma right now when I was the one who found the *Book of Secrets* to begin with. I took a deep breath and waited painfully for Eja to continue with Jemma's story.

"They had a daughter," he said, pointing to another symbol that was familiar to me. It was the same tattoo that emblazoned her arm, XXXI.

"So," I shrugged.

"She had a sister," he continued, pointing out another symbol.

Everything went fuzzy. The symbol he pointed out next was my earliest memory; perhaps the most permanent thing in my life. I traced my shaky fingers lightly over the fragile paper and the images began to blur. Whether it was from the tears in my eyes or the light-headedness I was feeling, I don't know, but no matter how indistinct the symbol was, I would've recognized it anywhere. LVX. My fingers instinctively went to my shoulder, where the very same symbol was permanently tattooed. LVX.

"Her name was Geneva. Geneva Sommers," Eja said, barely audible above the pounding of my rapid heart.

"We called her Eva," whispered Jemma, looking at me with such sorrow and pain that I barely recognized her. Her words where soft and held an unfamiliar tenderness. "You're my sister."

54

My name is Geneva Sommers. I didn't know that until today. Until today, I've lived the past thirteen years of my life as #65. Jane 65 to be exact. Janes, that's what they call us female orphans at the Troian Center. We live on Hullabee Island. Our way of life here is very simple, either you're one of the lucky ones, or you're not. I am not. Or at least that's what I thought, until I found out the **truth...**

NOTE FROM THE AUTHOR

I want to personally thank you for taking the time to seek out this great little indie series. Writing is truly my passion. I believe each of us can find a small part of ourselves in every book we read, and carry it with us, shaping our world, our adventures and our dreams.

Following my dream to write frees my soul, but knowing others find joy in my writing is indescribable. So thank you for your support and I hope your enjoyed your brief escape into the magic of these books.

If you enjoyed this story, don't worry, there's plenty more currently rattling around in my rambunctious imagination. Let me and others know your thoughts by sharing a review of this book. Reviews help shape my next writing projects. So if you want more books like this one be sure to shout it from the rooftops (or social media.) ;-)

- C.J. (Christina) Benjamin

Don't worry, this isn't the end of Geneva's story. You can start reading the next book now. ***Geneva Sommers and the Secret Legend*** begins on the next page.

Or

Order The Complete Book 2 Now

-THE LEGEND OF HULLABEE ISLAND-

GENEVA SOMMERS

and the Secret Legend

C.J. BENJAMIN

PROLOGUE

Some people come into your life by choice, some by chance, but others come in like a freight train, with certain uncontrollable force. Sometimes you can feel them coming, sometimes you are completely blindsided. Under either circumstance, you know your life will never be the same again. But don't waste time fretting in despair. You were on this collision course long before you knew it, before you had a choice or a chance to change it. Your only choice now, is what to do when that time comes. What will you do when these two worlds collide?

1

I squeezed my eyes shut and counted silently to ten. Maybe this was all a dream, a vivid and horrible dream. I mean honestly, when I thought about it, that almost seemed more plausible than the events of today being real. Isn't it possible I dreamt the whole thing up? I've always had an active imagination. Or maybe this was some new kind of magic power I'd just developed and it had me trapped in one of my daydreams. Perhaps when I opened my eyes I would wake up behind my favorite palm, in my secret hiding place in the Troian Center courtyard. Our headmistress Greeley would still be alive, the rainforest wouldn't be smoldering around me, my friends and I wouldn't be homeless and most importantly, Jemma would NOT be my sister.

I took a few more deep breaths and slowly opened my eyes. Then panic set in. It was all still there, all still in front of me, just as it had been before I closed my eyes. Jemma was staring at me and she seemed closer than before. Her face was twisted in some sort of quivering frown while tears created tiny winding rivers down her sooty cheeks.

Not possible, I thought to myself. *Jemma doesn't cry.*

I could feel my mind getting fuzzy and there was a dull buzzing in my ears that seemed to be making it really hard for me to connect my thoughts. I looked around to see where it was coming from and my eyes took in the devastating scenery surrounding me once more.

"This can't be real," I whispered, more to myself than anyone in particular. But it seemed Jemma thought I was talking to her because she launched herself toward me and crushed me in a desperate hug.

"It is! It is real!" She squeezed tighter and sobbed harder. "It's you! I can't believe this either, but it's you! You're my sister! I thought you were dead. They told me you died in the Flood."

It was all too much for me to take. I pushed her off of me, quickly wiping my eyes to hide my emotions, which were dangerously close to brimming over.

"I can't do this," was all I managed to squeak out before my voice betrayed me with a sob, so I turned on my heels and ran away.

"Wait! Eva!" Jemma called after me, but I didn't stop. I kept going, quickening my stride. I willed my legs to carry me far enough away, so I could have some privacy when I broke down.

"Let me talk to her," I heard Remi say. "You're overwhelming her, Jemma."

I tried to tune them out but my telepathy fed me a steady stream of their voices. I hurried my pace, sprinting away from their voices.

"I THINK she's probably in shock. She just needs some space to come to terms with all of this new information the *Book of*

Secrets has just dumped on her," Nova said, putting his arm up to stop Remi.

"Are you some sort of Geneva expert all of a sudden? You've known her for a second compared to me, so stop acting like you're the only one that knows what's best for her. I know her too and I think she needs someone to talk her through all of this," Remi challenged as he tried to push past Nova.

"She wants to be left alone," Nova said, stepping into Remi's path.

This time his tone was final and I didn't hear any more arguments from Remi. Maybe they'd stopped fighting or I was too far away to connect to them anymore. Either way, Nova was right. I know he only knew I wanted to be left alone because he was reading my thoughts again even though I'd asked him not to a million times. He probably couldn't help himself right now because my mind was practically screaming 'back off!' And honestly I was glad for Nova's mind reading abilities at the moment, because I truly did just want to be alone. I'm sure this probably hurt my best friend's feelings a bit, but right now, Remi's feelings weren't my focus. I was trying desperately not to freak out. I needed to keep breathing and calm myself down so I didn't lose control of my powers and so I could think of a solution.

ACKNOWLEDGMENTS

A giant thank you to all who have added time, love, and support. Geneva would be nothing more than a fantastic musing of mine without you. Thank you for helping me bring the magic to life. Thank you to my parents for always feeding my imagination and love of creation. Thank you to my husband for literally molding the words of my heart into a book that launched a hundred more. To my team of editors, narrators, artists, all the love you've giving to Geneva is stamped in every page. And to the fans, your excitement is a flame that will burn within me and these characters forever. I hope you hold onto the magic between the pages and never stop seeking new adventures.

ALSO BY C.J. BENJAMIN

YOUNG ADULT FANTASY/DYSTOPIAN SERIES

Geneva Sommers and the Quest for Truth (Book 1)

Geneva Sommers and the Secret Legend (Book 2)

Geneva Sommers and the Myth of Lies (Book 3)

Geneva Sommers and the Magic Destiny (Book 4)

Geneva Sommers and the First Fairytales (Prequels)

ABOUT THE AUTHOR

Award-Winning author, C.J. Benjamin, lives in Florida with her husband, and character inspiring pets, where she spends her free time working on her books and speaking to inspire fellow writers.

Her best-selling novel, *Geneva Sommers and the Quest for Truth,* has won multiple awards and stolen the hearts of YA readers everywhere. Packed with magic and imagination, her epic tale of adventure hooks fans of mega-hit YA fiction like Harry Potter, The Hunger Games and Percy Jackson.

C.J. Benjamin loves to read and write across genres. She also writes YA contemporary romance under the name, Christina Benjamin.

For more information visit
www.crownatlanticpublishing.com

Made in the USA
Middletown, DE
27 February 2021